THE DEMON KNIGHT

The black knight slammed his shield against the sword in Cray's left hand, and the blade shivered with the strength of the blow. Cray's fingers, unused to curling about a pommel, went numb; he was barely able to hold onto the weapon.

Cray found himself backing off; suddenly his shoulders were against a tree trunk and he could not sidestep fast enough. The black knight came on. Cray raised his sword far to his right and then swept leftward with a blow too weak to dent plate armor, but strong enough and high enough to cleave a human skull. The steel bit deep into the black knight's head.

In the instant that Cray expected to see bright blood gush from the sundered pate, the black knight burst into flame.

Cray screamed once and his sword arm fell to his side.

Fire engulfed him . . .

SORCERER'S SON

Phyllis Eisenstein

A Del Rey Book

BALLANTINE BOOKS • NEW YORK

A Del Rey Book
Published by Ballantine Books

Library of Congress Catalog Card Number: 78-71231

ISBN 0-345-27642-6

Manufactured in the United States of America

First Edition: April 1979

Cover art by Darrell Sweet

For MARTHA EISENSTEIN
with gratitude
for her love and encouragement

SORCERER'S
SON

❦ CHAPTER ONE

Behind his walls of demon-polished bronze, behind his windows so closely shuttered with copper scales that no sunlight penetrated, Smada Rezhyk brooded over a leaf. It was a bit of ivy, small enough to fit within the palm of his hand, and written upon it in letters spun of gray spidersilk was the single word, "No." A snake had deposited the leaf at the gate of Rezhyk's castle, and he needed no signature upon the smooth green surface to tell him who had sent the message.

His footsteps rang against the floor—studded boots upon the mirror-bright metal—as he strode to the workshop, to the brazier that had never cooled since the instant Castle Ringforge had been completed. His hand passed above the flames, let go the leaf, which danced briefly in the upwelling heat until the fire caught it, curled it, shriveled it to ash. In the flickering light, the jewels upon his fingers sparkled, the plainer bands gleamed warm; each ring was a demon at his command—a demon of fire, a demon to build or destroy at his whim. He tallied them slowly, his only friends in the universe. Then he summoned one, the first and best of them all, faithful companion since his youth; the simplest ring, red gold, was inscribed with that demon's secret name: Gildrum.

From some other part of Ringforge, Gildrum came in human guise, entering by the door as a human would. In appearance, the demon was a fourteen-year-old girl, slight and pretty, with long blond braids. Rezhyk had given her that semblance when they were

1

both young, and only he had changed with the passage of the years. He kept her near him most of the time and spoke his heart to her. She climbed atop a high stool by the brazier and waited for him to begin the conversation.

He was toying with glassware, with notebooks and pens and ink. He had not yet glanced up at her when he said, "She refused me."

In a high, fluty voice, Gildrum said, "Please accept my sympathy, lord."

"She refused me, Gildrum!" He turned to face the demon-girl, lines of anger set around his mouth. "I made her an honorable offer!"

"You did, my lord."

"Am I ugly? Are my manners churlish? Is my home unfit for such as she?"

"None of that, my lord."

"What have I done, then? How have I offended her? When? Where?"

"My lord," said Gildrum, "I do not profess to understand humans completely, but perhaps she is merely disinclined to marry *anyone*."

"You are too soft, my Gildrum." He leaned on a stack of notebooks, forehead braced against his interlaced fingers. "She hates me, I know it. It was a cold reply, brought by a cold creature. She meant to wound me."

"And has succeeded."

"For a moment only! Now I know my enemy. We must take precautions, my Gildrum, to make certain she never can wound me again."

The demon shrugged. "Never again ask her to marry you."

"Not enough! Who knows what evil she fancies I have done her? I must protect myself."

"I would think you are well protected in Ringforge."

"How?" He clutched a length of his dark cape in both fists. "I wear woven cloth; she could turn my very clothes against me."

"Inside your own castle?"

"Am I never to set foot outside again, then? Must I wear plate armor every time I walk abroad? Or felted garments hung together with bolts and glue? She rules too much, her hand is everywhere. What can I do, Gildrum?"

She smiled. "A fire demon could keep you warm enough if your vanity would permit you to walk the world naked, my lord."

"A sorcerer naked as a beggar? Hardly!"

"A beggar would not wear rings of power on all his fingers. People would know your rank."

"Don't try my patience so, Gildrum."

"Then I must think a moment, lord." Pursing her lips, crossing her arms over her bosom, she looked up at the ceiling. Just visible beneath the hem of her blue gown, her feet swung slow arcs between the legs of the stool, pendulums measuring the time of her thought. "My lord," she said at last, "if you are truly concerned about some danger from the lady, then I would advise you to construct a cloth-of-gold shirt, a fine mesh garment, supple enough to wear next to your skin. It must be made of virgin ring-metal, and you must draw and weave the strands yourself, without demonic help. Such a combination of your province and hers would be impervious to her spells and to any of your own that she might try to turn against you."

Rezhyk poked the coals in the brazier. "A fine notion, Gildrum, but what is to keep her from discovering that the shirt is being made long before I finish it? I am no weaver, after all; it would be a slow process."

"How will she discover it? You will do it here in Ringforge."

"How does she discover anything? Every spider is her spy."

"Even here in your own castle?"

"Even my own castle is not proof against vermin. They come and go as they please." He glanced about nervously. "There are none here now, but they might get in at any time."

"Well, then, you must do something about them. Post a watch of fire demons to burn every spider that approaches the outer wall."

"She *will* take that as an affront!"

Gildrum sighed. "Worse and worse. Perhaps if you just sent her a vase of flowers and begged her forgiveness . . . ?"

3

Rezhyk paced a slow circle about the brazier. "If only we could arrange for her to take a long sea voyage, or to go into seclusion in some distant cave for a while. How much time do you think the making of the shirt would require?"

"As you said, you are no weaver. Perhaps a month. Perhaps two. No more than that, I think, if I show you exactly what to do." She held up a hand to stop his pacing. "There is a way to weaken her powers for a month or two, my lord."

"Yes?"

"If she conceived a child, the child's aura would interfere with her own. She would be limited, severely limited."

"Enough . . . ?"

"Enough that she could hardly speak to a creature beyond her own castle walls."

Rezhyk shook his head. "She would abort the child. She would abort it as soon as she realized it existed. She could not allow that kind of vulnerability."

"A month or two, I said, my lord. Until she noticed the pregnancy. Until she noticed the curtailing of her powers."

"She might notice immediately."

Gildrum spread her hands, palms upward. "I have no other suggestions."

"We would have to work quickly. A month is too long. Could I do it in a week?"

"Working night and day, my lord, working with perfect efficiency, you might possibly do it in a week. At the end, you would be exhausted."

"I have no choice." He opened the drawer where he kept his stock of ring-metal. Gold lay within, and silver, copper, iron—wooden boxes held chips and chunks of each, surplus from old rings, and a few small ingots. "I have a gold bar, never used. Will that be enough?"

"Yes."

He hefted the bar in one hand. "This will be a heavy garment."

"You will grow strong wearing it."

He set the metal on his workbench. "We have only

4

one problem, my Gildrum." He glanced up at her. "How to bring about this pregnancy."

Gildrum smiled. "Leave that to me."

Rezhyk's gaze traveled the length of the demon's girl-body. "You suit me well; but for her . . . for her we must give you another form."

"Tall," said Gildrum. "Tall and lean and just past the first flush of youth."

Rezhyk worked two days and two nights to model Gildrum's new form in terra-cotta. Life-sized he made it, strong of arm and broad of shoulder, sinewy and lithe, the essence of young manhood. Other sorcerers, when they gave their servants palpable forms, made monsters, misshapen either by device or through lack of skill, but Rezhyk molded his to look as if they had been born of human women. Complete, the figure seemed almost to breathe in the flickering light of the brazier.

Satisfied with his work, Rezhyk set his seal upon it: an arm ring clasped above the left elbow, a band of plain red gold, twin to the one he wore on his finger, incised with Gildrum's name. Gently, but with a strength that would seem uncanny in so slight a body, were it truly human, Gildrum lifted the new-made figure in her arms and carried it across the workshop to a large kiln whose top and front stood open. She set the clay statue inside, upon a coarse grate.

Rezhyk nodded. "Enter now, my Gildrum."

The demon-as-girl smiled once at her lord's handiwork, and then she burst into flame, her body consumed in an instant, leaving only the flames themselves to dance in a wild torrent of light. Billowing, the fire rose toward the high ceiling, poised above the kiln and, like molten metal pouring into a mold, sank into the terra-cotta figure and disappeared. The clay glowed red and redder, then yellow, then white-hot.

Rezhyk turned away from the heat; by the light of the figure itself he entered its existence, the hour, and the date in the notebook marked with Gildrum's name. By the time he looked back, the clay was cooling rapidly. When it reached the color of ruddy human flesh, a dim glow compared to the yellow of the brazier, it began to crumble. First from the head, and then from every part, fine powder sifted, falling through the grate at its feet to form a mound in the bottom of the kiln. Yet the figure remained, though after some minutes every ounce of terra-cotta had been shed—the figure that was the demon, molded within the clay, remained, translucent now, still glowing faintly from the heat of its birth. The ring that had been set upon the clay now clasped the arm of the demon, its entire circle visible through the ghostly flesh. Then the last vestige of internal radiance faded, the form solidified, and the man that was Gildrum stepped forth from the kiln.

He stretched his new muscles, ran his fingers through his newly dark hair. "As always, my lord," he said in a clear tenor voice, "you have done well."

"I hope she thinks as much." He slipped the ring from Gildrum's arm and tossed it into the drawer from which he had taken the gold bar. "There must be nothing that smells of magic about you—above all, nothing to link you with me."

Gildrum nodded. "I shall steal human trappings. I know of a good source."

"You must not fail."

"Have I ever failed you, lord?"

"No, my Gildrum. Not yet."

"And not now." His form wavered, shrank, altered to that of the fourteen-year-old girl, naked in the light of the brazier. "Will you give me the seed for the child, my lord? Or must I find some beggar on the road?"

He took her hand. "I'll give it."

Rain poured down upon the forest from clouds crowded close above the treetops. On the muddy track below, a large black horse, tail and mane matted with wet and filth, trudged toward the nearest sign of life, a high-spired castle overgrown with ivy. The horse's rider slumped forward over the pommel of the saddle, one arm hanging limp on either side of his steed's drooping neck. He was dressed in chain mail, a mud-spattered surcoat plastered atop the links; he had no helm, and his shield hung by a loose strap, bouncing against his leg in the slow rhythm of the

6

horse's walk. On his left side, where the surcoat was ripped and the chain snapped to make a hole a hand-span wide, blood seeped out sluggishly, easing down his thigh in a rain-diluted wash.

As they neared the castle, the horse picked up its pace, sensing the shelter ahead. The storm drove from beyond the fortress, and so there was respite from both wind and wet in its lee. Almost at the arch of the gate, the animal stopped and bent to drink from a puddle and to crop a bit of soaked grass; its rider fell then, slid silently off its back and dropped to the mud in an awkward heap.

Inside, warm and dry and surrounded by the things she loved, was Delivev Ormoru, mistress of Castle Spinweb. She expected no visitors, neither on a stormy night nor a clear one; no one had knocked at the gates of Spinweb in many years, and she was pleased with that state of affairs. But when the ivy curled in her bedroom window, when a small brown spider scurried across its tendrils to report a stranger outside, she was curious. The stranger had not requested entry, had not pounded on the heavy wooden gate or shouted or beat sword upon shield to attract attention through the noise of the storm, yet why would he be there but to enter? She looked out her window, but the outer wall was too high for her to see anything close beneath it. She could have spun a web to view there, but walking would take no greater time, so she went.

The gateroom was wide, floored with polished stone, and hung with thick tapestries against drafts. Even so, she felt the storm there. Through a peephole in the carven portal, she saw darkness, streaming rain, and then, by a flash of lightning, him lying on the ground, the horse grazing nearby. She opened the door. Her first impulse was to step outside and turn him over with her own hands to see if he were dead, but she stifled that and sent a few snakes instead, in case he should be shamming with evil intent. The snakes were not happy to be out in the wet, but they obeyed. They nosed about the body, which did not move, and they reported it warm and breathing and leaking blood. She waved an arm, and they wriggled under him, a living mattress, living rollers to move him over the

7

rain-slick grass. They conveyed him through the door. The horse shied at the snakes, rearing wide-eyed and snorting, and Delivev had to grasp its bridle in her hands and murmur many calming words before she could coax it inside. She locked the gate behind it then, locked the storm out and the stranger and his horse in her home.

She led the animal to the roofed-over courtyard that sheltered many of her own pets and left it there with a mound of towels rubbing it down sans human assistance. She returned to the gateroom to find the snakes arrayed in a ring about the injured knight, who lay unmoving upon the floor, his limbs at odd angles, water dripping from his flesh and clothing. A red stain was forming at his left side. Delivev found the wound quickly, guessed it a mighty sword cut so to cleave through heavy chain mail, and wondered why the young knight's opponent had not finished him. Because the linking pattern of the chain lay within the province of her magic, though the metal itself did not, she scattered it with a nod. His clothing parted as well, exposing him naked to her ministrations, and while she bound his side she could not help admiring his youthful beauty. She felt of his head for fever and found none, though her fingers lingered long upon his cheeks. She leaned her ear against his chest and heard his heart beat strong and steady beneath the smooth skin, beneath the firm muscle. She chafed his wrists and spoke softly to him, and at last his eyelids flickered.

His eyes were the deepest blue she had ever seen.

"Who are you?" he whispered.

"I am Delivev Ormoru. Your horse brought you to my home."

"You are kind to take me in."

"I could not leave a wounded man to the storm."

"My name is Mellor," he said, and then he gasped and clutched with weak hands at his side.

"You must not speak. There will be time for that later." She summoned a blanket, wrapped him in it, motioned the snakes to crawl under him once more and transport him to an inner room and a couch. His eyes widened at the sight of the snakes, at their undulating touch, but he said nothing. "I am a sorceress," she said. "These are my servants, and they will not harm you."

He smiled his trust, and she smiled back, and as the snakes bore him into the heart of her castle, he found himself staring at her. She walked beside him, her gown of green feathers swaying with each step. She wore feathers, he knew, so that no one could turn her magic back upon her person, and even her hair, cut to many lengths, seemed like a crown of brown feathers on her head. *How beautiful she is,* thought Gildrum, who called himself Mellor.

✑ CHAPTER TWO

She found him walking in the small garden that her castle walls enclosed. The day was sunny and warm, the climbing roses were in full bloom, the morning glories just closing their petals to the noon light.

"Don't you think it too soon to be so far from your bed?" she asked, stepping close to take his arm and support him.

"I was feeling well. I heard the birds singing and I couldn't lie still any longer." He wore the robe of blue silk she had woven for him, to match his eyes.

"You look well," she said. "You heal quickly. Youth always heals quickly." She smiled. "Come, sit down with me. Don't push yourself too far; a wound like that needs gentle care."

"I can never thank you enough for *your* gentle care, Delivev." Stiffly, he eased himself to the sun-warmed stone bench. "I would have died that night if not for you."

"It was a foul night for swordplay."

"The swordplay was in the daytime, under a clear sky. It was quite finished when the storm began."

From the lush growth at her feet, she plucked a handful of varicolored flowers and began to twine their stems together in a wreath. "You have not told me your tale yet—where you come from, how you received that wound, what happened to your adversary. I have waited patiently while you slept the days away and drank my soup. I hope I won't have to wait any longer."

"I don't consider it a very interesting tale."

"Let me judge it."

"Very well. I am the younger son of a younger son, so far removed from nobility that I inherited nothing but the right to become a knight. When I gained my arms, I left home to travel the wide world. Since then, I have roamed far, serving petty men in their personal wars, surviving partly through skill and partly through luck. Most recently, I swore two years' allegiance to the Lord of the East March, a better man than some. I had been with him almost a year when he entrusted me with a message to his cousin at Falconhill—I was on my way there when I was stopped on the road and challenged by a rather large and angry-looking knight. I don't know what I did to provoke him; perhaps his teeth hurt and he was trying to find something to take his mind off the pain. We fought on foot, sword to sword, and he was a good fighter, but I was better. He did catch me in the side, but it was too late for him: at almost the same instant I struck him a mortal blow. At first, I hardly noticed that I had been touched, but when I tried to dig a grave for him, I almost fainted. I knew then that he would have to remain unburied, and I climbed on my horse and started out to look for help. I remember the sky darkening and the rain wetting me, but no more until I woke in your castle."

Delivev settled the wreath on her hair. "Knighthood," she said. "You like it?"

"I know nothing else."

"There are other trades. Safer trades."

"My father was a knight; I have no entry to another trade. Nor do I know of one that pleases me as well. Would I wish to be a tinker or a smith? I think not."

"You enjoy risking your life for petty men? You yourself called them petty."

He plucked a single blossom and held it cupped in his hand, looking down at its pale yellow against his ruddy flesh. "Someday I will find a lord I can love, and him I will serve without complaint." He glanced up at Delivev. "Shall I hear *your* tale now, my lady?"

"Mine?" She shook her head. "I have none to tell."

"What, a sorceress all alone in *this*," he waved an arm to include the whole of Castle Spinweb, "and no tale at all? Do you expect me to believe that?"

"I am a sorceress. They call me the Weaver sometimes. The castle was my mother's, and her mother's before her. None but my family have ever lived here, and I seldom leave. I lead a quiet life—you see all my world around you."

"The Weaver. What does that name mean?"

She pointed to a nearby trellis, cloaked with climbing roses. "You see the pattern there, the interlacing tendrils, the stems weaving in and out of the wooden support? Those roses are mine because of the way they grow. I could make them climb to my topmost tower in a few moments, or I could make them reach out to you, envelop you in their thorns, scratch your life away. Birds are mine, too, if they weave their nests, and snakes because they twine like living threads, and spiders that make webs—you'll find them in every room of Castle Spinweb."

"And cloth?" asked Gildrum.

"Cloth of course," and she nodded toward him, causing his silken robe to tighten in a brief embrace.

He laughed. "Do your guests ever worry that the blankets on their beds might turn against them?"

"If my guests meant me harm, they would do well to worry so. But I rarely have guests. You are the first . . . in a long time."

Softly, he said, "Is that your choice, my lady?"

"I have no need of human companionship. I have my plants, my pets." She gazed about her garden, stretched to pluck a rose from the trellis; carefully,

11

she stripped the thorns from its stem and then presented it to Gildrum. "Perhaps you would be surprised at how all this fills my life."

He accepted the rose and twined its stem with that of the yellow bloom he had plucked himself. "I wonder that you shun human society. Ordinary mortals, yes, I can comprehend how they might bore you, but there are other sorcerers—I know of several, at least by reputation, and once I even saw one from afar, casting a spell for the lord I served at the time."

"We know each other, we sorcerers, but we do not keep company. It is better so. Such powers would make for wild arguments, would they not, for even friends argue sometimes, and surely married couples do so. An argument over the seasoning of the soup might light the sky for miles, uproot trees, flood the land, destroy all that both of them held dear. Of what use would such a match be?"

"If that is your view of marriage, kind Delivev, then I, who have never married, cannot disagree."

"Between sorcerers, yes. The sorcerous breed have quick tempers, Mellor. They are happier solitary."

"You speak as if from experience. Forgive me if I pry, my lady, but . . . did you ever marry?"

She shook her head. "My mother married, to her sorrow. I saw, for a few years when I was very young, what life could be like for a sorcerous couple. We were better off, she and I, after my father died."

"And your mother? What happened to her?"

"She died, too. She was very old when I was born, though of course you could not tell from looking at her." She looked into Gildrum's eyes. "I am old, too, Mellor. Much older than you imagine. We sorcerers are a long-lived stock."

He held the flowers out to her on his open palm. "You are younger than these blossoms in my sight. And far more beautiful."

She took the blooms from his hand, her fingers resting warm against his flesh for a moment. "Is a flattering tongue part of your knight's weaponry, Mellor?"

"One learns soft words when the object is worthy of them, my lady."

12

"You should be a troubadour, then, instead of a knight, and spread soft words about the world instead of blood."

"What do you know of troubadours, my lady who rarely shelters a guest in her home? Are troubadours the lone exception to your aversion to humanity? If so, I might consider the change."

"I need not let the world into my castle; I can see it well enough if I wish, and hear it, too. Shall I show you a marvel?"

"Yes. I haven't seen many true marvels in my travels."

She rose. "Can you walk now?"

"I think so." He stood shakily.

"Lean upon my shoulder."

"With pleasure." He let his weight fall lightly upon her, just enough to let her feel that she was helping him. They moved slowly through the nearest doorway, down a corridor, and into a large room. Light spilling through a high window revealed the walls of the room to be festooned with spiderwebs. Gildrum hesitated at the threshold. "How long has it been since you last visited this place?"

"A few weeks," she said. "These webs are not signs of abandonment, merely of busy spiders. They do their best to satisfy my needs."

"How do spiderwebs satisfy your needs?"

"In many ways. You shall see one of them shortly. Come, sit down; you must be exhausted from that walk."

"Somewhat exhausted," he said.

The center of the room was occupied by a wide bed with thick velvet coverlet and mounds of cushions. Delivev seated Gildrum and herself upon it, and all around them the webs formed gossamer curtains. She pointed out one of the spiders, a tiny black creature sitting in the center of a web. At a gesture from its mistress, it scurried down a strand to spin a patch in a large open section of the net.

"Breezes sometimes break the silk," said Delivev, "or a bird or a snake will wander in here."

"Why don't you close off the room, then, and seal the window?"

"How would insects enter if I did that? My spiders have to *eat*, Mellor." She pressed him back against the cushions. "Relax now, and watch that web." She pointed to a fairly symmetrical segment of the drapery, eight strands radiating from a central point, joined by a myriad of closely spaced concentric rings. She stretched her hand out toward it, fingers splayed, palm parallel to the flat of the web, though many feet from it. Her hand moved slowly in a circular pattern, as if wiping a vertical surface with an invisible cloth. The center of the web became hazy, the strands blurring together into a uniform gray sheen, and upon that sheen dim shapes began to coalesce. As from a great distance, voices sounded in the web-draped room, their words indistinct at first but growing clearer, as if the speakers approached. The dim shapes turned into men, and their lips moved to match their voices. Gildrum and Delivev viewed a scene in the main hall of some castle as they would see through a window into the courtyard of Castle Spinweb.

"Pay no attention to their conversation," said Delivev. "Those two never discuss anything interesting. But there in the back—" One slim finger pointed to the left side of the scene. "There is the troubadour who is spending this season at the Castle of Three Towers. He will sing soon; it is almost time for dinner there."

"How are we seeing him?" asked Gildrum.

"There is a spiderweb on the wall beside the fireplace. The scullery maid cleans it off occasionally, but the spider keeps spinning afresh. It is a very industrious spider. The troubadour doesn't know that it hides in his pack every time he travels to a new castle."

"We are seeing this through that spiderweb?"

"Yes. And hearing, too. Ah, listen now; he is really quite a good singer." She leaned back on the cushions beside him and closed her eyes for the music. "You see," she said between songs, "I am not so isolated as you thought."

"Can you see anywhere in the world?"

"Oh, there are limits. I must know where to look. I must be interested in looking there. I know of many places that I *could* look, but I wouldn't want to bother.

14

There must be spiders, of course. I will never see the kitchens of certain very cleanly cooks because they don't give spiders a chance to spin more than a strand or two before they kill them. My curiosity is not piqued by such kitchens. And then there are the homes of other sorcerers—we respect each others' privacy, although I *could* look in on them if I wished to be rude."

"I can't imagine you being rude, my lady."

"Ssh. He sings again." He sang of love, as he had before, most plaintively. "I will weave a tapestry for that song someday," she murmured. "I see it as red and gold and brown—autumn colors."

"And send it to him?"

"Send it? Why should I? What would he do with it, a troubadour? Carry it on his shoulder from castle to castle?"

"Give it to someone, I suppose, to display for him. To insure that his memory outlives him."

"I shall remember him after he is dead. I don't care beyond that." She propped herself up on one elbow. "There are others, some better even than he."

"You have spiders traveling with them, too?"

"Yes. Though there is one of them that keeps finding the creatures, and they don't all escape his foot."

"How did you find them all?"

"With difficulty. The first was an accident: I was watching court politics in the bedchamber of a certain king, and he summoned a troubadour for diversion. I, too, was diverted, and I gave the singer a tiny companion for his travels. After that, I began to look for them. Now, through them, I see more of the world than ever before. Troubadours know no boundaries, after all, no politics, no loyalties, not if they wish to continue their travels. And none of them ever know that I am riding with them."

He gazed up at her face, so near his own, leaning upon the open palm of her hand. Her hair almost brushed his shoulder. "You cannot touch them, my lady Delivev. They are like images in a mirror; you reach out, but the surface is flat and it gives back no warmth. Nor will they speak to you, for you are like a ghost among them—less than a ghost if they never

15

sense you at all, not even by some inexplicable shiver running down their spines."

"So much the better," she replied. "I see and hear them, yet I need not tolerate their presence."

"I cannot believe that you so despise all other people."

"I despise no one. But I do not care to share my life with anyone I have ever seen in the web."

"Hosting a troubadour would hardly be sharing your life."

"A small part of my life."

"And yet, you took me in, a stranger, knowing that you would be sharing your life with me until I healed."

"I would have done the same for a wounded dog."

Lightly, he laid one hand upon her shoulder. "You are not as chill as you wish to seem. Your parents gave you an ugly view of life, but you know that what they had was not what might have been. Two people mismatched, nothing more. How can you judge all the world by them?"

"I have seen more than you suppose in my webs. I have seen great lords and their ladies, and they were different from my parents only in the limits of their powers—dishes thrown instead of lightning."

"And you must also have heard songs of great love from troubadours."

"Great loves that ended tragically, yes. Great lovers that died before they could drive each other mad."

He shook his head. "If your view of life were true, then no one would ever marry."

"I am not responsible for the mistakes of others. Only for my own. You are very young, Mellor. I would expect you to believe in many things that I have outgrown."

"I believe that individuals may love each other." He turned on his side to face her, very close, and she did not draw away. "I believe that I could love the kindest and most beautiful lady I have ever met."

"Mellor, what a foolish thing to say."

"And I believe that she could love me in return." His arms slid around her, and he pulled her to him. Her mouth was warm and yielding, and the cushions were soft beneath their bodies, the velvet coverlet voluptuous against their flesh. She whispered concern for his wound, that it might open from such exertion, but he sealed her mouth with his own and nothing more was said. Afterward, they slept in each other's arms on the bed surrounded by spiderweb draperies, and above them a troubadour in a distant castle sang of love.

From the balcony of the highest spire of Castle Spinweb, the stars seemed bright and hard and close enough to touch. Gildrum watched for hours as they wheeled about the Northern Star, as Delivev lay sleeping so far below in the bed they had shared this score of nights. Gildrum needed no sleep, of course, but he could feign well enough, and he had found great pleasure in holding her in his arms each night. Now he denied himself that pleasure. Now he found something inside himself griping like acid, like a small animal with sharp claws. His task was completed, and the will of his lord demanded his return to Ringforge. Not that Rezhyk knew what his servant had done—there was no communication between them while Gildrum was inside the walls of Spinweb—but that did not matter. The imperative was within Gildrum himself, the imperative of the ring, and he had no choice but to obey.

He did not wish to leave. In all the years he had been slave to a sorcerer, he had seen the human world, he had dealt with men and women in human guise; he thought he understood them better than any demon he knew. Sometimes he wondered if he no longer understood his own kind quite so well, for he had rarely been among *them* since he was captured by the power of the ring. He knew Rezhyk best, of course, through long contact, and he had puzzled over the sorcerer's proposal of marriage to Delivev the Weaver when first it was made. Rezhyk was a somber man, given to long nights alone in his workshop, poring over books brought him by his demons from the hidden corners of the world. He sought knowledge; material things meant little to him, except as the necessary comforts of life. Gildrum had thought a demon consort was the only sort that could please him, available when desired, in precisely the form that his mind could envision and his hands mold, never making demands, never impinging upon his life as a mortal woman would. And yet, the moment he had opened his eyes to Delivev, Gildrum had understood her attraction, compounded of cool serenity, beauty, kindness, and more than a touch of melancholy. He had never thought that a demon could love a human being, and though he spoke of it eloquently—for he, too, had listened to troubadours' songs, and to other things, in his travels about the earth—he was not sure that he knew at all what love was. He had never thought that a demon could want to be a man and stay forever with a human woman. He wanted that now, and if that was love, then he was a lover.

In the morning, he thought, *I shall use my well-planned excuse.*

He wished upon the fading stars that morning would never come, but the sky continued to brighten in spite of him.

"I understand," she said, but she sighed anyway. "You pledged yourself to carry the message to Falconhill, and you must go. I will not try to keep you against that pledge."

He took her hands between his own. "Never doubt that I love you, sweet Delivev."

"I have no doubts."

"I shall return as soon as my duty is done. I would that were tomorrow, believe me." He pressed her close against his heart. "I would not leave you out of choice, my love."

"I will be here tomorrow, and the next day," she murmured. "Whenever you return, I shall rejoice."

He kissed her lips one last time, and then they parted. His horse was ready, shuffling from hoof to hoof in animal impatience to be moving. He led it out the gate and mounted. His cleaned and mended surcoat rippled about his thighs in the fresh morning breeze, and his remade chain mail rustled at every move of his body. He lifted a hand in farewell, then wheeled and rode off into the forest. He did not look back. He did not see the tears that welled up in Delivev's eyes as the forest swallowed him.

She turned back to her home, bolted the door to shut the world away once more. Slowly she climbed the narrow flight of steps to the topmost tower, and there she set up her loom, to begin a tapestry to while away the days till he should return. She chose her colors carefully: pure black for the horse, white and red for the surcoat, and the deepest blue she had ever seen for his eyes. It would be a large tapestry, a long time in the finishing.

She did not discover her pregnancy very soon, for the tapestry held her attention and she lost track of time. One day, however, her stomach bothered her and she decided to lie down instead of working, to listen afar instead of dreaming along with her fingers. She lay down in the web-draped room, gestured with her hand, and the web she sought to transform into a window remained as it was. At first she thought the web at the other end of the rapport had been broken, and she tried another, and then another, but none responded. A little more testing showed her the newly circumscribed limits of her power, and then the roiling of her stomach and a swift count of days revealed the cause.

From the balcony of the highest spire of Castle Spinweb, she could see the tapestry if she turned toward the room—the horse's legs were complete, and the grass beneath and behind them; she would not reach the face for some time, though she could see it every moment in her mind's eye. If she turned away from the room, she could see the forest, and the path he would take returning to her. She had chosen the tower room because of that view. As he was leaving, she had thought of sending spiders with him but decided against it; she could not hang such chains upon her love, could not bear to torture herself with looking over his shoulder but never being able to touch him. The tapestry, an instant of his life frozen upon the threads, suited her better.

And now she carried his child. She pressed her hands against the flesh of her belly, as if she could feel the burgeoning life within. Her mother had told her

19

how it was—the blindness to the outside world, the sense of being cut off from the creatures that had been her own, like losing the use of arms and legs for nine months. Her mother had accepted the experience once, for love, but never again, not though her father raged for a son to match their daughter.

She could rid herself of the child now. That was a simple matter. She could abort it and return to her usual life, and the feeling in her stomach would be gone. Instead, she sat down before the tapestry and began to weave. She touched his spurs today, twining her woollen strands with silk to give the metal silver highlights. The tapestry would be finished when her time came, she thought, and then she would have flesh of his flesh as well as the portrait.

Summer passed, and winter, and she was still alone when she bore the child.

"Good work, my Gildrum, is it not?" said Rezhyk, admiring the cloth-of-gold shirt one last time before slipping it over his head. It was supple, finely woven, and lighter than he had expected—a piece of the gold bar remained unused. "I have never known such exhaustion." His cheeks were sunken, his eyes circled and pouchy, his beard grown out in disarray. He had paused from his weaving only to bolt the bare minimum of food that would sustain his strength. He had not slept at all in eleven days.

"Good work, my lord," said Gildrum. "You would make an excellent weaver."

"Bah! A tedious vocation, and I am glad to be rid of it. How long shall I sleep now? Three days?" He blinked and rubbed his eyes. By magic he had stayed awake so long, but still he was unsteady on his feet, and his hands shook. "Help me to my bed."

"Yes, my lord." Gildrum, as the fourteen-year-old girl, climbed down from the high stool from which she had guided her lord's activities. "Shall I carry you?"

"No, I can walk."

She took his arm and laid it across her shoulders and bore most of his weight as they moved from the workshop to his bedroom. She eased him to the wide bed and stripped off his clothes, save for the new shirt and the thin overshirt that concealed it.

Rezhyk drew the covers up to his chin. "Wake me tomorrow for dinner."

"My lord," said Gildrum, leaning over him. "I would ask a favor of you."

"A favor?" He opened one bloodshot eye. "What?"

"Let me go home for a little while. I need to get away from humans—I have been among them too much lately."

Yawning, Rezhyk shook his head, burrowing deep into the pillow. "I cannot do without you, my Gildrum. Not now. I need you to watch over me."

"You have other servants who can do that."

"Not like you. You always know what I want. We've been together so long."

She blew out the candle that illuminated the room. "Yes, my lord," she said. "I will be near if you need me." Silently, she glided from the room. She had a chamber of her own, on an upper floor, where she sometimes sat to watch the sky and wait for Rezhyk to summon her. She went there now. There were tasks to be done around the castle—there were always tasks —but she did not feel like doing any of them at this moment.

◆§ CHAPTER THREE

She called him Cray. She bore him without another human hand to help, while her animals looked on from a ring about her bed. When he was free of her body, cloths washed and swaddled him and laid him upon her breast, and the soiled bedding eased itself away from her, rolled into a ball, and tumbled away to burn itself in the fireplace while fresh sheets crept beneath her and fresh blankets tucked themselves about her and her new son. She slept then.

He was a happy child, laughing early, reaching out with curious but gentle fingers for the brightly colored flowers and birds of the garden. He grew fast and sturdy, with his mother's eyes and hair, with no hint of the young knight about him save for a love of fighting men. He would sit before the webs for hours to watch armored warriors strut across the view, to glimpse a sword and shield. He begged his mother to make her spiders move their webs outdoors, where he could watch sword practice and jousting, and she indulged him, as she did in most things. When he asked for a toy sword, she made it with her own hands, of a straight branch with a guard of twigs lashed to one end. She made a shield, too, a light frame covered with cloth, and she embroidered his father's arms upon the cloth—three red lances interlocked on a white field, just as they were upon the tapestry.

The tapestry was long completed. It hung in the room of its manufacture, the room from which the empty forest track could be seen. Delivev no longer climbed the stairs every day to look at either. But sometimes, late at night, after Cray was supposed to be asleep, she would visit the tower room and weep before the portrait. On those nights, she remembered the songs of troubadours too well. She listened to them less often these days, preferring to find absorption in her plants, her animals, and her son.

Cray had followed her to the tower a few times and crouched outside to hear her tears. He knew why she wept, and even when he was very young he wondered why any man would leave a woman to do that.

"He had pledged himself," his mother explained. "When a person makes a promise, he must fulfill it."

"Even if it means hurting someone?" Cray asked.

"Even so. That is the nature of a promise, Cray."

When he was older, he said, "He must have found Falconhill by now, Mother. He must have given his message. Why hasn't he returned? He promised you, too, after all."

"He did. He said, when his duty was done. Perhaps there was more than just the message itself. He never wished to speak of it, and I didn't press him." She was working on another tapestry now, with Cray as its central figure, but he was growing so fast that it no longer portrayed the Cray standing before her. "I will wait here and raise you, my son, waiting." She smiled sadly. "I never had better plans, before he came to me."

In a small voice, Cray said, "Do you think he's dead, Mother?"

She sighed. "I don't want to think that, Cray."

"Well, what else could have happened to him?"

"Perhaps he found some other woman he could love more than he loved me."

"More than you?" He threw his arms around her and hugged her tight. "How could anyone love someone else more than you?"

She kissed her son. "Someday, you may love someone more than you love me, and you will understand."

"Never!"

"Don't say never, Cray, not with a long life ahead of you."

He looked into her eyes. "Why don't you try to find him, Mother?"

"It would be difficult after so many years."

"You could *try!*"

She shook her head. "No. I told myself once that I wouldn't do that, and I have not changed my mind. He has some good reason for not returning; whether it be death or another woman, I have no desire to know."

With a new and heavier wooden blade, Cray practiced swordplay against a tree in the garden and then, when he learned a few of his mother's tricks, against a moving, man-shaped bundle of cloth. It dodged and ducked among the flowers, bucking a latticework wooden shield against him, occasionally tapping at him with a branch covered in leather braid. He had some trouble controlling its movements, but that was to the good, to his mind, because it made the bundle an unpredictable adversary. Unfortunately, it had a tendency to fall limp to the ground during Cray's moments of intense concentration on his own swordsmanship; when that happened too often, he went back to the tree.

He practiced riding, too, on a pony his mother acquired from another sorcerer whose passion was four-footed creatures; she traded a fine tapestry that her son might gallop about the forest with only a few spiders to keep watch over him. With a willow withe as a lance, he charged imaginary foes, and when he returned to Spinweb's sanctuary, he was as sweat-cloaked as his steed.

In time he asked for a real sword and a real shield, a helm, chain mail, and a man's horse. He was twelve years old.

His mother rose from her weaving, hands on her hips. "Don't you think, Cray, that you have played this game long enough? It is time for you to settle down to sorcery."

He leaned upon the stick that served him as sword, both hands upon its wooden hilt. "It is no game, Mother. I wish to be a knight."

Her mouth hardened into a white line. "I have indulged you out of love. I thought that while you played childish games your body would grow strong and straight. And it has. I never dreamed that your mind would not do the same."

"Mother, there is no shame in being a knight."

"There is death! If your father is dead, then knighthood was his killer!"

"Mother, I am not suited to the sorcerous life."

"Why not? You do it well, the little you have learned. There is far more to know."

He looked down at his hands and shook his head. "It holds no interest for me."

"You will grow to love it, as I have."

"I would rather go out in the world and earn my bread with strength of arms than conjure it by magic."

"You think you are ready to go out in the world as a knight? Oh, my son, don't think your prowess with a wooden sword and a tree make you ready to face a real opponent!"

Again he shook his head. "I know I am not ready. But I would practice here in Spinweb with a real sword, and then I would go out to seek a teacher to better my

24

skills." He raised his eyes to hers, and his gaze was level with her own though he had not yet reached his full growth. "Mother, this is truly what I want. If you love me, you will help me to be the kind of man I must be."

She turned away from him. "If I love you, I must lose you—is that what you say? How can you ask it of me?"

"I must go out in the world and meet other human beings."

"You can see them in the webs."

"I can see them, but I can't speak to them. I can't touch them."

"You are so young!"

He laid the wooden sword down and stepped close to her to wrap his arms about her. "I will make this promise," he said. "Give me the sword and the horse and the armor, and I will not leave you for another two years. I will stay here and laugh with you and be a loving son for another two years."

She leaned against him. "I have no sword and armor. I might find a horse that would suit you, but the choosing of arms should be up to you. I know too little of the matter. All sorcerers know too little of arms." She hugged him tight. "Oh, my son, you must go to a town where merchants deal in swords and shields, you must ask for advice from men who understand such things. If you had a father, he would instruct you, of course . . . if you had a father." Her voice broke and she clasped him ever more fiercely. "How can I bear to lose you, too?"

"Mother, every fledgling must fly from the nest at last."

"I never flew, not I!"

"Well, this one will."

She nodded, and tears leaked from her eyes.

Some days later, a vast dark cloud swept out of the east, blocked the sun above Castle Spinweb briefly, then descended, condensing, to the ground before the gate. By the time Cray and Delivev opened the portal, the dark and roiling mist was a sphere no more than ten feet in diameter. At their approach, it oozed back against the nearest trees, exposing the great horse that had been hidden in its depths. The horse whinnied and tossed its head, dancing restlessly on hooves as big as dinner plates, but it allowed the humans to touch it—indeed, it relaxed as their hands moved upon its sleek gray flanks.

"Very good," Delivev said to the cloud. She nodded toward the open castle gate, and a pair of rolled tapestries cartwheeled out to the grass. They spread themselves flat for the cloud's inspection, and it seemed satisfied, for it covered them and rose skyward with its new and lighter burden.

"I have never seen a demon yet that would say thank you," muttered Delivev. "Well, what are you waiting for? This is your horse—take it inside."

"I had not expected it to be . . . so large," said Cray.

"You will be heavy in your armor, my son; it must be large to bear your weight."

Cray stroked the horse's neck. "I shall call him Gallant."

In the misty dawn of a spring day, he saddled Gallant for the journey to the nearest town.

Delivev pressed silver money into his hands, to pay for the arms he wished to buy. "Don't flash the coins about," she warned him. "There are some men who would try to take it from you."

"I shall be careful, Mother. I've seen a few things in the webs, after all; I know there are evil folk out there. I'll have my knife and a stout staff, and no fear of using them."

"And don't worry about finding a chain shirt of perfect size; buy one too large and I'll refit the links to you better than any tailor could."

"I don't doubt it." He kissed her quickly, then grasped his horse's mane and pulled himself into the saddle.

"I want to hear from you, my son. Let one of the spiders spin a web each night just before sunset so that we may speak to one another."

"I will try, Mother. But if I am among ordinary people, it might be better that I avoid such sorcery."

"It might. I would worry . . . but you must do as you see fit. You have my love always. Hurry back." She waved till he disappeared down the forest track.

At first Cray traversed ground that he knew as well as his mother's castle, but soon he passed into unfamiliar territory. The nature of the forest did not change—it grew no denser, no darker, the trees did not bend over to clutch at him as, in younger days, he had thought they might. Smiling, he recalled other childhood fancies: that there was no world beyond a narrow stretch of woodland ringing Castle Spinweb; that the castle stood upon a disk of earth whose edge was the horizon, a cliff overlooking infinite depths. He had thought the scenes of the webs to be conjured from his mother's imagination, stories told for his sole benefit. He had assumed his mother and himself to be the only human beings in the universe, and when he viewed the tapestry portrait of his father, he thought that the handsome young knight had ridden too close to the edge of the disk and fallen into the vast nothing. When he finally spoke of these notions to his mother, she laughed and began to instruct him otherwise. Yet still, in his dreams, he sometimes peered over the edge of the world, and trees swayed close behind him, urging him to jump. In his dreams, he knew that his father was waiting, whole and strong, somewhere below.

He thought about his father more often than he would confess to Delivev. They had a tacit agreement between them that this one topic was not to be examined closely, but Cray could not help speculating, could not help measuring his life against the one he imagined his father had known. He could not remember when he had first vowed to be of his father's kind and not his mother's. He could not remember when he had first realized that he wanted his father to be proud of him.

The forest around Spinweb had few visitors. Its only hunters were Cray and his mother, and because they used magical nets that captured prey and carried it to the castle without human help, the forest dwellers had no fear of human beings. In his rambles, Cray had found deer to eat from his hands, and squirrels and rabbits to climb upon his lap and nuzzle him. His pony, too, had never frightened them, but before his great gray horse they now scattered, and all he saw of woodland creatures was an occasional rustle of leaves

27

in the undergrowth. He had no hunting plans, for his saddlebags held food enough and more for the whole round trip of six days, but he would have liked the companionship, however brief, of a deer or two. Instead, he had only a pack of spiders, and they were scant company, hiding in his boots, beneath his collar, behind the rolled brim of his hat. He held one on his finger for a time, but it didn't care for the breeze of his horse's motion and soon scuttled to the shelter of his sleeve. A couple of birds had followed him at first, flying around his head, lighting on his shoulder, but they had turned back before the morning was half gone. At noon he stopped at a spring, letting Gallant drink while he filled his flask; then he climbed the tallest tree he could find, to search behind him for Castle Spinweb. But it was gone, even its highest spire swallowed by the forest, which seemed to spread out in every direction, unbroken. Cray had never felt so alone in his life. He felt frightened by that, and elated, all at once.

That night, he camped in a grassy glade, and he set a spider to spin in a clump of rocks. Almost as soon as the web was done, its center blurred, and his mother's features coalesced upon the silk. They spoke briefly, she wished him good weather and a good night's sleep, and as her image faded, he caught the glitter of tears upon her lashes. He sniffled a bit himself, but only after she was gone. He missed her as much as she missed him, but not enough to turn him back.

On the third day, the forest track merged with another, wider one, and he began to encounter signs of humanity: an axe-cut tree stump, an abandoned shelter made of stout branches, rusted horseshoes, a lone, cracked wagon wheel. Soon the road acquired twin ruts where carts frequented it. At midafternoon he passed a hunter, the first human being he had ever seen face to face save his mother. The man wore deerskin leggings and a woollen shirt; he carried a longbow slung over his shoulder, and a quiver of arrows fletched with white goose feathers.

Cray meant to hail him politely, but his tongue clove to the roof of his mouth. He wanted to ask the distance to the town. He wanted to exchange civilized pleasantries. Instead, he could only wave and ride on quickly. The man watched in silence as he passed.

The reins felt suddenly slippery in Cray's hands, the leather wet with the new sweat on his palms, and he tightened his grip. Gallant felt the change in touch and tossed its head. He halted the animal, then turned in the saddle to see if the bowman were staring after him. He was not. He was walking the other way. He had seen nothing worth staring after in a boy on a large horse.

Cray kicked his mount to a trot. He was ashamed of himself. He had assumed that seeing a human being in the flesh would be no different from seeing him in a web. He had never thought to practice greeting as he had practiced fighting. Now he whispered as he rode: "Good morning, friend. How far is the town, good sir? Fare you well on this fine day, good wife." He hoped his heart would ease its clamor before his next encounter on the road.

The forest gave way to barley fields. Cray thought he saw a man standing among the grain, but on closer inspection the figure turned out to be a scarecrow. The afternoon was waning by the time he saw another human being—three of them at once, walking single file at the side of the track, bent-backed under huge bundles of wood. By that time he did not need to ask how far the town might be; he could see its walls in the distance, on high ground.

"Good morrow," he said as he trotted past them. They made some sort of reply, but he scarcely heard it, could not have said whether it was greeting or curse. He only knew that *he* had spoken to *them,* and with those two small words he felt some barrier dissolve within himself. He sat straighter on his horse after that, though he was tired from the day's riding, and he whistled a cheerful series of bird calls. As the road approached the town, other paths converged on it, and foot traffic from these—as well as that he had caught up with—enveloped him. He smiled and nodded at one and all, guiding his horse carefully among them, and when someone nodded tentatively in return, Cray made a verbal greeting. Soon he was speaking to everyone he passed, and if only a few answered with more than a tilt of the head, he was content.

The town gates were open; his horse was so tall that Cray had to bend at the waist to pass beneath their arch. Immediately within was the marketplace. It was quiet so late in the day, only a few woodcutters hawking their wares against the cool of the coming night. Cray dismounted near one of them.

"Good even, sir," he said. "Can you tell me where I might buy a sword?"

The woodcutter looked Cray up and down. "A bit young for a sword, aren't you?"

"Perhaps now," said Cray, "but the years will mend that. Can you direct me?"

The man shrugged. "The smith might know. Up that street." He gestured with a thumb. "You'll see the forge." He eyed Gallant. "Fine-looking horse you have there. Very fine—for such a young lad."

Cray smiled. "He has a vile temper, though. Watch you stay clear—he might kick."

The man stepped back, heels nudging the bundle of faggots behind him. "If he kicks me, I'll have your hide, lad."

"If he kicks you, you won't have anything, good sir." He waved a farewell and walked up the indicated street, Gallant ambling docilely after.

He found the smithy without any trouble. The smith, finished with his work for the day, was sitting in a large chair in front of the forge, watching the fire burn low.

"May I tie my horse to your rail and speak a moment with you, sir?" asked Cray.

The smith nodded. He was a short man but very broad of shoulder, with muscles hardened by metalwork. He looked at Cray only briefly, reserving the majority of his attention for Gallant. "That's a well-made animal," he said.

"I have been told so, sir, but I am no judge of horseflesh."

"He is well-shod, too, so what might you need of *me?*"

"I am looking for a sword, sir. And a shield and

30

helm and chain mail as well, but the sword comes first."

The smith shook his head. "I cannot help you, boy. Ask me to shoe your horse or mend your wagon, and I will do it easily. But I am no sword-maker."

"Where might I find one, then?"

"Not in this town." He frowned, fingering his chin. "The lord buys his weapons from a merchant of the south, and good weapons they are, so I hear. You might go up to the Great House and ask if they would sell you one."

"Thank you, sir." Cray bowed. "Will you direct me to the Great House?"

The smith waved one hand. "Follow this street to the wall, then take the east gate road. You will come to it shortly."

"Good day to you."

Beyond the wall, Cray saw the Great House immediately—a stone fortress that had been hidden from his sight previously by the bulk of the town itself. A wide, tree-lined road ran between cultivated fields from town to castle, and upon that rutted surface, a few late stragglers trudged townward. Cray guided Gallant past them, then allowed the impatient beast to trot, as if it were trying to overtake the long shadow that stretched like a herald before it. Summer twilight was settling slowly over the land as they drew up before the castle entry.

Two guards in studded leather jerkins challenged Cray. "You are not of this town," said one of them.

"Indeed, I am a stranger," he replied. "I seek a sword and armor and was told that I might be able to purchase them here."

The guard who had spoken studied him a moment, and then studied Gallant for another. He turned to his mate. "Who would we ask about such a thing?"

The other shrugged. "The captain might know." He, too, eyed Cray and the horse.

"Will you direct me to the captain, then?" asked Cray.

"I'll call him," said the first guard, and he stepped back through the gate and beckoned to someone inside the courtyard. In a few moments a very stocky man joined the guards; he wore a green leather badge on one shoulder to denote his rank.

"For whom do you wish to buy this sword and armor?" he asked.

"For myself," said Cray.

"Are you a knight, that you need such things?"

"I will be a knight, sir, like my father."

"Why does your father not supply you with a sword and armor, if he is a knight? Why does he let a lad so young rove the world alone in search of a knight's trappings?"

Cray had long since devised his explanation. "My father was killed far from home many years ago. His own armor was never recovered."

"You must have uncles, cousins to help you."

"I have no one but my mother, sir."

The captain squinted at Gallant. "There's a fine horse, I think. Your mother must be rich to buy him for you. Who is she?"

"Delivev Ormoru of Castle Spinweb."

The stocky man's florid complexion washed white. When he spoke next, his voice was very soft. "Your mother is the sorceress called the Weaver?"

"She is."

He bowed low. "If you will dismount, young sir, you may enter the Great House. The supper is being served even now in the main hall, and I am sure the lord will be pleased to seat you there. We will see to your horse."

Cray found himself surprised by the sudden respect engendered by his mother's name, but then he chided himself for that surprise. This town and this fortress were his mother's nearest neighbors, the ordinary mortals most likely to know of her. And obviously they feared her. He wondered what his sweet and gentle mother might have done that could make them fear her.

He slid from the saddle and handed Gallant's reins to the captain. "You are very kind, sir," he said.

"Please come this way," said the captain. He led Cray and the horse into the courtyard, where he passed the horse to the first subordinate he encountered, cautioning him to care well for the animal. Cray he conducted to the keep.

Inside the stone tower, a short corridor gave into a large, open room filled with people eating the evening meal. Tall slit windows admitted the last rays of the sun, and torches at short intervals along the walls added their flickering yellow to the scene. Upon a dais at the far end of the room, a small knot of talkers waved fowl joints to emphasize their words. One of the men was clothed in deep blue, with a gold necklet at his throat; the captain approached him, bowed low, and whispered in his ear. The man's bushy eyebrows rose as he listened, and the eyes that looked out at Cray from beneath those brows held both awe and disbelief. His hands tightened upon the arms of his chair, as if he felt he might be dragged from the seat at any moment.

"You say . . . you are the son of the Weaver of Spinweb," he said.

Cray bowed. "I am that, my lord. My name is Cray."

"You have come to buy . . . arms and armor—is that it?"

"Yes, my lord."

"There is no other reason? Your mother is not . . . displeased with us, I hope?"

"Not to my knowledge, my lord."

He spoke very quickly. "I know that a few of my people have been hunting in the forest that separates her land from mine. They have not trespassed, have they? I will punish any that do, I swear it. Or she may punish them herself, as she wishes, I will not say her nay."

"I know of no trespassers, my lord."

The man in blue relaxed visibly. "I wish to stay on good terms with her. You can understand that, I'm sure."

"Of course, my lord."

"Now . . . arms." He frowned. "Why would the child of a sorceress desire such things?"

"I intend to be a knight, as my father was."

"Your father was not a sorcerer?"

"No, my lord."

33

"Who was he, then?"

"His name was Mellor, and his device was three red lances interlocked on a white field."

The man in blue shook his head. "I do not recognize either."

"I would not expect it, my lord. My mother told me he was sworn to the Lord of the East March, and that is very far away for any of its knights to be known in these lands."

"Far indeed." His hands left the arms of his chair and came together, the palm of one slowly stroking the knuckles of the other. "Arms," he murmured.

"I can pay for them, my lord."

"Oh, I would sell them to the son of the Weaver for a fair price. But not to just anyone who came asking for them. Not, I think, to a boy who offered payment with stolen silver, for example." He leaned forward. "After all, how can I be sure you are who you say you are?"

Cray smiled. "I can prove it, my lord, if I must."

The man straightened, his shoulders striking the back of his chair with an audible thump. "How would you prove it, *if* I asked for proof?"

"You wear long sleeves, my lord. I could roll them to your elbows."

"Well, and so could I."

"But *I* would not touch them while doing so."

The lord set his palms flat on his thighs. "You may do so," he said.

Cray gestured with one outstretched hand, and the lord's left sleeve began to roll itself up his arm. All around him, people ceased their conversations and turned to look, and many of them stepped back, clutching their own sleeves, as if afraid they, too, might begin to move of their own volition.

"Enough!" shouted the lord of the fortress, and he stood up suddenly, brushing his sleeve down with the opposite hand as he might brush at an insect crawling on his skin.

"I can do more than that," said Cray, "but I would not wish to damage your property, my lord."

"No more is necessary, my curiosity is satisfied." He called over his shoulder, "Steward!"

The steward, who was among those who had reeled back from the magic of the sleeve, skittered to his liege's side. He was a small, slight man with a spade beard, and he held his hands curled to his chest as if protecting some treasure that lay within. "My lord?"

"Serve this young man supper, and then give him whatever arms and armor he requires. As a personal gift from me."

Cray bowed. "My lord, I have silver enough to pay."

The lord bowed in return. "As you wish. Let the price be a fair one, steward. And Master Cray—please convey my best wishes to your mother."

"I will, my lord."

"This way, sir," said the steward.

Cray bolted a quick supper, then followed the steward to the armory, which was a long narrow room with hundreds of steel pegs driven into its stone walls and all the trappings of combat hung upon those pegs. With the steward's help, Cray selected a blank shield, a simple bowl-shaped helm with movable visor, a shirt and hood and leg harnesses of chain, and a sword in a plain scabbard. All were in good condition, though all had seen use. The sword was nicked in two places; the steward offered to have the nicks ground out, but Cray refused.

"It will only get nicked again when I use it," he said. He tested the balance of the blade, swinging at an imaginary foe. His wooden sword had not been light, but steel was heavier, and he knew that the muscles in his arms were not yet strong enough to wield it for long. Yet its haft fit his grip well, for though his body was not full grown, his hands were already man-sized.

"It is large for you," said the steward.

"Not for the man I will be." He slid the blade into its scabbard and set the two atop the blank shield. "Steward, how long have you been with this House?"

"All my life, young sir. And my father before me."

Cray folded the chain mail into a manageable bundle, and the links chinked softly under his hands. "Thirteen years ago, my father may have stopped at this fortress. He was perhaps twenty years in age, and the device on his shield was three red lances interlocked upon a white field. Do you remember him?"

"You spoke of him to my lord, did you not? My lord did not recall him."

"Your lord is a man whose attention must be consumed by greater things. A steward, though, might notice one insignificant traveler."

The steward plucked thoughtfully at his beard. "We have few visitors. But, no." He shook his head. "I have no memory of such a one. Are you certain he came this way?"

Cray sighed. "No."

"Perhaps he passed us, not wishing to stop with strangers."

"Perhaps."

"If you wish, I will ask a few others who were here at that time. There may be someone who remembers him."

Cray smiled. "That would be kind of you."

The steward signaled one of the armory guards to come over and pick up Cray's bundle of knightly accoutrements. "We will pack these in your saddlebags, if there is nothing more you desire from this room."

"These are sufficient," said Cray.

"I have ordered a pallet laid for you in the main hall, that you may have a good sleep before you leave us."

"I thank you, steward. Now all we are left with is the matter of price."

"Ah . . . price." He waved the guard away, with instructions to ask the captain of the guard which animal was Cray's. "My lord said a fair price, but in truth I don't know what a fair price would be for these things. They are not new. And their loss is not significant to us, as you can easily see. I might say . . . six pieces of silver for the lot."

"That seems a small price," said Cray.

"Ah, doubtless you could conjure up whatever amount I asked. I hope it would not turn to ash as soon as you passed beyond the horizon."

Cray pulled the purse from his belt and spilled six silver pieces into his hand. "My mother does not

36

deal in magic metals," he said, "else I would not need to buy my armor from you, steward."

The steward nodded once. "A good point indeed."

"The money is real, I promise you." Cray offered the coins on his open palm. "You have set the price, sir. Take it."

Gingerly, the steward took it. After he had closed the money in his fist, he said, "I must confess, young sir, that I have never trafficked with a sorcerer before."

Cray smiled to hear himself so described, but he made no attempt to explain that he scarcely knew a hundredth of his mother's magic. "I will not harm you. You have dealt fairly with me. More than fairly."

The steward turned toward the door. "If you will follow me, then, I will show you to your bed."

The pallet was not as comfortable as his bed at home, but it was softer than a mossy pad under a tree. Cray was tired, and not even the snoring of other sleepers in the hall or the occasional bark of a restless dog could keep him awake. He roused at last to morning streaming through the high windows and a group of pages walking among the sleepers to announce breakfast and to clear the floor of pallets. The page who dragged Cray's pallet to a storage place in a far corner was not much younger than Cray himself. Cray wondered if the boy were bound to be a knight or if, like the steward, he would always remain a servant of the House. The boy was slight. If he planned to be a knight, he had not yet started training. Cray compared his own youthful muscles to the page's slenderness, and he felt he was well-begun in his life's goal. His father, he thought, would be proud of him.

A breakfast of bread and cheese and milk was set out on a long table below the dais, and as Cray was eating his share, the steward approached and motioned him aside.

"I have inquired, young sir, but there is none here who remembers your father. I am sorry."

Cray swallowed his milk at a draft. "I thank you for your efforts, good steward. Truthfully, I had no great hope of finding any trace of him here. But I could not visit without asking. Is my horse saddled and ready?"

"It is."

Scanning the room, Cray said, "I see your lord is not about. You will have to give him my farewell."

"I will do that, young sir."

They walked together to the stables and then with Gallant to the gate. While the steward stood beneath the arch, flanked by the men who guarded the entry to their fortress, Cray led his horse out into the open sunlight and mounted.

"Good luck with your quest," said the steward. "There is a quest, is there not?"

"There is," said Cray. He raised a hand in salute and wheeled his horse about. Before him, the road between the fortress and the town stretched out, full of foot traffic even so early in the day. He rode toward the town, but at the east gate, from which he had first seen the Great House, he turned Gallant aside and followed the wall around the settlement, to the track that had brought him there. He could not see the forest, save in his mind's eye, but he knew that afternoon would bring him to it. He would have one of his spiders spin a web then, between two trees, and he would tell his mother of his success. He hoped she had not waited up all night, worrying about him while her webs remained blank.

The chain mail in his saddlebags rustled to the rhythm of Gallant's pace, a metallic lullaby for a boy who yearned for knighthood. He daydreamed as he rode, of the years that lay ahead, of the feel of chain upon his body, of the heft of sword and shield. He would work hard and grow strong and sure, and then he would leave Spinweb for the wide world. Somewhere out there was his father, perhaps dead, perhaps alive and imprisoned by some enemy or enthralled by another woman—Cray would follow the trail to Falconhill, to the East March, to wherever it might lead. His mother had said she did not wish to know his father's fate, but Cray could not rest so. He had to know the truth, no matter how painful.

He did not plan to tell her of his quest, only that he

intended to search for a teacher to help him be the best knight he could. She would weep anyway, when they bade each other farewell. He thought it better not to burden her more than that.

✺§ CHAPTER FOUR

From the shelter of a tree hollow, a gray squirrel watched Cray practice combat against empty air. Its small head was turned sideways, one lustrous eye following the glint of the sword, both ears pricked to the sound of swinging chain mail. Its tiny paws balanced, humanlike, on the crumbling bark that rimmed its hiding place, and its broad, fluffy tail twitched over its back in rhythm to the boy's movements. The squirrel came often to that tree, and to others nearby, to watch Cray fight imaginary foes in the dappled sunlight of the forest outside Spinweb. It would have come more often yet, but it had a master who required its frequent presence at his castle, in the form of a young, blond girl.

Gildrum could see Spinweb's walls from that perch. It had come to the forest to see them, to catch a glimpse of *her* standing at the gate or the parapet or leaning from a window. It had come as a squirrel, many months after leaving as a man. In those intervening months, the demon had sought to drown itself in work, to fill its days and nights with fetching and carrying and traveling to the far corners of the world, to blot her face from its consciousness. It had even taken over tasks that would normally be assigned to lesser demons, on the pretense that Gildrum could do them better, faster, more precisely the way the master wished them done. Yet her face had been with it always, and at last it succumbed to her lure. Rezhyk never knew that there was a day after which every errand that took his faithful Gildrum from the confines of Castle Ringforge included a brief stop outside Spinweb.

It could not enter, not as squirrel nor as flame. No demon could enter a sorcerer's home without the owner's invitation, unless its own master were within. The knight could have gained admittance, of course, but Gildrum could not face the elaborate fabric of lies that would be necessary to explain visits only long enough for a greeting and a kiss. Rezhyk's command of secrecy still held; his servant could not reveal its true identity.

Rezhyk had given Gildrum the squirrel form once, that the demon might move among humans unobtrusively, and never had it used that shape so much as in the forest about Spinweb. It learned to know the other squirrels, the deer, the rabbits, the wind that whipped the castle walls and the rains that drenched them. It saw Spinweb in moonlight and in moonless starlight, in sunlight and storm, and at last that intermittent vigil was rewarded, on a bright spring morning when the dew was still fresh on the grass, shining like diamonds scattered beneath the trees: *she* stepped from the castle gate, the feathers of her dress rippling in the light breeze, a small child clinging to her hand.

Gildrum gazed long at the child, a brown-haired boy so like Delivev that he could be none other than her son—a sturdy, laughing boy who let go her hand to run barefoot through the wet grass. Cray, she called him, and she told him not to run out of sight. The gray squirrel chittered as they passed by its tree, and the child looked up eagerly and began to make small chittering noises of his own, holding his hand out to lure the squirrel closer. Gildrum was tempted for a moment to go to him, to be cuddled against that small breast, perchance to be touched as well by Delivev herself, but time weighed heavily against the demon; it had watched as long as it dared, and now it had to turn, to scamper back along the branch and dive into a hollow of the tree, to transform into something else, somewhere else.

It did not tell Rezhyk where it had been, what it had seen. Rezhyk, never dreaming that Delivev would bear the babe they had given her, never asked. He had other interests now that he was safe within his shirt of gold, and he had put her out of his mind.

Cray grew straight and strong and more interested in the world beyond Spinweb's walls than his mother was, and the gray squirrel saw her seldom and him often, if fleetingly. It saw him feed deer from his bare hands and tumble on the moss with wild rabbits. It saw him ride his pony through the dense woods, ducking low in the saddle to keep from being swept off by overhanging boughs. It saw him take up arms, first wooden ones and then steel, stalking the forest as a battlefield, slashing at the trees as if they were his mortal enemies. It saw . . . and Gildrum the demon found itself proud of Cray's accomplishments, as if the boy were its own child.

Gildrum knew other demons would laugh at that notion, as they would surely laugh at its love for a human woman; they would say Gildrum had lived too long among humans, that it had absorbed some of their madness. Yet Gildrum wondered why Rezhyk should be any more a father for giving the seed than a demon was for planting it.

My son, it thought, watching with dark, squirrel eyes as Cray rode his great gray horse away from Spinweb.

"I would not wish you to think that I am spying on you," said Delivev.

Cray sat patiently while she bound his hands to the loom with threads of many colors. "I understand, Mother. You have a right to know where I go."

"I don't care where you go, only that you are safe there. The tapestry will trace you like a map, recording not just the motion of your body but that of your heart as well. It will show me your joy and your anguish; it will let me share your triumph and your danger. And should you forget your poor mother for too long, it will show me where to send reminders of my love for you."

"I will try not to forget you, Mother," said Cray.

She kissed his forehead, then wrapped the threads about his temples, his eyes, his ears, his lips. In two years she had spun spool after spool from virgin wool, dyed with her own hands rather than by disembodied magic, and now she imbued the thread and the loom with Cray's aura by wrapping them together.

The loom was small, never before used. She had made it recently, felled the young tree with a stone axe, carved the straight-grained walnut with a blade of sharp obsidian, rubbed it smooth with fine sand, pegged it together lovingly. Metal had never touched it, nor was there a nail or a screw needed to hold it together. It lay wholly within her domain, responsive only to her will. She would command, and it would weave the thread into a tapestry of her son's travels.

She freed him slowly, one color at a time, winding the threads back onto the spools that were racked above the loom; only the uttermost end of each spool had participated directly in the magical process, yet the whole was affected, his aura seeping into the rest like oil penetrating silk. By the time he had ridden out of sight, the thread would be ready for weaving.

He stood up and drew on the gauntlets that had hung at his belt during the spell-making.

"Well," she said, "I can keep you no longer."

He kissed her cheek. "Be of good cheer, Mother. Think of the wonderful adventures that lie ahead of me. Don't weep."

"I lost you two years ago," she said, her hands flitting lightly over the sleeves of his surcoat, smoothing them against the chain mail beneath. "Why should I weep at losing you now?" Still, her eyes glittered, and her lips trembled as she spoke.

"The spiders will be with me, Mother. I'll talk to you often through the webs." Two years of growth had given him his full height, and now he looked down upon the top of her head when she stood so close to him. Two years of exercise with sword and shield and forty pounds of chain on his body had deepened his chest and filled out his limbs. He could lift her in

the crook of one arm. He could swing the sword tire-
lessly, blow after blow; there were trees in the forest
deeply gouged by his blade.

"Will you go to the Great House you visited before?"

He shook his head. "I think they fear me too much
there. Almost as much as they fear you."

"I don't know why they should fear me. Except that
all ordinary mortals fear our kind."

"They fear what they cannot understand."

She smiled sadly. "They would never fear you, then.
You are one of them. Oh, my son, I would call you
back to sorcery if I could!"

He took her hands in his own. "I am half of their
kind. And that half is the stronger, Mother. I can't
help it."

She pulled away. "No, Cray. It is the strangeness of
that life that draws you, not your father's blood. And
the first time you cross swords with another human
being, you may wish you were here, safe in sorcery."

"I think not. I think I have the courage to face an
armed adversary. And perhaps a fraction of the skill,
too."

She turned from him. "Go then. I have my pets,
still, to love; at least they will never take up arms and
leave me."

"I must do what I must do." He touched her shoulder. "You were alone before my father came to you.
You were alone for a very long time."

"And I was content. I will be content again, Cray.
We have nothing to gain from further farewells."

He passed through the arch of the gate to where
Gallant waited, cropping spring grass. Cray mounted
easily, remembering how arduous that simple action
had seemed when first he donned the chain. Now he
wore at least the shirt almost all the time, unless the
day was very hot and the padding that separated the
chain from his skin made him sweat too much.
Shield and helm hung at his saddle, the sword was
buckled at his waist, the saddlebags were full of provisions; nothing remained to keep him at Spinweb. He
lifted a hand in final good-bye, but his mother was not
there to see it, she had not followed him out. Only a

gray squirrel saw his farewell from a branch high above the forest track; he chirruped at it as he passed, but it scrambled away from him, claws clicking against the bark.

His first goal was Falconhill, to ask the lord what had become of a young knight named Mellor. He had only a vague notion of where it lay: to the west, his mother had told him when his was only a child's curiosity; some leagues to the west. He had hesitated to question her more recently, fearing that she might guess his motive. He had not reckoned on the tapestry tracking him, had not realized the extent of her power, though he had lived so close to it all his life. Yet he could not deny her the peace of mind she craved. And so she would see his route, know his destination, and when they spoke through the webs he would have to say that Falconhill was the nearest great holding he could find, where a youth might train under masters to be a knight. He thought she would want to believe that.

Westward he rode, opposite the direction he had taken two years before, and the forest stretched out before him as if there were nothing else in the world. The track narrowed for a time to an animal trail, but on the sixth day of his travels it widened abruptly, scattered with hacked-off trunks and the mushrooms that fed on their dead roots, and he knew that he was approaching the realms of men. The sun was high when he came upon the inn.

It was a rambling structure of weathered stone, with wooden cross braces bleached gray by many summers. Carven shutters flanked its many windows, open wide to the warm air, with white curtains fluttering gently. The inn stood in a narrow cleared space, great trees bending close to it, their leafy boughs brushing against the shingled roof, and among that greenery Cray could make out the thin plume of smoke spouting from the chimney.

A man labored in the yard before the building, cutting back grass with a scythe. He was a tall man, broad in girth, his face and bald pate red with exertion, framed by a peppery fringe of beard and hair.

When he saw Cray, he straightened slowly. "May I serve you, sir?"

Cray drew his horse up and smiled at the man. "Are you the landlord?"

He bowed. "I am, sir, and I welcome you to the Sign of the Partridge. We have a fine dinner this day, if you care to stop with us."

Cray eyed the yard, and the grass that was trimmed short into a fine lawn. Few horses, he guessed, had trampled that carpet in recent times. "Business has been poor lately, has it not?"

The landlord shrugged. "There have been better seasons. But truly, the food excels. I should know, for I am the cook."

"The cook would hardly be the first to admit that he lacks skill."

"No one has ever complained of my cooking, sir." He grinned. "And if you do not like it, you need not pay."

"In that case, I'll dine," said Cray, and he dismounted. He led Gallant across the grass to the front wall of the inn and threaded the reins loosely through an iron ring set in the stonework there. He gave the horse a quick pat, muttered some soothing nonsense in its ear and turned to find the landlord at the door, holding it open that Cray might enter.

Within was a single large room with high rafters and walls hung with hunting trophies. A long table occupied its center, with benches set in either side, and in the vast fireplace beyond, a brace of ducks was roasting, spitted, above a cheerful blaze.

"How many guests have you today?" asked Cray.

The landlord, who walked close behind him, said, "Only one, sir—yourself."

Cray gestured toward the hearth. "Then that is your dinner, and your wife's?"

He shook his head. "Mine alone, sir . . . or so it would have been had you not arrived. I have no wife, and no servants, either, just myself." He chuckled, a sound that seemed to emanate from the depths of his ample belly. "Do not underestimate the appetite of a man my size, young sir."

"I would not wish to eat your dinner," Cray said hesitantly.

The landlord placed his hands on Cray's shoulders and gently but firmly pushed him to a place on one of the benches. "The dinner is for my guests," he said, "and only for me when my guests have done with it. What landlord have you ever known who ate before his patrons?"

Cray shrugged. "I've never known any landlords but you. I have never visited an inn before."

"Never?" The man swung a leg over the bench and sat down facing Cray; seated, he was a head taller than the boy. "You mean you camp under the trees and cook your food over an open fire?"

"Yes. I cook quite well, too, or at least to my own taste."

"Pleasant enough for one night, perhaps, or two, but not for a long journey." He laughed again. "Else men like me would be hard pressed to earn a living."

"This is my first long journey," said Cray.

"Ah." The landlord lifted a quizzical eyebrow. "And how far have you to go?"

"To Falconhill."

"Falconhill? A fair distance, young sir. A fair distance indeed."

"Do you know it?"

"I have never been there, but travelers have spoken to me of the place. A mighty stronghold, they say." He nodded slowly. "And rich as well."

Cray interlaced his fingers and leaned forward, his elbows on the table. "Will this road take me there?"

"It will, yes, but . . . have you no map?"

"No."

"This road joins another, and then it forks and forks again . . . How is it that you journey to Falconhill without knowing how to find it?"

"I heard it was to the west," said Cray, "and I thought if I traveled far enough someone could advise me onward."

"I can advise you well enough, I think, at least to take you to the land it rules, and then you will surely have no further difficulty . . . but . . ." He grinned. "No, it would be unmannerly for me to ask what business takes you there." But he waited, expectantly, for Cray to respond to his prompting.

"I will find a master there," said the boy, "to train me in knighthood." He sniffed at the air, now redolent with the aroma of fowl juices. "Should you not be seeing to the ducks?" he asked.

The landlord rose unhurriedly. "I have not forgotten. They will be ready soon." He strode to the fireplace, a few paces for his long legs. He prodded the ducks with a long two-tined fork till the juices dripped into the flames, sputtering, and then he turned the spit halfway around. "They will be ready soon indeed," he called, and then he donned a thick gauntlet and reached into the flames, where a heavy, tightly covered iron pot rested on a grate; he pulled the pot out, setting it on the hearthstone. "I hope you like onions," he said.

"I like onions very much," replied Cray. He could feel his stomach roiling with hunger in response to the savory scent of the duck, and to take his mind off it, he stood up and made a circuit of the room, examining the trophies—antlers, tusks, claws, teeth, even a bear's skull, yellowed and cracked with age, the lower jaw fixed to the upper with wire. "Did you take these trophies?" he inquired.

"Me? Oh, no, young sir, except for a few of the very small ones. We used to have an excellent huntsman in these parts, in the days when this was a main trade route to the east and this inn was bursting every night with travelers. He hunted game for the table then, for my father, who was landlord here before me, and we thought the trophies gave the walls a friendly look. And something to keep the guests busy while they waited for their food."

"What happened to him?" asked Cray.

"Oh, that was many years ago, young sir. He is long dead. Nor have I any need for another like him in these times. I, poor hunter though I am, can take enough game to fill the pot, and there is a duck pond behind the inn, with more than enough birds for my needs. And flavorsome creatures they are, as you will soon discover. Will you take a cup of wine with your meal, young sir?"

"Yes, thank you."

A flagon hung on a hook in the wall some distance from the heat of the fireplace; the landlord took the vessel down, and one of the cups that hung nearby as well, and he poured red wine for Cray, setting both cup and flagon on the table. Then he returned to the roasting birds, sliding each off the spit onto one of the broad wooden trenchers that lay stacked on the floor beside the hearthstone. He opened the iron pot next, and the sweet aroma of onions cooked in butter rose from it in a moist cloud; he scooped golden onion slices up with a ladle and mounded them about one of the ducks like a nest, and this trencher he brought to Cray, leaving the other, onionless, close before the fire.

"You'll not need a knife to disjoint this bird, I promise you," he said. "The flesh will be as tender as the onions."

Cray's mouth watered as he plucked gingerly at one of the drumsticks; he could scarcely touch it, it was still so hot. He looked up at the landlord. "What of your own dinner?" He nodded toward the remaining duck. "It will dry out sitting there."

"It will keep well enough for a short time. And you might want more."

Cray freed the leg and took a small bite of the steaming meat. Warm juices invaded his mouth and dripped down his chin. The landlord proffered a kerchief.

"It is delicious," Cray said, somewhat indistinctly, as he chewed. "But I cannot eat more than one duck, I'm sure. You take the other."

"I'll wait."

"Truly, I know my own capacity. I am half your size, and so I have only half of your appetite, good landlord."

"Fine food sometimes increases the appetite," the man said, and he folded his arms across his breast and rocked forward and back as he watched Cray eat. When Cray's cup emptied, he poured another measure of wine. When Cray looked for salt, he fetched a cellar from the mantelpiece. "I have honeycakes to finish

48

the meal," he said when only the clean-picked carcass lay on Cray's trencher.

Cray shook his head. "I could eat neither a honey-cake nor a single extra scrap of duck. Have your dinner, landlord, and I hope that waiting before the fire has not damped its flavor. You spoke truly when you called yourself a good cook. Even my mother does not excel you."

The landlord bowed. Then he brought out the honeycakes from their cupboard by the hearth and set them in front of Cray before bringing his own meal to the table. "In case you change your mind, young sir," he said.

After some moments, Cray did change his mind, and he found the cakes excellent. By the time he had eaten a few of them and the food had settled deep enough in his stomach that he felt like riding again, the landlord had finished his meal and complimented his own cooking.

Cray stood up. "Now you can tell me of the route to Falconhill. You said the road forks more than once . . ."

"Considerably more. But if you follow the left-hand fork three times, twice west and the last time south, you'll find yourself among folk who can direct you more precisely. Falconhill rules that land, and the inhabitants surely know where to pay their taxes."

"Left three times. That sounds simple enough. And now, what is the charge for the fine meal I have just eaten?" He reached for the purse that hung at his belt.

"Two coppers, young sir."

"Two coppers," said Cray. He found a few of that sort of coin among his silver and passed two of them to the landlord. "And a good season to you. If I come back this way, I'll be sure to stop for another meal."

"Thank you, sir."

Gallant was waiting patiently at its tether on the wall, but as soon as Cray swung into the saddle, the horse began to toss its head and to dance from hoof to hoof, as if eager to continue their journey. The boy had only to twitch the reins, and his mount trotted across the grass to the road and headed west upon it.

"Farewell," called the landlord, walking a few paces down the path behind them. "And good luck."

Cray glanced over his shoulder once and lifted his arm in salute; the second time he looked back, the trees that overhung the road on either side had already closed in upon the inn and its proprietor, and all Cray could see was forest.

Behind, the landlord watched till the boy was out of sight, till the echo of his horse's hooves upon the hard ground faded to nothing, till there was no longer any likelihood that he would turn about. Then the big man's shoulders slumped, and he seemed to fall in upon himself, shrinking, shriveling, his clothes fading, his flesh melting, until all that stood where the burly landlord had been was a small gray squirrel. Gildrum scampered across the grass and up a tree. Beneath that perch, the inn resumed its normal appearance, great cracks showing in the stone walls, mortar crumbled, gaping holes where shingles had rested, wooden braces chipped and splintered with neglect. Inside, the demon knew, the fire had gone out, the flagon and cups crumbled, the table and benches rotted with damp, the floor overgrown with weeds. Before the front door, the lawn had sprung its full length, knee-high coarse grass, seed tops waving in the gentle breeze.

Magically, Gildrum flitted to another tree, farther along the road, and watched Cray pass beneath, then went to a third and did the same. After that, though it wished otherwise, it had to return to the errand its master had set it—an errand that should have taken a much smaller fraction of the day, although Rezhyk was not aware of that.

On its way, the demon stopped at Spinweb briefly. But Delivev did not show herself.

The tapestry drew a narrow line westward, with a stop every night and a few during the daytime, when she guessed he found game and paused to cook it, or to water his horse, or to admire wild flowers. He spoke to her occasionally, through the webs, perhaps two nights out of five, but he had little to say, only terse accounts of the vast forest, the birds, the beasts, the sun, the rain. She could see in the tapestry that he was

50

making his slow way to Falconhill, but she never mentioned that to him. She had known for some time that his goal would be either Falconhill or the East March. He had seen other holdings in the webs, richer ones, more powerful ones, no more distant than those two. But his father's name was not linked to any of *them*.

Spinweb seemed large and empty without Cray. Delivev had not realized, before he left, how much she depended on his voice, his smile, the clatter of his arms to fill her life, nor how much time she devoted to caring for him. Without his meals to prepare, his clothes to mend, his questions to answer, she felt incomplete. For days she wandered the halls of Spinweb, trying to recapture the life she had known before his birth, lavishing her love on plants and animals. She had thought herself lonely when Mellor left, but now she knew that had been nothing; Mellor, though she loved him, had only been with her a short time, like a dream, vanishing with the morn. Cray she had carried beneath her heart for nine months and kept at her knee for as many years and more; now, he was gone and she felt that part of her was gone as well.

I am getting old, she thought, though in sorcerous terms that was a lie.

She touched the tapestry as a few more threads were adding themselves to the weft; they moved under her fingers like snakes sliding under a door. Cray was probably camping for the night. She let a little time pass and then went to the chamber of the webs, in case he decided to speak to her.

He did not.

She lay sprawled upon the velvet-covered bed for a long while, staring up at the high, dark ceiling, and at last the thought came to her that she needed something new to take her mind off her son. She needed to see a new face, alive, not just in the webs. Castle Spinweb needed a guest. She stretched both hands out, and all around her, concentric rings of spider silk began to glow softly, their patterns blurring to grayness, to windows upon other climes. And all about Delivev the Weaver, people played out some moments of their lives, never knowing that she was picking and choosing among them.

The process took considerable thought and was diverting enough in itself that she hardly noticed how much time passed while she sought an appropriate selection. She weighed men against women, old against young, rich against poor. She rejected this one for being too ugly, this one for talking too much, this one because too many small children required her presence, this one because he had just married a passionate young wife. In the end, her choice narrowed to three footloose younger sons and a handful of troubadours; no one else was free to go wherever he wished without being missed by someone, and Delivev had no desire to cause another person the pain of loss that she herself knew so well, even if it was only for a short time. Of the younger sons, one was a fool, one had disgusting table manners, and one resembled Cray too closely for Delivev's peace of mind. The troubadours seemed equally witty, talented, and charming; it was their business to be so. Delivev chose the nearest one.

He was a man of middling years, tall and lean, his face craggy and weather-beaten by much outdoor living. His voice was low and full, his fingers nimble upon the strings of his lute, and he wore gold rings and bracelets when he stayed in places where they would not likely be stolen, gifts of wealthy patrons. At the moment Delivev selected him, he was reclining beside a garden pond, watching a king's young daughters play hide-and-seek. Occasionally, he tore crumbs from a loaf of stale bread and tossed them into the pond, and watched the fish glide to the surface to nibble.

The garden was full of spiders. A person who was not looking for them would scarcely see them, except perhaps for the black speck in the large web where two walls met. Delivev saw the garden from there, but there were other webs, small ones, scattered among the flowers, in the trees, and webless spiders as well, though Delivev had far less control over them. She prodded a small brown spider, and it came out of its hiding place between two stones and began to spin on a bush beside the pond.

The troubadour's eyes had swept past that very bush

a hundred times, but never be[...]
sage there, crude letters of spider s[...]
still spinning on the last of them:

TAKE THE NORTH ROAD

He stared long at those words, so long that Delivev
began to wonder if he knew how to read, despite the
movement of his eyes.

A second spider joined the first and added its share
while he watched:

GO TONIGHT

He jumped to his feet, staring down at the two
spiders. Then he called out hoarsely the names of all
the king's daughters, and he called again and again
until, reluctantly, they gave over their game and joined
him at the bush. By that time, though, the spiders had
been joined by others of their kind that pulled the
strands of web loose and pushed them together into a
formless tangle. The king's daughters were annoyed
that their game had been interrupted by a few spiders,
and they did not forgive the troubadour for the rest of
the afternoon.

Delivev watched through the evening as the troubadour sang for the king and his court, and she thought
he sang more poorly than usual, as if he were preoc-
cupied. The king sensed something amiss, too, and
asked if the troubadour were feeling ill, but the man
denied it. He sang another song and then he sat by
the fire with his lute, quite near the spiderweb at the
corner of the mantelpiece; he sat hunched over, his
eyes on the floor, or on some inner scene. At last,
quite late, when the king was about to retire to his
chambers, the troubadour approached him and sank
to one knee.

"Your Majesty," he said, "I have a need for air,
for the free moonlight and the open road. I would go
out tonight, perhaps for a day or two; I have certain
matters to think on."

"I had not expected you to leave us for a fortnight
yet," said the king. "What makes you change your
mind so suddenly?"

to speak of it, I will,

wise man, she thought,
magic, or of the tricks of his

he had he seen a spider ...
...he had the spider and the mes-

hand. "No, I would not press
, but I pray you, do not stay
me as last."

bowed low. "I shall not, Majesty."

billowing cloak, lute slung over his
shoulder crossed the drawbridge and bade the sleepy
sentries goodnight. The north road was deserted, the
travelers that used it during the day bedded down,
perhaps even dreaming of the next day's journey already. The troubadour did not see, as he walked, the
webs that hung in the trees on either side of the road,
nor did he know of the spiders that hid in the folds
of his cloak, but before the castle had slipped full out
of sight, he became aware of other spiders and other
webs. Where the road curved, a curtain of gossamer
strands enveloped him—a net, light as air, strung from
one tree to another, across the road. It clung to his
flesh and clothing a moment, and then he brushed it
away. Another moment passed before he resumed his
stride, and in that moment, something stepped into his
path.

By moonlight, it had the form of a war horse, standing still, blocking the road with its great body. It
dipped its head toward him. It bore no saddle, only
fringed reins hanging loose. He moved closer slowly.

"I am Lorien the troubadour," he said softly. "Is it
you that I seek on the north road?"

The creature dipped its head again and closed the
distance between them with one stride of its long legs.
Now he could see that though it had a horse's shape, it
was made of vines so tightly interlaced that they
formed a solid mass; the reins were plaited leaves.
Hesitantly, he touched the creature's neck with one
hand, and the tendrils that immediately curled about
his fingers made him jerk back as if he had thrust his
arm into a fire.

"What power has sent this thing to me?" he asked
loudly.

54

In answer, the creature knelt before him and bent its head to the ground at his feet.

"I am not afraid of you," he said, and he climbed onto its back. Tendrils clasped his hips and thighs, his knees, his ankles, held them close to the creature's body as it rose to its feet. He laid a hand on its neck, then pulled his fingers free of the clinging tendrils; his legs came free as well, with a sharp tug, but as soon as they touched the creature's sides again, they were claimed. He sat stiff at first, but when nothing further happened, he slumped and kicked impatiently with one foot. "Well?" he said. "Will you take me somewhere or not?"

The creature tossed its head and, turning, began to move northward along the moonlit road. It had a smooth and sinuous gait, not like a real horse at all, and it rustled as it went, like wind soughing through a hedge. It sped like the wind as well, as fast as a real horse could gallop, untiring through the night, its rider secured without benefit of saddle. The moon set, and first light dimmed the stars. Just after dawn the creature slowed, left the path to slide among the trees until it found a sunny, dew-decked glen, where it sank to the earth and fell apart, and he was left kneeling astride a pile of vines. He stood awkwardly and looked around, yawning and rubbing at his eyes with both hands. After a brief circuit of the open space, in which he saw no sign of human habitation, he eased his lute to the grass and himself after it, wrapping his body in his cloak as in a blanket. His eyelids sagged, though he had only a stone for a pillow, and then they parted abruptly, wide, as he saw the vines take root in the grassy soil and slim, pointed wands nose out from among the stalks, unrolling themselves into leaves that spread, broad and green, in the morning sunlight. The troubadour slipped one hand under his cheek and waited, and when nothing further happened, he finally fell asleep.

He woke late in the afternoon, found a brook in a dip at the far side of the glen, drank deep and splashed cold water on his face and neck. Then he paced a circle about the vines, which sprawled across the ground beneath their coat of leaves like any innocent plant, and he spoke to them: "Is this the end of the journey?" They rustled in answer, lifted toward him briefly, as if blown by a gust of air that he could not feel, and he stepped back hastily. He sat down then, some distance from the vines, and drew from the pouch at his belt a chunk of hard cheese; he sliced a piece off with his dagger and began to chew it.

Another rustling sound, much nearer than the vines, made him turn sharply to his left. Seeing the source of the noise, he froze in place, knife still poised over the cheese. A large snake approached him, sliding through rank grass and over stones, its body almost the thickness of his wrist. A loop of its heavy tail encircled a limp rabbit, which it dragged along the ground. The snake came to rest beside the troubadour's knee, and it lifted its head till its darting tongue was level with his throat. Still, he did not move, only stared back into the lidless eyes, and at last the snake swayed, dipped to the ground, and slithered away. It left the rabbit behind.

Lorien waited until spiders had gathered about the rabbit and spun a web on the grass, with one word upon it in many thicknesses of silk:

EAT

He built a fire and cooked and ate.

At sunset, the vines began to move. Their leaves rolled themselves into thin cylinders and dived beneath the stalks, which humped up and formed a familiar shape. The vine-horse tossed its head and knelt that the troubadour might mount. He did so, and they returned to the road and the ride.

Days passed in this manner—the vines a steed by night and a cluster of plants by day, snakes bearing small game for Lorien's meals each afternoon. Soon he was moving through lands he had never seen before, and one night, when the moon was on the wane, the road curved but the vine-horse did not. Into the trackless forest it galloped, and its rider was forced to duck low upon its back to avoid being swept off by hanging branches. The wide road had been faintly lit by moon and starlight, but the depths of the forest were dark, even the trees less individual shadows than a continuous gloom, yet the vine-steed galloped a sure course among them. In the morning, instead of stopping, it sped on, and before the sun had reached the zenith, it stood before Castle Spinweb.

The vines slumped below Lorien, and as he watched they slithered across the ground to the green-clad castle wall, rooted, unfurled their leaves, and blended among the other vines clinging there so perfectly that no one could have picked them out as having led a mobile, magical life.

Lorien knocked boldly at the castle gate, and the third time his fists struck the carven panel, it swung smoothly open. Sunlight streamed past him, washing out the radiance of many flambeaux within, illuminating a tapestry-hung room with floor of polished stone. He entered, and the door closed silently behind him. Turning about, he found himself facing a figure so cloaked and deeply hooded that no trace of human flesh showed anywhere upon it. Lorien inclined his head.

"You may tell your master that Lorien the troubadour is here."

The figure made no reply, only glided silently past him, moving as bonelessly as if it slid across an ice-covered pond, and it beckoned with one gloved hand that he should follow. He did so. Some distance down the curving corridor from the gateroom was a stairway, which they climbed. At the top, the figure paused at the first of two doors, opened it, and gestured for the troubadour to enter. Inside was a pleasant room, lit by the sun shining through tall windows. Tapestries covered two of the walls, and a third bore the windows, a cold fireplace between them. In one corner was a velvet-draped bed, in another a heavy table and two chairs; the table was set with wine flask and cup, salt-cellar, and a platter bearing a whole roasted fowl.

"My dinner?" asked Lorien.

The cloaked figure bowed.

"I see two chairs. Will your master be joining me?"

For answer, the figure glided through the doorway and pulled the door shut behind it. Lorien strode to the door, found it unlocked, and pulled it ajar. Then, tossing his lute to the bed and seating himself in the chair that faced the entrance, he consumed his meal. He had scarcely finished when the cloaked figure returned with a tray and bore away the scraps and tableware.

After it had gone, he went to the window and looked out upon the forest. His eyes were level with the tops of the shortest trees. Leaning out, he could see that he was in one of the castle's towers; above was another pair of windows, and beyond them a parapet. Below, too far to leap without breaking a leg, was the banquette, the narrow walkway just behind the outer wall.

He faced the room once more. "Am I a prisoner here?" he asked of tapestries red and gold and brown. They did not reply. One by one he turned them back, but he found nothing behind them save blank stone walls and cobwebs. He walked out the door then, and down a few steps; there was no sound from below, nor did he see any motion. The upper staircase was silent as well. On the landing once more, he hesitated a moment and reached for the handle of the second door.

He found himself in a room of mock weapons, wooden sword and shield, wooden mace and axe—they hung on the walls like hunting trophies. Beneath them stood chests, table, chair, all covered with a fine layer of dust. He opened one of the chests and found a boy's clothing laid neatly away, shirts and trews too small for a grown man, and tucked among them a stuffed animal so bedraggled that its identity was impossible to determine. He shut the chest, tried another, and found clothing more suitable to a man. He shut that, too, and having exhausted the room's secrets, he went out.

He yawned. "If no one objects," he said loudly, "I shall try the bed."

He slept soundly beneath the velvet cover.

The cloaked figure woke him. He had slept through the night, and morning light upon the tapestries made the room seem warm. Warm, too, was the glow of a small fire upon the hearth grate, and the room was filled with the rich scent of eggs frying in butter. The figure slipped away from the bed and bent to remove a pan from the flames. The table had already been set with bread and milk. Lorien pulled on his boots and shirt and sat down to eat.

"Your master is very generous," he said to the figure. "The bed is soft, the food is excellent. Shall I meet my host this day?" When the figure remained silent, he caught at its sleeve. "Can't you speak?" he asked.

The figure bowed to him and tried to pull the sleeve away, but his grip was too firm.

"Look at me!" he said sharply.

The hood turned to him, its rim hanging so low that it touched the front of the cloak.

"How can you see with that hood?" he asked, and with a swift movement of his free hand, he threw it back.

Beneath, the figure's head was a swaddle of cloth, lumpy, misshapen. There were no slits for eyes or nose or mouth.

Lorien stared, and his fingers loosened their hold on the sleeve and the figure pulled away, but not completely, not before he grasped at its gloved hand. The glove came off in his fist, revealing that the figure had no hand. The glove, which had picked a pan out of the fire and set it upon a trivet on the table, had been empty. He dropped the glove, now quite limp, as if it were a severed hand. The figure retrieved it with its other gloved hand, and in a moment it had two, as mobile as before. It used both to pull its hood up. Then it bowed and left Lorien to his breakfast. He ate slowly, his eyes upon the door, but no one entered as long as he was at the table.

Afterward, he sat on the bed, the lute cradled in his lap, and he plucked aimlessly at the strings. "You called me here," he said at last, no more loudly than if he were speaking to a person in the very same room. "Won't you show yourself?"

Long moments passed, and when no one came he began to relax, to stroke runs of melody from the lute, to hum with them. He was looking down at the strings when he heard the voice.

"Good morning. Welcome to Castle Spinweb."

His head jerked up, and he saw a woman standing in the doorway, a brown-haired woman in a long dress made of white feathers. He tossed the lute aside and scrambled to his feet. He bowed. "You are the lady of the castle?" he inquired.

"Spinweb is mine," Delivev said, smiling. "I hope you enjoyed your breakfast."

"It was excellent, my lady, most excellent."

"I trust your journey was not too arduous?"

"It was most interesting. I have never ridden such a steed before."

She laughed lightly. "I suspect that no one has. I hadn't thought of making one before." She half-turned, lifting one hand toward him. "Come see the garden, Master Lorien." He moved to obey, and she added, "And bring your lute, of course. What is a troubadour without his music?"

"Yes, yes, my lady. On the instant." He clutched the instrument by its short neck and followed her down the stairs. "I think you must be a mighty wizard," he said as they descended.

"I am." She glanced at him over one shoulder. "But I mean you no harm."

"I am glad to hear it."

"Have you never visited a sorcerer's castle, Master Lorien?"

"Never. I understood that they care little for music."

"Who told you that?"

"Why . . . I don't know. It's common knowledge, isn't it?"

"Common knowledge among ignorant folk, perhaps. We like music as well as ordinary mortals do."

"You have no other purpose in bringing me here . . . than to listen to my music?"

"What other purpose do you think I might have?"

He hesitated, lagging a little behind her. "I am only a troubadour," he said. "My imagination does not stretch so far."

She laughed again. "Oh, come along, don't be afraid."

"I am not afraid," he said staunchly, "else I would never have heeded your call."

On the ground floor they crossed the main corridor, passed through a series of arching portals, and stepped into the garden. Early sunlight splashed one corner of the open area; the rest was still shaded by the surrounding castle walls, cool and dew-decked. Delivev went to a pair of pale stone benches set in the sunshine, and she seated herself on one of them, gesturing him to the other.

"Play something for me," she said.

He laid the lute upon his lap. "Have you some preference?"

"Do you have a song of travel to far lands? Of eternal wandering? Of impossible quests?"

He thought for a moment. "Well, something of the sort, my lady."

"I will listen."

He strummed a chord, and then he smiled a little. "This seems so strange . . . I am not accustomed to playing for an audience of one, unless that audience were myself alone."

"There are others listening," she said.

He looked around. "I see no one. Do you mean behind those windows?" He pointed to slits in the masonry of the keep.

"There are birds," she said, and a small blue one landed on her shoulder and pecked gently at her earlobe. "And one of my dearest friends will be pleased to listen." The quick sound of horseshoes on the flagstones made Lorien turn about as a shaggy pony ambled from an open doorway on the shaded side of the garden and went straight to Delivev, nuzzling at her neck and displacing the bird, which jumped down to the bench beside her. She caressed the pony's face with one hand. "Do you like this audience better?" she asked.

"Is there no one in this castle but you and these animals . . . and that . . . servant who let me in yesterday?"

"Spinweb is full of life," she said, "of various kinds. You shall meet them all if you stay long."

"How long, fair lady, were you planning on having me here?"

She shrugged. "How long would you stay at any castle?"

"As long as the master let me."

"And at a wizard's castle? Not quite so long, yes? Not quite?"

61

"I don't know. This is a new experience for me, my lady."

The pony started toward Lorien and snorted, stretching its neck to reach the troubadour, to nose past the lute to a pouch at his belt. Lorien edged away, down the length of the bench, and the pony followed.

"Are you afraid of a pony?" Delivev asked, smiling at his discomfiture.

"What does he want?"

"An apple, I think, or a carrot. My son always kept something for him in a pouch on his belt. Come, Graylegs, come!" She slapped the pony's rump, and it lifted its head and looked back at her a moment, then turned about and walked slowly to her. She circled its neck with one arm. "We'll find you a tasty morsel, my darling, don't worry," she murmured. "Just stay here by me and leave the troubadour alone." To Lorien, she said, "He's an ordinary pony, I promise you. There's no magic in him at all. I merely caused the gate of his stall to unlatch, and so he came to me."

Lorien grinned sheepishly. "I don't know what to expect in this castle . . . after this morning's meal."

"Oh? Was something wrong with it?"

"No, no, it was excellent. But the servant who brought it . . . was rather peculiar."

"Really? I hadn't noticed."

"Her face . . . was all covered with cloths. I can't guess how she was able to see or even to breathe. And her hand . . ." His voice faded away as his gaze, which had been concentrating on Delivev, shifted to a spot beyond her shoulder.

A snake was slithering across the flags, bearing in its open jaws a large, rosy apple. It presented this apple to Delivev, rising to knee level to drop it in her lap. The pony did not startle at this apparition but rather dipped its head to take the fruit before Delivev could lay a finger on it.

"Greedy creature," she whispered as it crunched the apple loudly, and she stroked its shaggy mane. When the chewing noises had subsided, she said, "Play, Master Lorien. Play." She glanced sidelong at him, then down toward her knee, the direction of his gaze. The snake was still there, swaying slightly, looking up at her. "Does she disturb you?" she asked. "She isn't venomous. Ah, but she's quite deaf, so there's little for her to gain by staying. Be off with you, my pet." The snake's head dropped to the ground, and the animal slipped into the bushes. "I promise you," Delivev said to Lorien, "none of my creatures shall harm you as long as you conduct yourself as a proper guest."

"I am grateful for that promise, fair lady, but can you be certain . . . ?"

"I control them completely, I assure you. There is nothing in this castle that lies beyond my will. Except perhaps the pony." She smiled at it. "And you, of course, Master Lorien."

He inclined his head. "I, too, am yours to command."

"Then ply your trade, troubadour. Sing!"

He sang the tale of an endless quest through summer heat and winter frost, from one end of the world to the other. She had heard the song before, at a distant hearth, though not by him. She had heard it, she thought, before he was born. She sat in the sunlight and she listened, and she could almost imagine that he sang from a web spun in the garden, save that he looked at her as the music flowed from his lips.

When he was finished, she said, "Yes, I have always thought you sang quite well."

He laid the lute on the bench beside him. "Your pardon, lady . . . but we have never met before."

"No, we have not, but I have heard you."

"Ah . . . magic."

"Sing again."

"My lady . . . I would know for whom it is that I sing. You have a name, surely?"

"Surely. I am Delivev Ormoru, sometimes called the Weaver. Have you heard that name?"

He shook his head.

She smiled. "I have some local reputation. All undeserved. After you leave Spinweb, you may hear some people speak of me with fear. I hope the impression you carry with you will give you cause to discount their views."

"You have been only too kind to me, my lady, so far." He rubbed with two fingers at the varnished surface of his lute. "And I am reassured when I hear you refer to experiences I might have after leaving your castle. In truth, I was not sure that you intended for me to leave."

"I have no spells that require a troubadour's entrails, Master Lorien. I deal in quite a different sort of sorcery. Sing again; it's a beautiful day for singing, is it not?"

"It is a beautiful day," said Lorien, and he sang.

Outside the castle walls, the gray squirrel heard music rising from the garden. Gildrum had not seen the arrival of the vine-steed and its rider, and now the demon wondered if Delivev's spiders had spun a web in the garden instead of the web chamber, for her to view some distant scene. It wished it had a bird's form, to fly with seeming innocence close above the castle. But Rezhyk had never given it wings, and it could only fly in its true form. It looked up at the sky; a few clouds floated near the sun, but none across. The squirrel vanished as Gildrum passed from the human to the demon world, its normal mode of travel over long distances; it re-emerged as a flame against the sun, a bright spot invisible in the glow of that brilliant disk. It hung above the castle, far higher than the tallest trees, and below it Spinweb was laid out like a child's toy fortress. It could see Delivev, a doll-figure seated on a garden bench, and Cray's old pony stood close beside her. On another bench was a man, a lute cradled in his lap; from this height the music of both voice and strings was lost.

A man.

Gildrum perceived he was an ordinary mortal with an ordinary aura, no sorcerer. The flame that was Gildrum grew hotter, whiter even than the sun, and some moments slipped by before it recognized the emotion it was feeling.

Jealousy.

Gildrum returned to Ringforge, to the tower room that was its own, to the form of the girl with blond braids. She threw herself on the cold stone floor and wept hot, human tears.

What right have I to deny her a human lover? she asked herself. *None. None.*

Still, she wept. Gildrum had never wept before.

⊷§ CHAPTER FIVE

The ochre beeswax had all run out of the clay mold, which was now ready to receive molten metal. Rezhyk drew the long-handled cup from its small oven and tilted it carefully above the clay; liquid gold spilled in a thin, steady stream from the spout, filling the channels that led to the ring form. The air above the flow shimmered with its heat.

"This will be a fine one," said Rezhyk. "I can feel it in the smoothness of the pour."

"You have a steady hand," said Gildrum. She sat on the high stool by the brazier, holding the cloth with which he would wipe his sweating face when he was finished. "Have there been any but fine ones in the last dozen years?"

"There was the one we did the night of the storm."

"I don't count that one. Even *I* was startled by that clap of thunder."

"I count it," said Rezhyk, setting the spoon on a trivet and reaching for the cloth. "Many a good hour of spell-casting was wasted on that monstrosity."

"You could have used it still. You could have trimmed and polished it and set the stone in it. Only your own desire for perfection made you destroy it."

Rezhyk shook his head. "Even with your great experience, my Gildrum, you don't know everything. Nor do I, I confess it. I could not take the chance that the slave might use the imperfection to break free and do me some mischief. Not with that one. He was too powerful. And too angry at being caught."

"We are all angry at first," said Gildrum. "It fades."

"Does it? Well, perhaps with some. You, my Gildrum—you are not angry with me any more, are you?"

"You know the answer to that, my lord, or you would not care to keep me by your side."

"Not even a little?"

Her clear blue eyes gazed straight into his. "I bear you no grudge for summoning me. You have given me an interesting life in the human world, and I have learned much from it and from you."

Rezhyk turned his back to her. "Yet, when first I summoned you—how you raged! You would have liked to burn me to a cinder on the spot."

"Wouldn't you have felt the same, my lord, in my position? Stolen from home and friends, enslaved? I would have burned you. Truly, I would have, save for that ring on your finger."

He faced her. "The ring, yes! Can you doubt that it must be flawless?"

"Like all sorcerers," said Gildrum, "you know less about demons than you suppose. There are flaws and flaws. As long as the ring remains unbroken, minor imperfections are unimportant."

He circled the stool on which she sat and then, from behind, he fingered one of her blond braids. "I think not, my Gildrum. I think these things are subtler than you know. Or than you will admit. I have never asked your advice on ring-making, though you give it freely enough. As well ask a wild beast the best sort of trap to build for its littermates."

"Don't you trust me, lord?" asked Gildrum, her lips quirking in a smile.

"I trust you in many things. Other things, my Gildrum. We have been together many years, and I think I know you well enough by now."

"Do you, lord?"

"You think not? You think you can surprise me?"

She turned toward him and laid her hand lightly on

his shoulder. Her fingers perceived the golden shirt that lay beneath his tunic, though no human skin would have been so sensitive. "Would you be surprised to know that I wish my freedom?"

"So." He slid his arms about her waist. "My Gildrum wishes to be free of me."

"We have been together many years, lord. But you have better servants than I."

"None."

She nodded vehemently and grasped his ring-laden hands. "You have not fingers enough to wear all your servants. Where will you put this new ring? In the drawer with the others?"

"You are the first and the best," he said, drawing her down from the stool. She stood still in his embrace, her head against his chest, and she could hear his heart beat slow and steady in his breast. "What would I do without you, my Gildrum?"

"You could give another this form."

"But another would not be *you.*"

She pushed away from him gently. "After all these years, my lord, have we not, in some sense, become friends?"

"Of course we have."

"And would you deny a friend freedom?"

Rezhyk shook his head slowly and, clasping his hands behind his back, walked a few steps away from her. "It would not surprise me, my Gildrum, if a human slave wanted freedom. *Humans* always want all manner of ridiculous things. But what would you do if you were free? You find the human world interesting, yet without me you would have no place in it, nothing to do, nowhere to go, no reason for being here. And if you went back to your own world, you would find it much changed, I promise you. Many of your old friends would be gone, claimed by other sorcerers, and to those who were left, you would be a stranger. You have lived long among us; you are almost human in many ways." He looked sidelong at her. "You are neither human nor demon now, my Gildrum. What else could you be but a sorcerer's servant? Where else would you be content?"

"I would find some place for myself, somehow, somewhere, my lord."

He stretched his arms out to her. "Have I not been good to you, my Gildrum?"

"You have, my lord, but still . . . I have served your will, not my own."

"I need you, Gildrum."

"I think not, lord."

"I must be judge of that."

Gildrum looked down at the floor. "You fashioned the rings. You may dispose of me as you will."

"Perhaps I have heaped too much upon you these last years," he said. "Perhaps you feel you have no time to yourself." He took her shoulders in his hands. "Perhaps you need a holiday—a return to your own world for a little time. You'd see, then, that there is nothing for you there. Would that please you—a holiday?"

She lifted her eyes to his. "How long a holiday?"

"I don't know. A few days? A little longer, maybe."

"When? Now?"

He frowned. "No, not now, that's not possible. I have the ring to finish, and you must fetch me the proper gem for it from one of the deposits in the south. And then there are those books buried in the ruins of ancient Ushar—I know they must be there, even though you haven't found them yet—"

"You have other demons that could look for them as well as I."

"They haven't your fine touch, my Gildrum. I couldn't trust any of them to bring the books undamaged. And you know so well precisely what to look for. How long would it take me to teach that ignorant rabble to tell one volume of ancient lore from another? They would have me knee deep in genealogies and herbals, wasting my time with nonsense."

Gildrum let her shoulders slump. "I see I have served you too long. I have become . . . indispensable."

He shook her gently. "You shall have your holiday, my Gildrum. You shall. But not now. Later, when I have not so many projects in need of completion."

"That will be never," said Gildrum.

"Don't say that." ·

She bowed her head. "Yes, my lor

"Come, I want you to find that ge
begin the polishing. A fine, pale yel
be, the color of that wine we had
nights since—you recall I remarked or

"I recall, my lord. I recall."

Gallant trotted easily in the morning
making a fine rhythm on the hard-packed earth, its
trappings jingling as if taking joy from the sunshine.
The forest lay behind, with its leaf-shaded daylight,
and now horse and rider moved beneath the open sky,
between fields of nodding, golden grain. The road had
forked once, and they had borne left, according to the
innkeeper's directions. Ahead lay a village, a cluster
of huts on the north side of the path; Cray could just
make them out in the distance.

He sat straight in the saddle, even after so many
days of unremitting travel, even with the weight of
chain mail pulling continually at his shoulders. On his
head was a wide-brimmed hat, plaited this very morning of coarse grasses that grew by the side of the road
—plaited to shield his eyes from the glare of full sunlight. He thought he must look an odd sight in surcoat
and mail and straw hat. Thus far, though, he had not
encountered anyone on the road to tell him so.

Suddenly, not half a dozen paces ahead, a figure
emerged from the grain, a small, hunched figure that
stepped into the center of the road and halted there,
lifting an arm toward Cray. The boy had to jerk Gallant's reins sharply to keep from running the person
down. The horse took a few uneven strides beyond the
figure before turning back in response to its master's
touch.

"Don't you know better than to jump out in front of
a running horse?" Cray shouted. "You could have been
killed!"

The figure was cloaked and hooded in spite of the
pleasant warmth of the day. It cowered before Cray,
falling to its knees in the dust of the road, and in a
youthful masculine voice it begged his pardon. "I did
not mean to frighten your horse, my lord! But you are
the first person to come along this road today, and I

ɔr starving beggar with no one and nothing
…own. I implore you, my lord—alms. Alms,
… your heart and my belly. Good my lord, save
…rom starvation!" He looked up at last, and his
ɔod fell back, revealing the gaunt and sun-browned
face of a lad not much different in age from Cray. A
length of filthy rag was tied about his head so as to
cover his left eye.

Cray surveyed the youth's torn and dirty cloak, the
worn wrappings on his feet. "Is it food you want, beggar, or money?"

"Food first, good my lord, or I shall not live long
enough to reach yonder village. And after . . . whatever small coins you might be able to spare." He
clasped his hands and raised them toward Cray. "Anything, my lord. A crust of bread. A rind of cheese.
Anything."

Cray squinted up at the sun. "It may be a little early
in the day for a noon meal, but I shall eat anyway.
And you shall share it." He glanced down the road,
gestured with one hand. "I see a likely shade tree;
shall we sit there?"

The beggar nodded eagerly, and he ran beside Gallant as the horse took its rider to the designated place.

Cray dismounted and tied Gallant's reins to the tree.
Then he drew bread and cheese from his saddlebags,
and cold rabbit and a flask of water. He laid them on
the shield as on a table, to keep them from the dust of
the road.

Cray had seen cripples before, in the webs of his
mother's castle, but in his brief travels away from
home, he had never encountered one in the flesh. As
he divided the food with his knife and watched his
companion wolf that allotted him, he could not help
wondering what lay under the rag bandage. At last, as
they licked the last traces of grease from their fingers,
he said, "How did it happen?"

The other peered at him through one narrowed
brown eye. "How did what happen, my lord?"

"Your eye."

The beggar touched the rag with one hand, protec-
tively. "I was born this way."

"You can't see with it?"

70

"I can see . . . a little. But it isn't pretty. People don't like to look at it. So I keep it covered."

"What's your name?"

"Feldar Sepwin, my lord."

Cray grinned. "I'm not your lord. I'm not anybody's lord. My name is Cray Ormoru."

Sepwin bobbed his head. "Pleased to make your acquaintance, sir."

"And you needn't call me sir."

"I call everyone sir. A beggar must."

"Ah . . . or there wouldn't be any alms."

"You have it, young sir."

"Have you no family, Master Feldar?"

"They tossed me out, sir. Because of my eye."

"What sort of family would do that?" Cray asked.

"Farmers, sir. Plain peasant farmers."

"They tossed out a good pair of hands. Unless . . . there is something else amiss with you."

Sepwin shook his head. "Just the eye, sir. Folks don't like to look at it. Folks don't like to think about it."

"Can it be so ugly?"

Sepwin looked away. "You would think so, I'm sure."

Cray picked up his shield and hung it at its place on the saddle. "Where are you bound, Master Feldar?"

He shrugged. "Anywhere, sir. It doesn't matter."

"Would you care to ride behind me to the village? Gallant can easily carry both of us that far."

"My lord, that would be more than kind."

"Not 'my lord.' Just Cray." He mounted lightly. "Now up with you. Take my hand and put your foot in the stirrup there."

Awkwardly, Sepwin clambered upon the saddle, settling himself behind Cray. He was there only a moment when he pushed away and slid over Gallant's rump, landing heavily on the dusty road. He scrambled to his feet, one hand pressed to his right hip, which had taken the brunt of the fall. My lord," he said hastily, "the back of your neck is covered with spiders!"

Cray felt of his neck with gentle fingers, and the spiders crawled onto his hand and scurried up his sleeve. "They won't hurt you," he said.

71

Sepwin's single eye was wide. "You knew they were there?"

"They've been there ever since I left my home. They are my friends."

"Strange friends you have, my lord." Sepwin backed away, one limping step. "I was born a farmer, and I don't fear spiders, but I have never seen so many in one place at one time. And what a place!"

"They cling wherever they can," said Cray. "Usually, most of them are in my sleeve." He coaxed one brown-and-white mite onto his open palm and held it out to Sepwin. "You see?"

"Do they never bite you?" Sepwin asked.

"Never."

Slowly, Sepwin sank to his knees. "My lord," he murmured, "are you some sort of wizard?"

Cray smiled. "I know a few things, especially about spiders. That doesn't make me a wizard." He leaned down and extended his hand. "If you're not afraid of a few spiders, you can still have a ride to the village. I think after that fall you'd rather not walk."

Sepwin looked up and swallowed hard, his Adam's apple bobbing. "I am not afraid," he said, and he took Cray's hand and mounted Gallant.

"I haven't much silver," Cray said, kicking his horse to a slow walk, "but you're welcome to a piece of it."

"Where are you bound, my lord? I mean, Master Cray?"

"For Falconhill, Master Feldar."

"Where would that be?"

"You don't know?"

"No."

"Well, neither do I, precisely. It's in the west somewhere."

"I am from the south. Somewhere. Have you some business at this Falconhill?"

"Yes, Master Feldar. I seek word of my father, who went to Falconhill once and never returned."

"Perhaps it is a dangerous place."

"Perhaps. Would you care to go there?"

"I, sir? Not if it is dangerous."

"I have been traveling alone for a long time," said Cray, "and I was thinking that it's a dull journey without other ears than my horse's to talk to. And you have no pressing destination."

"True enough, Master Cray."

"And you would never go hungry as my companion."

"You have a compelling argument, young sir. But why would you wish to burden yourself and your horse with a cripple?"

"Are you so different from other men, Master Feldar?"

He was silent a moment, and then he said resolutely, "No, I am not."

"Then perhaps we will find you a horse for yourself in this village. Gallant would tire carrying both of us all the time."

"You would buy me a horse?"

"Don't expect another like Gallant, though."

"Master Cray, you are mad to treat a stranger so!"

"You asked for alms, did you not?" He shrugged. "Besides, we may find you some useful work at Falconhill. I have heard that it is a great holding."

"But your father—the danger—"

"You can always tell them you met me on the road and hardly know me at all." He kicked Gallant to a faster pace. "There is the village already. We can stop and fill our flasks at their well."

Small, dirty children ceased their play to point and exclaim at the beautiful horse as Gallant walked slowly past the low wall that marked the village boundary. The well was in the center of the enclosed space, and when Cray and Sepwin dismounted there, the children crowded around them, stroking the horse's legs and flanks, as high as they could reach. Although Gallant tolerated this attention quietly enough, with Cray standing at its head muttering soothing nonsense, a woman ran from one of the huts and pulled the children away one by one, scolding sharply.

"An animal that large," she said, her voice pitched to rise above the tumult of their complaints. "You don't know what he'll do, you little fools. Get away now, get away from him!"

"A fair morning to you, good wife," Cray said,

smiling broadly. "It's a wise mother that looks after her young ones so well."

She glared at him. "Who are you, stranger, and what do you want?"

"My friend and I have been long upon the road, good lady, and we came to ask if we might fill our flasks and water our horse at your well."

"I suppose you may. There's a trough for the horse." She flicked a thumb toward a low wooden basin some paces from the well. "Fill it at your pleasure." She walked away.

Cray smiled again and nodded at her retreating back, and then he dropped the bucket into the well and began hauling water up. He had scarcely splashed the first measure into the trough when he felt a small hand tugging at his surcoat. He looked down at a tow-headed child of six or seven summers. "Yes?"

"May I ride the horse?"

Cray squatted beside her. "It's a very big horse, child."

"I wouldn't fall off."

"Well, what would your mother say to that?"

"You could walk beside me."

"And what if you fell off on the other side?"

"Your friend could walk there."

Cray had to smile. "If you'll wait till my horse has had a drink, I'll let you ride him, but just for a little time, because we have a long journey ahead of us."

The child nodded and sat down with her back against the stones of the well. In the shade of the nearest hut, half a dozen paces away, her playmates whispered and giggled among themselves, but none dared join her.

Cray filled the trough and stood by while Gallant drank and Sepwin drew another bucket to replenish the flasks. Before long, three more villagers, men this time, approached the strangers, walking a wide circle about the well. Cray smiled at each of them in turn, and when he judged they had looked their fill, he hailed the brawniest of the lot.

"Would you have a horse for sale, good sir?"

The man crossed his arms upon a massive chest and said, "You have a horse, I see."

"But none for my friend," Cray replied. "His mount died some days ago, and we have not found another for him yet. We thought you might have an extra animal here."

"How did his horse die?" asked the man.

"A misstep upon the road. The poor creature broke its leg and we were forced to destroy it."

The man glanced at his fellows. "There might be an extra horse in the village." He beckoned to the others, and they moved together, speaking softly. After a time, one of them looked back to Cray.

"What can you pay?" he asked.

"I have a piece of silver," said Cray.

The villagers' conversation resumed, more loudly this time, and at last the brawny man broke away from the other two and said to Cray, "We seem to have three extra horses in this village."

"I need only one," said Cray.

"You may choose the best of the three, if you wish."

Cray nodded.

The men separated, and while each went in search of his horse, Cray lifted the little girl into Gallant's saddle and walked her around the well. She was very quiet on top of the horse, very wide-eyed, and she clung to its mane with both hands.

"Have you ever ridden a horse before?" Cray asked her.

"Yes, but not such a big one. It's so high!" And she loosed one hand for only a moment, to wave quickly at her playmates, who stared from the shade with envious eyes. "Does he have a name?" she asked Cray.

"I call him Gallant."

At the sound of its name, Gallant halted and turned its head inquiringly. Cray stroked its neck once and urged it forward.

"He's a good horse," said the girl.

"Oh, yes, a very good horse," agreed Cray.

"Are you a knight?"

Cray smiled. "Not yet. But I will be."

"I saw a knight once. He had a big horse, too."
She turned to Sepwin, walking on the other side of
Gallant. "You're not a knight."

"No, no, not I," replied the beggar.

"What's wrong with your eye?"

Sepwin hesitated, then said, "I hurt it."

"If you hurt it, where is the blood?"

"I hurt it a long time ago."

"If it was a long time ago, why do you need that
bandage?"

"Because it doesn't look nice."

"It doesn't?" The child leaned toward him. "Can I
see it?"

"Careful—you'll fall off if you lean like that!"

Even as he spoke, she began to slip sideways. Cray
called a warning and clutched at her leg as it went
over the top of the saddle, but he missed it. He halted
Gallant with a tug of the reins, then ducked under
the horse's neck to see what had happened. Sepwin
was just setting the child down on the ground. She
was gripping his rag bandage in one dirty hand.

"You said it didn't look nice," she said in an ac-
cusatory tone.

"Don't you think so?" he muttered, jerking the rag
away from her. He kept his left eye tightly closed as
he swiftly fastened the rag in place once more.

"No," she replied. She looked up at Cray. "Thank
you for the ride," she said, making a little curtsey, and
then she ran to join her playmates, to whisper and
giggle with them.

The brawny man returned with a small brown horse,
which he displayed to Cray proudly. "Not old at all,"
he said, prying the animal's mouth open to show the
teeth.

Cray, to whom the horse's teeth meant nothing, surveyed the animal and found nothing particularly wrong
with it. "This looks to be a reasonably good animal."

Sepwin tugged at his sleeve. "This animal is older
than you are, Master Cray."

"Oh? How can you tell?"

"The teeth. The pattern of the teeth."

Cray looked at his companion. "So you know horseflesh?"

"A little, sir. My father raised some."

"Good, then you can pick your own mount. Here comes another offer, if I'm not mistaken."

A second man approached, the tallest of the three, leading a horse whose dark coat was flecked with gray. Sepwin walked all around the animal, looked into its mouth, picked up its hooves one at a time and examined them. "Not bad," he said.

The third animal arrived shortly, a dark one with a white blaze on the forehead. Its back had a distinct slump in the middle. Sepwin looked it over, then looked at the others again. "Take the roan," he said at last, indicating the second animal.

Cray nodded. "Have you a saddle for it?" he asked its owner.

"This is a plowhorse," the man told him. "She's never known a saddle."

"Has she ever been ridden?" asked Sepwin.

"Oh, the children ride her all the time. And I have, too. She's gentle as a lamb, you'll see. She won't give you any trouble."

"Give me a blanket to throw over her back and I'll ride her," said Sepwin.

"The blanket will cost you extra," said the man.

Cray laughed. "I'll give you a copper penny besides the silver, if it's a good blanket."

"Oh, the best, my lord, the very best," he said, and he called a name toward the group of children who were whispering nearby. A small boy answered, whom Cray guessed was his son, ran to him, received orders to fetch a particular gray blanket, and scampered off to obey. The lad returned in a few moments with a heavy woollen bundle which his father unrolled and threw over the horse's back. In return for a silver coin and a copper one, the man handed the animal's reins over to Cray, who passed them on to Sepwin.

As they were preparing to mount, the small boy piped, "Before you leave, sir, may I see your eye?"

Sepwin looked at him, and with his free hand he pulled his cloak tighter about his shoulders. He said nothing.

The father cuffed his son. "What sort of question

77

is that?" To Sepwin he said, "Forgive the boy, sir. He's very young and full of curiosity."

His hand covering the cheek that had been struck, the boy said in somewhat muffled tones, "Eda says his eyes aren't both the same color, Father, and I don't believe her."

"What nonsense!" said his father.

The girl who had ridden Gallant ran to join them. "It's true—one is brown and the other is blue. Isn't it true, stranger?"

Sepwin shook his head. "The child is imagining things."

"The covered eye is blue, it really is! I saw it!"

"It is an empty socket," said Sepwin, and he grasped his horse's mane to pull himself up.

"Your father will beat you for lying when he comes home!" the boy shouted at his playmate.

"It's true!" she said.

The boy's father laid a hand on Sepwin's arm, kept him from mounting. "Is it true?" he asked.

Sepwin faced him. "What if it were?" he demanded.

The man opened his hand, showed the silver and copper. "I could not bargain with such a one."

"You have bargained with *me*," said Cray, one hand on the cantle of Gallant's saddle. "There is nothing wrong with *my* eyes."

"But the horse is for *him*," the man said, nodding toward Sepwin. "Let him show his eye."

"It is an ugly wound," said Sepwin.

"I have a strong stomach." He glanced at the boy and girl. "Go, children. There is nothing here for you to see."

"But father—" the boy began.

"I said go."

Reluctantly, the lad moved off, and at another glance from his father, the girl followed, casting many a backward look as she went.

"What nonsense is this?" asked Cray.

"Take off the bandage," said the man to Sepwin, "or you will not ride my horse beyond these walls." The other men, who had drawn back when Sepwin chose his horse, crowded close now, their own horses forgotten and ambling loose toward the water trough.

The men nodded to their fellow's demand. "Take off the bandage."

Sepwin stood with his back against his mount's flank, one hand clutching the crude rein that hung from its rope halter. His lips were tight, his face pale in spite of its tan. "Leave me alone," he said.

The boy's father threw the coins down into the dust. "I don't want a monster's money." Then he reached out slowly and pulled the rag from Sepwin's head. "Open your eye."

Blinking against the sunlight, the beggar obeyed.

Cray was too far away to see the color of the eye, but when the tall villager lunged forward to close his hands about Sepwin's throat, he could guess it. With one quick motion he jerked his sword from its scabbard at Gallant's saddle and, shouting, raised it high. All three villagers had fallen upon Sepwin by then and borne him to the ground under his horse's agitated feet; if they heard Cray's voice above their own wild cries, they paid it no attention. Cray kicked the nearest man with one booted foot and then, swinging the sword once above his head, he brought the flat of the blade down on the fellow's buttocks. The villager let go of Sepwin immediately and rolled over, scrambling away on his hands and knees, his terrified gaze on the sword. Cray brought it down again, and yet again, and added a few more judicious kicks, and Sepwin's attackers backed off.

"I'll kill the first one who lays another hand on him!" Cray shouted. With his free hand, he pulled Sepwin to his feet. "Get on that horse," he hissed, pushing the beggar toward the nervously dancing animal.

Sepwin staggered and coughed, clutching his throat, but he managed to mount, and he did not need another order from Cray to kick his horse to a gallop. By the time Cray vaulted into his saddle, Sepwin's horse was leaping the low wall at the edge of the village and speeding west along the road. Cray followed. He glanced back only once, to see the three villagers standing behind the wall, shaking their fists at the departing strangers. The children and a few other inhabitants of the settlement had joined them, and they all clustered close together, as if hemmed in by invisible boundaries. No one stepped beyond the wall.

Sepwin rode, his body bent low to his horse's back. Cray caught up and pulled abreast, calling for him to slow down, but Sepwin paid no attention. Soon his horse's sides were covered with white foam, and Gallant, too, had begun to sweat.

"You'll kill your horse!" shouted Cray.

Sepwin looked at him with wild eyes, and from this distance Cray could see the difference in color, the darkness of the right and the paleness of the left.

"They'll never catch us!" shouted Cray. "You must stop!"

Sepwin shook his head.

"You're safe!" Cray screamed, and then he eased back on his own reins, slowing Gallant to a prancing, snorting stop. He sat still in the middle of the road while Sepwin disappeared in the distance ahead.

"I didn't buy that horse to have you kill it!" he shouted, but he knew that the beggar was too far away to hear.

He let Gallant walk then and cool off, and he looked back occasionally, even though he was sure that no one was following. The afternoon had waned considerably when he came upon Sepwin and his horse in a stand of trees that marked the edge of the cultivated fields. The road forked there, the northerly path skirting the grain, the westerly leading into rolling land of intermittent forest and tall, wild grasses. Sepwin was rubbing his mount down vigorously with the gray blanket. Both of his eyes were uncovered, the rag bandage left behind in the village. At Cray's approach he moved behind his horse, placing it between them like a wall. Gallant, though, was so much taller than the village nag that Cray could look over the latter at Sepwin.

"Good evening," said Cray. "I trust you had a pleasant ride."

"You may jest," muttered Sepwin, "you with two eyes of the same color."

"You won't run away from *me*, will you, Master Feldar?"

"Should I?"

"I don't care about your eyes."

Sepwin leaned against his horse, arms crossed upon its back. "Everyone cares," he said. "This was not the first time that I've run from folk. Sometimes they throw stones instead of attacking me with their hands."

"But why?"

Sepwin closed the brown eye, then opened it and closed the blue. "Which one do you think is the evil eye?"

Cray shrugged. "Why don't you tell me?"

"Neither!" shouted Sepwin, and his horse started and tossed its head, and he had to soothe it with stroking hands. "Neither," he said more quietly. "Yet I have been driven from every human settlement where I've shown both of them. I've been stoned, spat upon, kicked, flogged. No honest work for me, no friends; even my parents finally cast me out!"

"I don't understand," said Cray.

"Don't you know what the evil eye means?"

"No."

"Have you led such a sheltered life, Master Cray?"

"I suppose so. Tell me."

Sepwin clasped his hands behind his back. "A cow dies, it's my fault. A horse goes lame, a plow breaks, the children sicken, everyone blames me. They say I've gazed upon them with evil intent."

"And have you?"

He looked up into Cray's face. "I have willed evil a few times, for revenge. I have willed it with all my heart . . . and nothing has happened. The cows die and the children sicken and all the other unhappy things run their course without any help from me. These eyes lie, Master Cray. They have no power."

"Very well," said Cray, and he swung a leg over his saddle and jumped to the ground. He tethered Gallant to the nearest tree. "Now that we have settled that, Master Feldar, what do you say to a cheery fire and a hot supper? I stopped off some distance back and netted a fine pheasant among the grain. I'm sure that between the two of us we can pluck and dress it in a very short time."

Sepwin took a single step toward him. "You are not an ordinary person."

Cray pulled the bird out of one of his leather saddle-bags. "Why? Because I believe you when you say you don't have the evil eye?"

"An ordinary person would have left me to my fate back there in the village. After all, you don't owe me anything."

"I've vowed to be a knight," said Cray. "How could I stand by and watch an innocent person killed?"

"I've been spat upon by knights."

"Then they were not proper knights."

"Who are you, Master Cray?"

Cray smiled. "No more than I seem—a boy looking to be a knight."

"You are more than that."

"Start the fire, Master Feldar, and I'll begin the plucking."

Sepwin stood motionless. "I've told you the truth about myself. Won't you do as much?"

"What do you think I am?"

"A wizard of some sort."

"Would you be frightened if I were?"

"Not now, my lord. Not now that I owe you my life."

"You owe me nothing," said Cray, "except the proper form of address."

"As you wish, Master Cray," said Sepwin. "I have never met a wizard before."

"I am not a wizard."

"Those spiders tell me you are. I see one on your hand right now."

Cray glanced down and saw a black mite gingerly investigating the pheasant feathers that brushed his right wrist. He blew on the creature gently, and it retreated up his sleeve. "I shall have to hide them better," Cray said, "if I want to move freely among ordinary mortals." He laid his hand on a branch of the tree where Gallant was tied, gave his elbow a sharp jerk, and a line of spiders trooped from his body to the wood; they began to spin immediately, anchoring lines to various twigs for a rough, radial pattern. "My mother is a sorceress," said Cray, "so don't be surprised by what you see next. She'll be interested to know that I've found a traveling companion." He gazed sidelong at Sepwin. "I have, haven't I?"

"You have," said Sepwin, and he bent to gather tinder for the fire. But his eyes never left the spiders and the web that they fashioned together in the trees.

The tapestry had woven the semblance of a sword upon the road that Cray traveled, and when Delivev laid her fingers upon it, she felt the heart thunder in her breast. Her son had drawn his sword, she knew, and used it for the first time against human beings. Yet there was no blood upon the cloth, and his path continued past the symbol; he had fought and run, unharmed, slaying no one. Delivev relaxed as she comprehended that, and then she smiled as she touched the sword again and found no fear there, only excitement. If he had to be a knight—and she still felt pain at that thought—he would at least be a properly brave one.

She turned away from the tapestry. Down the corridor, up the stairs, Lorien was waiting for his evening meal to arrive, expecting her to join him for it, but she felt no hunger now. Instead, she went to the web chamber and sought her son. The webs hung dark around her as she reached for the spiders that rode with him, willed them to find a place for spinning, even if it were the pommel of his saddle. They were not her spiders but his, raised in the influence of his aura, obedient to his will; yet they were spiders still, and her power over their kind was great. At last a small, bright spot appeared in the center of a web: Cray's chin and mouth, seen from below, swaying in and out of view with the rhythm of his steed's gait. Then the image crumpled, swept away by wind or a sleeve or a flick of the reins.

Delivev rose from the velvet-covered bed with a sigh. The moving horse was too chancy a support for spiderwebs; she would have to wait until Cray stopped for the night. Yet, having seen him with her own eyes, even the fraction of his face shown in the tiny web, she felt easier somehow; he was all right, the tapestry did not lie. Abruptly, she realized she was hungry.

In the kitchen, a bundle of cloth in the shape of a human being bent close to the hearth, turning the spit that bore a roasting joint of venison. At Delivev's signal, the cloth-servant removed the meat from the fire and set it on a platter; its glove-hands picked up an obsidian knife and began to carve the roast, heaping two trenchers with the steaming, fragrant slices. Delivev took one of the trenchers and ate, sitting on a stool by the table while the cloth-servant set the other on a tray with saltcellar and wine cup—that was Lorien's meal. Delivev hoped he did not mind eating alone. The only person she wished to see right now was Cray.

She had scarcely finished her meal when a spider descended from the ceiling on a long strand of silk, landing on her shoulder, scurrying to her neck to tickle her with tiny mandibles. She threw the trencher down and fairly ran to the web room. The largest web showed Cray against a vista of grain fields golden brown in low sunlight. He raised his arm in greeting when he saw her enter the room.

"I had an adventure today, Mother," he said, "at long last."

"You aren't hurt, are you?"

"Oh, no, not a scratch. And I want you to meet my new friend, Feldar Sepwin." He gestured to someone out of sight, once, and then more vehemently. "Come on, Master Feldar, let my mother take a look at you."

A thin lad of about Cray's age edged into view of the web, his eyes downcast. Slowly, he sank to his knees, his hands clasped at the level of his waist. "Good . . . good health to you, my lady," he said.

Delivev eyed his ragged, filthy clothing and said, "Good health to you, Feldar Sepwin. And good fortune to you—you seem to need some."

"Master Feldar has had considerable trouble in his life, Mother," said Cray, "because his eyes are two different colors. Show her your eyes, that's a good fellow."

Sepwin glanced up furtively. "I mean your son no harm, my lady,"

She leaned close to the web. "Two different colors indeed. How unusual. What sort of trouble does Cray speak of?"

"Folk say I have the evil eye, my lady," Sepwin replied. "But it isn't true." ·

"The evil eye? You mean, blighting crops, bringing disease—that sort of thing?"

He nodded, and then he shook his head violently. "It isn't true, really it isn't!"

"Where are you supposed to have learned this power?"

"Learned? My lady, they say I was born with it. My parents cast me out from fear of it."

"Merely because of your eyes? What ignorance!"

Sepwin looked at the ground. "It is widespread ignorance, my lady. I have met it everywhere."

Delivev placed her hands on her hips and half-turned from the web. "Cray," she said, "when I hear such foolishness, I am doubly saddened that you have forsaken the sorcerous life. Ordinary mortals know nothing of us. To think that a sorcerer would be marked with some physical sign, that he would have power from birth . . ."

"I am not a sorcerer!" said Sepwin.

"Of course not. Sorcery is not inborn; it is learned, and the learning takes more years than you have been alive. Accusing a child of sorcery is like accusing a cow."

"Well, Mother," said Cray, "I do know a few tricks."

"Children's games, my son. The evil eye is not acquired in a few summers of play. I knew of one who had it, and she worked long and hard."

"Why would anyone want such a power?"

Delivev shrugged. "One who finds happiness in the misery of others . . . The one I mentioned, though, had another reason. She wanted silver and gold. She threatened her neighbors with her evil eye, and they paid, lord and peasant alike—they paid whatever she asked, to keep their lands and families secure."

Cray nudged Sepwin. "See how you could have become rich, Master Feldar? You could have promised to keep your evil eye closed and wrung money from folk instead of beatings."

"And when the promises were not kept, Master Cray? When the cows died anyway?"

"You would have had to move on quickly."

"I would be homeless and friendless as I am now. But well-dressed."

Cray laid a hand on Sepwin's shoulder. "You are not friendless anymore."

Sepwin looked up at him for a long moment, then at Delivev. "You don't mind, my lady," he said, "that your son has a beggar as a friend?"

"You'll not have to beg while you're with me," said Cray.

"I'm sure he's been lonely since he left our home," said Delivev. "I know I have."

"I was lonely, Mother."

She smiled at him, a very small, sad smile. "But not so lonely that you wanted to turn back."

"No, not so lonely."

"And now you have a companion. That's well enough. I have one, too . . . or at least, Spinweb has a guest."

Cray cocked his head to one side. "A guest?"

"You would know him—Lorien the troubadour."

"Lorien?" Cray frowned. "Didn't he sing at Highmount last winter?"

"The same. He happened to be passing Spinweb, and I invited him to stay a while."

"A troubadour in Spinweb! I'm sorry I can't be there to hear him, Mother."

"You could be."

Cray shook his head. "You'll not lure me back with that sort of bait. I'll surely hear troubadours a-plenty on my journey."

"Perhaps not."

"Then I'll still have the memory of hearing them through the webs. Mother, this is hardly worthy of you."

She laughed softly. "Can you blame me if I would rather have you here than him?"

"Even though I don't sing at all well?"

"Even so."

"I love you, Mother. You know that."

For a moment she could not reply, her voice trapped by teeth clenched to hold back tears. Then, very low, she said, "Tell me about your adventure."

He waved it away with an open hand. "It was really nothing, Mother, though exciting enough for a journey as dull as this one. Some ignorant louts were trying to do mischief to Master Feldar, and I taught them a lesson."

"He saved my life, my lady," Sepwin said. "They would have killed me."

"What did you do to them?" she asked him.

"I showed them my eyes."

She wagged her head sadly. "Have you thought of wearing a patch over one eye?"

"I have done so, my lady."

"You move in the wrong world, Master Feldar. The sorcerous society would not treat you so poorly. You should have been born to us."

He bowed his head. "One is born as he is born. We cannot change ourselves to something else."

Delivev looked at her son. "I know one who thinks otherwise."

"I was born of two worlds, Mother," he said, "and I made my choice."

"Your choice, yes. Your free choice."

From behind her, Lorien said, "I thought I heard voices down here."

She whirled to face him, one arm stretched out to keep him from the room. His own clothing became his prison, frozen in the doorway, and he could not move against it.

"That is Lorien," Cray whispered to Sepwin. They had to look over Delivev's shoulder, for she stood in front of the web, barring it from the troubadour's view.

"You are not welcome in this room," she said. "Turn around and go back to your tower. I will call you when I want you."

Stiffly, without his volition, Lorien's clothing turned him about and walked him away.

"That was hardly a proper way to treat a guest, Mother," Cray said when the troubadour was gone.

"I will not share this room with him." She crossed her arms over her breasts and clutched her shoulders, as if feeling a sudden chill. "Only those I love may come here. Let him find some other entertainment for himself in Spinweb. Let him play his lute and divert me. The webs are not for him."

Cray bent and picked up a half-plucked pheasant from somewhere below the web's view. "We're about to prepare supper now, Mother. And soon the light will fail."

"I can watch you by fireglow," she said. "Make your supper. I'll just sit here by the web, as if I were with you."

"As you wish."

"Just for a little while."

The velvet coverlet was too smooth for her imagination to transform into the coarse grass she saw all about them, the air of the chamber too close to pass for night-damp. Nor could she reach out to touch her son as he readied for bed, to kiss his forehead as she had for so many evenings through his life. He gave a last wave in her direction and rolled in his blanket by the fire. He slept quickly, she knew, and deeply. Sepwin seemed to do the same.

A gesture of her hand made the web opaque. She rose from the wide bed and made her way to the corridor. She paused at the foot of the stairway to the tower where the troubadour waited. Almost, she walked on, her mood too heavy for music, but after much hesitation, she climbed instead.

He lay upon his bed, the lute at his side, slow, mournful notes rising from it.

At the doorway, she said, "Please accept my apology for treating you roughly, Master Lorien."

He sat up. "Will you come in?" he said.

She inclined her head, entered, and seated herself at the table. "You interrupted a conversation with my son. He has been gone some time now, and I don't speak to him often."

"Please accept my apology for interrupting," said Lorien. "Had I known, I would never have done so."

"That is a private room. I do not wish you to enter it."

"Whatever you say, my lady." He pulled the lute to his lap. "Shall I play for you?"

"No." She looked down at the thick rug upon the stone floor, at its bold pattern of green and gold. She

88

had knotted it with her own hands, and a little magic, after weaving the open canvas backing on her largest loom. She had crafted many such beautiful things in her long lifetime; Spinweb was full of them. Yet in her heart she felt no beauty now, only emptiness.

"Sing," she said at last. "Sing to me of love."

He sang a plaintive melody, his voice deep and mellow, his eyes never leaving her face. He sang, and after some verses he rose from the bed and moved closer to her, still singing, till he stood above her, and his music fell upon her hair like a coronet. He sang, and his fingers left the strings of the lute and reached out for her, gently, as for a wild bird. Almost, he touched her cheek. And then his sleeve tightened about his wrist and held it back.

She looked up at him. "No," she said, and she rushed from the room.

When he was able to move once more, he went to the door and found strands of spidersilk hung across it, strong and immovable as bars of steel. He could not leave his room. He could not follow her to another tower, to the chamber overlooking the forest track, to the tapestry that showed the face of a man he did not know.

She wept there, alone, as on many another night.

✑ CHAPTER SIX

After breakfast, she bade the troubadour leave.

He fell on his knees before her. "My lady, if my behavior last night offended you, believe me, I am most heartily sorry. When you asked to hear of love, in such a melancholy voice, I allowed myself to think . . . perhaps . . ." He smiled up at her, a sunny smile that transformed his rugged features almost to youth, and Delivev thought that many women must have been won with it. "You are so beautiful," he said. "Can you blame any man for wanting to cherish you?"

"Rise, Master Lorien. I am not offended. But I did call you most unexpectedly from a king's home, and I know the king was loath to let you go. He will be cheered to have you back."

"I have been here so brief a time," he said, standing straight once more, a head taller than she. "Do you really wish me to go?"

She turned away from him, toward the window of his room, and she looked out over the forest canopy as she fancied Cray must have done many times. This was his room, and she felt now that she had made a mistake in giving it over to a stranger. "You've changed your feelings in these few days, Master Lorien. You're no longer afraid of me."

"You are a kind and generous lady," he said. "You would grace any castle, magical or otherwise. And I was never afraid, only uncertain."

"You were afraid. I could see it in your eyes. You only came to Spinweb because you feared the consequences of disobedience to my command."

"I came out of curiosity, my lady."

She glanced back at him. "I think neither of us will convince the other. Fear or uncertainty—call it what you will; you'll have no more of it now. A steed will be waiting for you outside the gate." She gestured toward the door, and the cloth-servant entered, bearing a large, wool-wrapped bundle in its outstretched arms. "Here is some payment for your services."

The servant laid the package on the table and opened it. The wool wrapping was a mantle, its lining brown plush, and folded neatly inside were a fine brocade shirt, velvet trews, and knitted gloves.

"These are fine things, my lady," said the troubadour, "for such a short stay as mine."

"It was a long ride, was it not? The return will be no less." She waved, and the servant rewrapped the bundle and bore it away. "They will be waiting for you with your mount. And you will be cared for on your return journey as you were before."

He bowed. "I am grateful for your hospitality, both here and on the road."

"I would give you silver as well, but I have little use for it and so acquire it seldom."

"There is no need for silver, my lady. There is no need for payment of any kind. I will profit from this visit with you for many years to come."

"How so?"

He smiled again. "In the telling of the tale, of course. I warrant it will bring me silver enough for ten men. I have sung for a beautiful sorceress, ridden magical steeds, been served by all manner of wondrous creatures. This is a great gift you have given me, my lady. Far more than I have given you." He looked into her eyes. "I would that there were something I could give you, besides a few songs."

She shook her head. "Nothing that I want is within your power to give. Go now, Master Lorien. Spinweb is too lonely for one of your kind."

"Not too lonely for you, my lady?"

"No. Not for me."

He bowed once more. "As you wish."

The vine-steed waited in the warm morning air, the package of clothing like a pillow upon its back. Lorien mounted, and the tendrils clutched him and his reward alike.

"Will I ever see you again?" he asked of Delivev, standing before the gate of her home.

"No, never. But I will see you."

"As you saw your son last night?"

"Just so."

"Then . . . sometimes . . . should I seem to smile for no reason, you'll know that I smile for you."

"Thank you, Master Lorien. And farewell." She raised an arm, and the vine-steed wheeled and broke into a gallop.

Lorien waved once before the forest swallowed him up.

She stood there a moment, her back to the gate, her mind following the trail of his mount among the trees. A breeze stirred her hair, cool and damp, smelling of rain. She would make a shelter for him when it came, of interlaced branches and broad leaves.

"Yes, I am lonely, Master Lorien," she said, though he could not hear. "But not for you."

She went inside, and the gate barred itself behind her.

Gildrum passed briefly through the demon world, as it always did when leaving Ringforge; space lay differently there, and travel was faster than in the human world, and invisible to mortal eyes. Every demon had a personal portal there that only it could use; Gildrum's opened into its private dwelling, the place it had spent its time before answering the summons of the rings. To mortal perception, the place would seem a sea of blinding light, without visible boundaries, without furnishings. To Gildrum, it was comfort and quiet and the dream of freedom. The demon yearned to stop there and nevermore return to its master's demands. There had been a time when it had not felt so, when its home had merely been a way station for its travels, a convenience. It had found fascination in the ways of humans then, and in its work for Rezhyk, even in Rezhyk himself. It had been young then, though not in human terms. Now, with a long life yet stretching before it, Gildrum felt old and weary. It wanted to rest in its home. But it could not, for Rezhyk had commanded, and though the command might be delayed, it could not be denied.

Gildrum emerged into the human world at the ruins of Ushar.

Ushar was a city from the morning of time. Its people had been the first to find ways of enslaving demons, and thereby they had become a race of mighty sorcerers. But their petty jealousies, their rivalries in love and power, their greed, undid them at last: a war erupted among them, a conflict with no sides, with every combatant for himself, brother against brother, mother against son. When it was over, their civilization lay in ruins, their wealth and knowledge buried in the rubble, and their bodies, too. A few survivors, ringless, crippled, blind, scattered to tell the tale of their lost greatness. Generations passed before a new breed of sorcerer uncovered the keys to the demon world, and by then the lost knowledge of Ushar was legend only, a myth to frighten children when thunder rolled in the skies. Ultimately, through the demons themselves, the ruins were found. But excavation proved frustratingly difficult, and few sorcerers had gleaned more for their labors than a clay tablet or two, tallying herds of sheep and goats.

Rezhyk sought something greater.

He was a methodical man, and patient. While other sorcerers had dipped into the ruins, found nothing, and lost interest, he had spent the greater part of his life studying them. On one wall of his workshop hung a map of the city, showing squares, streets, buildings, even fountains, all located by his prying demons. He had even visited the site himself, though he had seen only the mound of grassy earth that marked it, that no demon had disturbed. A shepherd, chasing his unruly flock above the bones of Ushar, would never have suspected its existence.

Gildrum had been there many times and was responsible for large portions of the map. The demon slipped into the earth at its usual place, where a small patch of soil was baked and cracked from its entry, as by the desert sun. Beneath the soil lay hardened lava that glowed at its passage. Beneath that was the rubble—stone blackened by fire, cracked, crushed, pillars sifted with walls and floors, as if they had never seen separate existence. Gildrum followed a trail of lava around and among the debris of Ushar; though a boulevard was filled with broken buildings like fruit in a pie, the demon traversed it as easily as a human being would cross his bedroom. Yet the map was unfinished, even after so many years, and at last Gildrum came to the end of its own and others' explorations. Before it lay the remnants of a house, fallen pillars blocking the doorway, walls leaning inward, roof collapsed. The insignia of the resident was visible upon the brass fittings from the door, which lay upon the threshold, the wooden panel having burnt completely. Three interlocked rings marked the owner of the house as a member of the highest class of citizen, a most powerful sorcerer. As Gildrum entered through cracks the lava had filled, it wondered if this sorcerer had escaped the doom of his fellows.

Inside, the wooden floors had not survived the heat of entombment, and the roof had fallen all the way to the cellar in several pieces—Gildrum encountered that rubble there when, descending to the foundation, it began its search. In the darkness of solid rock, no eyes could see, no fingers trace the outlines of objects; the demon's perceptions were limited to the tactile sensations of its flame, to the material warmed by it, and its progress was as slow as that of a man plowing a field without a horse. Under the debris of the roof it discovered smashed ceramic pots and bronze boxes crushed flat, their contents forever unidentifiable. It found jewelry, too—gold and silver chain distorted by melting, cabochon gems cracked by heat, lumps that must have been brooches, pendants, diadems.

And a demon-master's ring.

It was a delicately crafted piece, the modeling of tiny leaves on the golden surface still perceptible in spite of the melting that had given the band an oval shape. There had been a gem once, but the prongs that had held it were mere nubbins now, the gem itself lost somewhere among the many others embedded in the lava. The ring encircled a small, charred finger bone, frozen there by the stone that had replaced the flesh. The rest of the skeleton huddled about it, as if the ring had been the center of the wearer's being, to be protected like a child in the womb. The whole skeleton lay beneath a rectangular slab of fine-grained marble that Gildrum guessed had been a tabletop.

The demon left the ring where it was. Crushed, broken, its maker dead, the circlet no longer had any power. To a living sorcerer, Ushar could offer only knowledge of the techniques of enslavement, never the slaves themselves. And so Gildrum searched for the ancient books that dealt with that knowledge, though it felt like a traitor to its race.

In a corner of the cellar, where the flags that lined the floor had buckled, it found the vault. Once, that hiding place had been well sealed with dressed stone and mortar, contents wrapped in greased oxhide against the damp. But lava had reached it in the final

94

cataclysm and within a jacket of stone, the oxhide was only a black and crumbly crust. With the most tenuous of fiery tendrils, Gildrum probed within the crust and found a stack of steel sheets. The folk of Ushar recorded their most important matters on demon-made steel, although to them herbals and genealogies were just as important as sorcerous lore. Still, Gildrum thought, in a home marked by three rings, a book of steel was likely to be what Rezhyk desired.

The demon withdrew from the steel and expanded to envelop the whole vault within its flame-body. It increased its heat then, till a sphere of rock containing its discovery floated free in a bed of molten lava, like a pebble in hot grease. It could cross to the demon world at that, and leave a hole, like a giant gas bubble, deep in the ruins of Ushar.

Gildrum left the sphere suspended in the brilliance of its home for a time, cooling, and when it judged that human flesh could touch the stone without damage, it delivered the dark mass to the workshop at Ringforge. Rezhyk hastened to examine the treasure while Gildrum, taking the form of the girl with blond braids, leaned against it to keep it from rolling across the polished floor.

"You could have made it a little smaller," said Rezhyk, tapping at the surface with hammer and chisel. The sphere stood only a head shorter than he did.

"There's a stone vault inside, with a melting point higher than lava. I was afraid the extra heat so close might damage the book beyond salvage."

Rezhyk grunted agreement. Dark flakes sprayed about him with every stroke of the hammer, and soon he had formed a broad, flat space on the sphere. Gildrum then rolled the rock mass over to rest on that surface, took the tools from her master, and set to work in his stead. She was quicker than he, her blows harder, because she did not worry about being injured by flying fragments. When the gray of the vault began to show, though, her progress slowed, for the harder, less porous rock of the vault yielded to force more reluctantly.

Rezhyk watched for a time, and then he turned to

other endeavors. Gildrum had been gone in the ruins many days, and her master had used that time for the final polishing of his new ring, and for the setting of its stone, the topaz pale as white wine that Gildrum had brought him. The ring lay on his workbench, and beside it was its larger counterpart, a plain circlet with the same metal content. Rezhyk set the large ring on the brazier, upon the coals that carried forth the low flame that had never died in Ringforge, and he set the other ring upon his own left index finger. As he began the chant that would call his new slave, the tapping of Gildrum's hammer behind his back fell into the rhythm of his voice.

In the center of the brazier, in the center of the ring, the reddish glow of a coal turned white-hot. Rezhyk chanted on, demanding, insisting, compelling. Abruptly, a pillar of flame roared from the brazier, rising through the ring, constricted there like sheaves of wheat clutched in a fist, but billowing above into a mushroom of fire. Over the roaring, whipping blaze, a voice shouted, "No! No!"

"Take your earthly form!" said Rezhyk. "I command it!"

The flames flickered against the ceiling, and in them a thousand shapes danced that might have been men, women, animals, creatures real and fantastical, all translucent, insubstantial. Flamelets broke away, skittered about the walls like leaves fluttering in an autumn wind, like butterflies about a tree in blossom, and then they swooped back into the pillar of fire, moths seeking death.

"Take your earthly form!" Rezhyk said again. "I command you!" He held his left hand out toward the flames, showing the ring, and the firelight glanced off the stone, bursting into a thousand rainbows. A limb of fire reached out for the gem, stopped short, played above it, throwing coruscations across the walls and floor, looped, spun, then dived back into the main body.

"Three times I command you to take your earthly form!" said Rezhyk.

The blaze shrank and coalesced into a creature no larger than a cat. It settled among the glowing coals of the brazier, the loose folds of its belly skin completely engulfing the large ring that lay there. It was an ugly and ungainly chimera, part scaly, part hairy, with long snout, great ears, and too many legs. Its tail, which roved restlessly among the coals, was studded with winking eyes. Its mouth was a wide, drooling slash across the top of its head.

It said, "My lord."

"Inscribe your name upon the ring," commanded Rezhyk.

The creature drooled. "It is done." Its voice was harsh and grating, as if torn from a throat that had not known speech in many years.

Rezhyk pulled the ring from his finger. On the inner surface of the band, the name Harolando now appeared. "Welcome to Ringforge, Harolando," he said. "You may go now, until I have had time to make a more pleasing form for you."

"As you wish, my lord," said Harolando. And then its head lifted and its tail twitched, and all of its many eyes gazed past Rezhyk's shoulder, to Gildrum, who still labored with hammer and chisel on the stone vault. "Greetings to you, cousin," the new demon said. There was no trace of cheer in its voice.

Gildrum, who had averted her eyes during the conjuring process, looked toward the brazier now, briefly. She did not know this demon. She guessed that it had not existed when she herself had been caught. Still, she said, "Greetings, cousin."

The new demon flared into flame and vanished. It left the coals glowing behind it, and Rezhyk had to remove the large ring from them with tongs. The name Harolando was inscribed on its inner surface.

He turned to Gildrum. "Are you finished with that yet, my Gildrum?"

"Almost, my lord." And she struck the chisel so hard that the remaining vertical section of the vault sheared away clean, leaving the small mass of lava that directly encased the sheets standing exposed on a dark stone pedestal. "Just a little more," she said.

She found herself remembering what her own first call had been like, so long ago, the summons that had cut her off from the other free demons forever. Before that moment, she and they had scorned the slaves; afterward, she had never looked at them without seeing their scorn. She pitied Harolando—the adjustment to captivity was not an easy one. But at least Harolando had demon companions about Ringforge. There had been no cousin slave to greet Gildrum, just Rezhyk himself, standing in a glade in the woods where Ringforge was to be built.

She could scarcely remember her own earthly form, save that it had been large and many-limbed. She had never used it beyond that once, the first time she had ever visited the human world. It must have been ugly, for Rezhyk had bade her stay in the flame-body until he could fashion a more pleasing one. By the time Ringforge was finished, he had given her the form she wore now, the first of many.

Already, he was molding clay for the new demon's first human semblance.

Delicately, Gildrum chipped at the dark stone. She had discarded the large hammer and chisel in favor of a very small pair, and with these she reached the thin layer of black that had been oxhide and then the metallic surface itself. As the lava crumbled under her taps, she perceived a pattern of markings incised on the steel.

"Ah," she said, and instantly Rezhyk was at her shoulder, brushing powdered lava from her work space with a tuft of camel's hair, reading the ancient words as she uncovered them. The first sheet was the hardest to clean; the rest were nested so snugly against it and each other that no lava had seeped between them —only their edges were sealed with once-hot stone.

"Gently, my Gildrum, gently," said Rezhyk. "The metal surely lost its temper during the slow cooling, and a sharp blow might crack it."

"I know, my lord."

"They are not . . . welded together, are they?"

"I think not," the demon replied, easing a thin blade between the top two sheets. "The lava was cooling by the time it reached the vault, and I suspect that it was never hot enough to weld steel. There!" The top plate separated from the others as the last bits of adhering rock broke.

Rezhyk snatched the freed sheet away, to examine it under the strong light of an oil lamp. "Fortunately," he said, "the sorcerers of Ushar recorded their wisdom on the most durable material they could find. If they had chosen copper instead of steel, this book would be a solid block of metal instead of individual, still legible pages."

Gildrum pulled the other sheets apart with little difficulty, passing them to Rezhyk one at a time until there were no more, and then she went to look over her master's shoulder.

"I'll be many months in deciphering all this," said the sorcerer. "But it appears, from the little I can make out, to be exactly what I was seeking." He smiled at the demon. "Once again you have served me well, my Gildrum."

"I made certain assumptions from my knowledge of Ushar as to the most likely locations for such books. We have legends of the city, too, we demons, and they are perhaps not so garbled as human legends, for they have not passed through so many generations."

"Ah, you would be perfect if only you could read these inscriptions as well as bring them to me."

She bowed her head. "I am sorry, my lord, but they who could have read those words are gone, every one of them. Even demons die at last." She peered up at Rezhyk through lowered lashes. "Nor do I think, were they alive yet, that they would reveal this ancient and powerful language to one who served a sorcerer. Freed by the destruction of Ushar, they would not wish to chance being enslaved again."

"Well, you and I shall puzzle this out." He brushed a trace of clinging powder from one of the sheets. "Look here—these are familiar lines: the conjuration of a minor fire demon, if I am not mistaken. Yes, yes." He bent close to make out a portion of the inscription that was not engraved as deeply as the rest. "But here he recommends a far greater proportion of nickel to gold than I have ever attempted. And this symbol here . . . do you think it might stand for jade? Could the sorcerers of Ushar have conjured demons with opaque stones as well as translucent? Bring me my notebook, Gildrum, and those sheets I

99

bought from Klarinn. He may have thought ancient history useless, but I suspect it shall aid me in this translation."

"Yes, my lord," said Gildrum, and after she got the notebook she pulled up the tall stool, foreseeing a long session ahead. She sighed. Rezhyk found the deciphering of ancient lore fascinating, but she found it tedious; she had no talent for such things, and her contribution was usually limited to a nod of her head or murmur of agreement or, at most, a reminder to the sorcerer of something he had already said. Rezhyk insisted this was all useful, and so he bade her sit by while he worked.

She sat, and if her mind was elsewhere, he did not notice. She thought of the skeleton in the lava—a woman's skeleton, she decided, too delicate for a man's, the hips too broad in proportion to the shoulders and rib cage. Many women had died with Ushar. Gildrum wondered if this one had been old or young, dark or fair, ugly or beautiful. Beautiful, she resolved, as all women should be—tall and brown-haired and beautiful. Unbidden, the image of Delivev rose in the demon's mind—beautiful and melancholy enough to tear the heart from any man's breast. Heartless in any anatomical sense, Gildrum still felt a pang deep within her being—not the human form worn like a mask upon the truth, but the demon essence, the intangible, inhuman reality. As her eyes could almost see Delivev, so her ears could almost hear the music drifting upward from Spinweb's garden. Her fingers interlaced tightly upon her lap, as if that tension could drive the memories from her. Resolutely, she turned her mind to thoughts of Cray, upon the road to Falconhill.

Upon his quest for a knight who never existed.

Cray and Feldar Sepwin arrived at the third fork in the road.

"We're to turn south here," said Cray, "and then we must ask directions of some local, for I have no further knowledge of the route."

Sepwin nodded, squinting up at the sky. "Does it look like rain to you? Perhaps we should seek shelter."

Cray glanced up at the clouds bunched gray about

the sun. "No rain for a few hours yet, I'd say. Let's go on."

The sky grew no darker, but in a short time they were forced to stop anyway because Gallant began to limp. Sepwin examined the favored hoof, found a sharp stone lodged there, and carefully removed it with the point of Cray's knife. He said, "He shouldn't walk on this foot anymore today."

"There's a hut up ahead," Cray said, gesturing with one hand. "I saw it from the last rise. We can stop there and be sheltered if the rain comes."

"Unless it's abandoned and has no roof," said Sepwin.

"Do you always think of the worst possible eventuality, Master Feldar?"

"For beggars, that is the usual one," Sepwin replied.

"But you are not a beggar any more. Come along. I predict that not only does the hut have a sturdy and weatherproof roof, but it is inhabited and we will find a hot supper there." He took Gallant's reins and walked ahead, the horse trailing after, still limping.

Pulling his own mount along, Sepwin fell into stride with Cray. "What is the source of this prediction, Master Cray? Wishful thinking?"

"Look at the grass encroaching on the road. Someone has cut it back recently, someone uses this road. Who more likely than the folk who live in yonder hut? We've seen no other dwelling in many miles."

"Perhaps the lord of this land sends his men to keep the roads clear," said Sepwin.

"Always the worst possible eventuality, as I said. Would you care to wager on it?"

"With what, Master Cray? My rags?" He halted abruptly. "Wait—I see smoke rising from that hut. Perhaps you are right after all." He lifted one hand to his face, covered his right eye with it. "Have you a rag, Master Cray? A scrap of something?"

"I have a kerchief. I'm sure that will do."

Sepwin nodded. "Quickly, before someone sees us."

Cray found the fine linen square in one of his saddlebags. It was embroidered with his initials.

"Rather an elegant eye patch," said Sepwin, folding

101

it into a bandage and tying it at the back of his head.

"It does make a bit of a contrast with your other clothing," remarked Cray. "For one thing, it's clean. Well, perhaps we can do something about that while we wait for Gallant's hoof to heal."

"My clothes have lasted me a long time, Master Cray. They may fall apart if washed."

"I have extra clothing in my saddlebags. It will fit you well enough, I think, if you need it."

Sepwin stared at him, one-eyed. "Why do you offer me such favors, Master Cray? First the horse, now clothing . . ."

"I have plenty of clothing, Master Feldar. And you could not travel with me on foot, after all."

"I don't understand."

Cray shrugged. "I grew up . . . alone . . . except for my mother. I had all the clothing I wanted, all the food, all the toys. There was a pony when I was old enough to ride it, and later Gallant here. My mother never denied me. But I never had a human friend. It was a long time before I realized that I wanted one." He smiled at Sepwin. "Now you are my friend. If I can give you a few small presents, what is the harm in that? It is no sacrifice for me to give you a horse and clothing. I can hunt excellently, I can weave a shelter from the weather if I must; I have no real need of my little silver save for luxuries. So I choose the luxury of a friend."

"I never had a friend either," said Sepwin, and his fingers brushed the bandage over his eye.

Cray's brows knit, and then he pointed to Sepwin's face. "Didn't you have the other eye covered before?"

"Does it matter?"

"No, I suppose not. But . . . isn't that patch uncomfortable?"

"I am used to it, Master Cray."

"But you must be frequently among people, and half blind. Do you never tire of having one eye covered? Do you never peek out from under the bandage, to see with both eyes?"

"I try not to, Master Cray. A one-eyed beggar, even if both of his eyes are the same color, dares not be seen as a fraud. This is my livelihood, or was until

I met you. People haven't near so much pity for a beggar without ills."

Cray nodded slowly.

"I am ready now; shall we go on?"

The thin plume of smoke they had seen rising from the hut actually came from a small fire built behind the structure. An old man sat close by the flames, feeding small twigs to them while a pot of porridge bubbled in the heat. He seemed not to notice his visitors until they came quite close, and then he jumped up and backed a few steps away, bowing jerkily.

"Your pardon, sirs," he said in a loud voice. "I did not hear you approach. Your pardon!"

"Good day," said Cray. "We are travelers on the road with a long journey both behind and ahead of us, and one of our horses has gone lame. We were wondering if we might stay here today and perhaps tomorrow, until he is fit to travel again."

"Eh?" said the old man. He cupped a hand to his right ear. "My hearing isn't what it used to be. You must speak loudly."

Cray repeated his request, and the man bobbed another bow. "Oh, stay, stay if you like," he said. "I haven't guested a traveler in many a year. Many, many a year. You're more than welcome to share my poor fare, though it is only yesterday's porridge." He smiled, showing a toothless jaw.

"A hot meal," muttered Sepwin.

"I'll hunt," said Cray softly. "The rain will hold off for a while yet. He probably doesn't eat meat very often."

"Meat? He can't chew meat without teeth."

"We can make soup from some of it for him then. Or do you want porridge?"

"I've eaten worse in my life."

"I'll hunt," Cray repeated firmly. "Take care of Gallant for me?" He took one of his magic nets from a saddlebag. "I won't be long."

"Can you hunt without that?" asked Sepwin.

Cray looked down at the gossamer-fine spidersilk in his hands. He hardly felt its weight, and in all but the brightest sunlight it was nigh invisible. "Why would I need to?"

"In case you lost it, of course."

Cray shrugged. "They are easy enough to make. My mother taught me when I was very young. You could learn the process without any difficulty, I am sure."

"Me?" said Sepwin.

"There's a little trick to it, but nothing a diligent student could not master."

"But I am not a sorcerer, nor even a sorcerer's child. How could an ordinary mortal learn something like that?"

"Sorcerers were once ordinary mortals," said Cray. "Or didn't you know that?"

"But they live so much longer . . ."

"They became sorcerers through knowledge," Cray told him. "Knowledge extended their lives as well as giving them power."

Sepwin cocked his head to one side and regarded Cray with his one uncovered eye. "And you? Half of one sort, half of another—which life span will you have?"

Cray fingered the gossamer net. "I don't know," he said slowly. "I don't know of any others like me, so . . . I don't know." He laughed then. "We're both a trifle young to be talking of death, don't you think?"

Sepwin took up Gallant's reins and those of his own mount. "I have thought about it," he said. "Someone like me . . . thinks about it often."

Cray clapped him on the shoulder. "Well, not now, Master Feldar. Not even though the day be cloudy and promising rain." He grinned. "And on such a day, I must be off to the hunt without further delay." With a last glance at the sky, he turned and jogged off into the trees.

As soon as he had passed well out of sight of the hut, Cray spread out his magic net. He laid it at the foot of a tall and gnarly oak, between mighty arching roots, where mushrooms sprouted. He baited the net with herbs from the woodland floor—thyme and marjoram sprigs elaborately knotted together. Then he climbed another tree and hid himself among its leaves to sit, quiet as a bluebird hiding in its nest from hunting hawks. Shortly, a pair of rabbits approached the oak roots; they circled the tree, nibbling bits of greenery that grew around it, sitting up sometimes, their pink noses twitching as they sniffed the air. First one, then the other edged toward the net, and neither seemed to notice it, even when they stepped upon the fine strands. When they stood head to head, their noses nudging the aromatic bait, Cray gestured with one finger, and the net wrapped about its quarry, enfolding them in webbing light as air but strong as steel. Again, the rabbits seemed unconcerned. Cray descended from his tree and dispatched them with his knife.

Back at the hut, Sepwin and the old man were getting on well, though Sepwin was swiftly becoming hoarse from so much shouting.

"His family is all gone," said Sepwin, helping Cray to skin and dress out the two rabbits as their host looked on. "The oldest son died of fever, the youngest ran off to be a tinker, the daughters married away, and his wife died in childbirth with her eighth. He's lived here alone for the past few years, and he wants us to stay for a month or two to keep him company."

Cray grinned. "We thank you for such a kind offer of hospitality, good sir," he said loudly, "but we cannot stay longer than it takes for the big horse to mend. We have a long journey ahead of us."

"A few days then, young sir," said the old man. "Just a few days. I haven't seen a human soul since the last daughter left. Too lonely here, she said. She met a man when we took a bull calf to market in the town, and she would marry him, no matter that it meant her old father would be left alone." He plucked at his short, scraggly white beard with fleshless fingers. "She waved all the way down the road, waved and waved, and then she turned her back and never waved again. I have been lonely, I can tell you."

"Why not go to one of your daughters, then, good sir?" said Cray. "Live with one of them, with your grandchildren about you."

The old man gazed at Cray with startled eyes. "And leave my home?"

"If you are so lonely . . ."

"I built this house with my own hands. I cleared my own fields, planted, cultivated, weeded, and when the horse died I pulled the plow myself, and one of the boys walked behind to guide it. My children were born here, and I will be buried here!"

Cray shrugged. "Then you must resign yourself to loneliness, I suppose. You can't force your children to come back."

The old man nodded. "I let them go. How could I stop them? Pen them like goats? Tie them to the trees? I let them go. Still . . . it is a lonely place." He looked out over his land, which stretched in the shape of a triangle with apex at the hut and base against distant trees. At one time, when it supported a large family, it must have been planted with neat, parallel rows of tall grain and low vegetables. Now all but the portion closest to the hut was overgrown with weeds, and here and there a spindly sapling showed above the scrub, the forest reclaiming its loss. "I am the farthest settler from the town," he said, his voice and his face suffused with pride in those words. "My father said that bandits would raid us, that wild boars would eat the grain, that wolves would kill my children; but none of that happened. We were too lonely even for those things. Certainly too lonely to guest many travelers." He smiled at Cray. "But I have tried to keep the road clear for any who might pass. I knew they would be grateful."

"Indeed we are," said Cray. "And I hope that the fine soup we will make from this rabbit will be some small recompense for your labors. Have you a pot, good sir? One without porridge in it?"

"A pot? Oh yes. A pot." He scrambled to his feet and ducked inside the hut to return in a moment with the twin to the porridge container. "This will do, won't it?"

"Admirably," said Cray, and he dumped bones and finely cut scraps into it, along with the herbs that he had used to bait his net. The old man added onions and carrots from his fields, salt from a small bag hung just inside the door of his hut, and water from his well, and they set the pot on the fire to boil. Cray was left with boneless rabbit steaks, which he wrapped in a cloth and stowed inside one of his saddle bags; they would be safe there, in case the old man had a dog or two about his place, in case there were weasels in the fields. Later, when the soup was done, Cray would broil the meat over open flames, and all three of them would share the evening meal.

When he turned back to the fire, the old man still sat there, stirring it and musing on the past, and Sepwin sat happily enough beside him, a green twig between his teeth. Cray settled beside them, lying down on his back on the bare, fire-warmed earth, arms behind his head, and he looked up at the sky, where the clouds had finally cleared away without loosing any rain at all.

"In twenty years," the old man was saying, "I have had only four guests. Others have passed on the road and, I suppose, found my hut too poor to stop at; one even waved to me as he galloped by. He bore a blue standard in his hand, and I always wondered where he came from, where he was going in such a hurry." He nodded, more to himself than to Cray or Sepwin. "Yes, some few have passed, but only four have stopped. You are two." He counted them off on the index and middle finger of his left hand. "And the other two— they were here together, too, but not *together,* not companions like you. The one came first. He was a pleasant young fellow. My wife liked him. She was alive then, and some of the children were still here, the three younger ones, I think. She wanted to know if I thought him handsome, I remember. Oh, quite handsome, quite. And he chopped enough wood to last us the rest of the year. The other came later. I never saw *his* face at all—he kept his visor down, just shouted a challenge to the first. They fought on the road, right out in front of the hut. I never found out exactly what it was they fought about. The second one —he rode away right after it was finished, didn't say another word. I had to bury the other one myself."

"They were knights?" asked Cray.

"They wore armor. I suppose they were knights. It was some private feud. I kept the children away after the fighting began, though they wanted to watch. Two wild men they were, with their swords in their hands, and I thought it would be easy for a watcher to be killed."

"Did they use only swords?"

"Yes, swords. And shields. And a mighty racket they made, too, bashing metal against metal. The loser's sword was all notched, and the edges of his shield were bent. Every time I look at them, I wonder how a man's arms can stand all that battering."

"You have the shield and sword of the man who was killed?"

"Oh, yes, yes." The old man bobbed his head. "I had his horse, too, to pull my plow until it died. The winner, he just rode off, never saying a word, leaving the dead body in the middle of the road. The bloodstains were there until the next rain."

Cray frowned. "He should have taken the shield, at least, to send to his opponent's lord. That would have been only courtesy. They did seem to know each other, did they not?"

"They knew each other well, I thought. Certainly, there was no time for them to argue before they met here and the fight began."

"It was wrong to leave the arms behind them. And wrong not to bury the body as well."

"Right or wrong," said the old man, "I would not have stopped him to demand either. He was a big man on a big horse, and his armor was black as pitch, with no device, without a scratch upon it. He had never lost a fight, I knew that. I let him go, and I thanked good fortune that he had no quarrel with me. My wife cried when we buried the other. She said he was too young to die." He shrugged, "Well, and so was she, and my eldest son. We all die, sooner or later. I think on that when I look on their graves, and I wonder why I have been spared so long. A grave is an excellent thing, to give a man pause in a long day, to remind him to be grateful for the little life given him. Don't you think so?"

"I don't know," said Cray. "I've never seen a grave."

"Never seen a grave?" The old man looked at him with bright, incredulous eyes. "Where have you lived that no one dies, young sir?"

"I have lived with my mother," said Cray. "Just the two of us, and I have never known anyone who died."

"But graves . . . surely the graves of your ancestors were somewhere nearby."

"None that I knew of, good sir." He did not mention that sorcerers, unless killed considerably before the normal span of their long lives, merely crumbled to dust and blew away at death. His grandmother, dead more than half a century, was part of the forest soil, and when Cray was a child one of his fancies was that she lived in every tree, in every herb, in every mushroom that sprouted there. His mother spoke of her sometimes, and Cray knew what she looked like from a tapestry that Delivev had woven before he was born.

Nor had he ever seen a grave in the webs. Delivev had no interest in graveyards.

"You may see a few this day then," said the old man. "And every one dug by these hands." He held them up, and they were knobby with age but still calloused. He rose. "Come. Come along."

Cray shrugged and followed him, glancing back once at Sepwin, who stayed still by the fire.

"I've seen enough graves for my taste," said Sepwin, and he stirred the soup with a clean stick.

Cray and the old man walked through the untended field, wading through coarse grass and grain gone wild that reached their waists and higher. Almost at the trees on the far side, they emerged from the tangle to a small open space, where the greenery was clipped short and scattered with wild flowers. Here were three graves, neatly mounded hillocks of earth side by side. The first was marked by a large stone cut into a rough slab, with symbols against evil incised deeply in the weathered surface.

"My eldest son," the old man said.

The second grave had two stones at its head, one large, one small, with carvings in proportion.

"My wife is there," said the old man, pointing. "And the baby, too. I thought she would not like to be separated from him."

But Cray's eyes tracked quickly past the first two graves, to the third. Its marker stone was rougher hewn than the others, rounded, more like an ordinary boulder. And tilted against it, their lower parts buried, anchored in the grass-grown earth, were a sword and shield. Both were rusty from long exposure to the elements, and much of the shield's paint had weathered away, but still there was enough left upon it that Cray could make out the bearings of its owner: three red lances interlocked on a white field. He stood before the grave and stared down at that shield, and the old man babbled behind him, unheeded.

"It is a moving experience, is it not?" the old man was saying when Cray could hear his words once more. "I weep, too, every time I come to tend them. I miss her, though she's been gone so long."

Cray blinked and realized that his cheeks and lashes were wet with salty tears. "His name," he said slowly, "was Mellor."

The old man came close to him. "You knew the man? But this happened many years ago, and you are very young."

"Fifteen years ago."

"Fifteen?" He rubbed at his bearded chin with one hand, then ticked off the years on those fingers. "Perhaps fifteen," he said after some moments. "Or fourteen. Since my last daughter left my house, I have not kept a careful count of the passing years."

"He was bound south for Falconhill from the East March."

"He was indeed! Bound for the hold of our very own lord with some business from the East March!"

Cray knelt by the grave and laid his hands upon it, as if some essence could pass from the corpse resting within to himself. He felt only grass beneath his palms, and the coarser texture of herbs scattered among the shorter growth. He touched the shield, the sword, and flakes of rust came away in his hand.

"He was my father," Cray said, and he closed his eyes and curled his fingers into the grave mound, into the rich black soil beneath the grass. Of a sudden, the chain was heavy on his body, and he could not rise against its weight for a long, long time.

Beside him, Gildrum stood silent, his lips closed over toothless gums. He wanted to touch the kneeling youth; he wanted to take him in his arms and hold him

110

close, but he held himself aloof instead, as a stranger would, leaving Cray alone in grief over a lie.

The demon had planned the simulated death well, thinking that Delivev would find some way to track her lover when he did not return. The victorious foe, a hulking knight in black armor, had been an illusion, the battle realistically wild, the witnesses frightened flesh and blood. But Delivev had not traced her lover, and in the years that followed the event, the witnesses had trickled away through marriage and death, until the hut lay abandoned, the fields overgrown, the graves lost in weeds and wild flowers.

Sitting on the high stool in Rezhyk's workshop, Gildrum had known that Cray was approaching the place, following the innkeeper's directions. With little time to spare, she had begun to voice a certain personal dissatisfaction to her master, a certain discontent with her own accomplishments. The steel plates, she had said, would be more easily translated if there were more of them, and so she offered to return to Ushar and search onward. She hinted, even, that she could almost guess where others might be found, and her arguments were so earnest and persuasive that Rezhyk agreed and gave the command she sought.

Gildrum had not lied to its master—the demon fully intended to return to Ushar, and it did have a notion of where to search next. But knowing that it would not be expected back at Ringforge soon, it went elsewhere first. It transformed the abandoned homestead into a place where an elderly man might live, for Rezhyk had given his servant that form once. It repaired the hut and cleared a patch around the structure, trimmed the sides of the road and tended the graves. Then it caused Cray's horse to go lame. If Cray had not stopped at the hut of his own volition, Gildrum would have contrived to go out into the road after him.

Cray stood up at last, and he gathered the shield and sword in his arms, wrenching them from the earth that anchored them. "These belong to me now," he said.

"I understand, young sir," said Gildrum. "It is only right that his kin should know what became of him."

And to himself, he said, *Tell her, my son. Tell her, and both of you will be free of someone who never existed.* He watched Cray walk stiffly through the tall wild grain, toward the hut, and before he followed he allowed himself to sigh so quietly that the youth could not hear. *But I,* he thought, *I shall never be free of you.*

"Master Feldar," Cray called hoarsely, "we shall not be going to Falconhill after all."

She knew something was wrong when she stepped past the threshold of the chamber where the tapestry wove itself. The whole room was dim, as if curtains of thick gauze veiled the bare windows, and the air was a heavy miasma that seemed to roll into the lungs like syrup. A thousand terrible thoughts filled her brain as she crossed the floor, images of Cray lying broken in some foreign land, robbed, tortured, dead. Even as she touched the cloth, tears were streaming from her eyes, and she could hear the blood of fear rushing in her ears. As her fingers met the threads, the shock of grief invaded her flesh, rising in her arms like poison from a snakebite. She shivered with ague and fell to the floor, powerless to move, her hands still clutching the cloth. She scarcely needed to see the bearings that the tapestry had pictured, the lances interlocked; she knew her son too well to doubt the source of that emotion. The knowledge she had never wanted was hers now, and the pain that it brought was fiercer by far than any she had ever known in so many years of uncertainty. She keened, harshly, brokenly, until her throat was afire, and even then she did not cease.

Slowly, her creatures joined her, the spiders and snakes creeping close to her prostrate form, the vines sliding in the window, the birds lighting on her shoulders and hips to peck at the feathers of her clothing, at her hair, her ears. Only the pony did not come, locked in its stall near the garden, but it sensed the pall that flowed from that room, and it whinnied its uneasiness. After a long time, she heard it, and she rose, heavy with the age she had never felt before, and went out to comfort it.

112

✦§ CHAPTER SEVEN

When he saw her in the web, Cray perceived some change in his mother. The soft, pale plumage she had always favored for her garments had been replaced by glossy raven feathers, and in contrast her skin seemed ashen. She sat too still and straight upon the velvet coverlet, only her fingers moving, the slender needles poised in their grasp twitching rhythmically upon some half-completed knitting. She did not smile, not even the sad smile that he knew so well, and there were dark circles beneath her eyes, as if she had been awake far too long.

"I know what you found, my son," she said. "You need not speak the words. What will you do now?"

"I'll go to the East March, Mother. He swore fealty to its lord, and I shall do the same. Surely they will accept his son."

"I don't know what ordinary mortals will accept," she said.

"Well, there's no point in going on to Falconhill now."

"No. No point. But the East March is far."

"Other places are farther."

She looked down at her knitting. "I suppose it is your proper destination now."

"I don't know of another."

"You can stop at home on your way. Rest. Replenish yourself. I can think of a few favorite foods you can't have tasted in quite some time. I'll even welcome your friend, if he's still with you by then."

Cray shook his head. "I'm not coming home, Mother. I'll take a different route."

She looked up at him. "Another route? But any other route would be longer."

"Once at home," he said, "it would be very hard to leave again. Even if you didn't cook any of my favorite foods." He smiled, hoping the expression would prompt an answer from her lips, but it did not. "I know you understand, Mother."

She lowered her eyes once more. "I understand. Do you plan to pass north or south of Spinweb?"

"South, I think. We have come some distance south already, and we can strike directly east from here."

"To the south, where the forest thins, there is a great swamp. Both men and roads have entered and never emerged. You must detour far around it, unless you have an excellent map."

"I have no map at all," said Cray. "I was hoping that you could provide me with one."

"I am no mapmaker," she said.

"Perhaps not, but I'd guess you know one."

Her fingers paused, stilling the needles. "Human roads and settlements have little interest for a sorcerer. And demons need no maps."

"A demon of the air could easily make a map," said Cray. "What of the sorcerer who sent Gallant for me? He has many such demons, and he has dealt fairly with you before."

"He has. But he does no favors. He would have to be paid."

"Give him something that belongs to me, then. Tapestries from my room, the rug, the coverlet. I don't care."

"You don't care," she murmured. "Because you'll not be using any of it again."

"Please, Mother. Do this for me." He reached out toward her with an open, pleading hand.

She sighed heavily. "Of course. Have I ever denied you anything?"

"Thank you, Mother."

"Stay where you are a day or two. The map shall come to you." Her image faded away, and the web became just a web strung between two bushes, bellying gently in the morning breeze.

Cray turned to Sepwin. "I have hurt her terribly," he said. "After so many years, she was still hoping that he might be alive."

"As you were," replied Sepwin.

Cray nodded. "At the very least, I never expected the trail to be so short."

Sepwin shrugged. "He was young, and youth usually means inexperience. He was pitted against a better man. And an angrier one, if we can believe the old man's tale."

Cray glanced down the road. They were some hours' travel from the hut, from the grave, and they had passed two other homesteads, both abandoned and overgrown with weeds, before stopping in a grove of trees. He had not wanted to speak to his mother where the old man might overhear, and then he had not found the heart to set his spiders spinning until the hot morning sun had burned some of the tears from his eyes. The corroded shield hung on Gallant's saddle behind his own, and the sword was wrapped in a linen shirt and thrust into one of the saddlebags; he could not look at his father's arms without feeling his heart tighten in his breast.

"He was young," Cray said at last. "Even by mortal standards."

"Not younger than you are, though, I'll warrant."

"Than I? No. But he was a knight, of course. If I started my training tomorrow, it would be years before I could be knighted."

"To me, Master Cray, you are already a knight. And a better one than most."

"Nonsense, Master Feldar. How many knights have you known?"

"I have never *known* one before, but I have encountered them a-plenty, thank you. Big, fierce men, without a care for anything but themselves. I once saw one trample a small child that happened to be playing in the road. He just rode over it, as if it had been a weed."

"He must not have seen it. Those visors, you know —sometimes they obscure the vision enormously."

"He saw it. But he didn't care. The mother cared, though. She screamed loud enough. But he rode on."

"Well, I suppose there must be evil knights as well as good ones, as there are of other men. You must not judge them all by the actions of a few. In the webs I have seen them courteous and kind, helping ladies with their knitting, playing with children, laughing, joking. The oath of knighthood demands that they be good and true to their friends. In battle, of course, toward their enemies, that is something quite different."

"Where did you see these knights?" Sepwin wondered.

"As I told you . . . in the webs."

"No, I mean where were *they?*"

"In various castles. Perhaps a dozen in all. So you see, I have seen a goodly number of knights."

"Well, I have never been in a castle, Master Cray. I only know the knights who have passed me on the road or in villages. Perhaps they are as you say among their own. A man would hardly do evil to the lady or children of his host, or to the man who might guard his back in battle. But among the peasants, among the people who are of no consequence, these knights are not so kind and courteous. I will not go so far as to say they are evil, no. But they are selfish and uncaring, and we who do not belong in castles, in fine clothes and jewels, we do not matter to them an eye blink."

"They protect you," said Cray.

"They protect themselves. We work the land to make them rich. Well . . . my father does. He pays his taxes promptly each year. I am not in a position to make anyone rich. Perhaps that is why they spit on me. A beggar pays no taxes. He is worth less than the poorest peasant."

Cray said, "You have had some bad experiences, Master Feldar. You see the world in a twisted way."

"Ah, no, Master Cray. It is you that sees the world twisted. The webs have limited your vision to the best side of these men, and you know nothing of the rest."

"You are wrong, Master Feldar," said Cray. "I know that evil exists in them; I do not delude myself on that score. The webs have shown me ugly things as

116

well as beautiful—theft and betrayal and even murder. Yes, murder. Still, I don't believe that every knight would ride down a child playing in the road. Perhaps if you did not have eyes of two different colors, you would see a more balanced version of the world."

Sepwin fingered the kerchief which had served as an eye patch; he had worn it about his throat since they had left the old man behind. "Perhaps because I have eyes of two different colors, I have seen things that you have not."

"I don't doubt it. Fear, I'm sure, is a potent force for evil."

"I am fortunate, then," Sepwin said, a slow grin curving his mouth, "that you have no fear." He touched the shoulder of his shirt, one of Cray's clean linen shirts. His trews, too, were Cray's. His old clothes, save for the worn cloak and sandals, had been thrown away; as predicted, they had not survived washing.

Cray folded his arms across his chest. "I have fears, Master Feldar, but I don't fear nonsense. And I don't fear magic, as you should not."

"It's easy to fear what one doesn't understand," said Sepwin.

Cray gestured up at the sky. "Do you fear the sun because you don't understand what keeps it aloft? Do you fear clouds, rain, the moon and stars?"

"But these are natural things," said Sepwin.

"As is magic."

"Not to me. I know that the sun will rise in the east and set in the west, and the moon and stars, too. I know that clouds float across the sky and sometimes loose rain, which falls down and makes me wet. But magic . . ."

"Magic is a tool," said Cray. "Like fire. Human beings make fire serve them, and they do the same with magic. One must treat the sorcerer with respect, as one would a man with a blazing torch in his hands. Each is in a position to do harm, but neither will attack the innocent." He frowned slightly, then added, "Unless, of course, he is mad."

"Of course," echoed Sepwin. "Tell me, Master Cray . . . are there many mad sorcerers about in the world?"

"I've heard of one or two."

"Only one or two?"

"How many would you expect? How many mad ordinary mortals do you know of?"

"Quite a few, Master Cray. Quite a few. There was a whole village went mad some years back, joined hands and went dancing across the countryside, every man, woman, and child. Except the youngest, who stayed behind in their cradles."

"What happened to them?"

"The babies? They starved, for their parents never came back."

"And the others?"

"They danced till they dropped," said Sepwin. "It took days, and whether it was hunger, thirst, or exhaustion that finally ended them all, I don't know. There's a road south of here lined with their graves—the local inhabitants buried each dancer where he or she died and marked their headstones with a sign to ward off evil. They said it was sorcery."

Cray shook his head slowly. "I don't know. I don't know what sort of magic could do that."

"There was an old woman they offended," said Sepwin. "She passed through their village and no one would give her hospitality because she was so very ugly. It's said that she laid a curse on them."

"Who said it?"

"Who?" Sepwin pursed his lips. "Well . . . I don't know. Someone from the village, I suppose, before he died. I heard the tale from a blacksmith."

"You never saw any of the dancers?"

"No, it happened a long time ago. Maybe before I was born."

Cray raised one eyebrow. "Are you sure it happened?"

"Well . . . no. But what reason would the blacksmith have to lie to me?"

"I have no idea. Perhaps he was merely passing on a diverting tale he'd heard from someone else. Do you always believe everything that people tell you, no matter how outlandish?"

"I don't know what is outlandish, Master Cray. I've

seen things on my journey with you that I would have thought outlandish before we met."

Cray inclined his head. "True enough, Master Feldar. I should not belittle your gullibility. I'm sure I could show you more marvels yet. Though nothing as wonderful as making a whole village dance." He rubbed at the side of his nose with an index finger. "Perhaps . . . if there were vermin in their clothes, biting them constantly, they might appear to be dancing . . . or flying insects buzzing around them, stinging them . . . But if the old woman were truly one of the sorcerous breed, she would hardly need their hospitality, she would be quite capable of looking after her own requirements. I wonder what they really did to her."

"You see," said Sepwin, "you accept it as magic."

"I accept it as a strange puzzle," Cray replied, "that may or may not have some basis in fact."

"Some basis, I think, or I wouldn't know so many similar stories."

"Of whole villages going mad?"

"Not quite that, no, but I know of crops that failed for no reason, wives and children who disappeared, homes that burned when there was no flame to touch them off—oh, we beggars pick up stories in our travels."

"I look forward to hearing them all," said Cray. "The road to the East March is a long one."

"Did your mother never tell you such stories when you were a child? Mine did."

"No, my mother's stories dealt with the natural world, with animals and plants and rivers and mountains. They didn't often include people or the things that concern people."

"Then you will have a few tales to tell me on our journey, too," said Sepwin. "Though I suspect we will run out of stories before we reach our destination."

"I am grateful for your companionship, Master Feldar."

Sepwin shrugged. "Falconhill or East March—it makes no difference to me where I go. But . . . do you think the second knight could have been from the East March?"

"What? And followed my father all that way? I doubt it greatly. If it were true, he would have been waiting outside Spinweb, surely, when my father left; he was inside quite long enough for anyone to catch up with him."

"Not if the pursuer left the East March much, much later than he."

"Are you seeking some danger at the East March, Master Feldar?"

"I am only being cautious."

"Well, I respect your caution," Cray said, "but I think it is misplaced in this instance. My own feeling is that my father and this other knight had some quarrel earlier upon the road. Perhaps they even clashed then, and the fight was indecisive. Perhaps the other knight was dazed, or perhaps he pretended to give over the fight and go another way and then, when my father arrived at the old man's hut, his enemy rushed after him, to surprise him."

"You spin a fine tale, Master Cray."

"Do I?" Cray sighed. "Well, I confess, it *is* only a tale, I won't try to make myself think otherwise. But it makes neither more nor less sense than an old enemy come from the East March to settle an old quarrel. Why journey so far from home to kill a man? And if the East March were not the other knight's home . . . then, Master Feldar, we have nothing to fear by going there and claiming my father's place."

"Perhaps he didn't want word of the deed to get back to the East March . . ."

"And if that is the case, and he *is* there, he won't dare to expose himself, and we will still be safe."

"Until you win your knighthood and leave on some quest . . ."

Cray half-turned away from him, arms akimbo. "All right, Master Feldar, we will be careful. With you to remind me of such dangers, I'll be jumping at every shadow in the East March. And I don't even know who he is."

"He wore black armor, you know that."

"With no device on his shield. That was a disguise, I'm sure. But if I should happen to encounter a black knight, I'll certainly be wary."

"You'll kill him, won't you?" asked Sepwin.

"I think he'd be more likely, just now, to kill me," replied Cray.

"He's fifteen years older."

"And fifteen years cannier. Don't let our little adventure at the village give you an exaggerated notion of my knightly prowess. I'd be no match for a real knight. I don't intend to throw my life away for vengeance."

"It's a better motive than some I could think of."

Cray gazed at him sidelong. "It wouldn't bring my father back."

Sepwin stared down at the ground. "I don't suppose there's any magical way . . ." he murmured.

"He's dead. Nothing can change that. Not even sorcery."

"I'm sorry, Cray. Truly I am."

Cray made no reply, only stood still and looked past Sepwin, at his horse, at the shield, half hidden behind his own; and the silence that had suddenly descended between the would-be knight and the former beggar stretched and stretched until it was broken by a powerful blast of wind.

"What's happening?" cried Sepwin, and he stumbled sideways, clutching at the branches of the nearest tree to keep from being knocked over.

"The map!" shouted Cray, and his voice could hardly be heard above the roaring that had risen from nowhere. Tree limbs swayed around him, branches dipping and crackling in the blow, leaves rattling wildly. Dust from the road kicked up, whipping against his skin like shards of glass, and he covered his eyes and nose and mouth against them with both hands.

The branch that Sepwin grasped broke with a loud snap, and he fell, rolling, till he fetched up against a tree trunk, and he huddled there, white-knuckled hands scrabbling for purchase on the rough bark.

"You wouldn't do this if my mother were here!" Cray shouted to no one visible, and then he was pushed against a tree and pinned there by empty air while leaves slapped him like so many hands.

Abruptly as it had begun, the wind ceased, and in

its wake floated light laughter, receding, ever receding into the dim distance.

At Cray's feet lay a roll of parchment. He bent to pick it up, to unroll it carefully. "The map," he said, turning it so that Sepwin could see their route laid out on the pale surface.

Sepwin was rising gingerly to his feet. He said, "Is it over?"

"I should think so. Look here—an excellent map."

"I . . . I think I'll bathe my hands first. They're pretty badly scraped." He edged to where the horses stood, his eyes never ceasing their search to one side and another, as if he thought he would see another wind coming. The horses stood unconcerned where they had been tied, not a hair of their manes or tails disheveled. "I wish I could be as calm as these two," said Sepwin, reaching for a water flask.

"They were beyond the range of the effect," said Cray. He sat on the ground now, the parchment spread across his knees as he studied it.

"Effect?"

"The demon's effect." Cray looked up at him. "That was an air demon. It was just having some fun with us."

"My hands don't think it was fun."

Cray tossed the parchment aside immediately and strode to where Sepwin was fumbling with the water. "Let me see." He scrutinized his companion's palms, found them abraded and bloody. "You shouldn't have tried to hold on to anything."

"Should I have let myself be blown away?"

"You wouldn't have gone far." He pulled the kerchief from Sepwin's neck and, wetting it, dabbed at the wounds, which were superficial and soon stopped bleeding.

"Next time you expect something like that," said Sepwin, "please warn me. Remember, I'm not as accustomed to magic as you are."

"I didn't expect such a playful demon."

"Playful?"

"We're neither of us really injured, so that was play. Air demons can be rough, but it's all innocent enough, if you're not an enemy. Be glad it wasn't a fire demon

—one visited my mother's castle once, and when it left, all the leaves within ten paces of where it had stood were singed. She had a word with its master for *that,* I'll tell you."

"Dangerous creatures, these demons."

"They have moods."

"Like human beings," said Sepwin.

"You might say that. Now come here and look at the map." He spread it out upon the grass and pointed with an index finger to a meandering line on the left side of the sheet. "This is the road we're on now. Here we are, you see, there's my name, and two horses to show both of us. The road goes south to Falconhill, down here, you see?"

"Certainly looks like a castle to me. I suppose those symbols say Falconhill."

"Yes." He looked at Sepwin sharply. "You can't read?"

"Not many people can, Master Cray. You don't need letters for farming."

"Hmm. Well, yes, that says Falconhill. Now, before then, you see there's a road crosses this one, and its eastward branch passes through the swamp and eventually meets another road here that veers northeast to our destination."

Sepwin's eyes tracked the route that Cray's finger had indicated. "How far would you say that is, Master Cray?"

"Well . . . judging from the distance to my mother's castle from where we are now . . . if the map is to scale . . . I'd say three months and more."

"Summer will be gone by the time we arrive."

"Nearly, yes."

"It might be a good place to winter, the East March."

"It might," said Cray. "Warm and dry, at any rate."

Sepwin peered at the parchment. "Where is your mother's castle?"

Cray smiled slightly. "You will not find it marked on any map. Sorcerers do not reveal their homes so. And I have no need of a map to find the place where I was born."

"I didn't mean to pry," said Sepwin. "I was only curious."

Cray clapped him on the back. "I understand, Master Sepwin. Now shall we find ourselves some lunch and then get on with our journey while the sky is still light?"

"By all means," replied his friend. "All this talk of traveling has given me a considerable appetite."

Eastward they rode, through the hot days of summer, and every cultivated field they passed bore grain stalks taller than the last. Some days it rained, and they sheltered with peasants, returning labor for hospitality, chopping wood or milking goats; or, if no humans lived nearby, Cray fashioned a lean-to of leafy branches woven so tightly together that the wet could not penetrate. On those rainy days in the lean-to, they played games with pebbles Cray had gathered, games ranging from the simplest of children's diversions to the most complex contests of strategy that Delivev had ever taught her son. Sepwin proved an apt pupil, and soon he and Cray were so evenly matched that one game could encompass an entire rainstorm. And sometimes the two players remained hunched over the pieces long after the rain had done.

"So this is how sorcerers amuse themselves when they don't feel like moving mountains," said Sepwin one gloomy afternoon.

"Not sorcerers, Master Feldar," said Cray. "Kings and queens. I have seen them in the webs, and learned some of my own strategy from them. Sometimes they even wager on the outcome."

"Well, I think I shall pass that opportunity, unless you'll accept a few leaves as a decent wager."

Cray laughed. "I've no doubt we'll see such wagering at the East March castle. My mother said it was a great holding, and I have noticed that the great holdings are always wealthy places indeed." He weighed a pebble in his hand before adding it to a half-finished pattern. "I think I'm a rather good player; I might be tempted. I have a little silver."

"You might have less after such wagering."

"I used to win sweets from my mother."

"And what did you offer on your side of the wager?" asked Sepwin.

"Kisses."

Sepwin laughed then. "Didn't you like kissing your mother?"

"Oh, I liked it very much. Sometimes I kissed her even if I won. Have you ever made a wager, Master Feldar?"

"Only once. I lost. I had to spread manure on the fields for days afterward. I have had no great desire to wager since then."

"But you play quite well."

"So you say, Master Cray. But perhaps if I played someone else, I would learn otherwise."

They passed through several villages and then, at the very edge of the great swamp, through a market town. At midafternoon, the market was bustling, men and women hawking everything from pigs to pots, cloth to cough remedies, and everywhere they offered the flapping, clip-winged waterfowl of the swamp. Cray and Sepwin stopped to buy a little wine to cheer their journey, but not the birds, which Cray thought he would be able to net easily enough once they were inside the swamp. As they stood sipping their first measure of wine, a vendor approached them, a bolt of fine, white gauze slung over his shoulder.

"Netting," he chanted. "Netting for the night, netting for travelers sleeping under the stars. Netting." He measured Cray and Sepwin with a glance. "I have enough here for a fine tent, young sirs, for you and your horses. Only two silver pieces."

Cray waved him away. "We've no need of a tent."

"If you plan to sleep in the open anywhere near this market, you'll need one. And after sunset, there won't be anyplace to buy it."

"Why not?"

"Because we all go to bed at sunset, when the insects come out," he said, "and we won't come out from behind our nets just to keep strangers from being bitten."

"Bitten? Well, what are a few insect bites? I've had my share."

"A few, young sir?" He smiled and wagged his head.

"They rise from the swamp by night, in their millions, hungry for blood. Why . . . a man was found dead in the swamp only last month. Stayed out past dark, hunting birds. He didn't take any netting at all, poor fellow. His wife said he must have gotten lost." He lifted the bundle of gauze from his shoulder and held it out to Cray. "You'd best buy, young sir, or else ride west past the hills to be safe; they don't fly that far."

"We came from those hills this morning," said Cray, "so we know they don't fly that far. Now we are eastbound, but we won't need your netting, thank you."

"If you're taking the road into the swamp, you will *surely* need it."

"Again, I thank you, but we won't need it."

"Reconsider, young sir! The biting will drive your horses mad! And if you should escape the swamp before succumbing, the ride to the hills would be a long and terrible one. Or the walk! If your horses should bolt from their agony and leave you behind . . . ! Reconsider, I beg you!"

Cray drained his wine cup, and set it on the counter of the wine stall. He bowed formally to the vendor and said, "Good day to you, sir," then walked away. Sepwin scuttled after.

At the horses, as Cray was preparing to mount, Sepwin whispered, "Don't you believe him?"

"About the man found dead in the swamp?"

"Well, yes, that and the insects."

Cray swung into the saddle. "There may have been a man found dead in the swamp, though possibly not from insect bites. I'm sure there are any number of deadly things in the swamp."

"And *we* are going into the swamp?"

"The road crosses it. We can, too."

Sepwin looked up at him anxiously. "Master Cray, I fear my heart fails me. At least . . . buy some netting!"

Cray stared down at his companion. "Do you really believe I need some of his netting to keep me safe?"

"But . . . what about me?"

"Master Feldar, you know that spiders *eat* insects."

"Y-yes."

"Then why are you worrying? Get on your horse."

126

After one more moment's hesitation, Sepwin mounted, and his horse followed Gallant's easy pace out of the market, eastward.

There was no obvious dividing line between the ordinary land and the swamp. The cultivated fields about the market gave way to a wild growth of grass pocked by occasional trees, and finally wet patches appeared, sparkling in the sunlight, ponds choked by cattails, streamlets sluggishly winding. The road turned muddy; in some places it disappeared entirely, drowned, only to reappear a few paces farther on. For a time, the way was well churned by hooves and the feet of human beings, but the longer they rode the less traveled the path became, until there were no marks at all of anyone else's recent passage.

"You're sure this road goes all the way through the swamp?" said Sepwin.

"The map shows it so."

"You're sure the mapmaker was telling the truth when he drew that? He wasn't just . . . being playful?"

"My mother is following my course, Master Feldar. If anything happens to me while I use this map, the sorcerer who had it made will be the first target of her anger." He looked down at Sepwin from the vantage of Gallant's height. "My mother would be a very dangerous person, angry. He would not dare to give her or her son anything but an accurate map."

"I am reassured," said Sepwin. "Now we only have to worry about the insects."

"Come," said Cray. "It's late enough to stop for the night already, and our sleeping preparations will take a little longer than usual."

"Will they?" asked Sepwin.

"You'll see."

They dismounted where a large tree overhung the road and the ground was reasonably dry, and Cray tethered the horses there. He climbed the tree then, and cracked the first broad bough so that it dipped to the ground while still partially attached to the trunk, forming a support for a lean-to large enough for two young men and their horses. He climbed higher after that, to break off leafy branches for the walls, and back on the ground he wove them together half by magic and half by the dexterity of his hands. Well before sunset he had completed the latticework structure and led the horses inside through an opening barely large enough to admit them. His final task was to plait a door for that aperture, and when that was ready to set in place, he turned to Sepwin with a smile.

"Will you step inside, Master Feldar?"

Sepwin eyed the lean-to uncertainly. "I know excellently well that this will keep the rain off, but . . . what spell have you woven into it to keep the insects away?"

"None," said Cray.

"I shall smother if I must sleep wrapped in my cloak from head to toe," said Sepwin.

"You shall not smother. Enter. The sky is fading."

With a last furtive glance at the setting sun, Sepwin obeyed.

Inside, Cray set the door securely in place, then laid both of his hands against it and closed his eyes. From his sleeves, the spiders scuttled, more than a score of them, all colors and sizes. They swarmed over the branches and immediately began spinning. Slowly, a fine net, layer upon layer of silk, spread over the walls and floor until a gray cocoon surrounded Cray and Sepwin and the horses. Gallant was not disturbed by the spinning, but Sepwin's horse swayed nervously from foot to foot, and its master had to soothe it until the last rays of sunlight had ceased filtering through the gray curtain and it could no longer see the moving spiders.

"I've slept in rooms this small," said Sepwin, "but never before with such a feeling of imprisonment." He laughed nervously. "But of course, this is hardly a prison; I could tear these walls apart with my hands, after all."

"Not these walls," said Cray.

"No?"

"Not even the horses could break down these walls, Master Feldar."

"I see." He was silent a moment, in the darkness, then he said, "What if I wanted to get out?"

"And face the insects? I can hear them humming already. Listen."

The sound was soft, but increasing, a high-pitched buzz rising all about them, and once more Sepwin's horse shifted uneasily and had to be soothed.

"Well, I don't want to go out now, of course," said Sepwin, "but just for the sake of argument, if I wanted for some reason to go out, how would I do it?"

"I thought you weren't afraid of spiders, Master Feldar. Or have you decided you're afraid of me?"

"Oh, no . . . but if something should happen to you. To be quite blunt, Master Cray, I don't fancy being locked in here forever."

Cray laughed. "Always worrying, Master Feldar. Well, let me assure you that even magic webs don't last forever. Especially my magic, which is of a very inferior kind. It would fall apart within a few days, and you would emerge none the worse except for a bit of hunger." He yawned. "But I don't plan to die or desert you right now, so why don't you go to sleep? We'll want an early start in the morning. I don't want to spend more time than absolutely necessary in this swamp."

In the morning, he gathered the spiders into his sleeves, and the webs broke apart at his touch, like any spiderwebs, letting the companions out into the sunshine. After a quick breakfast, they rode on. Deeper in the swamp, there were ever fewer trees and more coarse grass, more open water, and ever more waterfowl; about noon Cray netted a brace of ducks and hung them from his saddle for later. Shortly after that, the companions found themselves facing a wide sheet of water. They could see the road continuing on the far side, but on the near it ended at a pair of wooden posts.

"So much for the accuracy of the map," said Sepwin.

Cray dismounted to examine the wood, to pick at it with his fingers. "There was a bridge here. A fairly old bridge. I'd like to think that it washed away since the map was made."

"If there was a bridge," said Sepwin, "then the water is too deep to wade."

"I would presume so. We'll have to swim it."

"Swim? I don't know how to swim."

"Neither do I, but the horses probably do."

"Probably?"

"It should be easy. The current looks slow enough. You won't be swept away. Just hang on tight."

"Not I," said Sepwin.

"Don't be afraid."

"Easy for you to say."

Cray shook his head. "Have we come all this way to balk at a little water?"

"Can't we go around it?"

"If there had been an easy route around it, the road would go that way instead of crossing. Come along now. Or shall I leave you here to face the insects alone tonight?"

Sepwin stared at the water. "I'm really frightened, Master Cray. We don't know how deep the water is."

Cray looked all around. "I would build a raft for us," he said, "but there aren't enough trees around here." He rubbed at his cheek with one finger, frowning, and finally he said, "There may be another way, Master Feldar. A way you won't have to get wet. If you'll trust me."

"What way?"

"My mother could build us a raft of snakes. There must be enough snakes in these waters for that."

"Snakes?" He leaned forward on his horse's neck and peered at the water. "I haven't seen any snakes yet, have you?"

"A few." He grinned. "But don't worry about that. No snake will harm you as long as you're with me."

"You control snakes as well as spiders?"

"No, nothing like that. They just stay away from me unless I call them. Another trick my mother taught me, useful to a child growing up in a castle full of snakes."

"Your castle is full of snakes?"

"Oh, yes, and spiders, too."

"Then I'm glad we didn't stop there," said Sepwin.

"You would soon grow accustomed to it, Master Feldar. Now, what do you say to a raft of snakes?

130

I fear your horse will have to swim, though; snakes might be too much for her."

"We'll both swim," Sepwin said firmly.

"You're sure?"

"Let's do it already!"

Cray nodded, mounted, and guided Gallant into the stream. The water rose swiftly to the horse's knees, its chest, its neck, and then the sudden fluid motion of its limbs indicated to Cray that it was swimming. In midstream, Cray glanced back, saw Sepwin still on the bank. "Come along!" he called.

Clinging to his mount's neck with both arms, Sepwin spurred it into the river with a kick.

Gallant was already climbing the opposite bank when Cray realized that he should have taken his chain mail off before making the crossing, at least the leg harnesses, for they, like everything else he wore below the hips, were now very wet. He dismounted immediately, stripped off his surcoat and the leg sections of his chain and wrapped the wet metal in the dry cloth. While he was doing this, Sepwin emerged from the river and slipped off his horse to sit wearily on the ground. He watched Cray handle the chinking metal.

"I have never seen you take that off before," he said. "Do you really wear it all the time?"

"As often as I can." He unsheathed his sword then, and dried it on a patch of grass, leaving the scabbard propped upside down, dripping.

"You know . . . if you had fallen off your horse, it would have dragged you straight to the bottom."

"I doubt that. It's not really so heavy."

"Steel? Not heavy?"

"I'm accustomed to it."

Sepwin wriggled his shoulders. "I'm glad I don't want to be a knight. Too much weight for me."

"Far too much," said Cray, "for such a skinny frame. It's handy stuff, though, if someone goes at you with a blade."

"Well, I promise not to do that, so you can take it off if you like."

Cray shook his head. "One can never tell when it might be needed. Some enemies don't give warning of their attacks. In the village, for example, if I hadn't been wearing my chain, if someone had gone after you with a blade instead of bare hands . . . where would we be? My Gallant would be pulling a plow, and you and I would be fertilizer for the crops. Thank you, but I'll continue to wear my chain. Truth to tell, I'd feel strange without the shirt at least."

"Not comfortable for sleeping, is it?"

"The quilting beneath keeps it from annoying me."

"Hot in the summer sun, I'll warrant."

"Sometimes."

"I was thinking about last night's shelter . . . couldn't you have your spiders spin a suit of chain that would be just as strong as steel but far lighter?"

Cray smiled. "I suppose I could, though it would have to be spun fresh every few days as the spell wore away. And I'm not sure I could find a lord to accept the service of a man who wore magical armor. I have seen how little ordinary mortals care for being near the sorcerous breed, and I think I would do better to keep that part of my heritage a secret."

"You'll have to get rid of those spiders, then."

Cray lifted one of his arms to inspect the score of tiny bodies that clung to its inner surface, hiding themselves among the links of chain. "Perhaps," he said. "But for now, and until my future has some pattern to it, I'll keep them. They still disturb you?"

"Somewhat. But as long as they don't crawl over me, I can stand them."

"You'd hardly feel them. They won't bite you unless I order it. Not like lice."

"I haven't any lice!"

"I presume not, since I haven't seen you scratch." He clapped Sepwin on one shoulder. "Come along now, let's ride on. You've recovered from your swim."

"I'm still wet."

"Well, so am I. The sun will dry us."

"Will there be any other rivers to cross?"

Cray unrolled the map, which he had been wearing like a huge and unwieldy pendant on a thong about his neck. "The swamp is swampy," he said, peering at the parchment. "This is the only major river, but there's a lot of water still ahead of us. But the road is shown as unbroken all the way to the other side." He grinned at his companion. "And we can always turn back if it becomes impassable."

Sepwin grimaced. "If we turn back, I might take you up on that raft idea." He pulled himself up onto his horse. "I'm ready."

The sun soon dried their wet clothing, and Cray was able to slip the chain harnesses back into place over the quilting on his legs. His saddlebags, made of oiled leather, had scarcely been penetrated by their brief exposure to the river, and so the rest of his gear was virtually dry. The two ducks hanging from his saddle had shed water as if they were alive. Late in the afternoon, Cray and Sepwin stopped to build a fire and enjoy the birds for their evening meal.

"No trees this time," said Sepwin, looking around nervously. "Shouldn't we keep going until we find one for our shelter?"

"I don't think we will," replied Cray. "I haven't seen a tree in a good while, except for a couple growing right out of the water, and I won't spend *my* night bailing out the tent, thank you."

"What will we do then?"

"We don't need a tree, though it would make things simpler." He tossed the last of the duck bones aside, stood up, and walked over to where Gallant, tethered to a low bush, was peacefully cropping the coarse swamp grass. The animal nickered softly at his approach, and he stroked its neck and face, crooning softly. Then he dipped into one of the saddlebags and found a kerchief. He folded it into a bandage and tied it over Gallant's face as a blindfold. "Use that eye patch that you don't need here in the swamp," he said to Sepwin, "and do as I am doing to your own mount."

Sepwin obeyed, and while he stood by his blindfolded horse, he watched Cray climb into his own saddle and lean forward, stretching both arms out over Gallant's head. Spiders crept from his sleeves then and spun their strands, anchoring at their master's limbs and leaping to the ground on either side of Gallant's unseeing eyes, playing thread from their descending bodies. Soon two parallel sets of ribbons had formed from Cray's arms, and the spiders had begun to climb back up, swiftly weaving cross strands till the webwork was nigh opaque. Cray peeled the web from himself then, letting it settle upon Gallant's head, and he eased backward in the saddle. The spiders followed his movements, spinning from the saddle now and returning to his arms when sheets of webbing hung from that. Cray guided the final webwork to fall upon his horse's rump and then he slipped off over the tail. Gallant stood still, covered with a close-fitting tent of spidersilk.

"Your horse's turn now," said Cray, and he mounted that animal.

"Must you sit there and let them spin all over you?" asked Sepwin. "Can't they just spin directly on the horses themselves, as they did on the inside of last night's shelter?"

Cray nodded. "They could. But horses are skittish beasts. How would you like to feel a score of spiders crawling over *your* skin?"

Sepwin backed off. "No. No." He watched the tent-making process repeated on his own mount, and after a time he said, "You're not going to do the same thing for the two of us, are you?"

"I could," said Cray, "but somehow I don't think you'd care to spend the night quite so closely draped in spiderwebs. The horses won't mind—to them the webs are just blankets, but to you . . ." He smiled. "Well, the webs *are* just blankets, you know."

"Isn't there some other way?"

"Don't worry."

When he was done with Sepwin's horse, Cray took up his sword and shield, which he had removed from Gallant's saddle before the web-making. He thrust the sword point-first into the ground, and a body's length away, he hammered the shield into the ground, also point-first. The ground was soft enough to yield to them but hard enough that they remained upright, and he braced them with stones to insure that they would not tip over. Then he marked a perimeter about them with other stones and set his spiders free upon that frame. Soon they had fashioned a small tent, with the sword and shield as its supports and the perimeter stones anchoring their silk to the ground. The tent was large enough for two people to crawl inside and lie down.

"Not quite as roomy as last night," said Cray, "but at least we won't have to share it with the horses."

"You're sure they'll be all right?" Sepwin asked. "Those webs are so close-fitting . . . might not an insect be able to bite through to flesh without actually passing through the weave?"

"Not those webs. And now I think we should enter our own armor; I can hear the buzzing already."

Sepwin clutched at his own arms and looked about. "I wonder how big they are."

"I don't think I care to find out. Come on."

In the morning, Sepwin peered at the map. "How much farther does this swamp go on?"

Cray traced the road with one finger. "I think we're about here now, which means another day or two. The end of the swamp isn't clearly marked, but there's a town over here, and surely *that's* beyond the swamp."

Sepwin sighed. "Well, now we know why your father took the northern route."

"Oh, we're halfway through. We can last another two days, can't we, Master Feldar?"

Sepwin mounted his horse. About its feet, like a scatter of gray dust, lay the remains of the spidersilk netting; at Cray's touch it had fallen apart, freeing the animal, which appeared unperturbed by the night's shelter. "I only wish I knew," said Sepwin, "if the worst was behind us."

"I suspect every human being would wish to know that," Cray said, climbing onto Gallant's back. "And since we have no way of acquiring that knowledge, let us assume it. I don't feel in any mood to spend my time worrying about the future." He grinned at his companion. "I'm sure you'll worry enough for both of us."

The morning passed uneventfully, the road alternately dry and mucky; occasionally the horses splashed through water to their knees. It was in one of these stretches, where the exact location of the road was unclear, although it could be seen to continue some distance ahead in a drier condition, that Gallant tossed its head, whinnied loudly, and began to thrash. Cray perceived immediately that his mount was stuck in the mud that lay beneath the water. He turned in the saddle and shouted for Sepwin, who lagged a dozen strides behind, to stop. Even as he did so, he realized that he and Gallant were sinking.

"What's happening?" cried Sepwin.

"We're stuck! Stay where you are and keep your horse calm. I'm sending you spiders—use their silk as a rope to pull us out!" As if throwing invisible stones, his hands shot out, and spiders poured from his sleeves, struck the water, and danced lightly over the surface, laying down silk behind them. Some stayed by Gallant, weaving a net about the horse, and the rest raced for Sepwin, swarmed up his mount's legs and began to fashion a net about both steed and rider. Sepwin shuddered once as they arrived, but he had no time for more than that, for his shying horse required every scrap of his attention; he soothed the animal at last when the spiders had done and had gathered to rest upon his shoulders, like dark snowflakes. He moaned softly but did not try to brush them off.

"I can't pull you both out!" Sepwin said. "You weigh too much—you'll pull us in instead!"

"I'll come first," said Cray. Already the water was at his thighs, and he could feel the muck beneath, sucking at his feet. He slipped into the water as flat and gently as possible, clutching the filmy spider strands with both hands and crossing his ankles over them. His lifeline sagged under his weight and the weight of his chain, and he shouted, "Move back!" just before water filled his mouth. A moment later, as Sepwin obeyed, the silken rope drew taut, rising a handsbreadth above the surface. Cray shook the water from his eyes, spat, and breathed deep; then he began to crawl, slowly, his body almost completely immersed. Gallant, sinking, pulled the rope that was anchored to it ever deeper; the horse had ceased to whinny now, and to struggle, but its terrified panting carried across the water like the breath of a blacksmith's bellows. Cray heard it when his ears cleared the surface, and though the time after that seemed to stretch endlessly for him, it was actually only a few moments until he was able to stand up beside Sepwin's mount. The water was at his knees in that spot, but there were rocks beneath his feet, hard and unyielding. He turned to look at Gallant and saw only the horse's head and neck projecting above the water.

"We'll never get him out," said Sepwin.

"I won't let him die! Get off your horse—you can't use your own strength from up there!" He touched the spidersilk webbing that encompassed his companion's steed, and where his flesh passed, the silk parted, freeing Sepwin's legs and enabling him to dismount. The spiders leaped from his shoulders to the horse then, to spin again and repair their netting.

"Come now, pull with me," said Cray, and he grasped the silken line just in front of Sepwin's horse. Sepwin joined him, tugging and urging his horse backward in the water. "Come now, we can do it," Cray gasped. "He's just a dead weight, not working against us. Pull!"

"We're not strong enough," moaned Sepwin.

"Your horse has pulled a plow through stony earth. She can do this! Back, plowhorse, back!" Gritting his teeth, Cray added every fragment of his strength to the horse's effort.

"We'll never do it," gasped Sepwin, his voice harsh and strained.

"Pull!"

So gradual was their success that they did not realize it until Gallant began to thrash. The horse stumbled then, as the muck gave it up, and stood muddy and shivering upon the rocks beside its master.

Cray let go the silken rope and threw his arms around his horse's neck, stroking and murmuring to it until the shivering ceased and its breath settled down to a semblance of normalcy.

"We'll have to stop now," said Cray. "He needs a rest and a good rubdown. Poor Gallant—you'll be all right, old fellow, I promise."

"I could use a rest, too," said Sepwin, leaning against his own steed. Sweat was rolling down his face and neck, and his arms were shaking with the effort he had expended.

"Yes, yes, all of us." Cray laid a hand on Sepwin's horse, and all the spiders skittered to his dripping sleeve. "Let's find a dry piece of road and set up a camp." He pulled his sword from its sheath. Mud clung to the pommel, and he rinsed it in the water at his knees. Then, using the blade as a staff, he tested the hidden ground all around, found rocks to walk safely upon, and led his horse a long and circuitous route toward the nearest visible section of the road. Sepwin followed almost precisely in his footsteps.

They staggered out of the water, horses and humans, dripping, muddy, exhausted. Sepwin collapsed upon the dry ground, but Cray pulled up some handfuls of dry grass and began to rub his horse down with them.

"Where do you find the strength for that?" Sepwin muttered. "It must be magical."

"I wish it were," said Cray, and doggedly he rubbed on, until Gallant was dry. Then he leaned against the animal and closed his eyes. When he felt himself slipping, his legs giving way, he shook his head sharply and straightened. Sepwin was asleep curled in a patch of grass; his horse stood beside him, nibbling at his green mattress. Cray wanted to lie down, too, but he did not. The sun was still high, but if he slept they might be caught unprepared by night. With heavy limbs, he took up his sword and shield and set them as tent posts on either side of his sleeping friend. He set the spiders to spinning then, and they spun the tent with a human being already inside. He blindfolded the horses next, and made their shelters, and at last he was free to strip off his clothes and chain and to lie down beside Sepwin and sleep.

He awoke to find his mother's face looking down at him from one wall of the tent. He blinked and rubbed at his eyes. Gray light filtered through the dense webbing. "Is it morning?" he asked her.

"Late afternoon," she said, "and cloudy where you are. I saw that you were safe and decided not to wake you. I saw water danger in the tapestry. What happened?"

Briefly, he told her.

Her eyes narrowed. "Someone shall hear about

138

this. I asked for a good map; I did not expect one that neglected the dangers of the road."

Cray stretched, yawning. "Would a demon of the air have seen such danger from above?"

She pursed her lips. "Perhaps not."

"And I really should have known better than to walk right into the water without a thought. I shan't do that again, I promise you."

"I hope not." She sighed softly. "Oh, my son, the journey is not so easy as you thought it would be."

He grinned. "I'm learning a great deal, Mother. And think of the stories I'll have to tell to the lord of the East March. Surely he'll look favorably upon me for not being turned back by these things."

"There will be adventures enough, I'm sure, after you are a knight, Cray. Adventures and to spare."

"Yes," he said, and he lay back, interlacing his hands beneath his head. "Just think, Mother . . . someday a troubadour like Lorien might set *my* adventures to music. How wonderful that would be!"

"Wonderful indeed, Cray. And the adventures set to music might be considerably more wonderful than the adventures really were."

He tilted his head to look at her. "Are you saying that troubadours tend to exaggerate the deeds they sing of?"

"Lorien admitted as much to me."

Cray chuckled quietly. "Well, Mother, I never did believe that one man could slay a dozen lions single-handed."

"Lesser things than that."

He nodded. "But I shall have to do great things if I want songs composed about me. Those are the only kind that ever become songs. Great accomplishments and great failures. I know which of *those* two I'd select."

"I suggest you start small, my son."

"I have, Mother. I have. And now I must leave you to catch our dinner before the sun sets."

"Of course," she said, and her image faded from the web.

Cray rolled over and nudged Sepwin. "Wake up, Master Stayabed."

The former beggar opened one eye, the blue one. "You know, I've never heard a troubadour sing."

"You were awake all the time!"

"Most of the time, yes. But I thought it best not to interrupt your conversation. And I couldn't quite figure out how to bow while lying down."

"I'm sure my mother would have forgiven your discourtesy, under the circumstances." He threw open the tent flap. "Come on, let's find something to eat before the insects rise."

Sepwin clutched at Cray's elbow. "I'd be perfectly willing to go without supper if the day is almost spent. I'm quite used to that sort of thing, you know."

"We have some time yet," said Cray. "And the horses will be hungry, too. I don't think they eat much while they're blindfolded."

"Oh, the horses. Yes, can't let them starve. They've got to carry us out of this terrible place." He crawled into the daylight behind Cray, glanced up at the sky nervously. "I can't tell how high the sun is; it's too cloudy."

"Your ears will tell you quickly enough—when it's low," said Cray, slipping into his clothing and chain, now dry. His saddlebags, however, had not withstood their long drenching, and everything inside their oiled leather was wet. After setting out his nets for fish, Cray draped his belongings on low bushes to dry.

They ate broiled fish and returned to their shelter just as the nightly humming began.

A squirrel watched in the night, the only squirrel in the whole swamp. It heard the humming but cared nothing for that; no blood-lusting insects would touch it, no water could drown it, no mud could suck it down to dark death. By the faint light of the cloud-strewn sky, Gildrum watched over the webwork tent that wrapped the two young travelers. It had only a moment to stand in the tall grass, a moment between Ringforge and its master's bidding. It chittered softly to itself, feeling much as it always did outside Spinweb's walls—seeing nothing, unseen, powerless. Cray was bound for the East March; Gildrum had heard the youths speak of that, had realized that it could only delay, never prevent, the journey. Cray was too strong-willed to be turned aside from his goal.

I'm sorry, my son.

And then there were no squirrels at all in the swamp.

ᵉᔕ CHAPTER EIGHT

They had passed through many towns, and Sepwin had worn his eye patch continuously, by the time they reached the fortress of the lord of the East March. The structure had no name of its own; the local folk merely called it The Castle, for it was the only fortification within many days' ride, and most of them had never seen another. It was an imposing stronghold, with thick, multiple walls sprawling over the sides of the broad, low hilltop it commanded. All around it, spreading from the walls to the river at the base of the hill, and across to the far bank, linked to the near by many bridges, were buildings of every size and shape. Lining winding streets, stone cottages jostled thatched huts and plank cabins; and open stalls, their owners crying their wares, were frequent among them. The fortress itself was a town within that town, with dwellings along the inside walls and a marketplace in the vast courtyard, where all the goods and services of life were loudly available. The gates stood wide open, though guarded by rows of pikemen, and people passed in and out freely. Cray and Sepwin were paid little heed by the guards; they let themselves be swept inside with the foot and horse and donkey traffic, until they reached a wineshop hung with earthen jars of drink. Cray signaled to his friend to halt there. They tethered their mounts in an alcove beside the shop, next to a pair of wooden carts.

"I've never drunk so much wine before as with you, Master Cray," said Sepwin, raising a mug to his companion's health.

Cray smiled. "You've never drunk wine at all, then."

"True enough." He drained the vessel. "I'll wager you drank wine every night at home."

"Only on special occasions," said Cray. He looked down at the blood-dark fluid in his own cup. "And I see this whole journey as a special occasion." He finished the drink and returned the container to the shopkeeper. "Come, Master Feldar, let's see what the possibility of an audience with the lord may be."

Sepwin scanned the courtyard. "He must be a busy man, with so many subjects. The justice alone for this lot would take most of a man's day."

"Perhaps they don't quarrel as much as you suppose."

"Impossible."

They approached the gate of the keep, a fat cylindrical tower in the very center of the compound. This gate was closed, the massive iron-bound panel guarded by a double row of pikemen.

"Hallo," said Cray. "How may I arrange to see your master, the lord of the East March?"

"It is too late," said one of the pikemen, distinguished from the others by the device on his helm. "The lord sees no one after midday."

"Well, tomorrow, then, or the next day. I come on important business."

"Important to whom?"

"To me," said Cray.

The pikeman looked him up and down. "What is the nature of this business?"

"Forgive me," said Cray, bowing stiffly, "but it is personal."

The pikeman's lip curled. "Come back at dawn and wait your turn then, with everyone else."

"Thank you." Cray started to turn away, hesitated, and looked back at the pikeman. He saw a middle-aged man, beard grizzled and going gray, mouth flanked by deep creases—a man old enough and more to be his father. "Sir," he said, "how long has the present lord of the East March ruled here?"

"More years than you've been alive, boy," replied the man. "Thirty years it might be by now, and years left ahead of him, for he was young when he came into his own." He smiled, and an old scar on his cheek pulled his mouth to one side. "Were you hoping he had died lately and a new lord taken his place?"

Cray smiled back, as disarming a smile as he knew how to show. "Quite the contrary, good sir. And I thank you once more." He took Sepwin's arm and guided him away. "That was my one fear," he muttered. "That a new lord would have the seat and know nothing of him."

The proprietor of the wineshop was able to direct them to lodgings in the outer town, and they spent the night in a small hostel on pallets so hard that they might as well have been sleeping on the ground. It rained that night, though, and for the first time in many a day, they had no need of Cray's skills to keep them dry. Sepwin slept soundly, as always, but Cray tossed and turned and greeted first light at last with red eyes and a glad heart. He woke his companion, they bolted the bread and cheese they had bought the previous evening, and went out to The Castle, Cray carrying his father's shield.

At dawn the inner town was bustling, and a crowd had already gathered in the courtyard before the gate of the keep. They were a noisy crowd, chattering and arguing among themselves, jostling one another for places closer to the gate, elbows banging against ribs, feet stepping on other feet, and many a fistfight broke out while they waited to see their lord. Cray and Sepwin found themselves at the fringe, hardly able to see the iron-bound door for the press of bodies ahead of them.

"I wonder how many broken heads this crush will yield," muttered Sepwin.

At the front of the crowd, a pike was raised, a blue banner hanging limp from its tip, and a stentorian voice demanded silence. The clamor faded somewhat.

"The lord of the East March will hear his subjects now!" shouted the voice. Cray thought it might belong to the man he had spoken with the previous day. He could not see him, nor any of the other guards; only their pikes showed above the heads of the crowd.

The gate opened a crack; Cray could see a sliver of light, from a torch within. The crowd surged forward. Someone elbowed Cray to squeeze ahead of him, but he pushed the elbow aside and stood his ground, and the fellow merely glared at him. The gate closed.

"Did they let someone in?" wondered Sepwin.

"I couldn't tell," said Cray. "It opened wide enough for a body to pass through, so I suppose one did."

Sepwin looked around. "There are a lot of bodies here, eager bodies, and a very small opening. Is there no system for orderly admittance?"

A nearby woman turned to Sepwin and said, "You must come here early. Early!" She frowned. "Too late now—we'll never get in." She turned away, shaking her head, and plowed outward, pushing past the people who had arrived even later than Cray and Sepwin; they moved forward, eagerly closing up the small space the woman had left.

"If we're too late," said Sepwin, "why are so many people standing behind us?"

Cray cast him a sidelong glance. "Perhaps they are hoping that others ahead of them, like that woman, will give up and let them move forward."

The gate opened again, and this time Cray thought he saw a head pass through the aperture before it shut. "They must come out some other way. No one could push back through this crowd from up there."

Sepwin glanced over his shoulder. "It isn't easy to do it from here. I'd hate to fall down in this mob. You'd have to scrape me off the cobblestones."

"I don't think you *could* fall."

The gate opened again.

"He seems to be dealing with them quickly at least," said Sepwin. "Maybe we *will* get in."

The morning passed like an eternity, each movement of the gate bringing Cray and Sepwin fractionally closer to itself, while behind them the crowd deepened. At last the two companions could actually see the pikemen who guarded the door, standing with their pikes crossed before it, a latticework of steel that lifted every time the door opened. The head pikeman, the same man Cray had talked to, would seize a person from the crowd by an arm or an ear or a sleeve, and when the gate opened would thrust him or her through the opening. The choice of who entered was his, and the people nearest him held out their hands with coins of copper and silver to attract his attention. He gave most of his heed to the silver coins, but occasionally he would select someone with less of an offer, an attractive woman or a cripple, or a very old person. Once he accepted a chicken, which he passed inside when the gate opened.

Cray had a silver coin ready, glinting between thumb and forefinger, thrust toward the pikeman's face, over the shoulders of the people in front of him, when the gate closed for the last time.

"The lord is finished for today!" shouted the head pikeman. "Come back tomorrow if you wish!"

The crowd dispersed so swiftly that Cray and Sepwin were carried some distance from the gate in spite of their efforts to stand still. When the area before the gate had cleared completely, save for the guards, Cray returned, silver in hand, but he was turned away curtly.

"Come earlier tomorrow," said the head pikeman.

"Earlier indeed," said Sepwin, when they had walked back to the wineshop where their horses waited. "We shall have to arrive at dusk the night before to be early enough for *that* crowd."

"Then we shall do exactly that," said Cray.

"Stand all night in the courtyard?"

"You needn't keep me company, Feldar."

"Now, what sort of talk is that, Master Cray? I've come this far with you, and I shall go the rest of the way, too!"

Cray stretched his limbs, which were stiff from the long, cramped wait. "Then we should return to the hostel and sleep now, don't you think?"

Glumly, Sepwin nodded.

Waking near sunset, they made a swift meal of bread and cheese and then set out for the Castle, Cray carrying his father's shield on one arm as before. Although the sky was dark, torches had been lit inside the courtyard, and activity continued there little abated from the daytime. At the gate, six or seven people already clustered, sitting close to the pikemen on small stools. When Cray and Sepwin approached, the seated people tried to move even closer to the iron-bound portal, but the pikemen pushed them back. The head of the guards, not the same one Cray had seen before, looked him up and down and then thrust out his hand.

"To stay here the night, you must pay me," he said.

"I have a few coppers," said Cray. "You're welcome to them." He dipped two fingers into his pouch.

"Silver for me," said the guard. "You think I'd take less than the day guard?"

Cray indicated the people on the stools. "These others all paid you silver?"

"They did. And if you have no silver, you won't find this door so near."

Cray shrugged and handed over a silver piece.

"What about this one?" said the pikeman, pointing to Sepwin.

"He's with me," said Cray.

"He must pay, too."

Sepwin bowed low. "I was just about to say good-night, sir." He bowed to Cray. "No need to waste silver on me. I'll be with the horses."

Cray sat down cross-legged on the cold cobbles, the shield upon his lap. The people on the stools paid scant attention to him, and scant attention to each other. As the evening waned, a few more individuals joined the group, paid their silver, and sat down to stare at the door. The bustle of the market thinned, torches guttered and were replaced, stalls closed, and the last drunken man lay down upon the street to sleep where passing horses could step on him. Cray found himself dozing, more from boredom than from fatigue; he stood up and stamped his feet and paced a small circle behind the first row of stools. The seated people looked up at him, annoyed, and several of them who had arrived after him took the opportunity to move closer to the gate, hemming him in on one side. He glared at them for a moment and then very deliberately pushed the nearest out of his way. The man stood up, the stool between his legs, and he was taller than Cray, but thinner. His hands curled into fists, and he would have rammed one into Cray's stomach, but the youth saw it coming and parried the blow with the shield. Then he struck the fellow across the face with one chain-clad forearm, knocking him to the ground.

"Will you take another?" demanded Cray, standing over the prone man. "I've swung a sword these two years, and I promise you that I'm the stronger of us."

The man made no reply, only pulled his legs up to protect his belly, as if expecting a kick. But Cray only nudged the stool aside. The other people looked up at him apprehensively, and those who had moved to take his place eased their seats back and let him return to his original position.

The pikemen had watched and made no move to interfere.

The sky grew gray with dawn twilight, and the crowd thickened, pushing from the rear; and the more folk who arrived, the more blows were exchanged among them, until at last dawn came and the guard changed and the pikeman that Cray knew announced that the lord of the East March was ready to receive. Cray's silver was ready to be given, too, and he was the eighth person admitted to the keep.

The corridor beyond the gate was long and torchlit, for the slit window high above the door admitted but little sunlight at that hour. The way curved before Cray and the scarlet-garbed steward who conducted him, until it gave at last into a small, high-ceilinged room. There, the lord of the East March sat, in a high-backed, intricately carven chair behind a plain bare table. He was a big man, broad of shoulder, thick of arm, and the shaggy hair that spilled over his shoulders was iron-gray. His garment was dark velvet, a silken scarf at the throat against the cool of the stone building, and his hands were ringed in gold and silver. At either of his ears stood a man of his age, well-dressed in light woollens, holding parchment and quills, ink and sand, ready for use.

"Your name, young man," said the steward.

"I am Cray Ormoru of Castle Spinweb. My father, Mellor, served the lord of the East March before I was born; these are his bearings." He turned the shield to face the lord. "Three red lances interlocked on a field of white. They are mine now, and I would beg that you take me into your service in his stead, for he is dead."

The lord leaned forward, one elbow on the table, his fingers playing at his neck below the clean-shaven chin. "Three red lances on a white field, you say? One can hardly see them."

Cray traced the lines with one hand. "I found this shield on his grave. It has seen much weather, my lord. Fifteen years of weather."

"Fifteen years dead, hmm? What did you say his name was?"

"Mellor, my lord."

"I don't know the name. Or the arms."

"He had served you a year, my lord, when you sent him to Falconhill with a message for your cousin there. He never delivered that message, for he was killed along the way. Shortly before that, he met my mother and engendered me."

The lord of the East March shook his head. "I recall no such messenger, nor any such errand from that period." He glanced to left and right, at the two men who stood near. "Is my memory failing so soon, gentlemen? Do you know the name . . . Mellor? The arms? The event?"

Both shook their heads.

"He was very young," said Cray. "Perhaps the least of your knights, my lord."

"I know every one of my knights, young man, by name and bearings, from the greatest to the least. Your father has never been among them."

"Are you sure, my lord? He was not with you long."

"He was not with me at all." He waved one hand in dismissal. "Next case!"

"My lord!" Cray fell to his knees and raised his hands in supplication. "I beg you to inquire more closely into this matter!"

The lord of the East March looked down at the kneeling youth. "You are not much more than fifteen years old, lad. If your father is fifteen years dead, who told you he was my man?"

"My mother, my lord, who heard it from his own lips."

"May I suggest, then, that he lied to your mother?"

Cray swallowed with difficulty. "I can't believe that, my lord," he said.

"Perhaps you had best discuss it with your mother, then. Steward, show him out."

The steward hooked a hand under Cray's armpit and hauled him to his feet. In a daze, Cray allowed himself to be escorted from the room, down another corridor and out into the morning sunlight. Even after the rear gate of the keep had been shut behind him, even after the man who had followed him inside had been dismissed, jostling past him roughly, Cray still stood, leaning on the battered shield as a cripple might lean on a low chair. In the bright morning sunlight, tears coursed down his cheeks.

Sepwin found him there, directed to the rear gate by someone on the fringe of the waiting crowd. When he saw his friend, he said nothing, only took his arm gently and guided him to the alcove where the horses were tied. There, Cray let go the shield, which clattered to the ground, and he swayed against Gallant's great gray side.

"What shall I do now?" he whispered hoarsely.

"What did he say?" asked Sepwin.

Cray choked the story out, his fingers twining in Gallant's pale mane. "Never here, Feldar! Never here!" he said at the end. "Why would he have lied so to my mother?"

"He must have had a good reason," Sepwin said softly.

"A good reason?" Cray closed his eyes. "What reason would be good enough for such a lie? Was he a king-slayer running from justice?"

"Must you think of the worst possible reason first?"

"Is that the worst? No, I can think of worse yet. I could make you shudder Feldar, with my imaginings." He looked at his friend, red-eyed. "But I *must* know. I *must*."

Sepwin met his gaze. "Perhaps you are happier not knowing."

"Never. Whatever he was . . . I am his son. I must know."

"But . . . how will you find out? We've come to a dead end here at the East March."

Cray shook his head. "There is a way, I think. My mother shall advise me."

"And if he lied," said Delivev, "does that matter? Will the truth give him life again?" Her fingers moved swiftly, guiding a slender silver needle in embroidery upon white satin. "Since you showed me his grave, he has faded in my memory, like a dream, ill-remembered on waking. A dream is nothing, my son, no matter how lovely. You are my reality now."

"For my sake, then, Mother, not his, help me."

"Let him go, Cray. Let him rest in death. If he had wanted me to know the truth, he would have told it."

"Mother, you may be content with that attitude, but I am not."

She looked up at him through the web. "Will you take away the dream, too, Cray? Will you trade me something less for it? Do you think I want to know what crimes he committed?"

He gave her back stare for stare. "I can never hold my head up among other knights if I don't know who my father was."

"I loved him," she said. "Is that not enough?"

"No. Not for me."

"And will you hold your head up if the truth is something terrible?"

"I will deal with that when the time comes."

The needle flashed in her fingers, and she bent over the work once more, seeming to be speaking to it rather than to her son, very softly. "If the truth is something terrible . . . Cray . . . will you still wish to be a knight like your father? Or . . . will you come home to sorcery at last?"

He turned his face away from her. "I can't answer that now." He crossed his arms over his chest, felt of the hard chain beneath the surcoat. "You think too fast, Mother. You hope too hard. Let me find the truth, and then I will make some decision." He looked down to his feet, where the battered shield lay, painted side up, its markings barely visible in the dappled, late-afternoon sunlight. Cray's spiders had spun their web in a copse of trees a day's ride from the castle of the East March, where no stranger would see it.

Delivev sighed deeply. "There is a Seer," she said, "not far from you. Bring her the shield, and she will tell you its source. She will send you to your uncles, your grandfather, your cousins—whoever lives now at the home he left. I hope . . . they will welcome you."

"That depends on why he left, doesn't it?"

"The Seer's dwelling is not marked on the map," said Delivev, "but if you follow the southward road to the first fork, then bear west, you'll find it. She lives in a cave, and the entrance is through a great tree growing hard against the hillside. You won't have to tell her who you are. She will know."

Enough, thought Gildrum, sitting on the high stool by the brazier. Across the table. Rezhyk pored over the new marvels his demon had fetched from Ushar— stone tablets cracked from the heat, fragments from tombs of that lost civilization, their inscriptions in praise of the dead an aid to translation of the steel sheets. And on a piece of parchment, copies of other carvings, too damaged to remove from the ruins, faithfully reproduced by the demon's own hand, unto every ornamental serif.

"Ah, here is the word I was seeking, here precisely," said Rezhyk. "The writer was too careless on some of these sheets, too heavy-handed with the stylus, and the result is that some lines are punched through and those words nearly obliterated."

"Writing on steel is not so easy, my lord."

"So I would suppose. Parchment suits me well enough, even if it does burn."

"Had the folk of Ushar used parchment, my lord, you would not be reading their records now."

Rezhyk smiled. "How fortunate for me, then, that they did not. And how sad for other sorcerers to come that I have no wish to pass my knowledge on to posterity." He made a note on the sheet of parchment at his elbow, one of many awaiting his hand. "What flowery sentiments these are; they loved each other well enough, these folk, after death. You know, my Gildrum, I have always thought that their greatest mistake lay in banding together as a city. They should have separated instead. We are so much safer these days, and happier, too, each of us alone in his holding. We don't rub elbows and we don't prey upon each other's nerves."

"You may be right, my lord. Human beings have always seemed to me to be a source of endless irritation to each other. That is why so many of them make war."

Rezhyk looked up at his servant. "Are demons any better, my Gildrum?"

"We live in greater harmony, I think."

"Perhaps it only seems greater to you, because you are one of the stronger demons. The others defer to you, so of course there is harmony between you and them."

"Life is different among us, my lord. Our passions are not yours. Our desires are not as human desires."

"That is well," Rezhyk said, nodding, "else you would have stolen our world from us long ago."

Gildrum fingered one blond braid, remembering the texture of other hair, soft, brown, like a crown of downy feathers. *Our passions are not yours,* she thought, *except for mine.* She slipped off the stool and paced the length of the workshop.

"Gildrum?" said Rezhyk, glancing up from his work.

"Here, my lord. Just restless."

"I would think you'd want a bit of quiet after all your labors."

"No, my lord, for I feel that there is more yet to be done."

"I have all I can manage here; bring me no more for now, or I shall feel myself drowning."

"As you wish, my lord." She gazed at her image in the polished wall—small, slight, insignificant. He liked her thus near him, she thought, because the form befit a slave. "Shall I fetch some wine, my lord?"

"An excellent suggestion, my Gildrum. You know my mind well. Wine, indeed."

"I return in a moment, my lord."

Enough, she told herself, descending the bronze staircase to the cellar, where the wine lay cool and mellow in oaken casks. In an ordinary mortal's castle, bronze stairs would be long since corroded from the damp, but in Ringforge they were clean and smooth and shining; three of the rings on Rezhyk's hands called forth demons whose only task was the maintenance of the bright metal in its unblemished state. Rezhyk's own steps would have rung on this stairway, but Gildrum's were silent, her feet bare. The stairs were warm and dry beneath her tread, though she would not have cared if they were made of ice and slippery with slime. Ringforge awaited Rezhyk's pleasure, every room, every corner, ready for his visitation. Save for a special antechamber at the front gate, reserved for strangers, no other human being had ever been inside the castle. Only demons.

Would I have loved her if she had come here as the mistress of Ringforge?

Gildrum knew the answer was yes.

"Enough!" she shouted to the silent cellar, and her voice echoed off the metal walls and ceiling. In the cellar, with no one to see, Gildrum changed shape, became the dark-haired young knight and the bearded old man and the full-bodied landlord and the other shapes that Rezhyk's hands had formed—animal, plant, whatever had suited his purposes through the years. And when all had come and gone, the living flame was left in their place, cold now, dancing among the casks and never scorching any, growing, shrinking, dividing into a hundred flamelets and coalescing into a spark, a brilliant spark as blue as a young knight's eyes. Then, from the spark, there bloomed a body, tiny as a flea at first, but expanding like rising dough. It was black as coal and many-limbed, hairy, grotesque. It opened a dozen eyes and saw itself reflected in the ceiling, though there was no light for any human eye to see by.

This is myself, Gildrum thought. *This is my earthly form.* A shudder passed through it, and it remembered the other time it had used this body, so long ago in the woodland glade. Rezhyk had made the small blond girl that very day, while the flame of Gildrum hovered over his shoulder; Gildrum could not blame him for wanting something less horrible as his servant. *I am not human. I never was human, I can love no human woman. I can have no human son.*

The many-limbed body burst into clean, bright flame.

Enough, thought Gildrum. *I must leave them alone.*

The flame dimmed, became the blond servant girl once more. With shaking hands she filled a carafe at the nearest cask. Resolve had left her weak, despite her demon strength, and she felt a great need to sink down on the floor beside the cask, to rest in the cool cellar another moment before returning to her master. She thought of Cray, seeking the heritage that did not exist, anguished, thwarted. She had tortured herself with watching him; she would watch no more. He was a resourceful lad. He would find his own destiny. A demon slave had none to give him.

And the branches outside Spinweb's walls would never again bear the weight of a particular gray squirrel.

After all, she thought, closing her eyes and leaning her face against the cool cask. *It ended long ago.*

The Seer's home was easy to find. Not only was it marked by the tallest, broadest tree that Cray had ever seen, a great arching hole cut through its heart to form the entrance, but the Seer herself was waiting for him by the side of the road. She was a very tall, thin woman, straight of bearing, wearing a long black robe. Her skin was pale, and her hair was white as newfallen snow, worn in a single braid that hung over her left shoulder, sweeping down the length of her body to brush the ground. She lifted a hand in greeting as Cray pulled Gallant up before her.

"You are Cray Ormoru," she said.

"Good day, lady."

"And your friend Feldar Sepwin." She turned her gaze upon the former beggar. "No need for that eye patch in my presence, young man. Take it off."

He pulled the bandage from his face, stammering an apology.

"I am called Helaine," said the Seer. "You may enter my house."

The companions murmured their thanks, dismounted, and tied their horses to metal rings set in the vast trunk of the tree. Then they followed the Seer through the arch and into a torchlit stone corridor that stretched deep and cool into the hillside. At the end of the corridor was a large, almost circular room with a ceiling so high that torches at shoulder level could not illuminate it. The walls were dark stone, scattered everywhere with crystals that flashed and glittered in the flamelight. The floor was strewn with a pure white sand fine as flour, save at the center, where a raised rim encircled a pool of water no wider than the reach of a man's two arms. The Seer sat down on this rim and dabbled her fingers in the black water.

"Give me the shield," she said, and Cray, who had carried it slung over one arm, passed it to her. She touched its battered face, tracing the design with wet fingers. Her eyes closed, and the corners of her mouth drooped as she sought the metal's essence with her flesh. Watching her, Cray perceived her age for the first time. She had seemed neither old nor young in the sunlight, only timeless, in spite of the color of her hair. Now, from the transparency of her skin, from the fine lines that appeared with her concentration, he knew that she was old—older than Delivev; older than anyone he had ever seen, in web or in person.

"Cray Ormoru," the Seer said at last, eyes opening. Her irises were pale, like the rest of her, pale as brook water. "These arms are of the House of Ballat at Castle Mistwell, in the south."

"Can you direct me there, lady?"

"It is a long and hazardous journey."

"I care nothing for that. Only show me the way."

She pointed a slim finger at him. "For you, Cray Ormoru, there is sorrow at the end of this journey."

Sepwin leaned forward. "Death?" he whispered.

"No," said the Seer. "Not death."

"What sort of sorrow, then," said Cray, "beyond that which I have already known?" He touched the

155

rim of the shield with hesitant fingers. "What do you see here, lady, that I cannot see?"

She shook her head slowly. "Not in the shield, Cray, but in yourself. There, I see anguish and despair."

"I have known both."

"You shall know them again."

"For what cause?"

She gazed down at the shield. "I can tell you of the house that bears these arms: an old house, and strong. But the shield has passed through too many hands, has too many lives bound up in it. They call to me, a dozen voices, and I cannot tell which one is your father's. I would need a relic that belonged to him alone, or at least for the greater part of its existence, in order to tell you his tale."

"I have his sword."

"Give it to me."

Cray ran out to the horses and returned with the rusted blade. The Seer ran her wet fingers over the pitted surface, grasped the pommel, bent her forehead to the hilt. Then she thrust the sword into the white sand at her feet to dry it.

"It is the same," she said. "This has been used by many men."

Cray took the sword and shield from her. "Then I shall go to Castle Mistwell."

"You will find no happiness there."

"I don't expect happiness, lady. Only truth."

She smiled gently. "I give you the advice I would give a child of my own, Cray: you have a talent for sorcery; train it, and give over this desire to be a knight."

He bowed stiffly. "I thank you for your advice, lady. And now I ask only one more favor of you: guidance to Castle Mistwell."

"As you will." She rose. "I will give you a map." At the opposite end of the room from the corridor that led to the outside was a heavy wooden door. She opened it easily, slipped through the aperture, and returned a moment later with parchment and quill and ink. These she set down on the rim of the pool.

"Lady, this parchment is blank," said Cray.

"Hush. Have you no patience at all?" She gazed into

the pool a long moment, and then she took up the quill, dipped it in the ink and began drawing on the unmarred white surface. Never once did she look at what she drew, only into the pool, as if copying something from its dark surface. The map formed under her hand, cardinal points marked, major towns and castles named, the road curving this way and that, ever southward until it ended in a circle. She blinked then, and focused on her handiwork. "Here we are, here." She placed a star to locate her home; the road between it and the circle stretched the length of the sheet.

Cray looked at the map. "How far would you say that is, lady?"

"If you leave tomorrow, if you encounter no mishaps on the way, you may reach it before the snow flies."

"So far? Then we shall leave today and gain a few hours on winter. Now, lady, there is the matter of your fee. I have some silver with me, and if that is not enough, my mother can provide other payment. . . ."

"Keep your silver, young Cray," said the Seer. "We shall meet again, and then we will decide a proper fee."

"We shall meet again?"

"Yes. You think I don't know my own future?"

"As you say, lady. I do not doubt you."

She walked with them to their horses and stood silent while Cray secured the battered sword and shield to Gallant's saddle. When he had mounted, when he towered above her and raised his hand in salute, she said, "Watch for four men on horseback. Three will have beards. They are bandits."

"Where?"

"Eighteen days south of here."

He inclined his head. "Thank you."

"Don't be afraid to deal harshly with them. They have killed their share of travelers."

Sepwin leaned forward, grasping his horse's mane with both hands. "Perhaps you should have drawn us some other route, my lady."

"Any other would be so much longer that you would be stranded in the mountains for the winter. You might freeze to death. Would you prefer to chance that?"

"Mountains?" muttered Sepwin. "Can't we go around them?"

"You can . . . if you wish to measure your travel in years."

"Enough," said Cray. "We will follow your map. Farewell."

She lifted one pale hand. "Until next time, Cray Ormoru."

That night, Cray and Sepwin compared their two maps. They overlapped, though from the Seer's estimate of the distance covered by hers, they were not to the same scale.

"Do you think she was just trying to frighten us with the warning about the bandits?" said Sepwin. "After all, she said she'd see us again."

"Possibly," said Cray, tracing with two fingers the route they would be taking.

"She didn't say we *would* meet them. Maybe she meant only that we *might* meet them."

"I'm going to assume that we will. It would be foolish not to be prepared for such a thing after being warned."

Sepwin drew his knees up and clasped them with his arms, as if he were cold, though the nights were still pleasant enough, and they had a cheery fire. "Or . . . she said she'd see *you* again. Maybe . . . maybe something will happen to me when we meet the bandits."

Cray glanced at him sidelong. "Are you going to worry about that for the next eighteen days?"

"It seems like a reasonable thing to worry about."

"Perhaps you should stay behind, then."

Sepwin frowned. "And leave you to wander alone in dangerous territory?"

"Well, what use would you be in a fight, Feldar? You couldn't even defend yourself against a handful of unarmed men back in that village. What would you do against horsemen who would surely be armed with *something?*"

"You could teach me."

"Teach you what? We've only one sword. You can't count my father's blade—one solid blow and it would fly to pieces."

Sepwin pursed his lips. "She never said they would be armored men, did she?"

"No."

"Teach me to use a cudgel like a sword, then. I'll bash their heads in if they try to touch us."

Cray smiled. "You think you have the strength for that, Feldar?"

"Since I've been with you and eaten well, I've more strength than I ever thought possible."

"Eighteen days is not much for training a fighting man."

"Then we should begin at once!"

"We'll travel slower if we stop to practice combat."

"A small time every day, Cray. We can shorten our evening's rest."

Cray shook his head. "We'll need it more than ever after hacking at each other. Oh, very well, Feldar, I'll show you a thing or two. Come, cut yourself a staff from that tree over there, and I will do the same, and we'll see how well you take to swordplay."

When the cudgels were ready, Cray wove his friend a light, square shield of supple branches and spider-silk, as proof against sword and staff as his own metallic shield. Then they faced off, armed and armored alike. Cray tried not to strike too hard during this first session, but by the time Sepwin was winded and called for a halt, the former beggar was bruised and battered, red welts rising on his sword arm and the shoulder above his shield.

"The shield is a weapon, too," said Cray. "You must move it to deflect the other man's blows, not just hold it still before you."

"I'll remember," said Sepwin, dropping his battle array and rubbing his swollen arm with the hand that had gripped the shield.

"Not so easy as you thought, is it?"

"I never thought it would be easy. Just necessary. I'll be ready for more tomorrow."

"We'll see about that," said Cray. "You'll ache tomorrow, far more than you do today."

Sepwin resumed his place by the fire. "How do you know so much about fighting, Cray? Shut up in your

159

mother's castle, you never had another human being to fight with, did you?"

"Never," said Cray, sitting down beside him. "But I watched the webs. I imitated the swordsmen who were praised by their fellows. I didn't want to come to my training a complete novice."

"You handle the staff as if it were your arm. Are you as good with the sword?"

"Better."

"It's heavier."

"But it has a good grip, and balance. It has a different feel from a cudgel." He smiled. "I am very good with opponents who stand quite still. Like trees. You know, I never struck another human being till that day in the village. And now, with you, I really should be grateful for the practice."

"Well, I won't stand still, I promise that."

"Oh, you're much better than a tree." He looked into the fire, stirred it with a slender twig until the twig caught and he had to drop it into the flames. "The day after tomorrow, if you're feeling well enough, we'll try exchanging a few blows on horseback. We'll have to be very careful, though; we don't want to hurt the horses." He glanced at Sepwin. "The bandits' horses, of course, would be fair targets. If you aim for the face, I think even one of your blows would bring a horse down."

"They weren't very good, were they?"

"You strike too wild. You're too eager, and you tire quickly. These faults could be overcome, given time and dedication."

"I have dedication," said Sepwin.

Cray touched his shoulder lightly. "Listen, my friend: if the bandits do strike, ride away as fast as you can. Your plowhorse is swift—I know that well enough."

"I couldn't leave you!"

"When the time comes, you may find it easier than you think."

"No!"

"Well, this is a different Feldar Sepwin than I picked up on the road so long ago. Where have you found your courage?"

160

Sepwin shook his head. "It's not courage. It's madness. Your madness, Cray. But you saved my life back there in the village, and I owe you something for that."

"You owe me nothing."

"And if I ride away and leave you to die at the hands of bandits, I'll have no one, just as before. I'll be a beggar again." He gripped Cray's arm. "When you are a knight, will you let me be your squire?"

"You think too far ahead, Feldar. Right now, I am only concerned with arriving at Mistwell. Let us leave the rest for later." He smiled at Sepwin. "And there will be a later, for both of us, I promise you."

The next day they rode and then they slept; Sepwin was indeed too sore and too tired to lift staff or shield. The following day, though, they spent a little time in a clearing off the road, on horseback, sparring. Cray taught his companion to dodge and duck and still keep his seat, to swipe at the opposing horse's legs and neck. Having been raised among horses, Sepwin rode well and had hardly more trouble manipulating the staff and shield while mounted than he had while on his own feet. His motions were slow, though, his muscles still being sore, and Cray was careful to avoid hitting him with any real force. Still, he groaned considerably from his own exertion, and when they were finished he only wanted to lie down and be quiet.

He was better the next day.

And the next.

"I make a poor warrior, don't I?" he said on the tenth afternoon, nursing his newest bruises by the fire. That day they had seen the mountains for the first time, like blue clouds on the horizon.

"You haven't the brawn for it," said Cray. "That takes more than a few days."

"So we're left with one of us, and perhaps a small fraction added for me, against the four of them. And you don't seem worried at all." He frowned into the flames. "She didn't say we'd come back with all our arms and legs intact. Remember, she prophesied anguish and despair."

"I don't think that had anything to do with the bandits, Feldar."

"I wish I were as confident."

Cray nudged him in the ribs. "Listen, my friend—knowing how to defend yourself with a good, stout staff is an excellent thing. You could have used such knowledge, I think, in the past. But you probably won't need it when we meet the bandits."

"Why not?"

"Because I have my spiders."

"What good will they be?" demanded Sepwin. "Except perhaps to frighten the bandits to death by crawling all over them."

"You ask that after seeing them spin silk as strong as steel?"

Sepwin looked at him with knitted brows. "Will you make us armor out of it?"

"I'll make us weapons out of it."

"What—swords? That won't be much help to *me*."

Cray smiled. "How good is your aim, Feldar?"

"My aim? What do you mean?"

"Can you hit a target with a stone?"

Sepwin shrugged. "As well as anyone else can, I suppose. We used to amuse ourselves by throwing stones at rabbits, back at the village where I was born."

"Show me." He pointed to a tree half a dozen paces away. "The knot on the trunk, the one at about a man's height—hit it with a couple of pebbles. Here . . ." He scratched at the ground, uncovered several stones no larger than the nail of his little finger. "Use these."

Sepwin weighed the pebbles in his hand. "These are hardly deadly missiles."

"Go on."

"Well, you've picked an easy enough target." He tossed one stone, overhand, hard, and it ricocheted off the knot with a sharp cracking noise. He threw two more, and both struck the target, which was quite large. "Shall I carry a bag of stones with me from now on?"

Cray stood up and walked to the tree. "Throw one at me now. Aim at my shoulder. And throw softly, Feldar, as if you wanted the pebble to come to rest where it struck, not punch a hole there."

Sepwin obeyed, tossing the pebble lightly, under-hand, and it touched Cray's shoulder gently and tum-bled off, to drop at his feet.

"Now, can you do that to a moving target?" He dodged to one side, bouncing up and down on the balls of his feet, weaving, bobbing. "Come on, come on."

Sepwin scratched up more pebbles and threw them, and in spite of Cray's maneuverings, most of the stones found a mark somewhere on his body.

Cray called a halt. "You've done well so far," he said, nodding. "We'll try it with spiders next."

"Spiders?"

"Do you think I mean you to throw pebbles at the bandits?"

"I don't know what to think."

"Stand still and watch." He lifted his hand, cupped the palm, and a spider crawled out of his sleeve to crouch upon his bare flesh. Then, as if it were a stone, he tossed it at Sepwin. He tossed it in a high arc, and it spun as it sailed toward its target, a trail of fine silk playing out behind it. It landed on Sepwin's arm and scurried across his chest to the other arm and behind his back, laying down silk that clung to him; when it reached its landing point once more, the strand drew snug about him, pinning his arms to his sides.

"Three or four spiders," said Cray, "and you would be netted as surely as any animal I ever hunted." He touched the silk lightly and it fell away to nothing. The spider jumped back to his sleeve.

"But . . . I can't do that," said Sepwin, massaging his arms where the silk had pinched.

"Of course you can."

"You mean they'll spin like that for me?"

"If I want them to. Will you try it?"

Sepwin grimaced. "I don't like the idea of carrying spiders up my sleeve."

"You didn't mind them sitting on your shoulders."

"Just at the moment I was too busy trying to save your life to care."

"Well, this is the same sort of thing, isn't it? The bandits won't be playing games with us." He crossed his arms over his chest. "Or would you rather try to

163

bash their heads with your cudgel? I guarantee you, this is more likely to succeed."

Sepwin chewed at his lower lip.

"And you won't get sore muscles from this, either," said Cray.

"Let me think about it."

"Hold out your hand, Feldar."

"What are you going to do?"

"I'm going to give you a spider. Hold out your hand. I swear you'll not be bitten."

"Will the spider swear, too?"

"*I've* never been bitten."

"I didn't have your mother."

"Hold out your hand!"

His face grim, Sepwin obeyed. His hand was steady, palm upward, fingers cupped, and he stared at it as if he had never seen it before.

Cray grasped Sepwin's wrist tightly with his own left hand, and with his right he dropped a small black spider into his friend's open palm. The spider froze upon the pale flesh, resembling nothing so much as a small, dark pebble.

"You see, it won't do anything I don't want it to do," said Cray.

"I don't mind it on my hand," said Sepwin. "But in my clothes, hiding, crawling all over my body—how can you bear it, Cray?"

Cray shrugged. "I have difficulty understanding why it should bother you."

"They're ugly, filthy, evil—"

"Nonsense! They are as evil as your eye, Feldar! I would have thought that you, above all people, would not harbor silly superstitions. And they are clean, too, and—in their way—quite beautiful. There is grace in their movements, smooth as the sweep of a lady's skirt in the pavane. And they create beauty as well: I have never seen a lovelier sight than a dew-drenched web, sparkling in the morning sun like strands of pearls. Now let's have no more foolishness, Feldar. You can carry a dozen spiders, and if you don't think about that, you'll never be aware that they ride with you."

"I'll feel them," said Sepwin.

"Only when they walk to your hands to be tossed. I'll command them to be still otherwise. Observe." He pointed at the spider in his friend's hand, and it unfroze, moving slowly over his palm, across the wrist, up the forearm, to disappear in his sleeve. "It's stopped now, and there it will stay until I tell it to move again."

"I feel it there. I feel it standing on my gooseflesh."

"You'll soon forget about it."

"I don't think so," said Sepwin. He flexed his elbow hesitantly. "Won't I crush it accidentally?"

"They aren't easy to crush . . . accidentally. Bending your elbow won't do it. They have hard shells, after all."

Sepwin stared at his arm, as if he could see the spider through his clothing. "Must I carry this creature until we meet the bandits?"

"Carry it a while today," said Cray, "to become accustomed to it. I'll take it back before we sleep. Tomorrow we'll try you with several spiders. Then you'll practice throwing them. By the time we meet the bandits, you'll be comfortable with them."

"I find that hard to imagine."

That evening, as Cray spoke with his mother, Sepwin watched the fringe of the web instead of its heart; he watched the spiders that had spun it waiting for flying insects to blunder into the sticky strands. They fed each night like that, sharing the one large web, their bodies scattered like raisins on the gossamer surface. When a struggling insect became entangled in the silk, some spider would scurry to the spot, walking on the few strands that would not cling to its legs, to spin a cocoon about the prey. When all the spiders had done with their meals, the cocoons were left hanging in the silk, to be blown away with the web by the next day's wind, after Sepwin and Cray had resumed their journey.

"How glad I am that I am not a fly," Sepwin said before they went to sleep.

"If you don't learn to use those spiders," replied Cray, "you *will* be a fly, to the bandits."

The following day, Sepwin carried two spiders. But after he had practiced throwing them, in the evening, he still insisted on a sparring match with staves and shields. "In case I miss," he said.

The land began to rise, the trail to become rockier and more difficult to negotiate. The mountains loomed close, seeming every morning taller than the night before, and every day's progress was slower than the last. On the sixteenth evening, they halted in a copse of oaks, a level place beside the steeply climbing road. After dinner, Cray set all his spiders to forming a fence of fine netting to enclose the trees.

"I think we should start to take turns standing watch tonight," he said, "in the event that the bandits are not completely obedient to the Seer's prophecy. I'll take the first watch."

"Do you really think they might strike early? In the night?"

"No, but why be unprepared?" He strolled along the silken fence, which was almost invisible in the moonlight. "This will keep them out if they do, at least until they decide to climb it. And by that time, we'll both be roused and ready to deal with them." He glanced at Sepwin. "Which means, my friend, that you'll be sleeping with spiders from now on."

Sepwin sighed. "I suppose that's for the best."

"Kneel down and put your hands on the ground. They're waiting to climb into your sleeves."

"Very well." He knelt. "You know, if I close my eyes and pretend hard enough, they feel like dry leaves brushing my skin instead of spiders."

"Think of them that way, if it makes you feel better."

Sepwin lay down, wrapped in his cloak. "I wish you had some other animal to follow your magical orders. I wouldn't mind sleeping with a cat or a dog or any number of other creatures."

"I don't think Gallant would care much for carrying a pack of dogs about."

"One dog."

"What good would one dog be?"

"A magic dog."

"I suspect spiders are much more useful than any magic dog."

"If I were a sorcerer," said Sepwin, "I'd think of some use for a magic dog."

"I thought you liked horses best."

"A magic horse, then. It wouldn't matter to me. Just so it was something pleasing to look at." ·

"Spiders are pleasing to look at!"

"I will never understand sorcerers," muttered Sepwin, and he rolled over and went to sleep.

During the next day, he was nervous, always looking back over his shoulder, to one side or the other, peering ahead. He used any excuse to halt and listen for the sounds of horses other than their own. But there were none, only the whistling of the wind among the trees, and an occasional fall of loose stones somewhere out of sight.

That night they slept surrounded by silk again, though Sepwin hardly slept at all; he rose at last and took the watch far earlier than midnight. Cray did not argue with him over it, merely rolled in his blanket and went to sleep, leaving Sepwin to start at every hooting owl, at every cricket chirp, at every unidentifiable rustle. In the morning he was red-eyed, and his limbs shook.

"You haven't slept enough," said Cray. "Take a nap; we'll start out later in the day."

Sepwin shook his head violently. "I'd rather ride now, and get it over with."

"Well, today is the eighteenth day, isn't it?" Cray looked his friend over. "You won't be much use to me in this state."

"I'll be all right. Let's be off."

"Have something to eat. Here's cold pheasant from last night's dinner."

"I couldn't eat."

"Where will you find strength for your defense, Feldar, if you don't eat?"

"I'll eat afterward. I don't think it would stay with me right now."

"As you will." Cray made his own breakfast without haste, then tore down the webs that had surrounded their camp. When he mounted Gallant, Sepwin was already astride his own animal, waiting, and his anxiety had communicated itself to his mount, which rocked from leg to leg and snorted with flaring nostrils at every whisper of wind.

They were high in the mountains now, and the trail swung back and forth, transforming steep ascents into gentle but interminable inclines. The peaks were all about them, treeless and wind-scoured. Frequently, the path narrowed to a mere ledge, with granite wall rising on one side and sheer drop falling away on the other. At these places, Cray rode first, and Sepwin followed, always looking behind him for pursuit.

It was Cray who called a halt at the barrier.

Sepwin pulled up beside him; the road was wide enough for both of them here, and neither cliff nor rock wall hemmed them in, though the slopes to either side looked to be rough climbing for horses. The barrier was a gate of logs laid across the road. Beyond it, two men waited. Their mounts were small compared to Gallant.

"Good day!" shouted one of the men.

Cray leaned forward in his saddle. "Good day to you, sir. Is there some danger ahead, that you've put up this obstruction?"

"This is a toll gate," said the man. "You must pay the toll to pass."

"And what is the toll, sir?" asked Cray.

"How much silver do you have?"

"Very little, I'm afraid. No more than a piece or two."

The man smiled. He wore a dark beard, and his teeth were very white within its compass. His clothing was leather, as was his companion's, and he wore several knives about his person. In a sling attached to his saddle, just brushing his right knee, was a heavy club. "Only a piece or two?" he said. "Are you sure?"

"Quite sure," said Cray. "We live off the land and have little use for money."

"What a pity," said the man. "In that case, you will have to pay with your horses."

Cray's fingers tightened on the reins. "Our horses? Good sir, *my* horse has been my friend for a considerable time. I could not give him up. And how would we pass through the rest of the mountains without horses?"

"You have sturdy enough legs, lad. You can walk."

"You ask a high toll, sir."

The man shrugged. "Not higher than you can pay."

"I think it is," said Cray. A sharp tap on the knee caused him to turn to Sepwin, who had struck the blow and was now looking back at the road behind them. A dozen strides away, a pair of riders moved toward the young companions; Cray knew they must have come from nearby concealment, else he and Sepwin would have heard their horses' hoofbeats before this. Two of them wore beards, making a total of three bearded men among the four mounted strangers, just as the Seer had predicted.

"You will pay the toll," said the spokesman for the group.

Cray looked at him. "Are you the lord of this land?"

"There is no lord here."

"Then what right have you to collect a toll?"

"The right of strength, lad. What other right is there?"

Cray sought Sepwin's eye, caught it briefly and tilted his head toward the men on the far side of the gate. He could see his friend's hands clenching and unclenching in his horse's mane, and as soon as their mutual gaze broke, Sepwin's eyes returned to a restless search to left and right. He seemed to be looking for a way out.

"Off your horses, lads," said the spokesman of the bandits, "and be grateful we haven't asked for more than that."

Cray wheeled Gallant about, till he was facing the other two men. "The toll is too high," he said. "We'll turn back."

"You may do whatever you wish," said the man, "after paying the toll."

"Now, Feldar!" shouted Cray, and his arms shot out toward the two rear bandits, spraying spiders like fistfuls of grain. The men were startled and raised their hands to fend the tiny creatures off, but those gestures only gave the spiders easier targets; they spun their first silk about the very fingers that tried to brush them away, binding flailing hands with unbreakable wrappings, like steel mittens. Then the spiders

began to bind the mittens to the nearest anchor points
—the men's own bodies, their saddles, their horses.
The horses reared and struggled at the touch of the
spidersilk, and one of the men fell, thrashing, hanging
from his saddle by a few near-invisible strands while
his terrified mount kicked at him.

Cray turned to Sepwin as soon as he had loosed his
spiders, and it was barely soon enough. Either Sepwin
had been too far from his quarry or he had failed to
use the proper strength in his toss, for most of his
spiders fell short, landing on the gate, where they were
busily spinning useless silk. The few that had found
their human targets could not fashion enough silk to
bind the men before both could charge their horses
through the gate. The swinging gate had caught
Sepwin's horse in the chest and forelegs, knocking it
aside and tumbling Sepwin to the ground. When Cray
turned to his friend's assistance, Sepwin was scrambling to his feet, trying to dodge the milling, whinnying
horses and the two riders with heavy clubs in their
hands. Cray drew his sword and, shouting, charged
the pair.

The odds were two to one, but neither of the bandits
was armed with a sword, neither with a shield, and
neither with the anger that Cray felt rising in himself.
He laid into them with a will, swinging his blade ef-
fortlessly, as when his only targets had been trees.
The blade clove human flesh with greater ease than it
had ever sliced bark. One man rode away, a deep cut
in his shoulder, and the spokesman of the group fell,
to dampen the ground with his blood. His frightened
horse stepped on him twice, but he was already dead
when that happened.

Sepwin watched the final fight from one of the slopes
that flanked the road, where he had clambered when
Cray distracted his pursuers. He still stood there as
Cray dismounted and began to move among the
frightened horses, trying to soothe them with soft
words and caresses. Of the five horses clustered by the
open gate, only Gallant stood calm and silent, as if all
this had happened to it before.

One horse still bore a rider, upon whom Cray's
spiders had spun their steely cords; he slumped for-

ward over his mount's neck, motionless. When Cray touched him, turning steel to ordinary silk, he slid sideways, limply, and struck the ground like a sack of stones. Cray also touched the man who still hung from webbing attached to his mount, the man whose own animal had kicked him to death in its terror; that body had not so far to fall. Cray tied all the horses to the gate, and they were quiet enough at last, except that their occasionally flaring nostrils showed that they could smell the blood spilled on the road.

Sepwin descended the slope slowly, and he stopped some distance from his companion. "You didn't need me," he said. "You did it all yourself." He looked down at the ground. "I'm sorry I failed you."

"You did your best," said Cray. "I know that."

Sepwin shook his head. "I knew I was too far away. But I was afraid to go closer. I was afraid they would throw their knives."

"And chance harming good horseflesh? Hardly." Cray crossed the space that separated them and clapped his friend on the back. "Never mind. It's all over now." He stooped to pick up his sword, which lay upon a patch of coarse mountain grass, where he had set it before trying to calm the horses. The blade was bloody more than halfway to the hilt. He wiped it on the grass, back and forth, over and over again, until the red was gone. "My first man," he said, gripping the pommel in both hands so that the tip of the blade lightly touched the ground. His back was to the dead men. "I should feel different somehow, now. But I don't. It was like striking a tree, only easier. Flesh is soft, bone is hard, but not so hard as wood. I could have cut him in two without much more effort. He wore no armor." He leaned on the blade, letting it dig into the ground. "I never expected my first fight to be like that."

"Not your first," said Sepwin. "There was the village."

Cray shook his head. "They were unarmed. Not even a knife among them."

"They were armed enough for me," said Sepwin.

Cray looked at him. "You've been close to death before. This was my first time."

171

"The village . . ."

"They wouldn't have touched me. They were afraid of the sword. These men weren't." He turned away from the sword, leaving it to stand upright by itself. "Let's bury the bodies."

"We haven't a spade, have we?" said Sepwin.

"No, but we can pile rocks on top of them. Plenty of rocks around here."

"You think they deserve such decent treatment?"

"I think the next travelers who use this route deserve to be safe from the wild animals that would come to pick the carcasses. Come, there's a gully beyond that rise; we can throw them into it and then roll the rocks after." He bent over the man his blade had slain. "Take the feet, Feldar."

"What about the other man? The one who rode away."

"Well, I don't see how we'll be able to bury him. He's pretty far away by now."

"I mean, what if he comes back?"

"He won't come back."

"He might come back with friends."

Cray shook his head. "Two spiders went with him. He was riding too fast to notice their work. I've lost them forever, now, but he won't come back." He gestured toward the man who had been dead on his horse, wrapped in silk. "As with that one, a few strands looped about the throat, pulled tight. Even a very strong man could not break them without magic. I don't want to meet any bandits on this road when we come back. If we come back." He frowned. "I wouldn't have used the spiders in a fair fight."

Sepwin's right hand crept up to his own throat, rubbed slowly at the collarbone. "You'll be a very unusual sort of knight, I think," he murmured, "commanding an army of spiders."

Cray shook his head. "I don't have an army, just the few I carry with me, my own personal spiders. I can't command any others, not like my mother, who has sovereignty over all the spiders of the world. And I intend to put these aside, if there are any of them left, when I'm a knight. They don't belong with sword and shield."

172

"But they give you such an advantage!"

"A short-lived advantage, Feldar. I've lost a dozen in this fight—the bandits crushed them. How long would the rest last if I used them so again and again?"

"Can't you get replacements?"

"I could . . . with my mother's help. But I won't. They would keep me from acquiring the proper skills of knighthood; I would depend on them, and not on my good right arm, and so I would be an inferior knight. Besides . . ." His lips quirked in a small smile. "My fellow knights might not care for such a hybrid in their midst. I have noticed, in my travels, that the two worlds do not mix well. Eh, Feldar of the strange eyes?"

"You have a point there. I was only thinking that you should use all of your resources to stay alive. The spiders would be a handy reserve."

"Sword and shield shall be resources enough, when I am trained. I'll need no spiders then."

Sepwin shrugged. "As you will."

"Come now, lift the legs. I want to ride on before the sun sets."

They rode on, but not far; building a cairn of rocks over the three bodies had taken most of the afternoon. Cray and Sepwin camped that night between two peaks, and the next day the path took them upward, toward the farther of the pair. The wind cooled about them as they climbed, increasing in strength until it beat at them like icy cudgels and they had to lean into their horses' manes to remain mounted. All around, the trees and bushes grew smaller, stunted and gnarled, clinging close to the ground beneath the blasting wind. In Cray's sleeves, where he carried all the surviving spiders, the creatures retreated from the wrist openings to the upper arms, where the cold gusts could not reach them. On the plains, the trees had not yet begun to shed their leaves, but in the highest mountains, the breath of winter was already touching the land.

The first snowflakes had begun to fall by the time the two companions found themselves descending, ever descending, with only foothills still before them. Since dealing with the bandits, they had met no travelers upon the road and had begun to suspect that they were the last to pass that way for the season. Ahead, misty as its name, lay the hold that the Seer had sent them to. As they approached it, the peaks behind them whitened, barring their return.

It was a quiet time at Mistwell. The harvest was done, the grains stored away, the cellars full of apples, the animals fattening for cold-weather feasting. Mistwell was at peace, and the knights of the hold had gathered for the winter, to joust and gamble and drink the lengthening evenings away. The main hall of the keep was a noisy place and bright, full of rich velvets and brocades, of silk, satin, and gold. It smelled good, too—with well-spiced meat roasting in each of the two large fireplaces. Cray and Sepwin, having left their horses in the care of a servant, entered, conducted by a man who wore a white surcoat over his armor; upon his chest were figured the same bearings that Cray knew so well, the same interlocked red lances that the battered shield under his arm bore. The symbols were everywhere here, upon the outer gate, upon the men-at-arms, upon shields ranked along one wall of the hall. Cray felt that at last he had come home.

The lord of the hold, Fayr Ballat, was a man of middle age, blond and bearded, tall and loose-limbed. He received the travelers cordially and listened to Cray's tale, from which the youth excised all mention of sorcery. At the end, he examined the sword and shield, turning them over and over in his hands.

"These are my House's arms," he said at last. "This sword was made within these walls, and this shield, too. Here are the maker's marks." He indicated an intricate symbol pressed into the rear of the shield and the end of the sword's pommel. "Yet, who could have carried them . . . ? You are sure he was a knight?"

Cray frowned. "So he told my mother, my lord."

Fayr Ballat peered closely at the battered shield, not at the faded design but at other parts of the face, the top, the bottom, the edges. "I say that because this seems to be the sort of shield used by my foot soldiers. It is simply the shield of the House, without any apparent personal symbol upon it. My own shield is like this, but with the addition of a blue canton. The other knights of my family, my brothers and cousins, all have their own individual emblems added to the basic design. So you see, this does not seem to be a knight's shield at all."

"He said he was the younger son of a younger son . . ."

"Still," said Fayr Ballat. "He would have some mark to set him off from others of the House. Can you see one?"

"There is none," said Cray. "My mother made a tapestry with his shield upon it, and if there had been some other device, she would have shown it."

Fayr Ballat reached out to Cray with one hand, laid it lightly on the youth's shoulder. "I will ask among my men. I don't know the name you gave, or the face you described, but perhaps there is someone here who will remember him. He must have left a long time ago, and if he was one of the foot soldiers, I'd not likely recall him."

"A foot soldier," muttered Cray.

"For now . . . consider yourself a guest of the House of Ballat. Both of you, of course. It was a good harvest, and we've food and to spare for the winter."

Cray bowed. "Thank you, my lord. We appreciate such hospitality."

Dinner was excellent, and the lord of Mistwell was as kind and solicitous as the lord of the East March had been cold and abrupt. This was a smaller hold, tucked away in the foothills of the great mountains, a realm of red-cheeked, fair-haired people who loved laughter and gaiety. Sepwin was early drawn into their dancing, and at his urging Cray at last left the cup of dark wine that had been the mirror of his soul and joined the ring. He was light on his feet, for a youth wearing a suit of chain and a heavy heart. Later, he lay down on a pallet in a quiet corner of the hall, while members of the household remained by the fire, talking in low voices, their cheer not yet ready to dissipate in slumber. He lay on his back, staring up at the shadowed ceiling. Sepwin snored gently beside him, having no unknown father to haunt his night. But the darkness was long, with winter approaching, and the late dawnlight found Cray finally overtaken by sleep.

At midday, Fayr Ballat came into the hall. Cray, awakened by the burgeoning activity of the chamber, red-eyed and groggy, watched his host walk with his councillors, speak with the ladies of the castle, bend near the hearth where the meal was being prepared by fat cooks. The youth waited, sitting at the far end of a long bench, while Sepwin nosed about the room, telling extravagant tales of the loss of his eye. He had the blue one covered for their stay at Mistwell, and his brown eye was being well received by pages and women and the kitchen staff, which was moved to give him a taste of hot food before anyone else had any.

"Pity," said Sepwin, when he returned to Cray's side with a trencher of meat big enough for both of them, "can be a wonderful thing."

"You should know," said Cray. "You traded on it long enough."

"And the pity of a rich house," Sepwin continued, "is clearly superior to that of a hovel. I never begged food like this when I was alone on the road. I can think of a peasant or two who would envy me this meal." He grinned. "We could do worse than winter here."

Cray looked down at his hands, fingers interlaced upon his knee. His shoulders were hunched, his whole body bent forward, as if the chain were unusually heavy this day. "He has looked at me several times," he said. "But he chooses not to speak. That promises ill."

"The Seer promised ill, Cray. Why don't you ask him what he hesitates to tell you?"

"That would be rude, Feldar. He has his House's business to attend to. I am not so important that he would leave off his own affairs to deal with me."

"I think he would. He seems to have a kind heart. The way he spoke to you last night—it pained him to tell you about the shield, I could see that plainly."

Cray closed his eyes. "I am of two minds on the matter. I want to know, yet I dread the knowledge. This is the end of the road, Feldar. What he tells me will color my whole life."

Sepwin laid an arm across his friend's shoulders.

"Eat something," he advised. "The world always looks cheerier on a full stomach."

Cray shook his head. "It would be like lead inside me."

"Better lead than nothing." Sepwin thrust the trencher at him. "You didn't sleep well, I can see that. At least eat."

Cray sighed and took a morsel. He chewed without relish. "It's like dust in my mouth."

"Your stomach won't think it's dust."

The midday meal had ended for everyone in the hall before Fayr Ballat sent a page to fetch Cray to him.

"I hardly know what to tell you, Master Cray," he said. "The name Mellor means nothing to my household, nor does your description of him stir any memories, though a description secondhand, as yours, carries no great weight behind it. Still, the time, near sixteen years ago, proves to have some significance—the old steward tells me that a sword and shield and suit of chain were taken from the armory, and a horse from the stables, at about that time. Spring it was, he said. He remembers it because he was beaten for allowing such a thing to happen. The armory guards and the stableboys were punished severely, but the thief was never identified. Nor did anyone ever determine where the stolen items went."

Cray stared at him. "Thief?"

"I know nothing of this myself," said Fayr Ballat. "I was just a stripling then, my father was lord, and I paid no attention to household details. But I have no reason to doubt the old steward's memory. I think that sword and shield must be the ones you brought with you."

Cray's gaze drifted from his host's face to the floor at his feet, his head bowing as if the ceiling were pressing down on him. At last he laughed a dry, humorless laugh. "I was prepared to hear almost anything when I came here. I was prepared to discover that he had been driven away from his home for some terrible crime. Now I find the crime was real but petty. And I still don't know who he was."

"You have come a long way," said Fayr Ballat, "for so little. I am sorry indeed."

"I thank you for your sympathy, my lord. I will trouble you no more." He began to turn away, but Fayr Ballat's strong arm stayed him.

"What will you do now, Master Cray?"

"I don't know."

"You can't return over the mountains—winter has already closed the passes. Stay here the season. Begin your training with us; my knights are well versed in their arts."

"I have no claim on you, my lord," said Cray. "As my father appears to have been no one, so I am no one as well."

"You have a strong heart," said Fayr Ballat. "And, from what the stablemaster tells me, a fine horse. Sword, shield, chain—what more could an aspiring knight need? I care less for bloodlines than for determination and skill. You seem to have the one; we can try to give you the other here at Mistwell. We've a long winter ahead of us and only a few young men to train. Another mouth and another arm won't strain us." He glanced at Sepwin, sitting on the bench across the room. "Even two mouths."

"We travel together," said Cray.

"Does your friend wish to be a knight, too?"

"No, my lord."

"That's as well, I think. He hasn't the shoulders for it. You have. Will you accept Mistwell's hospitality?"

"You are very kind to offer it. I shall accept."

"Good lad."

As Cray crossed the room to tell Sepwin the news, he could not help feeling that something had died inside him this day. He wondered how much his mother could sense through her tapestry—the emptiness in the pit of the stomach, the heaviness of limbs and head, the world as gray as if the very color had drained away from it? There were spiders in his clothing, waiting for the command to spin a web in some secluded place, that he and she could talk, but somehow he could not bring himself to face her just now.

Maybe not for a long time.

◆§ CHAPTER NINE

Winter was gone, and the snows that still clung to the heights beneath the spring sun were fast melting into icy, rushing rivulets. On every slope, new green was burgeoning, thrusting up through the wet mulch of last year's growth, and the hares that frequented the passes were shedding their white coats for summer's brown. Cray and Sepwin had been picking their way northward for some days, moving slowly on a path treacherous with chilly mud. Pebbles rolled under their horses' steps, loosened by freeze and thaw and flowing water. Once, they encountered a section of the road sunk more than a man's reach below its former level, and they had to dismount and lead their steeds a precarious, tilting scramble around the hole. Shortly after this, they found a small cave which opened from a cul-de-sac off the road, and they halted there for the night, though the sun was still high. The cave smelled of wolves, but it contained none. The companions built a bright blaze in its entrance, in case any former occupants tried to return. It was their first dry camp since leaving Mistwell.

"I would have waited till a bit later in the season," said Sepwin, "if the decision had been mine."

Cray shook his head. He was watching his spiders spin a large web against the cave wall. "I had no patience for waiting. She said we would be back, so let it be soon."

Sepwin lay with his feet toward the fire, and the mud that encrusted his footgear steamed in the radiant heat, turning slowly to hard clay. "I could wish you weren't so eager to prove her power," he muttered.

The spiders had done, and even as they scuttled from the web it began to flow gray and opaque. From the silk-covered cave wall, as if from a window cut through the mountainside, light spilled. At Castle Spinweb, too, the sun was high, and the web chamber was brightly lit. A bluebird perched, twittering, on the velvet coverlet; as Cray and Sepwin watched, it took wing and flashed through the high window, into the garden. Not long after that, Delivev came into the room.

She wore black feathers still. Cray had seen her in nothing else all winter, the few times he had crept away from other humans and spun a web where there were no witnesses. She was still beautiful, he thought, but thinner now than when he had left her, and paler than ever from the wan winter sunshine.

"Where are you, Cray?" she asked.

"In a cave some days' ride north of Mistwell, Mother."

"A cave? Are you on some quest for your lord?"

Cray shook his head. "I've left Mistwell, Mother. I'm going back to the Seer."

"The Seer . . . ?" Delivev looked at his eyes. "I thought you were happy with the House of Ballat. I thought . . . that you would stay and find your knighthood among them. They want you, don't they?"

"They want me," said Cray. "And they have been more than kind. I have learned so much this winter that I can scarcely believe I knew so little before. And above all, at Mistwell I fought real men, not bundles of cloth or trees, but men who could dodge and strike back, men with far more skill than I. Though I gave a good account of myself, I think. I shall always be grateful to the House of Ballat for this winter's experience." He broke the line of their gaze and looked to the ground. "But I had a question when I arrived at Mistwell, and I found no answer there. I don't know where that answer lies, but I do know that the Seer foresaw my return to her home, and so I will go there because I can't think where else would be a better place."

Softly, his mother said, "You could come back to Spinweb."

He sighed heavily. "I don't doubt that she will advise me so. But perhaps she will have some other thought as well. I can only hope so." He lifted his gaze to hers, and there was pain in his face. "Mother, I must know. If there is any way in the world, I must know!"

Her features mirrored his. "And if there is no way, my son?"

He bit his lip very hard, tasted the blood, warm and metallic, on his tongue. "Then I will come home," he said at last, and his voice broke on the final word. His eyes brimmed suddenly. "Oh, how could he have done this to us?" he blurted.

"I respect his reasons," Delivev said. "Whatever they were."

Cray shook his head violently.

"I only wish," she went on, "that he could have known we had a son. You look very well, Cray. You look strong and hard." She paused, watching the silent tears streak his face. "Now is not the time for us to talk, I think. Take care of yourself. I love you always. Farewell."

As the web blanked itself, Cray covered his reddened eyes with both hands. "What shall I do, Feldar?" he whispered. "What shall I do if the Seer has nothing left to offer me?"

Sepwin looked out through the cave mouth, at the mountains which lay all about them. "It's a hard road back to Mistwell, but we know it, and we know what lies at its end."

Slowly, Cray held his palms out to the fire. He felt the warmth beat against his skin, but it did not seem to penetrate; his whole body felt cold and stiff. "My body may take that road," he murmured at last. "But where will my heart go?"

Sepwin, watching him stare into the flames, had no reply.

Delivev sat by the tapestry of Cray's travels. It made a strange map, his route picked out in crimson threads against the earthy colors representing moun-

181

tain, meadow, forest, and swamp. As he retraced his
steps northward, the fresh crimson squeezed among
darker threads laid down when first he passed that
way, paralleling his old path; if anything significant
happened on that second passage, threads of the
weft would unravel on the spot, pull behind the
warp, and knot themselves, leaving room for some
fresh symbol to take shape and hint at the event. Such
symbols were scattered about the design: here was his
father's grave, here the swamp where he might have
drowned, here the bandits he slew, here the terrible
disappointment of Mistwell. Each even had its own
aura, faded now, yet easy enough to recapture if she
but placed her hand upon the threads there. Delivev
never did so, for there was only grief to be gained
from that. The tapestry carried no joy in its threads;
Cray, who had been a joyful child, had shed that
quality like a broken toy when he left Spinweb. Often,
contemplating the tapestry as she did this day, Delivev
wondered how he could bear to wander the world
when he knew that nothing but misery awaited him.

You are braver than I, my son, she said to the tapestry.

But she was not sure that even joy would take her
out of Spinweb. She, who could have the world in her
web chamber, had always preferred that to meeting it
in the flesh. She had ventured away from Spinweb
only three or four times in her long life, and none of
those recently. Save for her son, all she desired lay
within easy reach of these castle walls—all she desired, at least, that could be gained by mortal flesh.
Often, she pitied the ordinary people she saw in the
webs, who strove to gain that which was so far beyond
their reach that they used a lifetime in pursuit, of gold,
of glory, of power. Some of them wandered far in the
chase, as Cray did. Thinking about such wanderings,
she could not help but recall the greatest wanderers of
all, the troubadours, and the one she had once singled
out, Lorien.

She did not smile at that memory. She thought now
that she had given him too much in exchange for his
songs, not just of fine clothing but of herself. She had
made the gifts of cloth to salve her conscience, to

recompense him for the shabby treatment he had seen at her hands and for the false impression he had gained from her behavior—that she wanted more of him than music. The gifts of herself she had not given freely, her words, her demeanor, her solitude that he had woven already into the cloth of songs, with the magic of his voice. She had heard him in the webs, and she knew when he sang of her, though he embellished her mystery into a tale with beginning and end that bore no resemblance to reality. Now part of her would always be in the world beyond Spinweb, though her body stayed within these walls, and she would never look into a distant castle through the webs without wondering what was known of her there.

He knew she watched him sometimes; she could see that knowledge in his eyes. And spiderwebs drew his gaze, so that he occasionally appeared to be looking straight at her, and she had the haunting sensation that he could see her face. He had found her spiders riding in his clothing, but he had made no attempt to destroy them. They had an unspoken agreement, he and she, and both had paid for it with fragments of their privacy.

She went to the web chamber and conjured his image on one gossamer curtain. Far away, he sat on a fine-carved chair with velvet upholstery and gilded lions' feet for legs. A rich house: he had been there some months already, and his hosts showed no sign of tiring of his company. At this moment, he sang in an upper room of the great keep, and half a dozen young women sat on cushions at his feet, enthralled by his music. His song was not of Delivev, however transmogrified, but of dragons and knights and brave deeds, and the listeners were flame-cheeked with the excitement of the tale. When the last note died away, they clapped their hands in delight, and when the delight wore off they sighed all around and complained of having to leave his music so early in the day. They shuffled out of his chamber with many a backward glance, many a maidenly blush at the smile he gave them all.

One stayed behind. She had wrapped herself in the arras as her sisters drifted out. So quiet she stood there that they never noticed she was not among them, or perhaps they did notice, but only after the door had shut firmly behind them. Their voices receded quickly beyond the heavy door, and Lorien turned away from it, laying his lute on the table as he often did. While his back was turned, she thrust the drapery aside and stepped toward him. The rustle of her skirts was loud in the new stillness of the room, and Lorien looked over his shoulder. She smiled at him then and held her arms out to him, and he moved toward her in a way that showed he had touched her before. They kissed and then he broke away from her, and his image loomed large in the web as he walked to it, bent close, and brushed it aside with a hand. The view of his room vanished as the silken latticework crumpled.

Delivev could have had her spiders spin afresh, but she did not. *Let them have their rendezvous if they wish, alone.* She found herself wondering what the young woman thought of her lover's action—perhaps that it was just a little quirk of his that he could not bear cobwebs in the corners of his room, nothing to pay any heed, even if it did seem to come over him at times when his mind should have been otherwise occupied. Delivev smiled sadly. In her observations of troubadours, she had noted that they never had any trouble finding love, no matter what their personal oddities, the ugly face, the crippled leg, the youth, the age; it was the music, she thought, and the tales they brought to women whose sole contact with the greater world they were. Only she, Delivev, with her silken windows to everywhere, was immune to the lure of the troubadour. She could hardly blame Lorien for thinking that she was the same as all the others, that she had brought him to her by magic for love.

I am too old, she thought, *for love.*

She raised an arm clad in black feathers and conjured a different castle upon the web, different faces, different voices. A piece of needlecraft rolled through the doorway of the web chamber and scrambled up the coverlet like a live creature, to give her hands something to work upon. In the web scene, too, a woman sat quiet in a high-backed chair, fingers busy with embroidery. But her clothing was bright, her smile

184

as sunny as the spring afternoon that entered her home through slitted windows. At her feet, two small boys were tumbling with a pair of dogs, laughing, squealing in their pleasure. Occasionally, their mother cautioned them not to be too rough with the animals.

Delivev thought of Cray, of course. She wished that she could hear him laugh once more.

The sun shone bright and dusty on the waxy leaves of the Seer's tree. Cray and Sepwin were dusty, too, from the long, dry ride. Gone were the chill, fast-flowing streams of the mountains, gone the muck that slowed their horses' steps, gone the pale green of spring's first growth, all far behind them. Summer had begun, hot, merciless, and the intermittent shade of the trees that overhung the road could scarcely moderate it.

In the entry to her home, she was waiting for them, a carafe of cool wine in her hands. "I knew you would come today."

They drank gratefully, then followed her inside to the room of the dark pool and the sandy floor, where the sun never penetrated. It was cold there, by contrast with the blazing summer outside, and within moments Cray's and Sepwin's sweat-soaked clothing was chill and clammy against their skin. Seeing them shiver, the Seer brought blankets from behind the door at the far end of the room, and they wrapped themselves snugly.

"You have had the bad news," said the Seer.

"I have," replied Cray, "and it was full as terrible as you foresaw. Now I hope you can tell me what to do next."

She sat him down on the rim of the pool, and seated herself beside him. With one hand she touched his forehead, where the sweat-damp hair clung in ringlets; with the other she caressed the surface of the water, as if it were a living creature to be petted. "How disappointing it was for you," she murmured. "And yet you put your time at Mistwell to good use."

"I took what I was offered, my lady. It was considerable."

"And you paid the price that was asked. You polished armor and chopped wood and fetched water and even buried offal in the frozen ground. And you did all these things without a word of complaint, without a surly glance, yes, with a smile and a cheerful word, though your heart ached within you. You are a good lad, Cray; I have seen that from the moment you first entered my house."

Cray shrugged. "They were kind to me. I did not want to seem ungrateful."

The Seer nodded at Sepwin, who sat huddled in his blanket on the sand at Cray's feet. "And your friend worked as well, though not without complaint; still, he did his share."

Sepwin looked up at her hesitantly. "He has muscles from swinging his sword, and I have none. It was harder for me. Still . . . I'd swear that both fireplaces in the main hall burned my choppings all winter. And not once did anyone kick me or spit on me for being a beggar. I'm not a beggar anymore. That's Cray's doing. What's a little wood-chopping in return for that? Even if I *did* complain."

Cray's hand snaked out of his blanket and delivered a playful cuff to Sepwin's ear. "You wouldn't be yourself if you didn't complain a bit."

"They would have you back at Mistwell," said the Seer. "Whenever you chose to go back, they would welcome both of you."

Cray looked at her steadily. "And will we go back?"

She dipped her hand into the water and lifted a cupped handful of it. Though the pool was night-dark, the liquid in her hand was clear and colorless, and it sparkled in the torchlight as she flattened her palm and let it dribble away. "Do you want to go back?" she said.

"I don't know."

"It would be a good place for you. You would make a name for yourself in service to the House of Ballat."

"Will I?"

She gazed at him sidelong, her hand uplifted, droplets of water still falling from her pale skin, like teardrop gemstones. "You still want to find your father. You would not have returned to me if the House of Ballat had been enough for you."

"Yes. Of course. Tell me what to do! You are my last hope. I have nowhere left to turn, my lady!"

"I could say . . . turn home. Or turn to Mistwell. But I know those are not the answers you seek." Her hand on his forehead moved down his face, to his cheek, to the line of his jaw, across his throat to the back of his neck. She cradled his head in her hand. "You have courage, lad. Courage must carry you to the only other means of answering your question."

"Tell me!"

Her wet hand touched his blanket-covered shoulder and gripped hard—through wool and chain and quilting he could feel the pressure. "You must go back to his grave," she said. "And you must dig up his bones and bring them to me. Every one of them. I need them all, don't leave a single bone behind."

He started, shrank away from her, but only a hairsbreadth, for she held him. "His bones?"

"I must have them. Then I can tell you where he was born, where raised. And you will go there and seek yourself. I can do no more than that."

"His bones," Cray whispered. He looked down at the pool, where the surface still rippled gently from the drops that had fallen from her hand. "I must disturb his bones?"

"There is no other way. His sword and shield have told us nothing. What else remains?"

"My lady . . . this is a hard request."

"I know."

"To tear him from the peace of the earth like a weed from a field of grain, to bundle his poor bones in a sack as if they were no more than billets of wood . . ." He swallowed against a thickness in his throat. "And . . . to expose to the light of day that which no longer belongs in it, wormy, rotting . . ." He closed his eyes against the vision that his words conjured.

"I promise you," the Seer said softly, "that after so many years in the earth there will be no worms. Just bones, clean bones. But you are the only one who can decide if your quest is important enough for this last effort." Her hands fell away from him.

Cray looked into her compassionate face, into her pale eyes that seemed to hold all the sorrows of the world in their depths . . . or at least all the sorrows of his own world. At that moment, she made him think of his mother, though it was only the expression and not the face itself that called that memory. He thought of his mother, and of all the nights of weeping that he knew, and all the nights there must have been before he was old enough to notice. Then he looked at Sepwin, companion of so many travels. "Feldar?" he said.

Wide-eyed, Sepwin returned his gaze. "What do you want me to say?"

"Will you come with me?"

Sepwin glanced from his friend to the Seer and back. "It's evil luck to dig up a grave. What has been buried must remain so, or the bones will curse you."

"I don't believe that," Cray said firmly. "I *do* believe that it is the ultimate disrespect to disturb a grave." He took a deep breath. "But he would understand that I have no other choice. I am too far along the trail to shirk now—I must follow it to the end, to whatever end."

"Well, he was your father," Sepwin said slowly. "I suppose if anyone has a right to disturb the grave, you have."

"You needn't come along if the prospect frightens you."

Sepwin's lips tightened. "I am not afraid. I, who have one eye blue and the other brown, am not afraid of silly superstitions! I'll go with you."

"Thank you, my friend." Cray's hand snaked out from beneath his blanket and met Sepwin's in midair, clasped tightly. "I will never forget this." He turned his face to the Seer. "What do you see now, lady, in my future?"

"I see a good friend," she replied, smiling.

"And what else? More misery?"

She touched his hand, their two hands, lightly. "I see considerable travel yet ahead of you; though you have journeyed far already, your quest has scarcely begun. There is misery, yes; how not? You are unraveling a lie, and therein dwells much misery. But I will not give you the advice I gave you once before; I know you will not take it. A good journey to you, Cray. I think I need not say . . . have courage."

Cray rose, throwing off the blanket, and he bowed to her. "I will see you again soon, my lady. Fare you well."

The summer sun seemed pleasantly warm after the chill of the cave. The two companions had ridden some distance, and their clothing had dried in the warm air and begun to dampen again with their sweat when Sepwin cleared his throat to speak.

"Will you tell your mother about this part of the quest?"

"No. She'd only try to talk me out of it. She'd have good reasons, too—all the reasons I've already thought of and rejected. Truly, though, she doesn't want to know who he was, nor anything about him. He was like a dream for her, and she doesn't want reality to spoil the dream. Perhaps if I had known him, I might feel the same." He shrugged. "But she will know, of course. The longer I am on this quest, the more I wish she were only an ordinary mortal, with no power to look over my shoulder, to know everything I do, everywhere I go. She will know, through her tapestry, but not until the deed is done."

"What will you tell her, then, when she asks what we're doing now?"

"I think . . . that the Seer asked for some soil from the grave to divine from. That I should have brought that before, along with the sword and shield, but I didn't know, of course, that it might be needed."

"You think she'll believe that?"

"Why not?"

"She might ask the Seer herself what you had been sent for."

"Only if the expression on your face is as it is now when next she sees you, Feldar. Perhaps you had best practice an innocent gaze until then."

"Innocent?"

"Yes. Just now you look like you've stolen a handful of gems and are afraid their owner is coming after you."

Sepwin looked down at his horse's mane. "I'll do my best."

"I, too," said Cray.

"You know," Sepwin murmured, after they had ridden on a bit, "we don't have a spade."

"We'll buy one along the way somewhere. There will be towns, Feldar, and wine and food and many a campsite between here and there." Cray sighed. "For once, I could wish to be a sorcerer and have the power to fly where I would instead of this endless riding."

"I'd rather ride," said Sepwin. "The fall from a horse is considerably less than the fall from the sky."

Cray smiled. "If I were a sorcerer, my friend, you would never fall. But I'd wager you'd keep your eyes closed the whole trip."

"What—these eyes closed to sorcery? After the things they have seen already?"

"They've seen precious little, Feldar."

"More than most mortal eyes." He grinned at his companion. "There aren't many ordinary folk who've had the chance to travel with such as you, Cray. You often say you're not a sorcerer, but you are sorcerer enough for me, believe me, or for anyone who has only a mortal's power over the world. When I tossed your spiders at those bandits, I felt your power, Cray, and though to you it is nothing, to me it was wondrous. Why you would give it up to be a mere knight is beyond my comprehension."

Cray regarded him sidelong. "If you had grown up with my paltry skills at sorcery, if you knew the greater powers that exist that are so far beyond me that they would take an ordinary mortal lifetime to learn properly, you would not think my few skills so wondrous."

"But you would have a longer life, as well, in which to learn them."

"What is that to me," asked Cray, "if I must spend that life in a way that gives me no contentment?"

"I could be content so, I think."

"You know who your father was."

"You care too much, Cray, about that. You are yourself, not him."

Cray shook his head. "I am not myself until I know who he was. I am no one without that knowledge." In his mind, he could hear his mother's soft weeping. "I don't expect you to understand, Feldar."

"I don't," said his friend. "But I will follow anyway, and hope for your sake that we will find an answer this time."

The hut was deserted. Its thatched roof had caved in since their visit the previous year, and the few pieces of simple furniture inside were ruined by snow and rain. Behind the hut, where the old man had kept his fire, where he had cultivated his grain and vegetables, was a tangle of weeds like the rest of the abandoned fields.

"He must have died this winter," said Sepwin.

"Or perhaps one of his children came back and took him away to a cheerier home," said Cray. He stood in the doorway, contemplating the ruined interior, lit by bright sunlight through the rent roof. "I don't see any body. There is his bed . . . empty."

"Some passerby may have buried him. Or he may lie in the fields somewhere."

"We'll look for him," said Cray. "We owe him a burial, surely."

They searched the overgrown fields and the woods nearby, but they found no trace of the old man, and at last they were forced to give up by the setting sun. In the twilight, they cleared the hut of its fallen roof, and Cray set his spiders to spin a new one of silk, to shelter them for the night.

Neither slept well, thinking of the task that awaited dawn light.

They had some small difficulty in finding the grave patch, so overgrown was it with weeds and grain gone wild. The three marker stones seemed like so many boulders among the tares, the mounds of the graves themselves like mere hummocks of the earth. The wild flowers that had decked them were lost now, in the rank greenery. Pulling tough stems out by the roots, Cray cleared the tangle from the third grave, the one with the roughest marker. Then he began to dig. The two companions only had one spade between them; when Cray tired of chopping at earth hardened with years of repose, Sepwin took over. They had burrowed almost the height of a man into the earth, marveling at

191

the diligent gravedigging of an old man, when Sepwin struck metal. Something chinked beneath the spade.

"Stop," said Cray, jumping down into the hole with his friend. "We'll damage them if we dig farther with that." He stooped and began to scrabble at the dirt with his knife and his bare hands. Sepwin tossed the spade up to the rim of the excavation and knelt to help him.

The sun was at its zenith, its rays illuminating as much of the bottom of the hole as they could at this season, by the time Cray and Sepwin had uncovered the entire suit of chain mail. The badly rusted chain was laid out flat, as if upon the body of a man; the rotted remnants of a surcoat covered the links, and the quilted padding was inside, brown and delicate, shredding at the lightest touch. Leather gloves and boots, half disintegrated, rested where hands and feet would have been.

There were no bones.

Cray dug on, after sending Sepwin to the surface with chain and cloth and leather. He dug on alone, with knife and bare hands, till the hole was too deep for him to climb from without a rope, till he needed a torch to show him the bottom, far from sunlight, far from the heat of the afternoon. He paid no heed to his friend's voice, falling continuously from above, begging him to come back to the daylight, pleading that no man, young or old, would dig a grave so deep. He dug on, till almost half of every clod he tossed upward to the rim fell back upon him, till water began to seep into his work and collapse the walls as quickly as he could dig out the floor. Only then, at last, did he rise to unsteady legs, fingers numb from the chilling mud, and allow his spiders to spin him a silken ladder for ascent to the realms of the living. Halfway up, he dropped the torch behind him, and it snuffed itself out in the wetness below. Black with muck, his hands bloody from long scrabbling, he clambered to the surface. He had found only stones.

Sepwin made him sit by their campfire, where a pot of stew was bubbling for the evening meal. The sun was low and red in the west, and already the summer air was beginning to cool. Cray could hardly believe he had been digging for so long. He stretched his hands out to the flames, and the numbness began to drain from them with that warmth, but they shook—his whole body shook, muscles overstrained, as if he had been swinging a sword all day. Sepwin brought a cloth and water and began to clean the dirt and blood from his companion's skin, from gouges and scrapes that bled afresh with the rubbing. Cray tried to help him, awkwardly, but his fingers were too weary, too leaden to grasp the cloth, so he gave up and merely sat still, letting Sepwin tend him.

"You'll hardly be able to move tomorrow," said Sepwin.

"I'll be all right." He stared down at the damp and rusty pile of chain near his feet. Earth still clung to it, and the scent of the earth as well, dank and moldy. "What reason could there be in the world, Feldar," he murmured, "for burying the armor without the man who wore it?"

Sepwin poured more water on the cloth and gently swabbed at his friend's face. "He said he buried the man."

"He couldn't have!"

Sepwin shrugged. "What motive would he have for lying, Cray? He didn't know who you were."

Cray's head drooped low. "Then the body must have been dug up since it was buried."

"The old man would have known about that, surely."

"Not if it happened after he was gone."

"The ground was hard," said Sepwin. "Too hard to have been disturbed so recently."

"You think so?"

"I've handled a plow. I know virgin soil. Fifteen years is time enough for a grave to become as firm."

"Then he was never there at all. We come back to a lie, the old man's lie."

"I think he spoke the truth," said Sepwin. "He buried a body there. It wore this suit of chain, the clothing."

Cray squinted at him in the fading light. "How do you explain the lack of bones, then, Master Feldar?"

Sepwin reached for the stew pot, poured a share into the bowl Cray used and another into his own. "I explain it as you would, if you were thinking properly, if you weren't so tired that you'll fall asleep before you've had dinner if you don't eat quickly. I explain it by magic."

"Magic?"

Sepwin nodded. "Where you are involved, my friend, I always suspect magic."

"But there was no magic involved in his death."

"No? Well, perhaps not, but . . . were you there to judge it?"

Cray frowned. "You think the old man was deceived somehow?"

"I don't know what to think. Only that there is no other explanation at all. How else would one draw a body out of its grave without disturbing the wrappings or the grave?"

Cray closed his eyes, let the savory smell from the bowl in his hands fill his nostrils. "How else indeed?" he murmured.

Sepwin poked him in the shoulder. "Eat now. We can talk about it tomorrow."

Cray ate.

In the morning, they gathered up the chain and the rotted cloth and a spiderweb sack full of the soil from the grave, to take back to the Seer with them.

"I seem to have told my mother the truth after all," Cray said, loading the parcel of earth into one of his saddlebags.

"Do you think the Seer will be able to see anything in that dirt?"

"I don't know. That's why we'll bring all of this." He shrugged. "I even have a few of the wild flowers here. The old man must have planted them years ago. Maybe they'll help."

"Something will help," said Sepwin. "Remember the lady Helaine said that you had a long journey still ahead of you, that your quest had barely begun."

"Yes," said Cray, mounting Gallant. "I take heart from that, from knowing that however bleak things look right now, this isn't the end. Come on now, this looks like a good day for traveling."

The Seer shook her head slowly. "None of this tells

me anything, Cray. The chain, the clothing, comes from the same place the sword and shield did. Nor have these any more identity than those had. The earth and flowers . . ." She gazed at him sadly. "They are empty. There was never a human body buried in that earth; human flesh never nourished these flowers. I know nothing more about him now than I did the last time you saw me, Cray." She reached out for him, to touch his shoulders lightly with both her hands. "I am sorry."

"It can't be true." He searched her pale eyes. "There must be more."

"There is nothing."

Cray covered his face with his hands. "What shall I do now?"

Sepwin, who had stood behind his friend while they spoke to the Seer, now fell to his knees before her in the sand. "Kind lady," he said, "if it be true that no human flesh was ever buried in this earth, then what was it that the old man saw and spoke to and buried? What was it that chopped his wood for the winter, if it was not a human being?"

The Seer gazed down at him, a frown marring the smooth whiteness of her forehead. "I don't know. An illusion, perhaps."

"Wearing real armor?"

"Even so."

"Then . . . if Cray's father was an illusion . . . who was his father?"

The Seer dipped one hand into her pool. "You must understand something about the limits of my power, Feldar Sepwin," she said. "Ordinary human beings are as books to me, the pages of the past transparent and full of bold, black writing, the pages of the future blurred and shadowy—yet I am accustomed to interpreting shadows. You are such a book, and you cannot close yourself to me. But Cray . . . Cray has lived most of his life within the walls of Castle Spinweb, and there I cannot see, nor into any sorcerer's home. I read only the pages of his book that were written beyond Spinweb's confines; there are enough of them, though, to show me the important facts of his life. Of his mother, I can see nothing; she and all the others of the sorcerous breed have lives forever beyond me." She nodded slowly. "There is sorcery at work here, and not just on Cray's mother's side. But I can give no aid in puzzling it out."

Cray gripped her arm. "Who can?"

"Oh, there are those who *can,* I am sure, but none who *will.*"

"What do you mean?"

"Whoever your father is, he has gone to great lengths to hide his identity, or someone has done so for him. There are sorcerers who can ferret out such information, they who command demons, but none of them would betray a fellow by giving it to you. They leave each other alone—you know that, Cray; they keep uneasy truces among themselves, and none will chance another's wrath by revealing his secrets."

"Not even for a price?"

She flicked her fingers against the water, making it ripple in overlapping circles. "You don't have that kind of price."

"I could earn it. Even if it took me years."

"It wouldn't be gold, Cray. A demon can find its master all the gold he needs."

. "What then?"

"Knowledge. Power."

Cray bowed his head.

"I know this is a hard end for you, lad," she said softly.

He clasped his hands and, elbows on his knees, leaned forward to rest his brow on the interlaced fingers. "Where is the long quest you prophesied? Where is the journey scarcely begun? Am I to rush away from here to search aimlessly through the world, asking at every door for my father? Am I to ride on until I drop, without plan or hope?"

She touched his hair with her wet fingers. "There is another way."

His head snapped up. "Tell me."

"I don't think you'll like it."

"Let me judge."

"The secrets of this world, even sorcerers' secrets, are available to the demons. They pass human information freely among them, like so much gossip, and they will give it to the person who knows how to ask for it. Learn to summon such a creature yourself, and it will answer your questions."

Cray's lips pursed whitely. "Become a sorcerer, you mean."

"Yes."

"And put aside all I have learned, all I have striven for, all I have *been* for my whole life?"

"If you would know your father's name, yes."

Cray rose heavily and turned away from her. The white sand yielded under his feet as he walked slowly from the pool. "My lady," he murmured, "that is a heavier price than gold." He lifted his eyes to the walls, to their flashing specks of crystal, like stars in a firmament of black rock. Wavering torchlight gave them the illusion of motion, and that made him feel dizzy. A whirlpool seemed to yawn beneath his feet, sucking at him like the muck of the swamp, and he reached out for some support to keep him from falling in, but there was none. And then, suddenly, there was: Sepwin, gripping his friend's arm with surprising strength.

"You have the courage," Sepwin said, "to do as the lady Helaine says, and afterward to go back to knighthood."

"I wanted him to be proud of me," Cray muttered. "What is knighthood to me now that I know he wasn't a knight?"

"You don't know anything of the sort."

"He was not a knight!" Cray said loudly, and his voice echoed from the walls. "No proper knight would have been involved in such a lie!"

"Perhaps not a *proper* knight . . ."

"Beggar or sorcerer, sage or fool—he could have been anyone!" He patted Sepwin's hand that clutched his arm. "Ah, Feldar, I thought it could be no worse than on that day at Mistwell. How wrong I was! And how right the lady Helaine . . . The apprenticeship will be long, a long journey indeed. But my mother will be pleased."

"What will you tell her?" asked Sepwin.

Cray looked at his free arm, slipped the sleeve up to expose the chain he had worn so long. Spiders rested

197

within some of the links, as if in tiny nests. "I shall tell her that I have changed my mind. No more than that. No more."

"Will she believe that, after all this time?"

"She'll want to believe it. And it's true enough." Without looking back at her, he said to the Seer, "Tell me how I may apprentice myself to the proper sort of sorcerer, my lady. I would do so as soon as possible."

"I can communicate your desire to the sorcerous community. Surely there will be some few who wish apprentices but have no children of their own. You are welcome to stay here, Cray, until one is found."

"Thank you, lady. You are very kind. But I cannot impose. I have not even paid your fee."

"There will be time for that, when you are a sorcerer and have something worth paying with."

He glanced back at her sharply. "You knew. You knew all the time that this would happen."

She smiled at him. "I knew that, one way or another, you would return to sorcery. I knew, because I could not see anything after this last journey of yours. But what sort of sorcery you would choose . . . I could only guess that. Don't be angry with me, Cray. I have given you choices, not made them for you." She rose from the rim of the pool and stretched a hand out to him. "Come. There are rooms and rooms beyond this one, and soft beds and every comfort of the finest castle. Accept my hospitality."

Stiffly, he bowed. "As you wish, my lady. But first, Master Feldar, will you help me shed this suit of chain? I haven't any further need for it."

Sepwin helped him, and so did the Seer, and both pretended not to notice the tears that streamed down his cheeks as the links rattled and chinked and dropped finally to the pure white sand.

ᵛᵍ CHAPTER TEN

Rezhyk stormed across the workshop, his metal-studded boots ringing like bronze bells upon the polished floor. All around him, the minor demons that lit the chamber cringed in response to his anger, their flames burning low in the sconces that had never held candles. Their master hardly noticed. "Why did you not tell me about the child?" he shouted.

Gildrum sat on her high stool, twisting one blond braid slowly in her hands. "We always assumed there would be no child," she said softly. "We were so certain, I never thought to question that certainty." From the corner of her eye, she watched him pace the confines of the room. Rarely had she seen him in such a rage, not since the day Delivev Ormoru spurned him. "You never sent any of us to find out if there was a child."

He shook a finger at her, sharply, as if he could spray lightning bolts from the tip, and gems and gold flashed on his rigid hand. "This is *your* fault! Your advice has brought us to this pass!"

Gildrum dipped her head meekly and stared down at the pale blue fabric that covered her knees. "As you say, my lord."

"Would that I had never listened to you!" His hand curled into a fist and then opened, to clutch at his own chest and the heavy brocade that cloaked the cloth-of-gold shirt. "A child," he muttered. "What sane woman, sorceress or no, would want to keep a stranger's child?" His free hand struck the workbench a resounding blow, and the brazier jumped with its force, scattering some of the coals upon the smooth work surface. Heedless of their heat, Rezhyk swept the embers to the floor with a bare palm and crushed them under his foot. "A momentary diversion—of course I can understand that, as who would not? But to keep the fruit of a few night's pleasure, to throw away a portion of one's life in raising the by-blow of an ordinary mortal—it is beyond belief! What can I think of a woman who would do such a thing?"

"That she is very different from yourself," Gildrum murmured.

"Unless—she suspects!"

"Suspects what, my lord?"

"That you were something more than a mere knight."

"I never gave cause for any such impression, my lord. I obeyed your command and used no magic near her. Nor did she ever demonstrate any suspicion . . ."

"Afterward, my Gildrum, when you were gone, when she had plenty of time to think, alone."

"To think on what, my lord? There was no evidence."

Rezhyk leaned over the brazier, where the few remaining coals barely glowed deep red. He picked up a glass rod which lay nearby and stirred the embers with it, prodding thin yellow flames from them before they crumbled to ash. "She has some motive here," he said. "She is a wily woman. Her hand is in his request for apprenticeship, I know it. What would the boy want with another sort of magic than his mother's, after all? He knows nothing of demons; why should he want to master them?"

"Do you find that so hard to understand, my lord?" asked Gildrum. "You chose them yourself."

"Both my parents were demon-masters; I never thought to be anything else. But his mother has power over creatures of the earth—spiders and snakes and other such low life. She thinks that a superior form of sorcery, deluded woman; she is too proud to consider that something else might be greater. She scorned my demon mastery. Why then would she advise a child of hers to apprentice to it?"

"Perhaps she did not advise him so, my lord. Perhaps he has chosen to ignore whatever advice she gave him. I have observed, in my travels among human beings, that children do not always listen to their parents' advice."

"I wish I dared believe that." He gripped the glass rod tightly, his eyes staring off into nothing.

Gildrum wound the curling end of one braid about her fingers, like ribbon around a spindle, waiting for her master's next statement, and when some moments had passed in silence, she murmured, "What else might you believe, my lord?"

His voice was low and distant. "That she has changed her mind. That she has decided to add the powers of a demon-master to her strength."

"But my lord, if she scorns them as inferior . . . ?"

"She scorns them, my Gildrum, but even she could not deny that they have their uses. With two kinds of sorcery at her command, she would be a formidable power indeed among sorcerers. Her enemies would lie awake at night, wondering how they could defend themselves, while she slept easy." He turned his head, and his eyes focused on the demon, a baleful stare. "I am her enemy, my Gildrum." His hand, which gripped the rod so tensely that the knuckles showed white, jerked convulsively, and the glass snapped between his thumb and forefinger. The broken end struck the workbench with a high, musical sound and rolled back across the smooth surface to the edge, over the edge, and shattered on the floor.

Gildrum slid off the stool. "Are you hurt, my lord?" she asked, reaching for his hand with both of hers.

He lowered his gaze to his hand then, as if only just realizing what he had done, and he opened his fingers. A bright bead of blood was collecting on the first knuckle. "It's nothing," he said.

Gildrum peered close at the injured flesh, found no glass in the wound, then knelt to gather the glittering fragments that lay at her master's feet. She swept them together as if they were crumbs of bread fallen from the dinner table, with hands that could not be cut. "You have your shirt, my lord," she said, "and your own demons. Why do you worry so?"

"I know the limits of her power now, and I am safe

201

from them," he replied. "But afterward, when she has control of rings . . ." He shook his head.

"It won't be *her* control," said Gildrum.

"No? He is her son, is he not, my Gildrum? He sees the world as she has taught him to see it. His enemies are her enemies. Will you tell me such a mother and son would not work together for their ends?"

"I don't know, my lord. Still, they are two separate people; their desires cannot be identical."

Rezhyk flicked the drop of blood from his finger into the embers of the brazier, where it hissed softly and was gone. "Of course she would do better to gain power by apprenticing herself," he muttered. "But what sorcerer would be mad enough to take her on? Or even to let her step inside the confines of his home? Even the most foolish of us—even one . . . besotted with love of her . . ." He grimaced, as if something bitter had just touched his tongue. "Well, such a one might let her in, but even he would never show her the secrets of his art." He turned his back to the workbench and leaned against it, crooking his elbows to rest them upon it. "Her unschooled child, though, is a different matter. Innocent. Unformed. There are those among us who would see no harm in his apprenticeship."

Gildrum dusted the glass particles from her hands into the bin that normally received ashes and discarded metal fragments. "You think someone will take him on, my lord?"

"Eventually, yes." He sighed. "And then I shall have seven years, or perhaps ten, in which to wonder what will happen when he is mature."

"She has never tried to do you any harm, my lord, in all the years you have been proof against her."

"It has not been so many years, my Gildrum. And perhaps she has only been waiting . . . until her partner was ready." He touched his chest with both palms. "Will this be enough then? Or must I spend the next seven years finding some better protection?" He bowed his head, and his eyes closed. "What shall I do, my Gildrum? What *can* I do?"

The demon climbed back onto the high stool and

swung her legs in the space below the seat. "My lord, you regretted taking the last advice I offered."

He raised his head to glare at her. "Have you a suggestion? Speak!"

Gildrum shrugged. "Become her friend."

Color rushed to Rezhyk's cheeks. "I expect no such nonsense from *you.*"

"Then trust the strength you have, my lord. Ringforge is solid; I built it as well as fortress could be built. Add in the shirt you wear, and what more defense could be devised?"

Rezhyk's lips tightened. "Well, I must know, at least, to whom he goes. You will discover that for me, my Gildrum."

"Yes, my lord; nothing easier."

"I must know the range available to him, how many and what sort of demons his master—when he has one —commands."

"Such information can be obtained, my lord," said Gildrum, "if you will give me leave to spend some time in my own world."

"Yes. Yes, I shall. I need you for many things, but this is more important than any of them." His hands closed into fists. "If only there were some way to steer him to a lesser sorcerer, to one whose powers were so circumscribed that I would have no need to worry. To trick him, somehow, into making a poor choice." He frowned mightily. "No, to convince some sorcerer of little skill to ask for him before a better one does— *there's* the nut. What does the boy know, after all? He'll probably go with the first to make an offer. Who could I ask, my Gildrum? Whose powers are so insignificant that I need not fear them?"

"I can think of one or two, my lord, but they owe you no favors."

"No one owes me favors, my Gildrum. But they fear me."

Gildrum shrugged. "Do they fear you enough to train a person they know nothing about, that they may have to fear as well someday?"

"No sorcerer need fear his own apprentice."

"The apprentice is usually one's flesh and blood, my

lord, and such a tie makes a good reason for that lack of fear. But in this case . . ."

"You think the teacher fears the pupil, my Gildrum? Hardly. Who is better suited to combat the student's sorcery than the one who taught it to him?"

Gildrum smiled. "Just so, my lord. That leaves a clear choice. There *is* a person to apprentice Delivev Ormoru's child in a way which will suit you."

"Who?"

"Don't you know, my lord?"

"Speak, demon!"

She laughed. "Why look in any mirror, my lord. Look to the bronze of yonder wall, and you shall see his face."

Cray and Sepwin listened at the door, held barely ajar by a dagger's blade. Beyond the panel lay the chamber of the pool, and the Seer, speaking softly to a great prince of the ordinary world. The youths had been in her house many days already, and this was the first visitation in that time, an old man seeking the future of his line. He wore much gold and heavy brocade, but his shoulders seemed to stoop under more than the load of garments.

"There will be sons yet, with a new wife," the Seer was telling him, "but *you* will see none of them grown."

Sepwin nudged Cray. "I could have told him that," he whispered. His eye to the aperture, he could see a sliver of the room—the Seer's black-clad back and her questioner, seated on the rim of the pool, his eyes magnetized by her fingers trailing in the water. "You don't need to be a Seer to know that one won't last another ten years."

"Hush," said Cray. "He'll hear you."

"Will my nephew inherit then?" asked the prince. His voice was thin and reedy, and staccato with his anxiety.

"There will be a joint regency," the Seer replied. "Your wife and her father, till her eldest by you comes of age. So choose her well, O prince; your people will suffer otherwise."

"Choose her and choose her father, too, you mean,"

he muttered. He shook his head. "Tell me whom it shall be!"

The Seer's fingers splashed in the pool. "Are you no judge of women that I must select your bride? Or of men? Go home and look around you. You are no beardless boy ruled by your heart alone."

"Tell me," he said again. "I've paid you well to read my future."

"Have you paid me also to govern your land? For that is what I do if I choose your wife for you."

"But you *know* the future . . ."

"I do. And if I should tell you, O prince . . . ever after you will wonder, I promise you, if you married her because it was wise or because I told you to."

The old man was silent for a long time, staring into the pool as if he could see more than blackness there. At last he stood up stiffly. "I thank you, lady, for your words. I must return to my country now; I have been gone too long already."

"You will find your people safe and happy and eager to greet you."

"And the fathers of the eligible girls the most eager of all?"

"Undoubtedly."

He bowed. "Well, I know, at least, which ones will be disappointed."

The Seer inclined her head. "That is the first step, O prince."

He turned and strode down the tunnel that led to sunlight, his step firmer than his voice and bearing would have suggested. Outside, his train waited, horses and men sweating in the heat of the day; the caravan was lighter by a chest of gold than when it had arrived. The chest lay at the Seer's feet, half buried in the sand. She had not bothered to open it and verify the contents—she needed neither sight nor smell nor touch of the coins to know they were sufficient.

"You may come out from behind the door now, lads," she said.

Rather sheepishly, they emerged. "We meant no discourtesy," Cray began. "We were only very curious, lady."

"And who would not be?" she said, smiling at them. "You think I took no account of that when I offered you my hospitality? Youth is all curiosity, is it not, Cray?"

"I suppose that must be true . . . if I am any sample, lady."

"And from your listening at the door, Cray—what have you learned?"

"That you are wise as well as skilled in your art. But I think I knew that already."

One of her eyebrows arched, white against her pale flesh. "At my age, I take that as my due, not as flattery. And you, Master Feldar—what say you?"

Sepwin grinned. "That a Seer must know which questions to answer and which to turn aside with a deft hand."

She trailed four fingers in the water, and ripples spread outward from them on the dark surface. "A Seer must know which are the true questions," she said, "and which are those best left unanswered. I gave the prince what he needed, no more."

"You gave him advice," insisted Sepwin, "that he could have found closer to home, and for less gold."

She fixed him with her eyes, a strong, steady gaze. "Do you think he would have listened, closer to home? He will choose well enough without my help. He is a lucky man, leaving his people in good hands. I have read other futures that were not so bright."

"I wouldn't call his future bright—to die before his children are grown."

"But now," said Cray, "at least he knows he'll live to beget them."

"Just so," said the Seer.

Sepwin shivered suddenly. "Death," he said. "That's what you see in every person who comes to you. At the end of the path, after all the twists and turns, the good fortune and bad—death."

"Everyone dies."

"And for yourself, lady?"

"I see my death, yes. At the moment, it is comfortably far away."

"And . . . mine?"

"Do you really want to know, Master Feldar? I think not."

"Is it by stoning? Hanging? Fire?"

The Seer shook her head slowly. "Where is the gold to pay me for this answer, Master Feldar? I give no free gift of the future."

"Are you saying I will never be able to pay you?"

"Lad, these are foolish questions. Why so concerned with death, when you have scarcely begun to live?"

"I don't know," he said, and his arms crossed over his chest, and his hands gripped his own shoulders. He stared into the pool. "Of a sudden, I feel uncertain. What will I do when Cray apprentices to sorcery? Where will I go?"

"Why, with me, of course," said Cray. Then he added, hesitantly, "If . . . that is your wish."

"Go with you as what? Your servant? You think a sorcerous household would even let such as me in the door? There isn't a scrap of magic about me—you've said that often enough yourself."

Cray frowned. "I hadn't thought about it."

"Well, I have. Oh, yes, I have indeed. And so I ask the future, to know if the old, beggar's life lies ahead of me, but my lady Seer tells me nothing."

"You worry too soon, Master Feldar," said the Seer.

"I have worried all my life," he replied. "Why leave off now? While I have been with you, Cray, I have looked out at the world with both eyes, I have talked freely, I have known friendship for the first time in my life. Now I must give it all up. I must go back to jeers and terror and loneliness."

Cray caught his shoulder. "Feldar, perhaps no one will take me as an apprentice."

"Someone will," said Sepwin. "You are one of them."

"Then . . ." He looked to the Seer. "My lady, what is the chance of finding a sorcerer to change one of Feldar's eyes to match the other?"

Sepwin's head snapped up. "I have nothing to pay such a sorcerer with."

"I will pay," said Cray.

"Cray . . ."

"Whatever the price. Well, lady, what say you?"

"I will search," she said.

"Diligently," said Cray.

"Of course."

Cray grinned at his friend. "Come, Feldar, we need a good gallop to stretch our bones. We've been underground too long. I feel my skin paling by the hour." When Sepwin nodded, wordless, Cray linked an arm with his and drew him down the tunnel toward the sunshine. "We'll be back for supper," he called to the Seer.

"I know," she said, but so softly that they did not hear her. She turned to the pool then and stroked the cool surface with the flat of both hands, crooning a tuneless lullaby, as if to a sleeping babe. Presently, the water cleared, to her eyes alone, and showed other times and other places, all scattered with the pinpoint reflections of the crystals set in the chamber walls. She was still there, watching distant events without much interest, when a flash of light in the depths of the pool heralded a change in the view it showed. Abruptly, the water was a cloud-flecked blue—the image of the sky just outside the entrance to the Seer's home. Through the clear air fell an object like a sheet of parchment, its edges curling slightly as it wafted downward; but sunlight glanced from its surface as from polished metal, flashing about the cave again and again. The lady Helaine rose slowly from her perch on the pool's rim and walked down the tunnel and through the tree trunk, arriving in real sunshine just as the object fluttered to earth at her feet. She stooped to pick it up, a sheet of the thinnest bronze foil, light as parchment, inscribed with a sorcerous message.

For Cray.

The lads returned with a kerchief full of mushrooms, a surprise for their hostess, gathered in the shady woods where they had rested after racing their mismatched steeds. But when they entered her kitchen, it was their own surprise that had to be smiled away, amid jesting on the futility of keeping secrets from a Seer, for she was waiting by the kitchen fire, with a pot of pale butter already melted for their forest bounty. Supper proved a simple meal, but Cray and

Sepwin ate with good appetite after their afternoon's exercise. When they had done, the lady Helaine brought out the message.

SMADA REZHYK DESIRES TO INTERVIEW CRAY OR-MORU FOR APPRENTICESHIP. TRANSPORTATION WILL BE PROVIDED AT DAWN.

Cray fingered the foil. "What does he mean—transportation will be provided?"

"I presume he'll send a demon for you," said the Seer. "He's master to any number of them and can surely spare one for this service."

"Does he live so far away that I can't ride my Gallant there?"

"Far enough. And why should he wait all those days for you to ride to him when his own devices can bring you there as swift as the wind?"

"But if he decides he doesn't want me . . . ?"

"He'll return you here, I'm sure. Then you can wait for the next offer." She leaned closer to him, across the supper table. "But you would be well advised, Cray, to be on your best behavior for Smada Rezhyk. Who knows how many other sorcerers will be in the market for apprentices in the near future?"

Cray smoothed the foil on the tabletop, ran his palm over the embossed writing in the mirrorlike surface. Among the words, he could see his own reflection, bronze-tinted. "What is he like, this Smada Rezhyk?"

The Seer shrugged. "Like most of the sorcerous breed, he avoids revealing much of himself to others. He is no longer young, I know. And he has considerable power. You could do far worse than becoming his apprentice."

"But is he . . . pleasant?"

"As to that, I cannot say. But you shall meet him yourself and be in a better position to judge than I. And if he should prove too unpleasant . . . well, he will not force you to stay with him, I am sure."

"I have never known any sorcerer but my mother."

She touched his hand. "Are you afraid to meet him, Cray?"

"Not afraid. Just . . . uneasy." He glanced at Sepwin. "I would feel more comfortable if Feldar could come along."

"The invitation did not include me," said Sepwin. "I'd rather not presume on a sorcerer's hospitality."

"He is wise," said the Seer.

"Careful. I've always tried to be careful."

"Listen, Feldar," said Cray. "If things don't work out . . . if you can't come with me on my apprentice-ship, and if . . . if the lady Helaine can't find some-one to make your eyes better, or if you decide you don't want that . . . I'm sure my mother would take you in. You could learn weaving magic and be one of us, and your eyes would never matter again."

"You mean, I should take your place back at Spin-web?" asked Sepwin.

"Yes, that's it. She's been lonely since I left, you know that."

"She's been lonely, but not for me, Cray."

"It would be good for both of you, I know it."

Sepwin looked away from his friend. "You want me to go and live in a castle full of spiders . . . and worse. If *you* were going there, I would consider it, but . . ."

"You don't hate spiders any more, Feldar."

"No, but I don't love them either. Or snakes." He shook his head. "That sort of magic is not for me, Cray."

Cray looked long at the Seer. "You must help him," he said at last.

"I will do my best," said the Seer. "But ultimately, the choice of his future lies with him."

Cray rose from the bench. He rolled the bronze foil into a thin cylinder and tucked it inside his shirt. "Dawn comes early, and I'll have to be ready for it. Therefore I must take my leave of you." He turned toward the door that opened on the outer chambers, the opposite direction from his sleeping place.

"Where are you going?" asked Sepwin.

"Outside. To spin a web and speak to my mother. It's time I did that. Past time."

"You can spin it here," said the Seer.

"Thank you, but . . . I'd rather be alone."

As Cray opened the door, he heard Sepwin remark

to the Seer, "You know, he walks different now that he doesn't wear the chain anymore."

"And he speaks of the sorcerous kind as 'us,'" she replied.

He shut the door firmly behind him.

In the first instant she saw him, Delivev wanted to reach out to her son and feel of his forehead. "You don't look well," she said. "Is that cave too damp for you?"

He shook his head. "I'm just tired. Mother . . . I have made a decision."

"Yes?"

"I'm going to apprentice myself to a sorcerer."

Her mouth twitched, and she folded her hands tightly in her lap. "Have you met one, in your travels, that you have some special feeling for?"

"No. The Seer has cast about for me, and one has answered her call. I speak to him tomorrow about taking me on."

"Who would this sorcerer be?"

"Smada Rezhyk."

"Rezhyk? That slave master?" She frowned. "Why in the world would you want to apprentice to him, my son?"

"He wants an apprentice. He is willing to interview me."

"Rezhyk!" She pursed her lips and stared out at Cray through the web. "And what is wrong with weaving, now that you've decided to come back to sorcery? And why? Why do you change your mind now, Cray? What happened to your quest for knighthood? I thought you enjoyed your winter at Mistwell." Her knuckles were white with the strain of clasping her own flesh, and she sat at the very edge of the velvet coverlet, leaning toward the web as if she could thereby come closer to her child. "You have kept yourself from me these last months, my son. This winter you used the webs little, and I thought I understood that, for you were surrounded by ordinary mortals. But since you left the Seer on your quest to fetch . . . to fetch soil . . . you have been vague. And the tapestry, too, has been vague, as if you were walking through a fog, with nothing of any consequence going on about you. Only sorrow and more sorrow. I can hardly bring myself to look at the tapestry these days. I know what it will show me. I only glance . . . to know that you are alive. And now you tell me that you've changed your mind. . . ."

"Mother, I have sufficient reason. The quest for knighthood has not brought me happiness. Perhaps I can find it in sorcery."

"Of course you can. But . . . why choose Rezhyk's kind of sorcery? You know nothing of it."

"Perhaps that is why it lures me."

"You have talent; I don't doubt you'll do well, Cray, but the demon-masters are cold creatures. They deal in metal and gems, lifeless things, and creatures as different from the flesh we know as stones are from butterflies. More so! You know something about the natural world; it is a healthier one, warmer, more real. If you want sorcery, my son, come home and I shall teach you marvels you've never dreamed of. There is so much to learn—"

"I have decided, Mother. I will be master to demons. Some of them are made of flame—surely they are warm enough."

"It is the heart that is cold, my son, not the demons."

"Do you know Smada Rezhyk?"

She nodded. "I knew him once, long ago. He is a hard and selfish man, and vain as well."

"All sorcerers are selfish—you told me that yourself. As for vanity . . . the Seer tells me he has great power, and a man of such power comes by his vanity honestly."

"I would be a more congenial teacher, I promise you."

"I think I will work harder for a stranger."

"Do you think, perhaps, that there is more power to be had in the mastering of demons than in the natural world? Is that the reason you choose this sort of sorcery, my son? It is not true."

Cray reached out toward her with one hand. "Don't think, Mother, that I love you any less because I have chosen another kind of magic than your own. But it is what I shall have, if he will take me, and you know you cannot change my mind."

"I know." She bowed her head. "Very well, Cray; if this is what you must do, I can't say I understand it, but I accept it. If you have found your future . . . I accept it." She loosed her hands, let them fall limp apart. "His castle's name is Ringforge; it is a vast place, far more impressive than Spinweb. If polished metal impresses you. The tapestry will cease the instant you step inside its walls. I won't know . . . but then, what can happen to you there? You'll be safer with him than out in the wide world as a knight. You'll be safe. But . . . I won't know what is happening to you."

"I'll try to speak to you as often as possible, Mother."

She looked up at him, and her lips twisted into a sad smile. "He won't want that, Cray. He knows, I suppose, that you are my son."

Cray nodded.

"Then he'll lock you fast away within his walls. He won't want you giving away his secrets to another sorcerer. Even if she be your mother."

"Well, if I must, I'll call you only in his presence, so that he'll see I give away no secrets. Surely he won't deny me contact with my only family!"

"No? He has no family. Why should he care for yours?"

Cray frowned. "I'll speak to him about it. And . . . if he is adamant . . . perhaps I shall seek some other, more lenient master."

Delivev shook her head gently. "I have shielded you, Cray. Or perhaps it is that you have shielded yourself, with all those dreams of knighthood. You never gave yourself time to understand the sorcerous community, never wanting to be part of it. You'll find no more lenient master. Oh, Rezhyk will be harder than some, I don't doubt it. I never cared much for the man—he wears a shell of bronze around his heart as well as his body. But you won't find a master who'll let an apprentice communicate with another sorcerer. Not and allow him to remain an apprentice. You must give up, you see, or else come home and learn from me as your teacher. Otherwise, we part now, my son, until you are a full-fledged sorcerer. And then . . . you may not want to associate with me, even though I am your mother. You may be as selfish as the rest of us."

"Not I!" said Cray.

"When you have power, you may think differently. Especially when it is a different kind of power than your mother's. You may even learn to look down on me as a lesser sort of creature who only manipulates the natural world and has no power over . . . what you may consider greater things. You will be wrong, of course, but you may think so anyway."

"Mother, I would never look down upon your sort of sorcery. Nor any sort. I would not pretend to compare your sphere with any other, any more than I would compare horses to flowers."

"I hope it will be so."

"It shall be."

"And Cray—I will always be your friend, I promise you."

"Mother! You have no need to say such a thing."

"Other parents and children have not remained friends in our art, Cray, when they separated as you and I are about to do."

"I shall always be your friend, Mother, no matter what happens."

"I am glad to hear it. Take care of yourself, my dear." Her voice cracked on the final word, and she could not help lifting her hand to her throat, to soothe the pain that was building there. "You must forgive me," she whispered. "I can say no more."

"I'll speak to you soon, Mother, to tell you how the interview was."

She nodded. "Good night."

"Good night."

The web darkened, but Delivev was no longer looking at it. Her sight turned inward, her eyes seeing her son as a babe, as a child, as a youth on his great gray horse. And she marveled that she could be losing him a second time. *His father, at least,* she thought, *I only lost once.*

The eagle swooped down out of the sky, its feathers glinting bronze in the dawnlight. Had it been a true bird it could have perched in the branches of the great tree that was the entrance to the Seer's home; but it was huge, vaster than fifty eagles rolled together, and its feathers were truly bronze, not merely the color of the metal. It landed on the road instead, then, and its enormous wings brushed the dewy grass on either side of the path before they folded at its sides. It opened its beak, but instead of emitting a bird's cry, it called Cray's name in thundering tones.

The Seer and Cray and Sepwin had been waiting just inside the arch in the tree trunk, wondering what form Rezhyk's demon transportation would take. Now Cray emerged and announced that he was ready, and the lady Helaine and his companion of so many months stayed within the shady shelter of the tree, peering out.

"You will take care of Gallant while I am gone," he had said to Sepwin.

"As if he were my own."

They had shaken hands then. "I'll ask him if I can bring you with me. I'm not afraid to ask. Do you truly want to come?"

"Yes, of course. But he won't—"

"Hush, Feldar. I will do my best to convince him."

Sepwin looked into his eyes. "I fear I will not see you for a long time, my friend."

"I'll see you after the interview," said Cray, and he walked out to the dawnlight.

The great eagle dipped its head toward Cray, turning first one dark eye upon the lad and then the other. When he was close beside it, Cray perceived that there were handholds among the metal feathers of its back, and straps to fasten the passenger securely aboard.

"I am ready," said Cray. "How shall I mount, O bird?"

"You may not mount," replied the bird, and its voice stirred the leaves on the Seer's tree and made the dew shake loose of the grass at the roadside.

"How not?" inquired Cray. "Have you not been sent for me by the sorcerer Smada Rezhyk?"

"For you," rumbled the bird, "but not for those others."

Cray flicked a thumb in the direction of the tree entrance. "They are not coming with me, O bird."

"Not those humans. But the *others*."

Cray frowned. "What do you mean?"

"Those that ride your arms and chest, that hide in your collar and huddle in your sleeves. They may not mount me, nor enter Castle Ringforge. None but you may enter, Cray Ormoru, so leave them behind or stay yourself."

Then Cray knew that the eagle meant his spiders, those other companions of his travels, that he carried without any thought. "Very well," he said, and he knelt upon the ground, placing his hands flat on the hard-trodden road, and from his sleeves the spiders scuttled. They paused a moment at his splayed fingertips, but when he rose to his feet once more, they scattered into the grass. "Wait for me here," he murmured. He felt twice naked now, without either spiders or chain mail. He gazed into one of the bird's great eyes. "I am ready now. Will you take me?"

In answer, the eagle sank to the ground, its bronze breast upon the rutted road. One wing stretched halfway out, and wide-placed metal feathers rose upon that surface, a crude ladder. "Climb," intoned the bird.

Grasping the upraised metal struts, warm with morning sunlight, Cray scrambled to the eagle's back.

"Fasten yourself tight," said the bird. "We will be flying high and swift."

Cray buckled the straps about his legs and torso and clasped the handholds firmly. When he was settled thus, the huge bird spread both wings to their fullest, lifted them once, and with a powerful downstroke was airborne. Cray was pressed against the bronze feathers and buffeted by a great wind; his stomach felt as if it had been left behind on the ground, and his cheek, where the metal feathers lay hard against his flesh, ached from their blunt edges. The tallest of the forest trees dropped away from his sight as if yanked by the hand of a giant. Blue sky rushed close, and then clouds engulfed him, their moisture instantly soaking his clothing, their whiteness blinding him to his own movement.

Once within the clouds, the eagle rose no longer but soared on almost motionless pinions. With difficulty, Cray lifted his head. The wind was a hammer against

216

him, from the front now, rather than above; he could scarcely keep his eyes open against it, and he could see nothing but whiteness, parting before him to reveal yet more whiteness waiting. He laid his face down again and closed his eyes. He spoke: "How long will we fly?" But the rushing wind whipped his voice away, drowning the words from even his own ears, and if the metal bird heard him, it did not deign to answer. "I would rather ride Gallant," he muttered, "no matter how long the journey."

He shivered, and not just with the chill of the clouds. He had never felt so alone before in his life.

ᵉᶳ CHAPTER ELEVEN

He caught his first glimpse of Ringforge when the great bronze bird tilted one wing down and slipped sideways through the air, describing a wide, swooping turn. Cray saw the ground then, tipped crazily to his eyes, roaring toward him with terrifying speed; he saw a broad, flat, circular open space, fringed by trees, and in the precise center of the circle was a huge building made of metal so highly polished that it flashed the sun back skyward from a dozen surfaces. A glimpse was all Cray managed at that moment; he could never have counted the turrets or walls, or even guessed the nature of that metal from its brilliant hue, for he was busy holding his breakfast behind his teeth. He closed his eyes as tight as the muscles of the lids would allow, but he could not shut out the vertigo that claimed him, that throbbed through his ears, his head, his throat. Every sinew of his body ached with the agony of that effort by the time a tremor, like the touch of a dinner dish on the smooth wooden surface of a table, marked the end of his journey. Shaking, sweating, still engulfed by the misery of motion sickness, Cray did not realize that his steed had ceased to move until he heard a voice. While his stomach still churned, some small portion of his mind marveled that he could hear anything above the rush of the wind. And then he realized that the wind no longer rushed. He opened his eyes and beheld a steady world, distant trees whose leaves seemed scarcely to move under the impetus of the mildest of summer breezes. Closer, the ground was yellow and sunbaked, just as it had been outside the Seer's home.

"Master Cray?" came the voice again. It was a young voice, feminine, light, high.

Cray turned his head slowly, and the air seemed to spin about him. He groaned. His breakfast, which had not settled back to his stomach since the bronze bird began its descent, pushed at the back of his throat once more, and he tasted the bitter acid of it before he swallowed thickly. He laid his cheek against the metal feathers, gasping, and when his vision ceased its rocking, he found himself looking down on the bronze wing, extended in a ramp for his descent, and at its far end waited a girl in a long blue gown.

"Are you injured, Master Cray?" she inquired in her high, musical voice. She was small in stature, with blond hair plaited in two braids that fell forward upon her bosom. She appeared to be quite young, younger even than Cray himself, and he wondered who she might be. Rezhyk's daughter was the first answer that leaped to his mind, but it only raised another question in its wake—if Rezhyk had a child, why would he offer someone else's child apprenticeship?

"Master Cray?" she said again, stepping forward to poise on the endmost feathers of the wing. "Shall I help you down?"

He took a deep breath. "I'm a little dizzy," he confessed.

She climbed the ladder of bronze feathers and bent to unstrap him. "This one is not accustomed to bearing human cargo," she said, nodding toward the bronze bird's head.

The creature turned its gaze upon them, and the feathers of its neck squeaked loudly as they scraped against each other for that contortion. "The human is not injured," it thundered.

"No, no, I'm all right," said Cray, holding the girl's arm to rise from his bronze perch. "Just a little shaky." He wobbled down the ramp and stepped heavily upon the solid yellow earth. "I've never flown before," he muttered, trying to smile.

"I would think not," she said. "Shall I fetch you some tea?"

He shook his head, grimacing as the motion set the world a-sway once more. "No, nothing, thank you. I'll just sit down here for a few moments." He sank, cross-legged, to the dust and held his head in his hands.

As if from a great distance, he heard the girl scolding the bronze bird for giving its passenger too rough a ride, he heard it answer in low rumbling tones, heard the vast pinions shift and shuffle, smelled the flicking clouds of dust raised by those gestures. Still caught up in his own misery, he marveled at the temerity of a puny human being raising her fragile voice to a monster that could slash her in two with one stroke of its beak; he marveled that she was master of the situation, that the bird sulked apologetically. Presently the voices fell silent, and soon after that the universe righted itself, leaving Cray able to look up, wan but steady.

The bronze eagle had vanished. Cray had not heard its wings surge in flight, had not felt the gust of wind that must have marked such an exit. The girl merely stood alone where the eagle had once rested, and she watched Cray.

"Where did it go?" asked Cray.

"Where demons go." She walked forward till she stood above him, and then she stretched out her hand. "Are you well enough to rise?"

"Yes." He took her hand and scrambled to his feet.

"Welcome to Castle Ringforge, Master Cray."

"Thank you. And what might your name be?"

"Gildrum."

He smiled. "A pretty name."

"Is it? I hadn't thought it so."

219

"A pretty name for a pretty girl."

Gildrum smiled then, but she only said, "Come. My lord awaits us inside."

And Cray thought that she could not be Rezhyk's daughter after all, for she would not call her father lord.

Ringforge towered skyward behind them, sheets of bronze vying with the sun for brilliance, crenelations sharp as if cut with a diamond blade, like teeth biting at the birds that passed in the summer sky. Cray could not resist touching the clean, bright line where two faces of a rampart met, to see if it would slice his flesh, and he scarcely felt the stroke, until dark, seeping blood began to sting the wound.

"What a surprise is this for an enemy," he murmured.

Gildrum drew him away from the knife-edge juncture. "There are no such dangers inside," she explained. "Your place is there, after all, Master Cray."

"So I hope," he said, and he let himself be ushered through the massive portal. Gildrum closed it silently behind him.

Within was mellow dimness. The room was small, the walls made of brushed metal that scattered the light of a few sconced candles as clouds scatter moonlight. Two chairs faced each other across the width of the chamber—plain, straight-backed chairs of ordinary wood; Gildrum bade Cray take one.

When he had sat for some few moments, his eyes gradually becoming accustomed to the low illumination, his body beginning to squirm on the hard, flat, unyielding seat of the chair, he turned to Gildrum, who stood nearby, her hands clasped upon the girdle of her gown, her eyes downcast. As if sensing his gaze, she raised her eyes to his at the instant he looked at her face, and for a moment, in his surprise, he lost the words he had been about to utter. They both smiled at the seeming coincidence. Then she broke the silence.

"Shall I fetch you something now, Master Cray? Some wine? Or even a cup of pure, sweet water? I think you must have had a thirsty journey."

He shook his head. His throat was thick and his mouth dry, but he did not wish to be left alone in the small, bare room. "Where is the master of the house?"

"He will come."

"Is he watching me, perhaps, by his magic?"

Gildrum shrugged. "You are of the sorcerous breed, Master Cray. You know how they are."

"Are you not one of them?"

"I? No, I am just a servant."

Cray looked all around him, even to the ceiling, which was as softly brushed as walls and floor and suffused with the same pale glow. "What a strange place this is. Are there always these two chairs here, or have they been set here specially for the occasion?"

"Sometimes there are more than two," said Gildrum. "This is the only room of Ringforge that visitors may enter."

"How many of them have come here?"

"A few."

"Sorcerers? Or ordinary mortals?"

"A few of each sort. A great king once sat where you are sitting now. In that very chair."

"Did he bring his own cushion?"

Gildrum smiled more broadly. "No, and his rump was soon as stiff and sore as yours will be."

"Well," said Cray, "it will make a good match for my arms, which are stiff and sore already, from clutching at your master's bronze steed."

Opposite his seat, behind the chair that faced him, a section of the wall swung inward on hidden hinges, and a man strode into the tiny room. He was a tall man, thin and dark, with creases in his cheeks as if they had been grooved by a sculptor's tool. His eyes, set deep in his head, reflected pinpoints of candlelight, and the black brocade in which he was clad glistened like scale armor. With each stride of his booted feet, the floor chimed beneath him like a great bronze bell.

"I am the lord of Ringforge," he said, and he halted beside the empty chair and rested one hand on its wooden back as he stared at Cray.

Cray bounced to his feet and made a low bow. "My lord," he said, "I am Cray Ormoru."

"Turn around and let me see you from all sides," said Rezhyk.

Cray obeyed, slowly, feeling akin to a horse being put up for auction in a marketplace.

"You look to be a sturdy lad."

"I am strong and healthy, my lord. I can lift my own weight without strain and ride all day before I tire. I can scarcely remember the last time I was sick."

Rezhyk stroked the side of his jaw with one finger. "You resemble your mother."

"I have thought so, my lord."

"She is a great sorceress in her own right. Why are you not her apprentice?"

"I wish to conjure demons, my lord, and she knows nothing of that art."

Rezhyk slipped into his chair and leaned against the high back, his arms folded upon his chest. "And why, Cray Ormoru, do you wish to conjure demons?"

Cray looked at him levelly and then decided that dissembling with this cool, dark figure would be a mistake; if he were to apprentice himself to this man, it must be on honest terms from the beginning, for he felt sure that if once he were caught in a lie, Rezhyk would never trust him again. "I never knew my father," he said. "He disappeared before I was born. I want to find him, or at least learn his name, his house, his history. I have followed his trail for many months without success, and now the only means left to me is through the conjuration of demons."

Rezhyk frowned, and his eyes narrowed as he gazed upon the lad. "A unique reason," he said at last.

"I will work hard, my lord. I am not afraid of effort. You will find me a willing student, and not without a certain talent, at least so my mother judged."

In a low voice, Rezhyk replied, "Your mother is not the best judge of these things. The talent that may suit her sort of sorcery may be totally at odds with mine." He rose abruptly. "I must consider your request, Cray Ormoru. I must consider if your mother's son is the sort of apprentice I would wish."

"I have great hopes that you will take me on, my lord. I know that I could hardly find a better teacher."

Rezhyk's eyes seemed to flare in the dim room, or perhaps, Cray thought, it was the way he turned toward the candlelight. "Flattery means nothing to me," he said. He wheeled about and stalked to the opening in the wall. Within its compass, he glanced over his shoulder. "Gildrum will fetch whatever you may need for your refreshment and then join me in the workshop. I will weigh your suit there and return with a decision quite soon."

"I need nothing," said Cray. "Only your consent, my lord."

"To me, then, my Gildrum."

With a swift smile for Cray, Gildrum scurried to join her master, and the wall sealed behind them, leaving a surface so smooth that even when he examined it from a finger's breadth distance, Cray could not see the juncture. He sat down again then, trying not to feel as if he had been sealed in a tomb. The candles burned low, lower, but somehow they never guttered.

Rezhyk leaned against the bench where the brazier burned, his hands flat on the smooth work surface, fingers spread stiffly, pressing until the flesh whitened and the fingernails blushed deep pink with trapped blood. By the ruddy light of lazily burning coals, his face was pale in spite of its olive tint, ghastly, as if he had been ill for months. His eyes were wide, the whites showing beneath the dark irises, tiny vessels webbing that whiteness with red.

"I saw her, my Gildrum," he whispered, his voice rasping, as from a throat choked with phlegm. "I saw her staring at me through his eyes."

"An illusion, my lord," said Gildrum, touching his arm gently. "Surely her powers do not extend to human beings."

He turned a baleful stare upon the demon. "Don't be foolish; I know that well enough." He closed his eyes a moment, squeezing them shut with brows knitted so tight they seemed to merge into one line of darkness across his forehead. "Yet, he is her flesh and blood. It was . . . almost as if she were here herself."

"He is your flesh and blood, too."

Rezhyk's eyes snapped open, and he pulled away from the demon's touch. "Mine? Oh no, not mine, not of my desire!"

"The seed was yours, my lord. You cannot deny him."

"I can! I never asked for a child, my Gildrum!"

"Still, you have one."

"Oh, I have one; I have one indeed." He locked his hands together behind his back and began to pace, marking the length of the workshop with long-legged strides. "This game is not so simple as it looked some days since, my Gildrum. Oh, now how I wish it were as uncomplicated as I guessed. If only it were merely a bid for power by my enemy Delivev. If only she merely wished to increase her strength through alliance with another sort of magic."

"That never seemed uncomplicated to me, my lord," said Gildrum.

"You think not? Well, what have we here, then? He comes to me, my Gildrum, to find me out! She has sent him, I know it. She suspects, and now I have only to wait a few years before the truth is revealed to her. What will happen then, my Gildrum? When she knows the truth . . . will it be war between us? Will she find herself allies among my other enemies, perhaps, so that the shirt will not be enough to protect me? I could defeat her alone, I trust I could. Perhaps it would not be easy, but it could be done. But if her hate is strong enough . . . who will she find to help her? I have no friends, my Gildrum. I have no one to turn to for aid!"

Gildrum followed his progress with her eyes, while her body remained still. Softly, she said, "Has the lady Delivev any friends, my lord?"

"What? Friends? I suppose she must, somewhere. She will buy them if she must; her works are always in demand, those tapestries, those fine fabrics she makes. Oh, she'll have friends. She'll be ready for me. What shall I do, my Gildrum? What shall I do?"

Gildrum eased herself up onto the tall stool. "Are you sure my lord," she said slowly, "that she will hate you?"

"How not? After what I have done to her?"

"Perhaps she would not consider your actions so hateful. She raised the boy, after all; she must have

224

some feeling for him. She must love him. And you gave him to her."

He glared at the demon. "Were I Delivev, I would not love the one who did such a thing to me. It was not done out of love."

"You need not tell her that, my lord."

His gaze softened a bit. "What would I tell her, then, my Gildrum?"

"That you did it from love of her. That you gave her the child you wanted."

"You tell me to lie, my Gildrum."

"Yes, my lord. Lie, if you fear her so. Lie to save yourself."

Rezhyk stalked to the workbench, and with one slashing gesture knocked the brazier across the smooth surface, scattering flaming coals in a wide arc; most of them struck Gildrum, who did not even flinch but merely began methodically to snuff with bare hands the smoldering spots on her blue gown.

"No!" said Rezhyk. "I will not lie. I will not spout love at that cunning enemy. You think she'd believe for a single moment? No! I'd abase myself for nothing. And she would realize exactly how weak I must be. Better that she never knows, my Gildrum! Better that you and I hold the secret still inside us!"

"But what will you do then, my lord? If the boy stays and learns your sorcery, he will find out, he must."

"He must," echoed Rezhyk. "Yet I dare not turn him away. Another master would teach him as well as I, well enough to find the truth. Any demon-master would do for that." He shook his head violently, as if to rid himself of some unpleasant substance clinging to it. "What can I do indeed, my Gildrum? What is there to do that can prevent him . . . ?"

Gildrum spread her hands in a gesture of perplexity. "My lord, I know not."

Rezhyk looked down at the floor, where the polished bronze threw his own brocade-clad reflection back at him, foreshortened and squat, like some inhuman creature, scaly, wet, risen from the depths of the sea. "I can kill him," he said softly.

Gildrum stared at his bent head a moment and then

down at her hands, ashy gray from the crushing of embers. Her dress was speckled with char, and here and there a hole had burned through well enough to show the human-seeming flesh beneath. She caught up the hem, where fewer coals had struck, and wiped her palms upon the fabric.

"I can kill him," Rezhyk repeated.

She murmured. "Do you think that wise, my lord?"

"Wise?" He raised one clenched fist, shaking it at his reflection. "There is no wise course now. There is only swift action! If the boy is dead, then he can't discover the truth!"

Gildrum slipped off the stool and reached to the workbench to right the brazier. "And what will the lady Delivev do if the boy dies at your hand, my lord?"

"Not at *my* hand!"

"How then?"

Rezhyk dropped his fist to his side. "I will send him on a quest to fetch certain materials for me; he will have to pass through dangerous territory. It will not be my fault if he is killed."

"No?"

"No!"

"On your errand, my lord? On an errand that could surely be accomplished by any one of your demons?"

"One which requires human hands alone."

Gildrum stooped to gather up the coals that had fallen to the floor, the ones which still glowed cherry-red beneath a thin film of ash. These she poured back into the brazier. Then she opened a bin under the workbench and drew from its substantial supply a handful of the small, hard briquets that fueled the brazier's flames, and she stacked them atop the live coals. Their slate-smooth surfaces caught quickly, with little flamelets licking all around them, like flowers tossing in a high wind. Gazing into those flames, Gildrum said, "Somehow I feel that the lady Delivev will question the necessity of sending the new apprentice on an errand that some other human being could perform as well. Some other human being not her child."

"An accident then!" shouted Rezhyk. "Something caused by his own stupidity. He can lock himself in the kiln and burn to death!"

"In your house," murmured Gildrum.

"Yes, but an accident nevertheless. There must be a hundred ways of being killed beneath this roof!"

"Beneath this roof."

"Don't echo me, demon!"

Their eyes met. His face was red, veins standing out on his forehead, lips compressed to whiteness; her face was pale, guileless. She lifted one hand toward him, in supplication, in apology.

"My lord," she said, "your fear blinds you. If the lady is truly your implacable enemy, then she will not believe in any accident that claims her child's life. She will blame you, even though you be innocent as a virgin girl. You will have brought her wrath upon yourself, not seven or ten years hence, but now, when you have not yet the means to deal with it."

He tore his gaze away from her, and when he spoke, his voice had lost its edge of anger and was bleak instead, and hollow with despair. "You are right, my Gildrum. You see clearly. Human emotions do not cloud your vision."

"There must be another course, my lord."

"Must there? I know it not. There is no course at all, it seems. No matter what I do, I can only stave off the final conflict. It was inevitable. It has been coming for sixteen years now, and I have closed my eyes and trusted this shirt when I should have been preparing. Has she been preparing, I wonder? Surely. Perhaps the shirt is already nothing to her. Perhaps she knows of it and scorns it as she scorns me."

"She cannot know, my lord. We were too careful for that."

"She is clever, my Gildrum. Perhaps she has guessed all and merely wants . . . confirmation." He took a deep, shaky breath. "And he will give it to her, won't he." It was not a question, but a statement, and the voice that uttered it was tired, weak, as if its owner had run hours before speaking that sentence. Rezhyk looked behind himself for a stool, found one against the nearest wall, and sat down heavily, as if his bones were tired of carrying his flesh about.

"Perhaps not," said Gildrum.

Rezhyk looked up at her, his face grooved deep with lines of pain. "Perhaps not what?"

"Perhaps he won't be able to give her confirmation."

"What nonsense are you spouting?"

She leaned her elbows on the workbench, interlacing her fingers beneath her chin. "He said he had talent. What if he has not?"

"His mother said it, so he said. She would know."

"But she was wrong."

Rezhyk frowned. "How can you know?"

"My lord, he has no talent at all, for sorcery. He cannot learn the simplest conjuration. He will never become a demon-master."

"What are you saying, my Gildrum? Where have you found this knowledge?"

"I have invented it, my lord. And you will demonstrate its truth. You will teach him, but he will not learn."

"I doubt that. Delivev's child . . . and mine . . . I would think he would learn well enough."

"He will learn nothing." She nodded slowly, her chin brushing the backs of her fingers. "You will teach him nonsense, and when, after some reasonable time, he is totally unable to conjure the meanest demon, you will declare him incapable of mastering the art. He will go home then, or at least he will go away, and he will know nothing of his father—or of the trick you played on his mother."

Rezhyk clasped one hand over the other fist. "But . . . he will suspect. *She* will suspect."

"How, my lord? Neither knows anything of your art. How will they judge between true and false training?" She pointed one slim finger at him. "You are the master; they will accept your word that the lad is a failure."

"He will go to another master then."

"After seven years? Or ten? Or whatever limit you may set? He is a human being, my lord. He will run home to his mother and surrender himself to *her* tutelage, I think, when he has failed at yours."

Rezhyk covered his face with his hands. "Perhaps you are right," he said between his fingers. He nodded.

"Yes, it is a good plan, my Gildrum. I cannot think of a better."

"And it gives you time, my lord."

"Yes. Time. To prepare . . . for whatever lies ahead. For her." He rubbed at his eyes, grinding the pads of his fingers against them as if they were full of grit, as if he were just rising from a deep sleep, or had been awake too long. "I feel," he murmured, "like a man standing at the brink of an abyss. I see doom before me, my Gildrum. We should never have done it. Never. I should have searched further for a way to deal with her." He sighed. "No, I can't blame you. I grasped at it myself. It seemed . . . so likely at the time. Not your fault, my Gildrum. You have always given me the best advice you knew. It is my choice, after all, whether to take it or no." He heaved himself to his feet. "I suppose we must tell him the good news."

"Yes, my lord," said Gildrum, and she followed her master's slow and heavy step out of the workshop.

Rezhyk let the wall swing aside for him, but he did not enter the tiny, dim chamber. "Well, Cray Ormoru," he said quite loudly, "there is room for you at Ringforge, if your mind is still bent toward apprenticing to me."

Cray bowed low, smiling a trifle. "It is, my lord."

"Then there are certain rules that you must know. First among them is that no other sort of magic than my own may be practiced within these walls. If ever I catch you using any tricks your mother might have taught you, your time at Ringforge will be ended. Second, you must obey me in all things, without question and without quibbling; I know far better than you do what you must learn and how you must learn it. Third, there are chambers in this castle that you may not enter; their doors will not open for you, so do not attempt to force them or find some other means of entry—if I find you prowling about them, I shall mete out proper punishment. If any of these rules seems unjust or overly harsh to you, speak now."

"My lord, this is your home, and I am your guest. I would not abuse your hospitality."

Rezhyk nodded stiffly. "Gildrum will show you to

your quarters, then, and all the other places in my castle where you may roam freely. I leave you to her mercies." He turned abruptly and took one quick step away before Cray's voice halted him.

"A moment, my lord?"

Rezhyk glanced back over his shoulder. "What is it?"

"I have a friend, my lord," Cray said. "He and I have been together for many months now, shared many adventures, and we would share this one as well."

The sorcerer gazed at Cray with narrowed eyes. "I take only one apprentice, Cray Ormoru."

"Not as an apprentice, sir, he would never expect that. But he would serve willingly in the castle, I know. And he has no family, nowhere to go save with me."

"He will have to find somewhere then," Rezhyk replied. "He shall not come here. One outsider is enough."

"He is a most unusual fellow, my lord—diligent, faithful, and he is accustomed to sorcery now."

"An ordinary mortal, is he?"

"Yes."

"Then all the more reason to bar him from my home."

"Not even . . . as my own personal servant?"

"We have plenty of servants here, Cray Ormoru, and none of them with weak, human limitations."

"My lord, he is like a brother to me."

Rezhyk scowled at Cray, his lips pursed to whiteness in his dark face. "Would you prefer to find some other master who will take you both?"

Cray bowed again. "No, my lord. It shall be as you say."

"Very well." Rezhyk stalked away, leaving the wall open for Cray and Gildrum to follow.

Gildrum waited until Rezhyk was well gone, and then she turned to Cray and said, "His anger can be bitter. You would do well to keep silence when he is displeased. It passes then, more quickly than if you continue to speak."

"I had to ask," replied Cray. "I promised."

"Your friend will simply have to find his own way in the world from now on."

"He predicted it would be so. He was wiser than I in this." He looked questioningly at the demon. "What of my possessions, the things that I left behind me with the lady Helaine? I have a pair of saddlebags full of clothing."

"We shall send for them, never fear. The bird can carry saddlebags as well as a human being. Better, since *they* don't become ill on the way."

"I have a horse, too."

"Ah, a horse." Gildrum touched one finger to her lips. "We haven't any stable for a horse here at Ringforge. My lord never uses the creatures."

"I can build a shelter for him just outside the walls."

Gildrum shook her head.

"Is there some spot inside, then?"

"I fear you will have to give up the horse, Master Cray."

Cray started back one step, as if physically repelled. "Give up Gallant? No!"

"Yes."

"Never. He has been my constant companion for years."

"You will have no time for him here."

"I will make the time."

Gildrum shook her head again. "You have no concept of the sort of work that awaits you, Master Cray. It leaves no room for the exercise that a horse requires, for the grooming and feeding."

"Will he forbid me to have the horse here?"

"He will forbid you to waste your time caring for it." Gildrum glanced at the opening in the wall. "As you have seen, he is a severe master. You would be wise to bend with him instead of trying to stand firm. A horse is such a little thing to give up, if it makes your life smoother."

Cray eyed Gildrum, eyed the slight, fair form that appeared even younger than himself. "Have you served him long that you know him so well?"

She nodded.

"Are you . . . related to him somehow?"

"No." She smiled at Cray. "I am a demon, like all

231

the other servants you will meet in Ringforge. There are only two human beings here—you and my lord Rezhyk."

"A demon?" Cray found himself peering at her more closely, searching for some sign of her origin in the form or texture of her body. "You look . . . completely human."

"My lord gave me this shape. He is very good at such things."

"May I . . . may I touch you?" Cray lifted his hand toward her, halting the gesture in mid-air, an arm's length away from her face.

"If you wish." She stepped forward, took his hand in her own and laid the palm flat against her cheek. "I am not cold and slimy, I promise you." She smiled. "Fire demons rarely are."

Cray traced the line of her jaw and then drew his hand away slowly. "It feels like human flesh."

"Of course. My lord is master of his art."

"But are you not . . . made of fire?"

"Yes. Sometimes. I am sure you will learn about me in the course of your apprenticeship. Eventually, you will be able to conjure others of my kind yourself. That is what you wish, is it not?"

"Yes. That is what I wish."

"I will show you to your room, if you will follow me, Master Cray, and after that I shall send the bronze bird for your saddlebags."

Cray sighed. "But not . . . my horse."

Gildrum's voice softened. "Will he be well cared for, do you think, at the lady Helaine's home?"

Cray nodded. "My friend will look after him." He hesitated a moment. "Can I send a message with the bird?"

"Instructions for the care of the horse? And . . . a farewell to your friend?"

"Yes. And my thanks to the lady for all her help. And one other thing: a request to tell my mother that I am here, well, and accepted for apprenticeship."

"Ah, yes," said Gildrum. "Your mother would certainly want to know."

The tapestry ended abruptly at Castle Ringforge,

that many-turreted structure represented by a simple brown-edged rectangle, empty in the center, the pale warp strands untouched by weft. As long as he stayed within those sorcerous walls, she would know nothing of his life, his health, his hazards: He might even die, and no sign would mark the cloth. The weft threads hung loose, the bobbins dangling beneath the fabric like spiders hanging from their own silk, swaying gently in the breeze created by her passage.

In the garden, his pony waited for the touch of her hands. Its head came up at the sound of her step, and flower petals dripped from its slowly moving jaws. She had begun to reprimand it, gently, for eating these small, immobile companions of her loneliness when a scurrying spider apprised her of a message in the chamber of webs. She bolted from the garden, startling the pony, flowers forgotten.

The image in the web was dim, and it rippled constantly, like a reflection in restless water. The face was pale, the hair pulled back in a tight, white braid. The mouth was motionless, transfixed timelessly upon the web until a listener should arrive and bid it speak. Delivev recognized the lady Helaine and gestured that the message might begin.

"Lord Rezhyk has accepted him," said the Seer, her eyes staring out of the web, seeing nothing, attempting to see nothing. "He sends you his love. He is a good lad and has much enterprise. I think he will do well." The eyes closed, and the image faded away, leaving only blank strands of gossamer behind.

Delivev bowed her head. *Then I will hear nothing more,* she thought, and the finality of those words, silent as they were, brought the tears to her cheeks that she thought had been all spent on Cray's behalf. She realized then that she had been hoping against hope that Rezhyk would reject him, that all demon-masters would find him somehow unfit for their service, that he would be forced by that to come home at last and give himself back to her. Now she had to put that hope aside, once and for all; and with that final inward gesture, instead of finding the bleak agony that she had feared, she found a faint pride: pride in her son, that she had borne and raised alone, who had until recently known no other sources of instruction than herself and the images she conjured for him in the webs—pride that such a child could be considered worthy by one so different from herself as Smada Rezhyk.

He will be a man of power, my son, she thought. She reached out to the nearest web, grazed the silk with her fingertips, and it clung, nigh weightless, to her flesh. A spider skittered across the lattice, a brown-and-white mite no larger than her smallest fingernail; it came to rest on her upturned palm, and it, too, was as light as air, its tiny legs tickling at her skin like the merest puffs of air. She regarded it with tender eyes, with softly curving lips. "You must be my child now," she whispered. "You must all be my children, as before."

She tipped the creature back onto the web, then crossed her arms over her bosom. She thought of her own mother, dead so many years, dead so soon after passing the last of her knowledge to her daughter. Delivev was young; her life and her son's would overlap for a long time. *When he is a man of power,* she wondered, *will he still know me?*

Walking the central corridor of Castle Ringforge, Cray knew that he would be slow in adjusting to his new surroundings. His eyes were already baffled by the soft illumination from sconces that bore no candles and from the reflections of those sconces in many a polished wall. He thought himself in a maze of intersecting hallways, until he perceived his own image and Gildrum's walking among them and understood that most of them were phantoms in the flawless bronze, ruddy and dim as his own flesh was ruddy and dim when he raised a hand before his eyes.

"I'll soon tire of the sight of my own face," he remarked to Gildrum, who guided him to a staircase where they climbed close beside their reflections. The staircase was long, requiring half the length of the corridor to rise to the second story, and its steps were shallow, ridged with a bold pattern of parallel lines that provided a better purchase for booted feet than the smooth, level floor.

"You'll stop noticing it after a time," said Gildrum. She seemed to glide up the stairway, her skirt sweeping lightly behind her—it would have stirred up dust on a less perfectly clean surface. Cray suddenly felt dirty in his shirt and trews, his worn boots, and he wondered at the enormous effort of scrubbing and polishing that must be expended in the keeping of Ringforge.

"I have never seen bronze so bright," he said. "Almost like pale gold. How long has Ringforge stood, that it has not yet begun to darken with age?"

"A long time, Master Cray. My lord prefers it bright, and so his servants keep it for him."

"I feel as if I'm walking inside some great jewel."

She smiled back at him over one shoulder. "You may have divined my lord's intention, Master Cray. Of all the substances of the earth, he loves gems best."

"I saw—on his hands."

At the top of the stairs they turned left sharply, into the corridor that lay directly above that on the first floor. Gildrum paused after a few paces. "Here is your room," she said, pointing to the bare, smooth wall with one index finger. A section of the surface, rectangular, taller and broader than the biggest man, swung aside to reveal a dark interior.

Cray glanced from the aperture to Gildrum. "Are there no ordinary doors in this castle?"

"None with knobs and locks, Master Cray. My lord says such would mar the symmetry of the place." She gestured toward darkness. "Will you go in?"

"Have you a candle?"

"We need no candle. Step across the threshold."

He did as she bade, and the instant that he entered the chamber, sconces on every wall came alight, their images multiplied in polished bronze on every side, above and below. He squinted at the nearest sconce. "What is the source of that light?"

"Fire demons."

"I would rather have a candle."

"We don't use candles in Ringforge."

"There were candles in the room where I spoke to Lord Rezhyk."

"Were there?"

235

"Of course. I saw them."

"You saw what outsiders see, Master Cray." Standing beneath the light, she stretched up on her toes and passed her hand through the flame; when she pulled back, the fire was on her fingertips instead of in the sconce, and it played there, bouncing from one finger to another as she held her hand before his eyes. "A very minor demon," she said. "It can look like a candle if it so desires. It has a few other little tricks, too. Not much. My lord has any number of such creatures."

"Wouldn't candles be simpler?" said Cray, watching her flaming fingers with fascination.

She shrugged and flipped the fire away as if it were water dripping from her hand; it sailed in a smooth arc to the sconce and settled there, burning without ash, without soot. "When one is a demon-master," she said, "demons are simpler than anything else. My lord has no desire to waste his time in the making of candles. We would use quite a lot of them, you know."

"The demons could make candles."

Gildrum laughed softly. "Why make flames when you *are* a flame?"

Cray peered at the sconce, at the warm, steady flame, yellow as butter, and then his gaze shifted to Gildrum, whose hair matched the flame. "You . . . really look like *that?*"

"Not quite like that, Master Cray. I am rather grander than that."

"Larger?"

"If I wish to be."

"Can I . . . can I see you as a flame?"

"That is for my lord to say, not me." She turned away from him, crossed the room to open a cabinet taller than herself. Inside were deep shelves, empty save for bed linens. "When your belongings arrive, you can put them in here. If this is not enough room, we can easily provide another cabinet."

"I'm sure it will be enough." He looked about the room, trying to ignore the walls. It was a large room, seeming larger with the multiple reflections, and it was sparsely furnished. Aside from the cabinet, there was a bedstead in one corner, a desk and chair in another, a washstand with pitcher and bowl in the third. All the furniture was of brass, save the mattress and the cushions of the chair; even the pitcher was shining yellow brass, a harsh hue beside the mellow walls. Cray strolled over to the desk and chair. "I have never seen furniture made of brass before."

"We had quite a lot of brass," said Gildrum, "and my lord directed that the apprentice's furniture be made from it, rather than bronze, which he reserves for himself."

"There's quite enough bronze in this room already. Quite enough metal of any kind, in fact. Is there no possibility of something . . . softer-looking? Wood, perhaps? A wooden chair and desk?"

Gildrum closed the cabinet. "Fire demons do not get on well with wood, Master Cray."

"There are wooden chairs in this castle. I sat on one today."

"They are reserved for that room. They are not used elsewhere in Ringforge."

Cray eased himself onto the desk. "What of tapestries, then? To cover these bare walls and keep out the winter drafts?"

"There are no winter drafts in Ringforge. I built it stout, and it does not leak."

"*You* built it?"

Gildrum straightened her back and set her fists on her hips. "I did, and there is no fault to be found in it. Don't let this human frame deceive you, Master Cray. I am a powerful creature, the greatest my lord commands."

Cray shook his head slowly. "He chose an unlikely vessel for those powers."

"That is something you must discuss with him." And in a lower voice, she added, "But I would suggest that you wait until you know him better before you broach the subject."

Cray pushed away from the desk and stood in the center of the room, looking down at his image in the floor. "That still leaves us with the question of tapestries for the walls, and a rug to hide this mirror floor."

"We have nothing of the kind in Ringforge."

He tilted his head sidewise to look up at her. "My mother could provide them."

"No."

"There would be no cost, not for her own son."

"Again, no. I'm surprised you dare ask that."

"Ordinary tapestries. Nothing magical about them."

"My lord would never allow them in his home. Other sorcerers may take in magics not their own, but he does not."

"Not magic, I said."

"You won't be able to convince him of that, Master Cray."

He spread his hands in helplessness. "I haven't enough money left to go to a town and buy them of an ordinary weaver."

"That hardly matters," said Gildrum. "Even if you had the money, he would not allow it. With your background, he could not be sure that you would not use ordinary weaving magically."

"I wouldn't. I said I would never use my mother's powers inside these walls."

"Best you not be tempted."

"Tempted? With tapestries? As well I might be tempted with my own garments. Tempted to do what?"

"I don't know, Master Cray. Neither does my lord. Still, he would not understand the hanging of tapestries."

"I shall not be able to sleep in this room."

Gildrum smiled. "Of course you shall, with the lights out. They'll obey your commands, you know, individually or in concert. Try it. Speak, or just point. These demons understand language quite well."

"I believe you." He ambled over to the bed, sat down, sinking deep into the feather comforter. He punched the pillow. "You have woven things everywhere here, you know. Even your own clothes. I would not have your master suspecting I would use them for sorcerous purposes." He curled his fingers about the closest bedpost. "Perhaps I am the wrong sort of apprentice for him."

"He will be watching you," acknowledged Gildrum. "All of us will be watching you."

Cray pointed to the wall opposite the bed. "Even those demon lights?"

"Even they."

"Everything I do?"

Gildrum smiled with one corner of her mouth. "Only my lord has privacy in his own home."

Cray sighed. "Well, then, I shall have to show him what a fine apprentice I can be. I mean to work hard, Gildrum. I mean to make him proud of me, proud that he chose to take me in."

"I wish you luck, Master Cray. And now, if you wish, you may rest here, sleep, wash, whatever you like, until the midday meal. Afterward, you shall see more of Ringforge. If you should need anything while I am gone, call my name, or simply ask the air for assistance; I will come." She moved toward the doorway, open all this time to the light of the corridor.

"Don't close it behind you!" he called out sharply. "I don't know how to open it!"

She glided across the threshold. "The door will do your bidding, Master Cray. If you wish it closed, you must command it so." She passed beyond the aperture and beyond his sight, though her image in the opposite wall remained visible for another moment. Cray leaned sideways to follow it, wondering if she would transform into a flame outside the room, but the image was only that of a human girl, and it slipped away as a human reflection would, as the original walked on. He decided against running to the door to watch her longer.

"The door may close," he said, and it obeyed silently. When it was sealed, he could not see the line of its juncture with the wall.

He kicked his boots off and lay back on the bed. He saw his own image in the ceiling, encased in the billowing comforter. "Let all the lights go out but one," he said, and the sconces darkened obediently, except for the nearest to him. He could no longer make out his reflection, save as an indistinct shape above him. But all about him, that single flame shone ghostly upon every surface. "That final light," he said at last, "out."

The blackness was profound. Cray knew that beyond the walls of Ringforge, bright summer scorched the land, the high sun dazzling the eyes of travelers. Yet inside his room was moonless, starless night. He listened, straining for the sounds that moved commonly throughout the rest of the world—rustlings of vermin, birdsong, wind, waving grass and trees. He heard none. Ringforge was silent. The very air was still. Cray found his breaths deepening, as if his lungs could not fill, as if the cool air were close and hot and palpably thick. He felt the room crowd in about him, the walls bending inward, the ceiling looming till it hovered just above his face. He reached out to push it away, feeling foolish with the gesture, for there was nothing but emptiness as far as his arms could stretch. Yet, lying there enveloped in the comforter, he found himself smothering.

He sat up abruptly and called for light. Flames sprang into existence in every sconce, brilliant to his dark-widened eyes, each doubled by its nearby reflection in the bronze, and tripled, quadrupled in the other mirrored surfaces. Cray clutched at his throat, which was constricted, squeezing his voice like a pair of strong, evil hands. "Are there no windows in this room?" he demanded of the empty air. "Open the door! Open the windows!"

The door gaped, but none of the other walls was breached. Cray rolled from the bed, padded barefoot to the aperture and looked out into the corridor. Nothing stirred there; in all the expanse of uninterrupted mirror, there was no motion save that of his own image. "Gildrum!" he shouted. "Gildrum, where are you?" He strode down the hall, started down the staircase, and had nearly descended the entire flight when she turned in at the foot.

"Why do you shout, Master Cray?" she asked, climbing four steps to meet him. She caught his arm. "I can hear your normal tone well enough when you speak my name, no matter where I am in Ringforge."

"I would have a room with windows," he said. "I'm not . . . accustomed to being so closed in."

"You are not closed in. The room is large. There are larger still; I can speak to my lord for you and perhaps change you to one of those, if you wish."

"If it has a window. I feel in need of air."

She tightened her grip on his arm. "Are you ill?"

"No . . ." He hesitated, not quite able to express the sensations that had overwhelmed him inside the darkened room, nor willing to admit to a fear that, in retrospect, seemed childish. At last, he sat down on the steps, perforce pulling her with him, for she would not relinquish her hold. "I have lived a great part of my life outdoors," he said. "And my mother's castle has many windows. The prospect of being sealed into that room every night . . . it seems unnatural to me. I would prefer to be able to look out at the sky and the trees, to breathe fresh air and not be trapped into staring at myself repeated in all the walls." He smiled thinly. "A window instead of a tapestry—is that a fair enough exchange?"

"The air in Ringforge is fresh, Master Cray. We demons keep it so."

"I don't doubt that. Still . . . I would prefer sunlight and starlight to flamelight."

She let go his arm, dropping her hand to the step, palm flat on the metal, and she leaned there, looking down, not at his face. "I am sorry. It is impossible."

"How so? There are windows in Castle Ringforge. I saw them myself, high up along the walls."

"They are closely shuttered."

"Surely the shutters will open."

"Only to my lord's command, and he prefers that they be closed."

Cray stared at her. "One small window . . ."

"No."

"But why not?"

Gildrum shrugged. "My lord commands, and I obey. I know no more than that."

"Does he never open them?"

"He did, many years ago. Not lately. Not for a long time. He has no need of the outside, save what we demons bring him of it."

Cray's brow creased in puzzlement. "Do you mean . . . that he never goes out?"

"He has set no foot beyond the walls of Ringforge in some time."

"He stays inside all day, all night? He never opens

241

a window? He never sees anything but himself reflected a million times in these walls?"

Gildrum's lips quirked in a brief smile. "I doubt that he notices those reflections, Master Cray. He has too much to keep him busy." She rose from the step on which he sat, and she lifted one foot to the next, her blue-covered knee close beside his face. "As you will, Master Cray, I promise you. You will be too busy to look at yourself in these walls, and too tired as well, when you go to bed at night. Your apprenticeship will not be an easy time. Remember, I said you would not have time to spare on a horse. Nor, I think, will there be much to spare for lying on your back under an open sky. Today, you may dwell on such notions; tomorrow they will be pushed out of your mind by work. Come now; if we return to your room, the meal will still be hot." She offered her hand to help him up, and he took it, marveling at the strength that was in that frail-seeming girl's hand.

They climbed the stairs, and only then, though he had been walking on the bronze some time in his bare feet, did he realize that the metal floor was warm to his skin, not cold as he had expected.

In his room, the lights blazed brightly, and the brightest were above his desk, almost as glaring as sunshine, accenting the tray that waited there—bronze, crowded with bronze-domed dishes. He lifted one of the covers, found a broiled fish beneath it, a fat fish with four large fins; he did not recognize the variety, but its sweet aroma brought saliva to his mouth and a sharp rumbling to his stomach. He pulled the knife from his belt and fell to.

Gildrum seated herself on the desk beside the tray and pulled the lids from the other dishes, revealing steaming vegetables drenched in butter, new-baked bread, and fruit preserves. She poured white wine from a slim carafe and offered Cray salt from a crystal bowl.

"Will you join me?" Cray asked between mouthfuls. "There seems to be plenty here."

"Demons don't usually eat this sort of food," she replied.

"Oh? What *do* demons usually eat?"

She handed him the wine cup. "It isn't precisely 'eating,' Master Cray. We absorb certain forces from all around us. Beyond that, I don't really think I can explain it to you."

"Do you like . . . human food?"

"I like my own cooking. In my travels about the world, I have been able to observe human beings considerably, fine cooks among them. My lord says I cook well, so there are two of us of that opinion."

"Did you cook this?"

"Not directly, but I taught the kitchen staff most of what it knows."

"The kitchen staff?"

Gildrum nodded. "Demons, of course. Cooking comes easy to fire demons. And why should it not?"

"This fish is excellent," said Cray. "I have never tasted fish quite like it before. Nor seen any. Where did it come from?"

"From the tropic ocean," said Gildrum, "where it spent its days flying over the waves like a bird. Almost like a bird. It splashed into the water occasionally. An easy fish to catch, for a demon fisher, and my lord relishes it."

Cray looked down at his plate with skeptical eyes. "A fish that flies? I can hardly believe that."

"It's true enough. I have seen it myself."

"A magical fish?"

She smiled. "Not at all. Merely one of the small marvels of the ordinary world. If you were a seafarer, Master Cray, it would not seem unusual to you."

He finished the last morsel of fish and pushed his chair away from the desk, leaning back against the cushioned bronze. "Well, I suppose I will have to accustom myself to the unusual here in Castle Ringforge."

"To more unusual things than a meal of strange fish," Gildrum said. "Now, if you have quite done with eating, I will take you on a tour of the fortress, and of the doors that will open to you when you ask, and when my lord bids them so."

Cray tipped a last measure of wine into his cup and gulped it down before rising. Then he went to the bed to retrieve his boots. "Tell me, Gildrum," he said, easing the stiff leather over his heels, "if you are Lord Rezhyk's greatest demon, why are you spending your valuable time on his apprentice? Surely you have other, more important tasks to perform for him."

She slipped off the desk and stood by the open door. "Nothing is more important than his apprentice," she said, raising one hand to touch the slab of bronze, leaning lightly upon it; the door did not move beneath her touch. "You are the first human being besides my lord to walk the halls of Ringforge. Until this day, the visitors' room was the only one in which other people had stood. You are the first for whom doors will open, lights will blaze and snuff, meals will be prepared. You are not a guest but a resident. Of course you are important, Master Cray. That is why you are my charge. My lord desires you to be properly instructed in the ways of Ringforge, and there is no better and more trustworthy teacher here than I."

Cray joined her at the door. "Trustworthy?" he echoed. "Does that mean, perhaps, that you are as much my keeper as my teacher?"

"You might consider me so," she said, leading him into the corridor. "After all, you are a stranger to him."

"Well, I hope to prove myself a diligent and trustworthy apprentice so that you may soon leave off teaching me and return to Lord Rezhyk's other business."

Gildrum glanced at him with one eyebrow raised. "You dislike my company, Master Cray?"

"Oh no, not at all," he blurted, grinning sheepishly in his embarrassment. "Indeed, I feel that you are my one friend, so far, in all of Ringforge."

She halted abruptly, her eyes seeking his, holding them in an unwinking gaze. "Master Cray, I am a demon," she said. "You must not assume that I am able to be your friend, as a human would be your friend. I am my lord's slave, first, always, and his word directs my actions."

He frowned. "Can you not be my friend and Lord Rezhyk's servant at the same time?"

"I can, so long as the two are not in conflict."

"Well, I hope that they never shall be. I will do my

best to stay on good terms with your master, as a proper apprentice should."

"Remember," she said, "only remember. Now look—" She pointed down the corridor, where two doors were opening in the mirror-smooth walls. "These are storerooms, Master Cray, where you will be sent frequently, to fetch materials for my lord. Gauge their locations by the distance from the head of the stairway, and when you stand before them and command, they will open for you."

She watched Cray stride forward to look inside the nearest aperture. He walked, she thought, with a sense of power about him, as if still carrying sword and shield and chain mail. Youth was in his tread, vital but controlled. Gildrum could not help comparing his sure step with Rezhyk's habitual nervous pacing. Would the one metamorphose into the other, she wondered, after a few years of apprenticeship?

Or is there too much of his mother in him for that?

She thought of Delivev with a pang, as if the human heart that she did not possess were being squeezed by a cruel fist; and she realized that she would always think of Delivev now, every time she looked at Cray.

Our son.

CHAPTER TWELVE

Cray was awakened by the simultaneous flashing on of all the lights in his room, and by a loud knocking at the door. He stretched, rubbed knuckles into both eyes, and assumed by his easy wakefulness that it was morning, though all times of day seemed equal inside Castle Ringforge.

245

"Let the door open," he said loudly.

The panel swung aside, admitting Gildrum, who carried a tray in her arms. "I think you'll like to break fast with this," she said. "You slept well?"

"Well enough, even though I lacked a window. All that tramping about yesterday, up and down the stairs, tired me out, as I suppose you intended." He rolled out of bed and padded barefoot, clad only in a long shirt, to the desk, where she had set the tray. The covered dishes yielded hot buttered porridge, bacon crisp-fried, soft-boiled eggs, and fresh bread. "Looking at your wand-slim lord, I would never have expected the lavish food that has been served me. I'll have a belly big as a washtub before I've been here a year."

"My lord will keep you running, I think. As for himself—he eats well and never gains weight. He is a man of considerable energy. He will require that you match him in that."

"I shall do my best."

"He awaits you in the workshop. As soon as you have done with the meal, dress quickly and descend the stairs. I will be waiting for you at the bottom." She smiled at him and glided out the door.

He found his gear in the cabinet, and in addition to his own clothing, which had been cleaned and neatly stacked on one of the lower shelves, there were fresh garments of similar cut—tunics and trews and hose, and even a pair of boots made to his measure, the leather smooth and unscuffed, even the heels. He chose from the new apparel, which felt crisp against his skin, not worn soft like his old things, which shredded at a touch too violent. He gazed at himself in the wall, purposely for the first time in his stay at Ringforge, and he turned this way and that to see himself from all angles, all around the room. He thought he looked different from the would-be knight who had traveled so far in a quest without a resolution. He had been as worn as his clothing, and now the fresh garments gave his body a fresh posture, his face a fresh expression. Now he felt ready to begin his new life as apprentice to Lord Rezhyk the sorcerer.

He galloped down the stairs, and at the bottom

he grinned at Gildrum and linked his arm with hers to go to the workshop.

The entry was at a location along the mirrored wall of the ground floor, and like all the other doors, it was not marked in any special way, save that it opened to Gildrum's voice.

"It will open to you, too," she told Cray, "when my lord wishes you to enter."

Rezhyk stood in the center of the huge room, at a long table; he leaned upon it with both elbows, his hands interlaced as a support for his forehead, and between his elbows rested a thick book, open. He did not look at Cray and Gildrum as they approached him.

Cray loosed his hold on the demon and bowed from the waist. "My lord, I am here as you called."

Rezhyk did not bother to look up. "Clean out the kiln."

"Come," whispered Gildrum, plucking at Cray's arm. "I'll show you how."

The kiln was large enough to house a man, its walls made of double layers of red brick. In its lowest section, beneath a coarse steel grate, was a mound of fine-sifted powder, ruddy as terra-cotta, dry as desert sand.

From a nearby cabinet, Gildrum drew a wide-mouthed leather sack, a bronze trowel, and a horse-hair brush, and she bade Cray scoop and sweep the powder into the sack. "Even the last faint film of dust must be removed, if you have to use your bare hands to gather it up; the kiln must be clean for the next firing."

"What is this?" he wondered, filling the sack carefully. "Smashed pottery?"

"Something of the sort," said Gildrum.

"But where are the ashes?"

"Fire demons produce no ash, Master Cray." She directed him to tie the sack up tightly with a thong, leaving a long, loose end hanging, and then she looked back to Rezhyk. "Is the label ready, my lord?"

He nodded without raising his head, his hand pushing something small and flat across the table toward her.

Cray retrieved the object, a palm-sized square of

bronze incised with symbols meaningless to his eyes. In one corner of the metal wafer, a small hole had been punched, and through this he threaded the end of the thong, knotting it securely at Gildrum's instruction. He lifted the sack in his arms. "Lead," he said to Gildrum. "I will follow."

The sack's destination was immediately next to the workshop, a long narrow room lined with shelves, that Cray had not seen the day before. The shelves were deep, row on row, and the lowest were stepped, one above the other, so that a person could climb them like stairs to reach the highest. Sacks lay upon the shelves, most of them singly, with wide intervals between neighbors, a few clumped together like sheep huddling against the cold. Some of the shelves were entirely empty: Gildrum led Cray to one of these and had him deposit his burden there.

"What is all of this?" he asked. He peered at the labels of several of the closest sacks but could read none of them any better than that of the one he had delivered. "How does Lord Rezhyk use this powder, and why does he save it? And why could it not be gathered up by the lowest of his demons?"

"It may not be contaminated," said Gildrum. "You will find, Master Cray, that there are certain things in Ringforge that no demon may touch, certain procedures that must be carried out by human hands alone. Until now, my lord has handled all these matters himself, low and time-consuming as some of them may be. His apprentice can do many of them just as well, and I presume that he will delegate those to you."

"Gathering up dust?"

"These are demon residues, not ordinary dust. As long as my lord has any use for the contents of one of these sacks, it may not be touched by any demon save that one it represents. And this particular demon is away on my lord's business right now."

Cray looked all about him, wide-eyed. "These are demons? These . . . flour sacks?"

"No, only demon residues. These are the bodies that my lord has fashioned for his servants, but not the servants themselves." At his puzzled expression, she added, "You will understand better when my lord shows you the process."

"And you can't touch any of them, not even the outsides of the sacks?"

She smiled. "Well, I could have carried the sealed sack in here, Master Cray, but you were so eager to do it yourself . . ."

"It was a heavy load for a slight thing like you, Gildrum. I assumed you meant me to take it."

"I am stronger than I appear," she said, and wrapping one hand about the thong-tied neck of the sack, she lifted the great weight without strain and held it steadily at arm's length. "I'm sure you would become quite bored in the time that I could stand here like this. And my lord would surely wonder what had become of us." She set it down carefully. "He will have more work for you. Come."

Rezhyk had begun to wonder already. He straightened as they re-entered the workshop. "I expect your tasks to be accomplished a bit more swiftly in the future, Cray Ormoru. You have much work ahead of you and little time for dawdling."

"My fault, my lord," said Gildrum. "I was convincing him that he cannot judge demons by human standards."

"Come over here, lad," said Rezhyk. "I want to teach you the first thing you must know about sorcery."

Cray approached him.

Rezhyk slapped the open book that lay on the table before him. "This is the source of all knowledge, lad. Look well, and understand what you see." He pushed the book at Cray. "Tell me what it is."

The volume was larger than any Cray had ever seen, either in the webs or with his own eyes—as tall as his forearm and equally broad, and thick as his four fingers together. The pages were heavy vellum, covered with close, crabbed writing, some of it in plain language, some in incomprehensible symbols. Occasionally, as he turned the sheets, he saw diagrams, but what they signified he could not guess. He tipped the book shut to examine the cover—it was rich red leather, emblazoned with the large numerals "54" tooled deep in the surface and embellished with bronze leaf. He opened to the first page and found that empty save for the numerals repeated in black ink and Rezhyk's name writ in large letters at the bottom, followed by a date several years gone.

He peered at the name and then at the first page which was filled with words. "My lord," he said, "is this perhaps your own handwriting?"

"It is."

He turned a few more pages, noting that each had a date written at its head, and not all were completely filled; some had blank space at the bottom, though nowhere else. He skipped through the sheets more quickly and found the final entry, dated the previous day, followed by a score or more of unused pages. He closed the book once more.

"These are your records," Cray said. "This is the fifty-fourth volume to record your work."

Rezhyk pulled the book back close to himself, laying one arm across it in almost a protective gesture. "You are near it, lad. Not precise, but near. This is indeed a record of my work, but only of a particular project, the fifty-fourth I have undertaken. There are other volumes and other projects, more of them than I think you could guess. This is not the most recent I have begun. I am careful to keep them separate and detailed. That is the first lesson you must learn, Cray Ormoru—careful record-keeping. You must never lose track of where you are." He pulled open one of the many drawers beneath the table; inside lay a volume of similar size and appearance, but plainer, in black, and without a number on the cover. He drew it out of the drawer and proffered it to Cray. "This will be yours. In it, you will record everything you learn, every sorcerous move you make, every lesson, every drill. I will examine it from time to time to make certain it is properly done. I expect you to write legibly and to draw clearly."

Cray hefted the tome, then swung it under his arm. "This is a different sorcery indeed," he said, "from that I know. My mother keeps no books of this kind."

"I have my methods," Rezhyk replied sharply. "If you will learn from me, you must use them."

"I understand, my lord. I only meant that I am more ignorant than I thought."

"You are entirely ignorant. I can't even guess if you are fit to become a demon-master; but I suppose we shall determine that soon enough. Come along." He made a peremptory gesture with the same hand that had given Cray the book, then he wheeled about and walked swiftly to the door. Cray hurried after.

They walked far—as far as one could walk in Castle Ringforge—and at the end of a mirrored corridor, Rezhyk called for a door to open on a small, brightly lit room. He entered, Cray close behind, and he went to a long table that occupied the center of the floor. There were drawers beneath it and an open brazier atop the smooth black slate of the work surface. It was a duplicate, though smaller, of the table in his own workshop.

"This will be yours," said Rezhyk, waving to encompass the whole chamber. "You will bring my instructions here and practice the arts I give you. Gildrum!"

The demon, who had followed their trek unobtrusively, glided up to the table. "My lord?"

"Light the fire."

She removed coal briquets from a low drawer, heaped them expertly, with air spaces properly distributed, and then she applied her finger to the center of the pile. Flame leaped from her fingertip, licking up over the black lumps, fluttering in yellow ribbons above them. In a moment, their edges caught, graying quickly with superficial ash, reddening with the heat of their own combustion. Gildrum drew back, and the flames sank, leaving glowing coals that made the air above the brazier shimmer.

"If you are wise," Rezhyk said to Cray, "you will feed this fire regularly and never let it die. Gildrum will show you how to bank it for the night."

"Could I not relight it from one of the sconces?" Cray inquired.

"You can answer that question yourself by passing your hand through one of the sconce flames. Go ahead. Do it."

"My lord?"

"You won't be injured. Go on."

Cray went to the wall and lifted his hand to the sconce. Even a finger's breadth away from the flame, he could feel no heat. He swept his thumb through the fire quickly, once, then again, then settled it there, and the blaze, bright as a beeswax candle, bright enough to read fine print by, engulfed his flesh to the knuckle. He felt only cool air, though his eyes told him that he should be screaming in pain. He drew his hand back slowly, and by that same light he inspected the thumb; it was not even soot-blackened.

Rezhyk said, "I advise you not to try that with the coals of the brazier, or with any other flame than these on the walls."

"Yes, my lord." Cray returned to the table. "I will take good care of this fire, I promise you."

"Very well. You will find various materials in the drawers appropriately marked. You may examine them at your leisure. Do not *use* them except at my direction. You will learn all their próperties soon enough. Every morning, I will expect you to come to my workshop first, immediately after your breakfast, and there I will set you the day's tasks. When you have finished *my* work, then you may retire up here to pursue your own. I do not require you to go to bed at any specific time, but I suggest that you do so early, for I shall have you called early every morning, and I shall accept no excuses for tardiness save dire illness."

"I have never had a dire illness, my lord."

"I am glad to hear it. I trust you shall not begin now." He pulled open a drawer at the far end of the table. "You will find sundries in here—pen and ink and blotting sand, straightedge and compass and so forth. I suggest you mark your notebook with your name and today's date and all that I have told you already."

Cray dipped the quill and inscribed the first page of his book, dutifully noting: *Never let the fire in the brazier go out.*

"Now," said Rezhyk, "the kiln must be scrubbed with soap and water before I can use it again, and there are other matters about my workshop that require your hand, so we shall return there, Cray Ormoru, apprentice."

As they passed through the doorway, the lights in Cray's new workroom dimmed, leaving only the glow of the brazier, ruddy and flickering, to be reflected in the walls. Cray bade the door close and hurried after his master, who was already several paces down the corridor.

In the following months, Cray learned that Rezhyk rushed everywhere, that he could not sit still for more than a moment save when engrossed in reading or writing. He expected Cray to be the same and set him endless tasks to fill up his time—cleaning, polishing, removing ashes, fetching stores from every part of Ringforge. And every time Cray wondered if all these things had to be done by human hands, his master would nod and say that *he* had done them before Cray's arrival. The lad marveled, then, that the man had had any time for sorcery.

"I was more efficient than you are, apprentice," Rezhyk told him.

Between chores, Rezhyk instructed Cray in certain basic sorcerous techniques: the crushing and smelting of ores, the assaying of alloys, the making of molds, and the passes to be performed and words uttered at every step of each process to insure safety and success. All these things he demonstrated in Cray's workroom, with Cray's allotted materials; rarely did he allow the youth to observe him with his own projects, and then only for the most trivial procedures. Cray took dutiful notes, and in the limited span of time left after all of this, he practiced his lessons over and over again. Some nights he crawled to bed long past the time his eyelids began to feel heavy, long past the time that flashing sconces warned him of a reasonable hour of retirement. Sometimes Gildrum would come up to his workroom on those late nights, bearing a tray of cheese and mulled wine.

"You work too hard, too late," she would say.

And he would reply, "I must."

One night the demon was standing by, watching him weigh a quantity of greenish powder. She leafed through his notebook. "He can find no fault with this," she said, scanning page after page.

"He has found fault," replied Cray. "With my handwriting, which he says is none too clear, with my addition and subtraction, which he says are frequently wrong, and with my lack of organization."

"As to the figuring . . . well, you must do better there, of course. But if you can read your handwriting, and if you can understand your organization, what fault lies there?"

Using a fine, camel's hair brush, Cray swept another pinch of powder into the left-hand balance pan. "He says I may not be able to read my own handwriting years from now."

"Ah." She squinted at the page that lay beneath her fingers. "It seems not so bad to me. And how much will you need these early lessons, anyway, later in your career?"

He grinned at her. "Are you suggesting that I slough your master's instructions, Gildrum?"

"No, no—you do well to follow them to the letter. He is a stern master."

With one more breath of powder, the two sides of the scales matched exactly. Carefully, Cray emptied the weighed substance into a small stone crucible that already contained a heap of black dust and one of white, side by side. With the green added, Cray stirred the three together with a glass rod, until the mix was a sickly gray.

"What are you making now, Master Cray?"

"Brass. Again. I swear there are as many different kinds of brasses as there are flowers in a meadow. And I have made none of them properly yet. I will never reach gold at this rate." He carried the crucible to the far end of the workroom, where a small oven stood hard against the wall. In the bottom of the oven a bright blaze, lit from a coal of the ever-burning brazier, was roaring; the coals glowed uniformly orange, with yellow flames dancing all about them, and the heat that spilled from the opened door was greater than any needed to roast a haunch of boar. Cray set the crucible in the claw of a pair of tongs and maneuvered it into the oven, loosing the tongs with a tiny shake and drawing them back. He closed the oven door and stepped away, his face red with the heat, perspiration popping out on his cheeks and forehead.

"Every time, I have done something wrong," he said. "Either the zinc ore was ill-roasted or the copper ore not pulverized fine enough, or there was too much charcoal or too little, or the additional trace materials were measured out wrong. . . . I have tried to be careful, but when Lord Rezhyk examines my work, he finds a thousand faults." He began to work the bellows attached to the side of the oven, to inject air into the heating mixture.

"You need more practice in these techniques," said Gildrum. "I am sure they did not come easy to him, either."

Cray sighed. "I suppose not. I've scarcely been here two months—how can I expect to master the art so quickly, even a small fraction of it? There is far more to learn than I ever dreamed. Still . . . I thought myself a better student than I have proved. Perhaps I am just better adapted to the other things that I have learned."

Gildrum pulled herself up onto the table. "Are you sorry that you chose this sort of sorcery?" she inquired, nodding slightly to the steady rhythm of the bellows.

"No. My reasons are as good as ever." He opened the oven door a crack, peered in, shut it again, and kept the bellows going. "And it is interesting of itself. Haven't you found it so, Gildrum?"

"I?"

"You must have learned a great deal over the years you've been associated with Lord Rezhyk. Enough to be a sorcerer yourself, I'll wager."

Gildrum crossed her legs tailor-fashion, smoothing her long skirt over them. "I suppose I have. Though I would never practice it, if I were free to do so. No demon would ever attempt to enslave another."

"No?"

"There would be no reason for it."

"No greed among demons? No lust for control over the world?"

"I've told you before, Master Cray—you cannot judge us by human standards."

Cray opened the oven again, and this time he was

satisfied with what he saw and let the door gape wide. He eased the tongs about the crucible and drew it out as gently as he might lift a newborn babe. The powders had fused into a glowing yellow bubble of liquid brass. Atop the oven lay a shallow clay mold, a featureless rectangle; Cray filled it with the molten metal.

"How glad I am," he said, wiping his sweaty brow with one sleeve, "that demons are drawing most of the fumes and heat away from this work. I'd have suffocated long since without them . . . without a window."

"Still thinking about windows, Master Cray? Even now that you know how little Ringforge needs them?"

"Yes, I still think about them. My mind knows that the demons supply better ventilation than any window, but my heart still yearns." He glanced back at her. "How many demons are there watching over me?"

"Oh, quite a number."

"Yet since the bronze bird brought me here, I have seen only you."

Gildrum made a sweeping gesture with one hand that included all the sconces on the walls. "You see a dozen or more of them every day, Master Cray."

"I mean in human form."

"Ah. Well, my lord has not given all his servants human forms."

"Why not?"

"Because the human form does not serve all purposes. It catches ocean fish poorly. It delves for gems poorly. It flies to the far corners of the world quite poorly."

"Yet," said Cray, "it serves well enough for Lord Rezhyk's greatest demon."

"I have other forms as well. But I wear this one most because my lord so bids me."

Cray sauntered over to the table, set the tongs beside the brazier and leaned on the warm slate, looking up at her curiously, as if searching for the telltale clue that would betray her inhumanity. "You seem quite human to me. A little cool, perhaps, and aloof, but I have met cooler. From your example, I can hardly believe that demons are so different from us."

"I have been among your kind a long time," she replied. "My lord says that has made me a misfit among my fellows."

"Do you like it—being among us?"

She stared down at him, that penetrating, unwinking stare, and after a long moment she said, "It does not matter whether I like it or no. A slave must accept the master's orders."

"But if you had a choice," Cray persisted, "would you choose to stay among humans, in human form?"

"It serves no purpose to consider such questions," Gildrum said, and she punctuated the remark by sliding off the table. "The hour is late, Master Cray, and your mold will not be cool for some time. Should you not seek your bed now?"

"I have a few other things to do." He glanced down at his feet. "If I have offended you, I apologize, Gildrum; I did not mean to do so."

"You cannot offend a slave," said Gildrum. "We are not allowed to be offended. Good night, Master Cray."

He weighed and measured and sealed powders into boxes for a time after she had gone, and he thought about the pain that had been so evident in her voice. He had encountered that tone before, that strained, hard-edged betrayal of grief. He had heard it from his mother and from Sepwin and—he realized suddenly—from himself. How harsh was slavery for a demon, he wondered, that it brought such sorrow? Was there home and family somewhere that mourned for Gildrum and she for them? Were there dreams unattainable, valuables lost, because Rezhyk required her presence?

Cray had never thought of demons being other than mindless forces, mere things without any real will or action of their own, until he met Gildrum. She was flesh and blood, or at least the semblance of flesh and blood, warm and palpable and human-seeming as anyone he had ever met. More human, he thought wryly, than some. Were all demons like her? He glanced about the room, and he could not will himself to believe that the flames that lit his work could change themselves into people and speak to him as equals.

Nor that she could turn into a flame like them.

He shook his head, then set about banking the brazier fire for the night, as she had taught him.

In the morning, he broke the wafer of brass out of its mold and presented it for Rezhyk's inspection. Rezhyk turned it over in his hands, peering close by the light of the brazier in his own workshop. Then he licked it with the tip of his tongue.

"Not quite right," he said. "Too much copper." He glared at Cray. "How many times must I tell you to be more careful?"

Cray sighed. "My lord, I am sorry. I will try again."

And so the first months of his apprenticeship passed, with Cray studying much but rarely completing his lessons to his master's satisfaction.

"Am I so incompetent, Gildrum?" he asked her. He sat on the floor of his workroom, a brick of the inevitable brass on the floor in front of him. He leaned forward and nudged it with one finger. His hands were red and raw from scrubbing the kiln that afternoon; Rezhyk had been sharper with him than usual after examining the latest piece of brass and had found fault even with his scrubbing, making him do it twice over for good measure.

Gildrum had just entered the room; he had seen her image in the bronze, a small, light-footed form poised at the open door, and he had bid her enter before she had a chance to ask. Even then, he did not look directly at her but stared glumly into the space between the brass brick and the near wall.

"This is not an easy art you seek to master," she said, standing behind him. "You cannot expect to learn everything in a few short months."

"I expect to learn *something*. I thought that I had. But no. Nothing comes out right for me. Yet . . . I don't know what greater care I can take. Perhaps I should give up." He frowned painfully. "He is a harsh man, your master, and I know he is not well pleased with me."

"He is harsh," said Gildrum.

"I can see the contempt on his face. Contempt for me and my failure. Sometimes I think he wants me to admit defeat and give up, stop wasting his time."

She sank to the floor beside him. "Do you want to give up?"

"I can't. There is no other way to find the answer I must have. But it seems farther away than ever." He gazed sidelong at her. "What shall I do, Gildrum?"

Gildrum drew her knees up and clasped her hands about them. Softly, she said, "How can I give you advice, Master Cray? To tell you to give up would be to contradict your own desires, and to tell you to persevere would be a betrayal of my own kind." She bent forward to rest her forehead on her knees. "I know what you want me to say, but do you really expect me to encourage you to enslave other demons?"

Cray sighed deeply. "I haven't any interest in enslaving demons. I only want an answer. One answer."

"It will not stop there, Master Cray. Power will awaken greed in your heart. After the question is answered, you will find other desires that demons can fulfill."

"No."

"You are young to be so sure."

"I have no other reason for apprenticing to Lord Rezhyk. Afterward . . . I don't know. That depends on the answer. But I never wanted power, Gildrum, I swear it."

"My lord was something of that sort once. He only wanted knowledge. Still, he only wants knowledge. But he has needed demons to gather it for him. There are scores of us in this fortress, slaves to him. We had lives of our own, before. Now we live for him alone, at his whim every hour of the day. Some he lets go back to the world we came from for shorter or longer visits, but the rings always call them back eventually. Some, like the demon-lights, never leave the human world."

"Like you."

She nodded, her forehead rubbing against her cloth-covered knees. "I have seen very little of my home since he called me to him."

"Do you miss it, Gildrum?"

Her face turned toward him, and one long braid slid over her shoulder to drape against her neck. "There are things that I miss. Home is one of them."

"And what are the others?"

"While I serve my lord," she said, "they do not exist."

"I pity you, Gildrum."

She smiled a trifle. "No more than I do myself, I'm sure."

"You know, Gildrum, if it were not for you, I *would* be tempted to leave here. You are my only friend in Ringforge. You are more human than he is."

Gildrum straightened. "I'm sure my lord would disagree with you on that."

"In your heart."

"Well, I haven't any heart, Master Cray. Don't forget that. It is this young and pretty body that charms you. If I had the semblance of an ugly old crone, you would undoubtedly rush me off quickly every time I came near you."

"No, I would not, for the Gildrum inside would be the same. But perhaps I would treat you with more deference, as befits a grandmother."

"I am old enough to be your grandmother and more."

Cray looked at her closely, as he always seemed to be looking at her, every time she reminded him that she was something other than human. And as before, he found no flaw in her appearance; he saw beside him only a girl several years younger than himself, just barely beyond childhood. "How long have you served him?"

"Since the beginning. I was the first. He worked seven years on the rings that captured me."

"And you have not aged."

"He would not allow this form to age. And, in demon terms, I am still young."

"How long do demons usually live?"

"Far longer than human beings, even sorcerers."

"Then you will outlive Lord Rezhyk?"

"I don't doubt it."

"And after he dies . . . will you be free, or will you pass to the next owner of the rings?"

"I'll be free, at least until some other sorcerer claims me as Lord Rezhyk did."

"Is that likely?"

Gildrum shrugged. "I'll be free for a time; who can

260

say how long? Perhaps the rest of my life. Perhaps not."

"But you'll be able to go home then. For a while, anyway."

"Yes," she said hollowly. "Home will be there, waiting for me."

"And . . . the other things?"

"I have no hope on that account."

Hesitantly, he touched her shoulder. "Poor Gildrum," he murmured. "Is it some demon lover who won't wait for you?"

She raised her head slowly, and he was startled to see a tear in her eye. "Master Cray," she said, "let us speak no further on these matters."

"So demons cry," he whispered.

"This demon cries. It has been too long among you." She scrambled to her feet, wiping away that single tear with the back of her hand. "I ask you not to tell my lord that you have seen me weep, Master Cray. I know he would not wish to think his most powerful demon as weak as a real human being."

"I won't tell him."

She bent to grasp his shoulder with one tense hand. "I wish you luck, Master Cray. With everything."

"I'll need some," he replied.

Rezhyk examined the rough-cast ring closely, holding it up to his eye with two fingers; the unpolished surface appeared to be covered with a fine yellow powder. "It goes well indeed, my Gildrum," he said. "Another year, I think, with this one, and we'll be ready to conjure." He waved at the demon with his free hand. "You'd better make some more entries for me in the false notebook. Something about lead."

Gildrum fetched the volume marked "54" from its special drawer and set it on the end of the worktable, open to the first blank sheet. From another drawer she took a quill and inkpot that her master did not need for his real work, then climbed onto her stool and hunched over the book to inscribe it with a perfect imitation of Rezhyk's crabbed script. "What shall I say about lead?"

"Add a little to the ring that's described there. As much as you like, it doesn't really matter."

"You've never added lead to your gold."

"So much the better. We've concocted a truly creative ring in those pages. What a pity it's so useless."

"You know, my lord, you needn't bother to keep this notebook anymore," she said, writing more quickly than her master would. "He'll believe whatever you tell him."

"I want to stay consistent, my Gildrum. His lessons may be a sham, but they are a logical sham. What do you have there?" He peered over her shoulder. "Good. Good. It certainly sounds likely. Very good." He picked up a round steel file and began to stroke the inner curve of the ring. "Do you think he is beginning to feel discouraged?"

"He has expressed his self-doubts to me several times, my lord, but he always finds the strength to continue." She waved her hand above the page, shedding enough mild warmth upon it to dry the ink without need for sand. She closed the book. "He has a strong will, that lad."

"This last task I set him—he did very well with it, my Gildrum. He has the touch, the exactitude the art requires. He could do well as a demon-master. I expressed my disappointment most strongly."

"He told me, my lord," she said, leaning her elbows on the red leather cover of the volume.

"Perhaps this should be the last chance I give him. I can tell him that he'll never do any better than with this most recent work." His lips tightened into a travesty of a smile. "And it will be true, certainly." He fell silent, and for a long time the only sound in the room was the rasping of the file against the gold of the ring. Soon fine golden dust speckled Rezhyk's hands and the slate surface over which he worked.

"No, my lord," Gildrum said at last. "It is too soon to turn him out."

"Too soon, my Gildrum? Almost a year already. The weather has come around pleasant again, good traveling weather. It would be no cruelty to send him on his way now."

"I said too soon, my lord. What is a year in a sorcerer's apprenticeship? If he does not object, his mother surely will. She will say that you have hardly given him a chance."

Rezhyk sighed over his filing. "You are right, of course, my Gildrum. He has barely begun his apprenticeship." He frowned. "But I cannot be comfortable while he is near me. It is as if *she* were here. My flesh crawls when I see him, and I want to shut him away and be done with him."

"I shall endeavor to keep him out of your sight, my lord, if you wish it. I can even oversee most of his lessons."

"Yes. Yes, do that."

"You have been with us a year today," said Gildrum, leaning close to Cray's elbow to watch him write. His script had shrunk in the time he had been keeping the notebook, and each day's work required less space than the previous, though it was no less lengthy. He had nearly filled the volume Rezhyk had given him.

"Has it been so long?" he muttered. "Without the passage of the seasons to gauge time by, I have lost track."

"You have the date on every page."

"That is just a number. Winter has come and gone, it tells me, but my body still lives in the summer of my arrival. Ringforge is always the same, summer and winter. I might have been here a year or a hundred years." He measured the thickness of the used pages with a finger and thumb. "Sometimes it seems like a hundred."

"A year only, and it is summer again."

Cray blew on the writing to dry it. "A whole year—and I have not once been outside these walls. I, who used to spend my days in the open air." He shook his head ruefully. "I have grown pale."

She peered into his face. "Your cheeks are pale," she agreed.

"My heart, too."

She cocked her head to one side. "Well, I think my lord might agree to a brief holiday, for this anniversary afternoon, if you are so inclined."

He smiled at her. "I am inclined, but I have too much work to do. I have this batch right at last, I'm sure; he'll find no fault this time. If I can persuade him to look at it."

"Oh, he'll look at it, no doubt about that, Master Cray. I'll take it to him myself as soon as it's cool."

"He must be quite disgusted with me, to avoid me as he has lately."

"He has been very busy."

"So busy that he stays away from his own workshop when I am there?"

"There are other rooms in Castle Ringforge, Master Cray. He does not spend every waking hour in the workshop."

"And he takes care that my work there shall be completed in those hours that he is absent." Cray tipped his book shut. "Well, I find I cannot blame him. I have hardly become the sort of apprentice that would make him proud."

Gildrum turned to saunter away from him, around the table, one small hand brushing lightly along the smooth surface. She turned two corners and came to a halt directly opposite him; she leaned toward him, arms crossed upon the table, her eyes following the motions of his hands as he scrubbed the top clean of many-hued powders. "He hasn't given you much help," she murmured.

"Apprenticeship has been a trifle lonelier than I expected." He grinned at her. "Which has made me more grateful for your visits, Gildrum."

"You will get no more personal attention from him in the future than you have in the past. Less."

"Oh, after he sees this batch of brass, I think his attitude will change."

"Are you so poor a judge of human beings, Master Cray?"

He laid his hands upon the book. "A little success . . ."

"He is a harsh man. You think your success will make him less so?"

"Well . . . yes, of course." His brow knit quizzically. "Why take an apprentice if you find no joy in his successes?"

With one slim finger, she swiped at a speck of dust, giving the gesture a long moment of her attention, as if it were intrinsically fascinating. Then quietly, she said, "You think my lord took an apprentice to build himself a rival?"

Cray stared at the top of her blond head. "Well . . . no, perhaps not. Perhaps just to sweat for him at tasks he no longer wishes to do himself. Still, he is bound by custom to teach me his art in return for my labor."

"Is he?"

"Of course."

"You say that so easily, Master Cray. Have you learned nothing in this year?"

"What are you saying, Gildrum? That he cares nothing about teaching me sorcery? That he apprenticed me . . . as a human slave to do the things that his demon slaves must not?"

She gazed at him from beneath raised eyebrows. "Can you bear to think that?"

Cray shook his head sharply. "He wouldn't do that. It's . . . it's dishonorable."

"Is the sorcerous breed such an honorable one?"

"Why are you saying such things, Gildrum? What trick are you trying to play on me?"

"No trick, Master Cray. I only wonder how you have lived in Ringforge a year now with your eyes tight shut."

He wheeled away from her but was confronted with her image and his own in the wall. He looked down at the floor, where only his own foreshortened self stared back. "You are his creature, Gildrum. Why are you trying to turn me against him?"

Her voice was high, light, piercing. "I do his bidding, Master Cray, but I think my own thoughts. You think I love the one who has power over me?"

"Can you speak such words within the very walls of his own fortress?"

"I spy for my lord, Master Cray; he does not spy on me. He trusts me completely. Yet, the slaves may mutter when the master is out of earshot, even though they grovel to kiss his feet when he is near."

Cray eyed her over one shoulder. "So I should believe you when you say that I am a fellow slave . . .

and nothing more." He gestured abruptly at the book, his arm rigid, fingers splayed. "What is this then? Nonsense?"

Gildrum said, "What do you think it must be?"

"He wouldn't dare!" cried Cray. "He wouldn't dare treat me so shabbily. If my mother found out, she would be furious; and her fury is a force to be reckoned with—he must know that."

"Your mother's fury does not concern him."

"Well, it should! She is no weakling to be disregarded!"

"He does not fear her." Gildrum straightened up stiffly. "Master Cray, I told you that my lord trusts me, and that is true enough. Yet when it was decided that you come here, he gave me certain instructions . . . he forbade me to speak of certain matters. One of these matters is a thing which would, I think, prove to you the truth of everything I have said today. If you could only see that thing, you would no longer doubt me."

"Show it to me then."

"Ah—that will be no simple task. It will require that you disobey my lord's command and enter where he has not sent you . . . where he would never send you."

"Where?"

"His bedroom."

"He keeps this . . . thing there?"

"Sometimes. That is the place where you may see it most readily."

Cray's lips tightened. "Do you swear to me, Gildrum, that this thing is proof?"

"I know of no better, Master Cray. Believe me, your eyes and your understanding will open when you see it."

Beside his thigh, Cray's right hand clenched into a fist. "Very well. How may I enter his bedroom if he gives me no permission?"

Gildrum smiled slightly. "I can arrange that. But there is a complicating condition."

"Yes?"

"The thing to which I refer is only there when my lord is there, and only readily visible when he is about to retire. We must hide you, therefore, somewhere in the room before he enters. You will have to stay the whole night, utterly silent, closed up in one of the cabinets, with only a hinge crack for light and air. I will make certain that the thing will be visible to you from your vantage."

"A complicating condition indeed," said Cray. "You ask quite a bit of me. What if I am discovered?"

Gildrum inclined her head. "There is that chance. But the cabinet is the likeliest hiding place—better than under the bed. I will contrive to cover any noises you make, as long as I am there. After I leave . . . well, he sleeps soundly."

"You are asking me to risk my apprenticeship, Gildrum. If he discovers me, that will be the end of it."

She shrugged. "You have nothing now. You risk nothing."

"So *you* say."

"Do you wish to wait until he rejects your latest bar of brass? Will my words seem more likely then?"

Cray glanced toward the oven, where the metal lay cooling, almost cool enough to break out of the mold. "I don't want to believe you, Gildrum. But . . . if he rejects this one . . . Well, I can do no better than it. I would feel obliged to leave anyway; he wouldn't have to throw me out." His gaze swerved to her face, so childlike and innocent to belong to an inhuman creature. "And if there *is* proof—what then? What shall I do?"

"We can discuss that afterward, Master Cray. I have a suggestion for you, when the time comes."

"You want something from me."

She nodded. "I only hope it may lie within your power."

"I have no power. And you have said that your lord will give me none."

She smiled. "Let us discuss that later."

"I can make no promises, Gildrum; not till I've seen what you would show me."

"Well enough."

"And I'll take this brass bar to him myself, if you don't mind."

"It will not do!" raged the sorcerer Rezhyk. "Is it

that your hand is so unsteady, boy? Or is your eye so blind that you cannot see the scales balance?"

Cray stood quiet under his wrath, his eyes fixed on the brass ingot that lay before the brazier on his master's workbench. One edge of the bar had been scraped, and the fragments of metal so removed dissolved into tinted liquids in several flasks. Rezhyk clutched one in his hands, his fingers wound so tight about its narrow neck that they seemed likely to snap it any moment.

"Am I close, my lord?" Cray inquired.

"Close? Close will not do, lad! You must learn to be exact! Have you been here so many months and still not learned how to measure?"

Cray hung his head. "I thought I had learned, my lord."

Rezhyk set the flask down heavily. "I waste materials on you, Cray Ormoru. I might as well be throwing them to the wind."

"I will try harder, my lord," Cray whispered.

"You must! Or I shall find myself another apprentice! Out of my sight now! Out!"

As soon as he stepped into his workroom and closed the door, Cray heaved the brass bar the length of the chamber; it struck the far wall, clanging against the bronze like a clapper in a bell, and the whole room reverberated with the note.

"You wanted to see him yourself," said Gildrum, watching Cray as he stood in the center of the floor, his arms tight against his sides, his fists white-knuckled. "I have not lied to you on that."

"No," he replied. "And now I shall see what comes next. When does Lord Rezhyk retire?"

"We have plenty of time. No need to hasten to make yourself uncomfortable."

"I won't be uncomfortable," said Cray.

"Perhaps not at first, but toward dawn you'll find yourself cramped. And in need of facilities that will not be inside the cabinet."

"I don't intend to be inside the cabinet. I don't like your plan, Gildrum. I have a better one: a little trick my mother taught me."

268

"Sorcery?"

"Won't my mother's sorcery work inside Ring-forge?"

"Of course it will. That is why my lord forbids it."

"Good. As well disobey one way as another." Slowly, he turned to look at her. "Unless you choose to expose me."

"Not I."

"And you have control over these others, I perceive, or you would never have spoken so freely to me in front of them." He opened one fist to wave at shoulder level, at the sconces, and on the palm of his hand were the imprints of his fingernails.

"I have a certain hegemony here, Master Cray," said Gildrum, "when my lord makes no demands. He gave you into my care some time ago, and so what he knows of you is now entirely filtered through me."

"Well enough. We are conspirators now, Gildrum. You have knowledge of my disobedience, and I have knowledge of yours. I know that discovery means I will be cast out. What will it mean to you?"

Gildrum lowered her eyes. "He will not discover anything . . . if you are not foolish."

"But *if* . . ."

"There are punishments that I would prefer not to contemplate. Being sealed in solid rock until my lord dies is perhaps the least of them."

"Yet you dare this punishment." Cray frowned mightily. "Why?"

She raised her gaze to him, and in the liquid depths of her eyes he saw beyond the guileless youth of her body; he saw a darkness like the still, cold waters of the lady Helaine's pool, and he shivered with a sudden chill. She seemed to look into his heart with those eyes, into his marrow.

"You are my friend," she said.

He shook his head. "You told me, once, that we could not be friends if it conflicted with your lord's commands. Have you changed your mind on that?"

"I told you that I could not be your friend, not that you could not be mine." She rubbed her palms together, as if human sweat had accumulated there, sweat of nervous anticipation, and Cray found himself wishing to touch her hands to see if it were really there. But he stood where he was, not even reaching out across the small space that separated them.

"I tread a narrow path, Master Cray," she continued. "Narrower than any demon before me. I have not lied to my master, but I have . . . avoided speaking of certain matters. So long as he does not ask, I can go on as I have." Her lips tightened briefly. "You must not cause him to ask, Master Cray. My fate is in your hands. And now we must be on our way. I will guide you to his chamber."

"Carry me instead," said Cray. "I'll hide up your sleeve, and he won't even see me in a suspicious corridor. You can bring me back here, too, afterward."

"Up my sleeve?" said Gildrum.

Cray nodded. "I'll be ready in just a moment."

Swiftly, he stripped off his clothes and shut them in a drawer. Then, standing naked and pale on the mirrored floor, he bent forward from the waist, slowly, reaching with outstretched fingertips for the reflection beneath his feet. He murmured softly, unintelligibly, and the skin all over his body began to shudder, as if a thousand snakes were crawling just beneath the surface. His paleness flushed and darkened, tanning as under a hundred afternoons of sunshine, and as the pigment intensified, his body contours began to alter. His limbs shortened, his head absorbed his neck and pulled tight against his shoulders, his torso compressed into his abdomen, and all the time his entire frame was shriveling and shrinking, like a wineskin spilling its contents. He sprouted dark hair and strange mandibles, and his fingers and toes turned spindly as straw till they were his legs, eight fragile legs supporting the diminishing weight of his bulbous abdomen and tiny head. Within the space of a score of heartbeats, he had transformed himself into a spider no larger than the last joint of a grown man's thumb.

Gildrum stared down at him. "A wonderful little trick," she said. "Can you speak?"

Silence answered her question. She scooped him up, and he scuttled into her sleeve, just as his own spiders had done with his own sleeve, so many months before.

As a spider, Cray's viewpoint was limited. His eyes

and ears were sharp, still human, though altered in appearance and proportion to his body and veiled by his dark hair; no natural spider had ever borne the senses with which Cray contemplated his environment. But the world was a vaster place to him in that guise —human works were like nature's monuments to him, human sounds like nature's thunder. And, as a spider, he always found himself extraordinarily attracted to flies. He could hear three of them buzzing about the corridors of Ringforge now, as if they were the castle's only occupants, and he yearned to settle himself in some dark corner and spin a web to catch them. He had never eaten a fly—his mother had frowned upon such indulgence in the course of magic—and he wondered what they tasted like.

Gildrum carried her arm stiffly, unaccustomed to bearing a spider, but to her passenger the ride was a bad voyage through stormy seas, and he was relieved when it ended at last. Peeking out of her cuff, he watched a section of the wall open to her and reveal Rezhyk's private chamber. It was furnished simply, not unlike his own, except all the furniture was of bronze, with black cushioning. Gildrum set Cray in the shadow beneath a bar of the bedstead and bade him stay there without stirring. Rezhyk, she said, did not like spiders and might do something unpleasant if he noticed one crawling on his bed. Cray laid a tiny ring of sticky web to the underside of the bar and clung there comfortably, dark hidden by dark.

Shortly, Rezhyk retired. He came in with Gildrum, who had gone out of the room as soon as she had seen Cray settled, and now she helped him undress, slipping the mantle from his shoulders and hanging it in the nearest cabinet, pulling off his bronze-studded boots, his silken hose, his linen shirt.

And Cray saw what he was meant to see.

The light from many sconces glinted from the threads of Rezhyk's cloth-of-gold shirt, and beside the pure glory of that lustrous garment, the bronze walls dimmed to dross. Mirrors they were, only mirrors on every wall, and cold metal, cold as a winter's night behind the sunny cheer of yellow gold. Cray could make out the delicate weaving that had shaped the garment, and the flaws that marred it here and there, betraying an amateur's hand. And hot fury grew in his frail spider's body, for he perceived that a garment woven of metal was a trespass upon his mother's province and an insult to her—all the more so because Rezhyk wore it hidden beneath his other clothing, next to the warm skin that enveloped his heart. He was not at all surprised that he had never seen the shirt before; he understood that Rezhyk would never dare to show it to Delivev Ormoru's son.

Gildrum slipped a nightshirt over her master's head, and the gleam of gold disappeared beneath ordinary fabric. Then she stepped back, easing toward the foot of the bed as she bid him good night, and her hands trailed lightly over the bedstead; when they passed Cray's hiding place, he leaped to her cuff. Rezhyk had already turned over and pulled the blankets up to his chin; he did not bother to watch his oldest slave leave the room.

In his own workshop, Cray regained his human form as easily as he had shed it, and he stretched and flexed his muscles, which had cramped up with the transformation. To Gildrum, who watched him with impassive eyes, he said, "The shirt seems fairly well made. Is it his own work?"

"He is a diligent worker and independent."

"And what purpose does it serve?"

"Can't you guess, Master Cray?"

"Armor?" He regarded her skeptically. "How can he need armor when he is surrounded by demons? Surely they are better protection than any golden shirt, no matter what spells are impressed upon it."

Gildrum shrugged. "He had certain fears, Master Cray, at one time."

"What did he fear?"

"Not what. Whom."

"Whom, then?"

"Don't you know?"

"My mother is not his enemy!" Cray sputtered. "She doesn't care about him one way or the other!"

"Are you quite sure about that?"

"In all the years I lived with her, I don't remember her mentioning his name once. If she had had any feelings about him at all, surely I would have heard *something*."

Gildrum clasped her hands behind her back, tightly. "The events which caused my lord to make what you have just seen happened before you were born, Master Cray, and I fear I cannot discuss them with you. Suffice it to say that my lord had his feelings, no matter what your mother's may have been. And so the thing was made. And so, I hope, you now understand why it is that my lord treats you as he does."

Cray shook his head and heaved a loud sigh. "I do not understand at all, but I do perceive that my apprenticeship in Ringforge will never give me what I want." His hands flexed into fists. "I must leave, then, Gildrum, and find some other, more honest master. I have wasted a year; there's little point in wasting another day. I shall leave tomorrow."

"You needn't leave, Master Cray," said Gildrum. "I will miss you, I know."

"You can stay and learn."

"Learn what? How to scrub out a kiln? I know that already, thank you."

"I will be your teacher."

Cray looked at her speculatively. "Is it possible?"

"I know everything my master knows. I could conjure demons if I wished, if the very thought did not repel me. I will teach you."

"Teach me to enslave your kind? When the very thought of it repels you? Would you *really* do that?"

"For a price."

Cray rocked back on his heels. "Ah . . . a price."

"I will teach you," said Gildrum, "in return for my freedom."

They stared at each other for a long moment then, he with brows knit tight above questioning eyes, she with a bland, steady expression. At last he said, "How could I give you your freedom when you belong to Lord Rezhyk?"

"When I have done teaching you, you will know how."

"And . . . he will be my enemy."

"If he is still alive."

"Will I have to kill him to free you?"

273

"Not necessarily."

"But . . . perhaps?"

"Not if you don't want to."

"What would he do afterward, though—after I have stolen away his oldest and best demon?"

"You will not be without resources—I will see to that." She stepped toward him, one hand outstretched, as if offering the future on a platter of flesh. "I can teach you his art and more. He has spent years seeking knowledge; I will give you what he knows and what he has not found yet. You will be greater than he is, in a fraction of the time. He will not be able to stand against you." Her hand reached for him, hovering just below his face, and he could not help staring down at it, though it held nothing but invisible promises. "Live here in Ringforge," she said. "Feign my lord's apprenticeship while you serve a truer one to me. I promise you, you shall not regret it."

He lifted his gaze from her soft pink palm to her eyes. "You would betray your kind to me . . . for your own freedom?"

"If you find another master, we are as well betrayed. This, at least, will profit one of us." Her dark eyes narrowed. "And did you not tell me that you would be different from him? That you were not interested in demon-mastery but in something else?"

"You know what I want," said Cray.

"Then we shall both have what we want. Will you stay?"

"Won't Lord Rezhyk find out?"

"Not if you are circumspect. You will have to continue to scrub the kiln and other such drudgery, but you needn't waste your time with the lessons he sets you. I will report to him on your progress, and you can keep a book of nonsense to show him whenever he visits. *That* will not be often."

"Shall I believe you, Gildrum? Or are you tricking me as much as he is?"

Her hand dropped slowly away from his face. "Believe me," she said, "I want my freedom more than I can tell you. Without you, I have no hope."

Cray bowed his head. "I don't know what to say, Gildrum. I want an answer, not a war with another

274

sorcerer. The answer may determine the course of the rest of my life. Or it may do nothing at all. I don't know. I can't make you any kind of promise with a good conscience. Perhaps I should just find another master."

"No!"

"You'd be no worse off than you are now."

"Master Cray—I beg you . . ."

"And I don't know if I want to learn that much sorcery. I only want . . . an answer. If you could give me that answer, I'd leave Ringforge now."

Gildrum stood silent.

Cray gazed at her through lowered lashes. "If you were my slave, you'd find that answer for me."

"I can show you how to conjure a slave that will."

"Will you show me that, then, Gildrum? Only that? I don't want the rest."

"You might decide you do want it. Later."

"That would be later. For now . . ." He shook his head. "I can't make you a promise, Gildrum. I'm sorry."

She turned away from him. "I will teach you then," she said heavily, "in hope that later your heart will soften toward me."

"Gildrum! I don't mean to hurt you, but . . ." He waved his hands uncomfortably. "Gildrum, I am very young. I don't really know what it is that you're offering me, nor if I want it, nor if I ought to have it. My life is too much of a turmoil for that sort of decision here and now. You ask a great deal of me, and I am not even prepared to contemplate it."

She cast a glance back over her shoulder. "There will be time for contemplation if you stay."

He took a deep breath. "Then I will stay. Until I find my answer. Beyond that . . ." He shrugged.

"I accept that," said Gildrum. "You are young. I forget sometimes how very young you are." She smiled, tentatively. "You're a good lad, Master Cray. Another might have given me his promise without ever intending to keep it."

"We must be honest with each other," said Cray, "if we are to work together."

She looked away from him. "I am limited in my

275

honesty, Master Cray. My lord commands, and so there are things I must keep from you. I hope you will forgive me for them."

"As long as you do not lead me astray, Gildrum."

"I shall endeavor not to."

"Then there is something I must ask of you, to seal our bargain. But perhaps Lord Rezhyk has commanded you to keep it from me."

"What?"

"Your true form."

She threw her head back, lifting her gaze to the ceiling, and her long yellow plaits swung behind her, brushing the blue fabric of her skirt. "My true form," she echoed. "No, he has not forbidden it. But this is the shape I wear in his presence. You would prefer it, I know, to my true form."

"Still," said Cray. "I would see it."

"Very well, Master Cray. I suggest you step back from me. My flame shall be cool and shall not sear your flesh, but it will be bright."

He saw her watching his reflection in the far wall as he backed off. When another wall prevented him from moving further, she nodded once. Then, in a single instant, between one heartbeat and the next, blond girl and blue dress vanished in a burst of flame.

Cray started violently, clutching at the smooth surface behind him as if it were his mother's skirts. His mind could hardly fathom what he had seen, and his eyes could only stare glassily, unblinking, at the fire that spilled about the room, bounced off the walls and was multiplied a hundredfold in polished bronze.

Her voice, when it came at last, was whispery, crackling, like damp logs burning on a hearthfire—not the girl's voice but something inhuman and unknown. "Are you satisfied, Cray Ormoru?"

He pressed hard against the wall, and then the flames splashed toward him, engulfing him in yellow light. He started again and closed his eyes involuntarily, and when they were closed he could still see the light, blood red, beyond his eyelids. But he felt nothing. He opened his eyes again and found himself still enveloped, flame like a robe about him, dancing on his arms and legs, veiling the room from his sight like a tenuous yellow curtain. He raised a hand before his face, and it was alight, a living wick. He looked past his hand, to the far wall, and he saw his whole body blazing.

In another moment, the flame had drawn away from him, was flowing toward a corner of the room, coalescing into a small, bright ball, pinching into an elliptical shape. The fire dimmed then and solidified into a small, blond girl. "You have seen," she said in her human voice. "And now, I think, our friendship will never be the same."

Cray tried to swallow, but his throat was desert-dry. He whispered, "Now I know why the ancients worshiped fire."

Slowly, she walked toward him. "Are you afraid of me?" she asked.

He pushed himself away from the wall with one hand. "No!" he said loudly.

"Are you quite certain?"

They met at the center of the room, halting when there was a single arm's length between them. He looked down at her. "I feel like a fool," he said. "I, the child of a sorcerer, and an apprentice in my own right—I cringed from a show of sorcery. I am ashamed of myself, and I ask you to excuse my behavior."

"Your mind knew I was a demon," said Gildrum. "Now your heart knows, too."

He offered her his hand. "I reaffirm our friendship, Gildrum."

She gazed at his extended hand a time, and then she took it firmly. "Our friendship," she said. "As much as it can be."

❧ CHAPTER THIRTEEN

As the years passed, Cray's features hardened. He had been a boy when he set out on his quest, no matter what his mother thought, or what he thought himself. He had had his full stature and his adult strength, but his face had been still soft and rounded, his cheeks full, his chin downy. Now the subtle changes of maturity crept upon him, hollowing the spaces beneath his cheekbones, narrowing his once-wide eyes and etching them with shadows. He grew a pale beard and a mustache that veiled his upper lip like dandelion fluff. In the mirror of his walls, he saw himself every day and was not startled by the gradual alteration in his appearance, but on each anniversary of his arrival at Ringforge he paused to stare at himself and wonder what his mother would say if she could see him.

"I look more like her now than ever before," he mused one time. "Except for the beard, of course."

At his shoulder, Gildrum looked at his reflection and then away, saying nothing.

He was an excellent student. He found that sorcery could be fascinating if the frustration of constant failure were removed. His workroom was alight through more nights than not, as he strove to master Gildrum's instructions, as he smelted brass and bronze and silver, as he practiced the gestures and intonations that would bring him his goal. He hardly saw Rezhyk anymore; Gildrum was their go-between, relaying even the orders to perform menial tasks and reporting fraudulent training and results to her master. Cray kept his notebook of nonsense, though Rezhyk rarely looked at it, and in the meantime his true notebooks multiplied with the intensity of his concentration.

Occasionally, after he had grown the beard, after he realized his talents truly lay in the direction of sorcery, he would think about his life as it had been. In the moments while the oven was baking ores, while a new mold was cooling, or while he was scrubbing the kiln for Rezhyk, his mind would drift back and he would feel an ache deep inside himself, a loss, an emptiness. At last, he succumbed to these feelings, one night when a new alloy lay cooling atop the oven; he opened the cabinet where his old gear had lain untouched for so long. His sword was there, his shield, his chain mail. There was no dust upon them, no dust anywhere in Castle Ringforge, thanks to the diligent demons. He drew the sword from its scabbard, slowly, and the steel blade seemed a cold thing in the warm bronze light of the room. It seemed heavy, too, to his muscles long unaccustomed to hefting its weight. He took up the shield then, and his left arm sagged, tendons protesting sharply below the elbow.

Has it been so long? he wondered.

He swung the sword experimentally, and he felt his joints creak, like those of an arthritic old man trying to rise in the morning. He let the tip of the blade dip till it touched the floor. His hand clasped the hilt tightly. He felt shame rise within him, for his body no longer obeyed him with the ease of yesterday.

From that day on, he began to exercise. He had little enough time for such things, yet he found some opportunities, which otherwise he might have spent in reverie. In the workroom, he stretched, he tumbled, he ran in place, he lifted bars of metal over and over again. And in his bedchamber, each night before sleeping, he swung his sword at the reflections in the walls. There was no opponent with unanticipated reflexes, nor even a tree to beat at, yet Cray found himself enjoying the activity. The skills came back quickly, the stamina followed. Soon Cray carried the shield and swung the sword with the old ease, as if they were extensions of his body, and if he never struck a solid target, at least he never ran any risk of shattering his weapon from the impact.

He never wore the chain.

Gildrum found him feinting at his reflection one evening. She said nothing, but her quizzical expression prompted him to offer an explanation.

"I've grown soft here in Ringforge," he said. "The exercise is good for me."

She said nothing. She was frequently silent these days, except during the lessons. Cray had begun to work with gold already, and they both knew that the time of his first conjuration was fast approaching. Though Gildrum had vowed to speak of the future to him, she had not done so, had shied away when the topic came up between them, as if she were afraid that the mere mention of what could be would make him reject it.

"I suppose I can't forget completely," Cray said, gazing at his reflection. "This is what I was for so very long. I look more the part now, with the beard, don't you think?" He smiled with one side of his mouth. "No more the stripling, Gildrum. There's none could deny I'm a man now."

"You are still young," she murmured.

"I'll be twenty soon enough. Not young anymore."

She shook her head. "Still."

She was not with him when he conjured the demon.

The rings had taken him more than a month to make, simple bands, smooth and slim, one fitting the little finger of his left hand, the other larger, an armlet for the slave. They bore no stones, no figured devices, and Cray knew that whatever demon would be drawn to them would be scarcely greater than one of Rezhyk's sconce lights. Yet Gildrum had assured him that his answer could be extracted even from such a one.

He had begun with virgin ore, the greater part gold, with a small admixture of silver for hardness. He had smelted the two together, poured the molten metal into a pair of clay molds and then soaked the resulting circlets in an acid bath before filing, polishing, and buffing them to a mellow luster. His meticulous notes showed the painstaking precision of the process, and the magical essence which had been imbued at every stage, with words and gestures and particularly with every stroke of file, emery, and rouge.

His brazier was ready, packed with coals glowing fitfully with ruddy light. At Gildrum's instruction, he had put out the original fire lit by her finger and started a fresh, unmagical one with flint and steel. He set the arm ring upon it and the finger ring on his own hand. He had never worn a ring before, and the tiny weight felt odd to him, as if some small animal clutched at his finger, a spider sitting there with legs clasping his flesh. He covered the ring-bearing finger with his other hand and began the chant that would summon his servant.

So hypnotized was he by the steady rhythm of his own words that he did not notice at first that the flames of the brazier leaped yellow before him, sputtering in a column that rose a full arm's length from the center of the arm ring. He had expected more, a pillar that would brush the ceiling at least, but when it remained diminutive, pulsing like a living heart caught fast by the circle of the ring, he ceased his chant, and with his arms outflung, he cried, "Take your earthly form! I command it!"

The flame wavered and shrank till it seemed no more than a burning twig lying upon the coals, and then it solidified into a creature no larger than a twig, than a flower stem. It stood upright within the ring, mantislike with jointed limbs and large-eyed head; its greenish skin was covered with stubby thorns. Beneath its feet, the coals glowed red and flameless.

It said, "My lord."

"Inscribe your name upon the ring," commanded Cray.

In a tiny, crackling voice, the creature said, "It is done."

Among the coals, Cray could see the spidery script taking form upon the inner surface of the armlet. He pulled his own ring off to confirm that it was there, too. He read the name Yra. He slipped the ring back on. "Welcome to Ringforge, Yra," he said. "Now I have a question for you, and you must not rest until you have found me the answer."

"Speak, my lord," it said, and Cray wondered if the sound came from the tiny throat or from the movement of the serrated legs, like insect chirping.

"You must discover me the name and house of my father, whether he is alive now, and where I may find him."

"It shall be done, my lord."

"Go."

The creature turned back to flame and melted to nothing like golden sunlight before a cloud.

With a long-handled pair of tongs, Cray removed the armlet from the brazier and set it upon the slate surface of the table. He passed his hand above it, and when he felt no radiant heat, he touched the metal and found it merely warm. After inscribing Yra's name in the appropriate notebook, he dropped the arm ring into a drawer; he contemplated it there, before shutting it away from his sight, wondering if any other ring would ever lie beside it. He felt that the end of his quest—and a portion of his life—was imminent, and though he had felt that way before and been disappointed, he could not resist the sense of elation that made his heart beat hard in his breast and his hand shake a trifle where it rested on the lip of the drawer.

Gildrum brought him dinner, and he said nothing to her of his afternoon's work. Nor did she ask, but he guessed that she could read excitement in his eyes and that she must know what had transpired; the sconce-demons, at least, would have told her what they had seen.

Later, Cray lay upon his bed, sleepless, staring at his reflection in the ceiling. He watched himself finger his beard, toss his head from side to side, twist and turn upon the sheets, seeking some comfortable position. At last he arose, and there in his bedchamber he commanded his servant to appear.

It came as a flame again, a yellow teardrop shape, burning silently in the middle of the air, shedding no heat. Even the sconces seemed brighter.

"Have you found my answer yet, Yra?" Cray demanded.

In the crackling whisper of flame, it replied, "My

lord, I am small and weak. The task you have set me will take time."

"How much time?"

"I cannot say, my lord. I am doing my best."

"Of course you are. Continue, Yra, and report to me the instant you have the information."

"Yes, my lord." The flame shrank immediately to a pinpoint and vanished.

Still, Cray could not sleep, so he fetched the sword and shield from their cabinet and spent the remainder of the night beheading invisible enemies. Gildrum found him so, sweating and panting, when she brought him breakfast. She stood by while he ate, and more than once he fancied she was about to speak, but apparently she thought better of it and held off. She left, as she had come, in silence, and for all the rest of that long day she did not come near him save to bring him food. He could not have spoken to her if she had, for his mind was a-rush with anxiety, and every beat of his heart was a club striking his flesh, every flicker of sconce-flame a knife blade feinting toward his throat. He could not sit still, he could not pace the floor. He began a thousand tasks and put each aside unfinished. Even sword and shield could not divert him now, as he marked endless time with the singing of his nerves.

That night, haggard and red-eyed, he hunched over his desk, scribbling aimlessly, correcting notes that were already accurate, elaborating drawings that were already sufficient. His hand could hardly hold the pen, his script was nigh illegible and the drawing no better, but he could hardly tell, for his vision swam with the light and dark of exhaustion. Once, he looked at himself in the mirrored wall, and the face he saw so close to his own was alien to him, tired, old. He shook his head sharply to clear the vision, but the image remained, for it was a true picture of himself. He shut his eyes to blot it out, and he could scarcely open them again; he felt heavy with years, with hope, with desperation. The sconce lights danced about him, and he found himself peering from one to another, trying to determine which was the creature he commanded. He asked his question of them, his voice slurred beyond comprehensibility, and when none answered, he shouted and slammed his fist against the desk. He rose, tumbling the chair backward, and staggered to the center of the room and stood there, surrounded by all his selves. He raised his arms above his head, though they seemed weighted with steel.

"Tell me!" he shouted. "Tell me!"

And then the steel was too much for him, and he sagged beneath it. The floor was hard against his knees, his hip, his shoulder. His hand struck the floor with a loud clack—the ring, gold against bronze. He rolled over onto his back, crusty eyes blinking dryly. At last even that effort was too great, and he let his lids shut. He slept.

He woke in bed and knew that Gildrum had carried him there. A covered meal waited on the desk; a bowl of rich stew, fresh bread and butter—it had the look of supper. By that and the emptiness of his stomach, he guessed that he had slept till evening, though without a window he could not confirm that guess with a glance at the sky. Nor did he care. Whatever the time might be beyond the walls of Ringforge, his morning would come with his demon.

As the stew soothed his growling stomach, he realized that his anxiety was gone. He felt himself suspended in time and space, without future or past, only an unpredictable present; he existed only to see the yellow flame of his servant, nothing else mattered. He had no responsibilities, no desires, no thoughts until that moment. He could not even summon the concentration to call the demon to him; he could only wait. He lay down after eating, and he floated like a leaf upon the sea, bobbing in and out of shallow slumber, thinking nothing.

And his calm was rewarded.

The crackling whisper brought him to full consciousness.

"My lord, I have your answer."

Cray sat up slowly, staring at the butter-yellow flame of his servant. The words he had longed to hear fell on his ears like the tolling of a huge bell. He shivered suddenly, feeling a wild impulse to flee. Confronted with the imminence of truth, he found himself

284

shrinking from it. Too many years had passed, too much effort, too much sorrow. Abruptly, he saw the truth as a burden. He had always thought it would free him; now he realized that it would bind him instead. Deep within his breast a voice cried out that as long as he didn't know, he couldn't suffer more than he had already.

He bent his knees up to his chest and clasped them with both arms. He wished, for a moment, that his mother could be near to hold him tight. He dug his fingers into the flesh of his own arms to reassure himself that he was truly awake, that this experience, that these feelings were not simply part of a nightmare. His voice was very low when he said, "Tell me."

The demon replied, "Your father is Lord Smada Rezhyk of Ringforge."

Cray felt himself blanch. "What?"

"Smada Rezhyk, master of Ringforge, my lord."

"That's not possible."

"Yes, it is, my lord. There is no doubt. You are flesh of his flesh."

"But how can it be?" He stared through the flame, eyes focused on nothing. "Rezhyk, the handsome young knight my mother loved? Never! He might have disguised his body, but never his heart. She knew him from years past; she would have recognized his coldness, his bleakness. She wouldn't have let his outward appearance sway her. . . ." His gaze was stark, and he shivered as he began to wonder how well he knew his mother after all. "Surely she would have sensed magic in his semblance. Surely . . ." He turned to the nearest wall, focused on his own face, searched it for some aspect of Rezhyk. He had his mother's features, chiseled to manhood but unmistakable. Of either Rezhyk or the young knight, there was no trace.

He looked back at the demon's steady yellow flame. "There is no doubt at all?"

"None, my lord."

"Why, then? Why did he father me?"

The flame fluttered at the edges, wisps dancing as on a ball of pitch alight. "My lord, the demon world is full of facts, and if one searches far enough, one can find them all. But motives are another thing apart. I cannot search inside a human heart."

"Go then. I need you no longer." And when the flame had winked out, Cray raised his voice to a shout: "Gildrum!"

She came too swiftly, as if she had been waiting nearby for his summons.

He directed the door to close behind her, sealing them alone together with their multitudinous reflections. "You knew," he said tightly. "You knew all the time."

She looked down at the floor and made no reply.

"No need to shrink from speaking, Gildrum. I have the truth now. I made my conjuration and found a servant to bring me my answer." He slid off the bed and padded, barefoot, to her, and he took her slim shoulders between his hands, as if she were a human girl, and he shook her hard. "Why did he do it, Gildrum? Why did he want a child? He hates me, I know it well; he has used me ill, Gildrum, not as the child of his flesh should be treated, and he has taught me nonsense and tried to divert me from a proper master to prevent me from knowing the truth. He will never claim me. Why do I exist, then?"

She let him shake her with a tightening grip that would at last have made a real human girl scream in pain. "Master Cray," she murmured, "this is a subject which I may not discuss."

"I would think not, Gildrum! It wasn't me he wanted, was it? It was my mother. And the coward had to go to her disguised. Was he afraid to try in his own form, afraid she'd spurn him for the cold, unfeeling man he is? And so I am the fruit of his vile deception. When did he make the shirt, Gildrum—before or after he deceived her? After, was it? In case she should discover him and vent her anger?"

"Master Cray, I can tell you nothing."

He pushed her away, and a real girl would have staggered and fallen from the force of the gesture, but Gildrum only stepped back lightly. Cray's hands curled into fists, as if he would strike her, but he wheeled away instead, took two long strides, and stood

286

rigid before the cabinet that held his belongings. In its bright surface, he saw his face, saw sweat streaming from his forehead, though the room was pleasantly cool. To the bearded man who was his weary self, he said, "And after Lord Rezhyk had slaked his passion with my mother, he left her, and left a false trail of death for her to find, just one more lie among the many he had given her. Perhaps he thought he was being *kind*." He spat the words out now, like the bitter kernels that hid in the pits of sweet apricots. "Of course he dared not train me. He dared not let me learn the truth." He raised his fists to the cabinet door and leaned his forehead upon them. "And you knew, Gildrum," he rasped. "You knew. All these years, what have you thought of me?"

Very softly, she said, "I have thought that someday perhaps you would hate him as much as I do."

He took a deep breath. "Hate? No. I am too empty for hate. I thought someday to give my mother the gift of her lover's identity. But now . . ." He shook his head, eyes closed. "How can I give her this? How can I sully her memories with truth?" His fists loosened, and the fingers interlaced upon the brass. "Does he love her, Gildrum? Did he ever love her?"

She was silent a moment, and he thought that his question had trespassed on forbidden territory, but she answered at last: "I don't know, Master Cray. I don't think I understand human love."

"You were his servant . . . when it happened. His oldest, his best . . ."

"Master Cray," she said, "there is only one way you can find out what I know of those events. Give me my freedom, and I promise you I shall not keep anything from you."

His arms fell limp at his sides. "I cannot blame you for hiding the truth. You are only his slave." He shook his head. "Keep your knowledge, Gildrum. I want no more. I have stayed overlong in Ringforge already." He pulled the cabinet doors open and clawed at his belongings. The sword and shield clattered to the floor, the mail spilled after like water tumbling over a precipice.

The demon took a single step toward him. "You're leaving?"

He drew on his boots, then knelt to pack his saddlebags, empty save for that other, rusted sword and shield, wrapped in soft linen during the years of his apprenticeship. The garments he had been given in that time filled the remaining space. "If you would be so kind as to summon the bronze bird, I would appreciate it. Or if I must, I shall walk away from Ringforge."

She ran to him, long skirts swirling about her legs, and she fell on her knees beside him, halting his hands with her own. "No, please, Master Cray. You have so much more to learn. You are such an apt pupil. In a few short years more you could free me, I know it!"

He shook his head. "You will be no more worse off than when I came."

"Oh, yes, much worse. When you came, I saw hope. Now you'll take it away with you. Master Cray, you know what hope is!"

"And I know what sorrow is, too." In spite of her clutching hands, he finished packing and strapped the bags shut. "I cannot stay here, Gildrum. Not even to help you. You'll have to find someone else for that."

"Who will help a demon, Master Cray?" She caught at his head, one hand on either cheek, and she held it tight so that he was forced to look at her. The expression on her face was one that he had seen on his own in the mirror-bright bronze. "I have nowhere else to turn."

He pulled away from her. "I can't think now, Gildrum. I only know I must leave. How much longer would Lord Rezhyk keep me, anyhow? We have stretched this failed apprenticeship further than I thought possible. I must leave. I must get out from behind these walls, to the open sunlight, and think." He cast her a stricken glance. "I never promised, Gildrum. Remember?"

Still kneeling, she murmured, "No." Her body sagged, until she lay prone. "I remember."

He swallowed with difficulty, clutching the saddlebags, the sword and shield in his arms. "I must think," he repeated. "Afterward . . . perhaps I will come back . . ." He felt his eyes brimming. "Gildrum, I must think."

She did not rise. "Go," she said. "Go now. The walls will not keep you in. You'll find the bird waiting to take you back to the lady Helaine. You need not even say good-bye to Lord Rezhyk. He will understand." There was a catch in her voice, as if she, too, were weeping, but she did not look up at him, so he could not see any tears on her cheeks. "Go," she said. "I cannot hold you."

"You have been a good friend to me, Gildrum."

"Go."

The door opened for him, and he raced down the hall, down the stairs. At the end of the first-floor corridor he could see the entry to the antechamber waiting ajar for him, and as he passed through the tiny room, he saw that the two chairs were still there, still facing each other as they had on his very first day in Ringforge. In the farther wall was the only ordinary portal in the castle, a massive door of bronze, studded and figured in high relief; it swung wide at his approach, and a brisk, damp wind entered through the opening, engulfing Cray in its tenuous embrace. He welcomed it and welcomed the dank, gray sky of morning twilight. The instant he stepped beyond the threshold, the gate of Castle Ringforge clanged shut behind him.

The bird was waiting. It took his baggage in its cavernous beak and raised its hackles for Cray to mount. When he was settled in the straps, it swooped into the dawn, feathers rustling in flight like coins jingling against one another in a heavy purse. Cray closed his eyes and let his tears of anguish mix with the mist of the sky, knowing that they could never corrode that shining plumage.

When Rezhyk woke, he found Gildrum standing by his bed, as on many another morning, holding a breakfast tray. He sat up, accepting the meal onto his lap, eating swiftly. Between bites, he said, "I need a piece of cinnabar today, my Gildrum; there's a fine deposit of it in the west, not far from the falls of the river Beorn. The vein runs deep, though—it may give you a bit of trouble."

Gildrum focused her gaze on the foot of the bed, on the bar where Cray had once hidden in spider guise. "He is gone," she said.

Rezhyk looked up at her. "Gone? Who? Where?"

"Cray Ormoru gave up his apprenticeship this morning. I have sent him back whence he came."

"The boy? Gave up?" He pushed the tray aside and rose from the bed, flinging a light mantle over his shoulders. "How did it happen? Why?"

Gildrum transferred her gaze to his face. "Why not, my lord?" she murmured. "After so long? He was unhappy when I saw him this morning. He felt he could no longer stay in Ringforge. He said . . . he wanted sunlight."

Rezhyk clasped himself with arms crossed over his chest. "Good enough. Better this way, by his own choice, than if I had dismissed him. I did wonder when the years of failure would begin to tell on him." He smiled, showing his teeth like an animal snarling. "There has been a pall hanging over Castle Ringforge these years. Now it has lifted. We can resume our normal life, my Gildrum." He turned away from her slowly, toward the cabinet which held his clothing. "Still," he said, "I shall miss another set of human hands about the place. I have grown lazy these years, not needing to do certain things myself."

Gildrum leaned against the bedstead. "You could take another apprentice."

His head jerked around, and the eyes that glared at his servant from that swarthy face were ice and molten steel at the same instant. "No more apprentices," he said. "Never again."

"As you say, my lord."

Rezhyk dropped his mantle and slipped off the light nightshirt he had worn to bed. Against his naked skin, the cloth-of-gold shirt gleamed warm; he looked down at it for a moment, the tunic that would cover it clutched in one hand. He looked down, and then his free fingers touched the golden threads lightly, over his heart. "Where have you sent him?" he said.

"Back to the lady Helaine, from whom he came, my lord."

"The Seer. What will he tell her, I wonder? And what will she tell him?" He glanced sidelong at the demon. "Do you think he suspected what we were doing, my Gildrum?"

Gildrum replied, "I am sure that he thought he was being taught proper sorcery, my lord. I did my best to convince him so."

Rezhyk shrugged the tunic over his head. "Still, perhaps he thinks another sorcerer might be a better teacher."

"I don't know, my lord. He said nothing about seeking one."

"He's a stubborn lad. Only a stubborn one would have stayed so long in the face of so much failure." He pulled on trews and hose and stepped into his boots. "I think she might tell him to try another teacher."

"My lord, how will she be able to find him a better one than yourself? Surely she will tell him there is no hope for him."

"Surely?" Rezhyk belted his tunic. "Are you so relieved at his departure that your reason no longer functions, my Gildrum? There is nothing sure in this world. The longer I live, the more uncertain I grow. Except of one thing."

Gildrum frowned. "My lord?"

His thumbs hooked over his belt on either side of the bronze buckle, and his fingers tightened on the leather till the knuckles showed white. "Death, my Gildrum," he said coldly. "We all die. Even you. Even I. Even Master Cray Ormoru." He turned his face toward her, and his expression was hard. "Kill him for me, my Gildrum, before he finds a new master, and make sure the deed hasn't any look of sorcery about it."

She met his eyes, and softly she said, "My lord, do you think that's wise?"

"Do you think not? No one will suspect me. I have done my best over these years to teach the boy my art. I had faith in him. I was sorry to see him go. Why would I kill him?"

291

Gildrum inclined her head. "As you will, my lord. He is with the lady Helaine already; I presume you do not wish the deed done in her home."

"No. She would sense your presence, you mustn't enter there. But you said he wanted sunlight."

"Yes, my lord, he told me that."

"Then he won't be spending much time inside her cave. She won't find him a new teacher tomorrow or the next day; there will be time for him to roam outdoors, and he'll be restless enough for it, with nothing to do but wait. Go there, my Gildrum. Find yourself a hiding place nearby and watch for your opportunity."

"And . . . if there is no opportunity?"

"Then you must make one."

She vanished, and in her own bright home in the demon world she paused, an inhuman flame blazing anger, hate, and helplessness. *I am only a slave, my son. Only a slave.*

A moment later, high in the tree that was the entrance to the Seer's cave, a squirrel leaped among the branches, chittering in the sunshine.

✑ CHAPTER FOURTEEN

The great bronze bird shrugged him off and spat out his possessions, and then, without a word of farewell, it rose again on flashing pinions, swooping upward into the sun. He watched it dwindle in the distance, one hand shading his eyes from the glare of day, and it had disappeared before the dust stirred by its passage had cleared from the summer air. Cray coughed, scrambling to his feet, slapping the yellow powder from his hands and clothes. The giddiness of flight ebbed as he stood there, swaying, and he was soon sure enough of his balance that he could scoop the saddlebags into his arms and start for the nearby entry to the Seer's cave. The tree was in full leaf, as when he had left, and if it had added some feet to its prodigious height in the time he had been gone, he could not tell. He stepped through the arch in the trunk, into the light, cool breath of the cave.

She was waiting by the pool, looking toward the corridor from which he emerged, and he knew at once that she had been expecting him.

"It is not good news, I see," she said, "that brings you back to me."

"Has the pool told you that?" he asked, letting his burdens slip to the pale sand.

"I need no pool to tell me; it's written on your face. Come, sit down, Cray Ormoru, and share some wine with me."

"Gladly," he said, and he perched on the rim of the pool facing her. Involuntarily, he glanced at the dark waters, and he saw his own reflection there, but it moved with him, not magical at all.

The far door opened, and Feldar Sepwin entered, bearing a carafe and cups. He was taller than Cray remembered, and better fleshed out, and a drooping mustache hid his upper lip. He grinned at his old comrade and poured wine redder than blood into a fat mug. "Welcome," he said, offering the cup. "Welcome indeed."

Ignoring the wine, Cray threw his arms around Sepwin and gave him a bone-crushing hug. "Feldar, you're here!"

"I never left," Sepwin replied, laughing. "Here now, let go before we dye the sand red." He stepped back and lifted the full mug up to Cray's face. "Take it, take it; you don't expect me to hold it forever, do you?"

Cray seized the mug and drained it, and while he did so, Sepwin poured other mugs for himself and the Seer, which they raised in silent toasting.

When Cray caught his breath, he said, "What do you mean, you never left?"

"I am apprenticed to the lady Helaine," Sepwin replied, nodding toward her.

"And a good apprentice he is," she added. "I saw it in him before you left, Cray. I thank you for bringing him to me."

Cray looked into his friend's face. "Your eyes—they're as they were."

"We never found a sorcerer to make them match," said Sepwin. "But that doesn't matter anymore. People expect stranger things of a Seer than mismated eyes."

Cray set the cup down on the pool rim and took his friend's shoulders between his hands. "You're happy here?"

"Yes."

"Then some good came of our quest after all."

Sepwin's grin softened to sympathy. "Not for you?"

"I came to the end of it." His hands dropped to his sides, suddenly heavy. "I found my father."

"That was what you wanted."

"Yes." He turned to the Seer, and his smile had pain in it. "But you were right. It didn't make me happy."

"Knowledge seldom does," she said. She swept two fingers across the dark surface of the pool. "They come to me in fear, Cray, to hear me say that what they fear is false. Most of them don't even look for happiness, only relief."

Cray sighed. "I did not even find that, lady. I could almost wish that I had never discovered the truth." He sank down upon the sand at her knees and leaned his head against the cool rocks that restrained the pool. His grip on the cup loosened by degrees, and at last the vessel tipped over, shedding one drop of red wine, like blood, upon the pure white powder. "I have more questions than I had before, more doubts, more confusion. Now I have truly come to a dead end, and I don't know where to turn. I only know that I can't tell my mother who he was."

"Do you want to tell us?" asked the Seer.

Cray pulled his knees up, clasping them with both arms, and he did not look anywhere but at the sand between his feet when he spoke. "Lord Rezhyk is my father," he said. "Lord Rezhyk himself." His voice broke on the last word, and then the whole tale of his strange apprenticeship poured out of him in a wild, disjointed torrent—demons, ores, mirrored walls, failure, success, all, until Cray was clutching at the sand as at a spar floating in the open sea. But the sand ran through his fingers, and he was left only with his own flesh, and his nails bit deep into the calluses of his palms. When he gave over speaking at last, he slumped, head falling forward to his knees, exhausted by the very telling of the tale.

The lady Helaine let a soothing silence cloak the three of them for a moment, and then she said, "And you did not confront Lord Rezhyk with your knowledge?"

Cray shook his head.

"Were you afraid?"

Cray shook his head again. "I couldn't betray Gildrum. It would have gone hard with her."

"Noble sentiments, Cray; but now you will never know *why*."

"I don't think I want to know."

"Oh, come—that is precisely what you want to know. And you could know . . . by continuing your apprenticeship under the demon until you were strong enough to free her from her silence. Obviously, she knows everything you want to know; she is the key. Why have you run away from her, then?"

He raised his head to gaze at her. "How could I stay? How could I spend another night under the same roof with him? I am not a son to him. I am not even another human being to him. I am a slave for his convenience. How could I work for him and know that he would never claim me, never show a spark of father's love?"

She bent to lay a pale hand on his shoulder. "But, Cray, you knew that if your father were alive he would not acknowledge you. He had years for that and never did it; why would he suddenly change his mind?"

"Lady, I thought that if I showed myself worthy . . ."

Her eyes were sad and infinitely old in her pale

face. "And so, when you thought him a knight, you trained yourself for knighthood. And when you thought him a sorcerer, you found yourself an apprenticeship for that. What if he had been a merchant, Cray? Or a peasant? Or a beggar? What would you have done then?"

"What shall I do now, lady?" he whispered. "Tell me. Give me the good advice that you give to others."

"I gave it once, and you would not take it then."

"Go back to Mistwell? Or . . . home?"

"You must decide what you want from life, Cray. And what you have the courage to pursue."

"Look into the pool, my lady, and tell me what lies ahead."

Her hand slipped from his shoulder to his cheek. "No," she said. "I will not read the waters for you again."

"Why not? Is it because I've never paid you? Yet you yourself always said to wait, to pay later, always later. Name your price, lady, and I will bring it to you."

"You have paid me well," she said, and she glanced at Sepwin, still standing with the carafe and an empty mug in his hands. "You have paid me for a thousand futures."

Cray rose to his knees before her. "Then why will you not give me one more?"

Her hand pressed his cheek, her fingers curling under the curve of his jaw, hooking there, holding his head as if it were a naked skull. "Listen to me, Cray Ormoru: you are too young to let an old woman command your actions. How many men have come here for cheer and left wishing they had never asked their questions? How many have given up their fight in life because of a few moments by this pool? I was young once, and I would have given you what you ask then. But not now. Through me you have found your father, and that is the end of my work for you. Leave here, and make your future what *you* will, not what *I* say." She loosed his head suddenly, and he rocked back in reaction, catching himself with one outstretched hand before he could tumble over on the pale sand.

Sepwin set the carafe down and extended a wiry arm to help his old comrade up. For a moment, the two young men stood eye to eye, regarding each other over the handsbreadth that separated them, and the years.

"I suppose I can't ask you to come along," said Cray.

"No. I have my place here. I am content."

Cray dusted his tunic and trews of the clinging white powder. "Can you find me a horse, since I haven't magical transportation anymore?"

"There's Gallant," said Sepwin. "I have kept him trim for you, ridden him every day."

"I gave him to you, Feldar."

"And now I give him back. I have the other horse, if I should need a mount. But I don't foresee leaving here."

Cray gripped Sepwin's arm. "You are a good friend, Feldar. Better than I have been."

"You did your best, Cray."

"Perhaps . . . for you." He turned away. "I'll leave now, my lady, if that is well with you."

"It is best, I think." She transferred her gaze to her apprentice. "Feldar, get the packet of food for his journey."

He went through the far door and returned in a moment. The parcel was a large one, provisions for many days.

"You knew I would be leaving immediately," Cray said, tucking it under his arm. He reached for the saddlebags, but Sepwin hefted them first. Cray was left with only his sword and shield in addition to the food.

"I know what happens in my own home," said the Seer. She followed the two young men down the corridor and out into the morning sunshine.

Sepwin set the saddlebags down. "I'll fetch Gallant. I built him a stout shelter among the trees; it isn't far." He crossed the road and entered the forest that grew thick on the other side. Shortly, he returned, with Gallant saddled for the trip, though there had not been time for the saddling.

Cray stroked the horse's neck and murmured, "Do

you remember me, I wonder, my good old Gallant?"
Sepwin had a carrot in his pocket, and he gave it to
Cray to feed to the animal. "I've changed with the
years, haven't I?" Cray whispered, as Gallant's warm,
soft lips moved against his palm, his strong teeth grinding the hard carrot to mush. "But you haven't changed
at all. It might have been yesterday that I left you
here. So, Gallant, my old friend, we travel together
once more, just you and I."

He strapped the saddlebags in place, the sword and
shield. He grasped the pommel of the saddle in one
hand and the cantle in the other and was about to
mount when he thought better of it and let his arms
fall to his sides. He looked down then, at his horse's
feet, peering at the bare earth of the road. After a
few heartbeats, he moved half a dozen paces away, into the grass, and he stooped there, squatting on his
heels, touching his fingertips to the moister, green-
cloaked soil. He closed his eyes. Nearby, he could hear
Gallant snorting and easing from foot to foot, as if
impatient to be off. He heard the soft breeze rustling
the leaves all around him, and the creak of branches
swaying before the force of mere air. He heard a squirrel chittering far away.

Before long, a tickle on his right index finger advised him of a new presence: a small spider. Of all the
spiders he had discharged in the road before the
Seer's home, only this one had been near enough and
long-lived enough to hear his call. As he straightened,
it scuttled up his sleeve. He turned back to Gallant.
"Now there are three of us," he said.

Sepwin watched him vault into the saddle. "I would
you had stayed with us a while," he said.

Cray gazed at him from the great height of Gallant's
back. "But you knew I would not."

"*She* knew. My skills are still quite limited."

"He does well," said the Seer. "As well as any
apprentice I've ever heard of." She smiled at Sepwin, who smiled in return.

"I owe my life to you, Cray," he said, his hand
resting lightly on Gallant's reins, on the pommel of the
saddle. "I'd still be a beggar if not for you. A beggar
or worse."

"You don't owe me anything," said Cray. "You kept faith. I couldn't ask more."

"I looked into the pool for you, Cray. I'm not very good at it yet, but I saw danger ahead."

"What sort of danger?"

"I don't know, but you'll raise your sword and shield to it."

"Well . . . a bandit perhaps. Or a wild animal." He shrugged. "I haven't forgotten how to use the sword."

"Be careful."

"I shall."

"Where will you go now?"

"I don't know. Ask her, after I'm gone. Take care of yourself, Feldar. Perhaps we'll meet again."

"Good luck to you, my friend. I have never stopped thinking of you. I never shall."

"And good-bye to you, my lady. And thank you." Cray wheeled Gallant about and guided him westward, away from the golden morning sun. He looked back twice, and both times Sepwin and the lady Helaine still stood in the road, their arms upraised in farewell. The third time, the road had bent, and they were beyond his sight.

The horse felt strange to him, after so many years of sitting on chairs and stools, and he knew that on the morrow the muscles of his thighs would protest the unaccustomed exercise; still, he did not cut his day's travel short because of that. He ached already, as he stopped with the advent of twilight, but he welcomed the ache, as he had welcomed the steed—a sign of the end of the apprentice life and the beginning of the unknown. His route led toward Spinweb, but he could as well have turned south to Mistwell from that road, or to somewhere new. He had passed the day without thinking beyond it, without thinking of more than the next five strides of his horse. Now, as he gathered dry twigs and struck sparks to kindle a small fire, he found himself contemplating other fires that burned only in his mind's eye, until a tickle at his wrist reminded him that with his freedom from Ringforce came other responsibilities. He dropped his tiny passenger at the fork of two branches on a drooping oak limb, and he watched for a time while it anchored its web among the surrounding twigs. When he turned away to eat his dinner, the sun had set completely, and the spider had only finished the radiant strands that would support its close spiral; alone, though it spun swiftly, it could not finish before Cray settled for sleep. He ate his dinner and left the mite working, left his use of the fruit of its labor for morning.

When he woke, he ached, but he ignored that. The web hung above his sleeping place, glistening with a myriad of dewdrops. The spider rested in its center, a black spot, with dew glinting, too, on legs and back. Cray took it up in his sleeve, dampness and all, and then he stretched his hand to the web, palm parallel to the plane of the spiral, halting just a finger's width away from the diamond-speckled surface. Silently, he called to her.

Time passed while he stood stiff, his arm upraised, and at last the web turned misty gray, opaque, and a familiar image coalesced upon it. The first thing that Cray noticed was that she still wore black.

"Where are you, my son?" she said. "Is something wrong?"

He looked at her across the vast distance that separated them—a distance not of space but of knowledge. He said, "I've left Ringforge, Mother. I've ended my apprenticeship with Lord Rezhyk."

A frown creased her brow. "Did you quarrel?"

"No. But . . . as master and apprentice, we were not suited to each other. He was . . . too chill for me."

She nodded. "Chill indeed, in spite of his mastery of fire demons. They don't warm the heart, Cray; you understand that now."

"I don't think he liked me, either."

"Did you behave ill to him, my son?"

"No. I tried very hard to be useful and obedient and friendly. But . . . he was cold from the first. Mother . . . did you and he have some sort of conflict years ago, perhaps even before I was born, that he would be so cold to your son?"

"We knew each other, years ago." She shrugged. "I never cared much for him, but I was civil. He took that civility for friendship, at one time, knowing nothing warmer himself. He even proposed marriage. I refused. I didn't want to marry anyone then." She looked down into her lap, where her hands clasped each other. "That was before I met your father."

"You never told me," said Cray.

"It never seemed important." She lifted her head again. "Oh, when you said he had accepted your apprenticeship, I thought perhaps there was some remnant of his feeling for me after all these years, that he was doing it to show his good will—such good will as a man like him might have. It's a rare sorcerer who takes on another's child for apprenticeship." She shrugged. "I suppose he changed his mind after you had been with him a while. I suppose he decided that the gesture was too much for him—"

"I suppose so."

"What will you do now? Find another master?"

Cray shook his head. "I don't know yet. I thought . . . I might come home for a while."

Delivev smiled. "I would be very happy to welcome you."

"I'm not sure, Mother. I want to travel a time yet. I want to . . . to think out my life."

"I understand, my son. I am grateful that you called me. If you want to come home . . . well, it is always open to you. And I will teach you sorcery, if you wish it."

"I know, Mother."

"And Cray . . . I like the beard."

He grinned at her. "It makes me feel full-grown."

"Yes," she said. "I'm sure it does."

"You look well, Mother."

"I am well. You look like you could do with a bit of sunshine."

"I'll get it now," said Cray. "Good-bye, Mother. Don't worry about me. I love you."

"And I love you."

Her face faded, and the web was just a web, dewdrops shrinking in the gathering sunlight. Cray left it on the tree for the wind to tear apart, and he resumed his westward travel. He walked for a time, leading Gallant, until his legs had limbered enough for him to climb into the saddle without gritting his teeth.

Afternoon shadows were long across the road when he met the stranger. He had seen no human beings since leaving the Seer's home, save his mother; only a few rabbits and squirrels and a flock of calling birds had crossed his path. On a stretch of road no different from any other, the stranger moved out from behind a thick-boled oak to block the way: a tall, broad person in night-black plate armor, riding a horse of the same hue, so that Cray could scarcely discern where rider ended and horse began. The stranger carried a blank black shield.

"Hold!" he said in a deep, rumbling voice.

Cray pulled Gallant up short.

"No one passes this way without facing me," shouted the stranger.

"Good sir," said Cray, "I know I am no match for you. I am a man of peace. Let me pass, I beg you; I have no wish or skill for a fight."

"Draw your sword or I strike you down where you sit, and that fine horse, too!"

"Sir, I wear no armor! Hold off!"

The black knight spurred his mount, which launched itself as if from a crossbow, nostrils flaring, teeth bared. Cray twitched his reins, and Gallant stepped aside, letting the black knight thunder past. And then the chase began, as Cray raced westward with the black knight, wheeling quickly, in hot pursuit. Their horses were well matched, and Cray thought that the heavy armor of his pursuer would hold the man's mount back, but it gained instead, slowly, steadily, until the horses raced nearly side by side. In desperation, Cray turned off the road, guiding Gallant among the close-packed trees, but he lost speed there, and the black knight drew near once more, near enough to swing his blade and miss Cray's neck by a narrow margin. Cray answered with a flick of his right arm, tossing his lone spider at the knight in hopes of catching the sword and tangling it fast with webwork to the helm, the shield, the saddle pommel, anything, but the stranger batted the tiny creature aside, as if he knew how dangerous it could be.

Gripping Gallant with his knees, Cray eased his shield from its hook and slung it over his left arm just in time to deflect a blow from his opponent's sword; then Cray drew his own blade and returned a stroke. The horses slowed as the men joined combat, until they were barely walking, and neither animal shied from the force of sword on shield, though both riders were rocked in their saddles by the blows. Cray looked for an opening, but the black knight was sealed into steel while he himself was nearly naked to a heavy blade, without even chain to turn the edge. He drew his exposed leg up behind the shield. The motion over-balanced him a moment, and before he could recover, a solid strike at the top edge of his shield sent him tumbling off his horse.

He scrambled to his feet, dodged behind the nearest tree, and the black knight and his dark horse followed relentlessly. Now Cray's opponent had the advantage of height, and Cray raised the shield to protect his head, taking blows on the steel sheet that shook his whole body. Desperately, though it was an unchivalric act, he cut at the dark horse's legs. The animal foundered, throwing its rider to the forest floor.

Cray ran toward Gallant, waiting quietly under the trees. Most men, he knew, could not rise from a fall in plate armor, but behind him he heard the squeak of metal on metal, and then the rattle and clank of an armored man running. The sound came close, too close, and Cray had to turn, though Gallant was still half a dozen paces away. The black knight loomed toward him, huge and ponderous, like some great beast driven by madness. His sword arm swung at Cray, who tipped his shield up to receive the blow and danced away. Cray was light, spurred by desperation; the black knight was heavy but tireless. They moved through the forest, away from the horses, to where only the over-hanging trees would judge their wild combat.

Cray saw the opening and took it without thinking—he drove the point of his sword into the exposed eye slit of the black knight's helm, and the helm broke loose of its moorings and slipped upward, blinding the knight and toppling him backward. Cray leaped to the man's chest as he went down, one foot pinning an armored shoulder, the other stamping hard on the mailed hand that held the sword, crushing it to the earth and forcing the pommel out of the clenched fist. He grabbed up the sword then and tossed it as far as his strength would allow, and then he dropped to his knees on the black knight's body, one knee hard against the man's chain-covered throat. He forced the black helm completely free of the man's head. Although Cray's sword had lodged in the eye slit, it had not penetrated to the flesh, and there was no blood on the face that he exposed.

He recognized it.

Years had passed since he had seen those features, but he had no difficulty recalling them. That salt-and-pepper fringe of beard, that bald dome—they belonged to the landlord of the very first inn he had stopped at, at the beginning of his long quest. The man had given him directions to Falconhill.

"You!" said Cray. "A knight?"

The man stared up at him, saying nothing.

"Yield yourself to me, sir, or I cut your throat!"

In answer, the man thrust upward with his shield, and Cray went tumbling.

Cray lunged for the other sword, scooped it up and bounced to his feet. The black knight circled him warily, helmless, his shield held stiffly before him.

"This is nonsense!" shouted Cray. "I have no wish to kill you!"

The black knight eased closer.

"Let us stop here and now!" said Cray. "I declare a truce!"

The black knight thrust his shield toward Cray, like a battering ram on the end of his long, thick arm, and Cray danced sideways, striking a light blow on the edge of the shield with one sword and a heavier one on an armored thigh with the other.

"You have no weapon," said Cray, thinking quite otherwise as he watched the shield move. "Leave off!"

The black knight slammed his shield against the sword in Cray's left hand, and the blade shivered with the strength of the blow, and Cray's left fingers, unused to curling about a pommel, went numb; he was barely able to hold onto the weapon.

Cray found himself backing off, and suddenly his shoulders were against a tree trunk and he could not sidestep fast enough. The black knight came on, and Cray raised his sword far to his right and then swept leftward with a blow too weak to dent plate armor, but strong enough and high enough to cleave a human skull. The steel bit deep into the black knight's head, and in the instant that Cray expected to see bright blood gush from the sundered pate, the black knight burst into flame.

Cray screamed once, and his sword arm, freed, fell to his side, the blade rapping bark with a hard, dull sound. Fire engulfed him, no warmer nor yellower than afternoon sunlight. He looked at the forest through it as through a gauzy veil, and when he had blinked a few times and straightened up and twitched his shoulders free of clinging scraps of bark, he said, "Gildrum?"

The flame retreated from him, shrank to a short pillar, and solidified into her familiar form.

"He bade me kill you," she said, "before you found another master."

Cray's grip on both swords tightened. "Why?"

"He is afraid of what you might find out. Still."

"But I already know."

"I didn't tell him that. But it wouldn't matter. He would be even more afraid then."

"I don't plan to find another master."

"Not your mother?"

He shook his head.

"You may change your mind."

"Not if I know you'll kill me if I do."

She clasped her hands behind her back. "He doesn't realize what he said. He wants you dead *now,* that I know. But that is not what his *command* was, as you so clearly perceive. Still, I must have something to tell him when I return. And I cannot lie outright, only sidestep the truth."

Cray raised the sword. "What, then? You've tried once and failed."

"Purposely, I'm a better knight than that. Still . . ." She smiled her guileless smile. "It was a pretty show, wasn't it?"

"Don't toy with me, Gildrum."

"Master Cray, I don't want to kill you. I hope you understand that."

"Then don't do it."

"I must obey my lord's commands."

"But he left you an out. If I never apprentice again . . ."

"Eventually, he will call me back and give another command. One which will not be subject to variant interpretation. There are compulsions attached to ring-slaves, Master Cray. Our wills are not our own. Though we may fight hard, still the master is the master."

"Then why do you delay?" Cray cried. "Why do you torture me with conversation? Why not kill me and have done?"

"Because I have a plan."

The sword tip wavered and dropped to the ground, as if the blade were as exhausted as Cray himself. He eased his body to the mossy hollow between two of the tree's roots, using the swords as staffs to lean upon. He crossed his legs tailor-fashion, though they ached unmercifully from riding and running and dodging. "What is your plan?"

"If I must kill you before you find a new master, then you must return to an old one instead."

"Return? But you said he wants me killed—"

"Not to Lord Rezhyk. To me." .

Cray shook his head. "I don't understand."

She sank to her knees before him and took one of his hands in both of hers, brushing the sword out of his palm as if it were a dead flower. "You have a bold heart," she said. "Now I ask you for the boldest decision of your life. I ask you to come with me to my own world and continue your studies until you are so strong that Lord Rezhyk has more to fear from you than you from him."

"Your world?"

Gildrum nodded. "It is a fearsome place to human senses, and you will be the first human ever to visit it. But you will be safe there; I will be able to tell my lord that you no longer walk the earth."

"And in return, I suppose you still want your freedom?"

"Yes."

"You have risked so much to get that freedom, Gildrum. What if he discovers this new treachery?"

"I will chance that. He has never suspected me of treachery before."

Cray tried to read her eyes, but all he saw was darkness in them. "Is it so precious to you, Gildrum? So very precious?"

"Yes. Yes."

"Why?"

She looked away from him, still clutching his hand. "When I am free I will be able to tell you."

He leaned toward her. "It has something to do with me? With my birth?"

She said nothing, only gripped his hand harder.

"Did you know, Gildrum, that Lord Rezhyk once asked my mother to marry him? And she said no?" When the demon made no reply, he added, "Was that when he went to her and made me?"

She turned her gaze to him once more. "Don't ask me such things, Master Cray. I have done my best to help you find the truth yourself. I have walked the narrowest path a demon ever trod, between obeying my master and obeying my heart. Or whatever it is that demons have instead of hearts. Sometimes I am so close to forbidden ground that my mouth opens and no words come—it is the power of the ring, holding me back. Believe me, I want to tell you everything!"

Cray shook his head sadly. "At this moment, the only thing I want to know is . . . how could she love him—*him*, Rezhyk, whatever his form."

Gildrum let go his hand. "Yes," she said. "I would wonder at that, too."

"I am not surprised that he could love her."

"No, that doesn't surprise me either."

Cray eyed her sidelong. "You've met her?"

Gildrum looked down to the moss at her knees.

"You've met her?" Cray asked more loudly.

Gildrum did not raise her eyes.

Cray reached for her shoulders and shook her sharply. "Is that part of the secret, that you've met her?"

"You cannot shake answers out of me, Master Cray," the demon said softly. "Nor beat them, nor

307

burn them. This is not human flesh that you hold be-tween your hands."

"No," said Cray. "This is demon flesh, masquerad-ing as human. It looks so fragile, so deceptively frag-ile. Yet a little time ago you were taller and broader than I am. What other forms can you take, Gildrum?"

"I have been a squirrel. And there are others."

"Show me the others. All of them."

In rapid succession, Gildrum displayed the squirrel, the old man, an oak sapling, a pebble. She shrank, she grew, she sprouted fur, wrinkles, and green leaves with equal facility. And when she had done with all four shapes, she returned to the young girl in the blue dress, kneeling on the moss.

"Is that all?" Cray asked of her. He had sat silent while her semblance warped and flowed before him. Only his eyes had moved, lids narrowing momentarily with each change. "Are there no more?"

"You saw the black knight."

"And . . . ?"

Her lips pursed, and she said nothing.

"Is there another yet—one that I am not supposed to see?"

Still, no reply.

Cray rose to his feet and turned his back to her, one hand raised to the rough texture of the tree trunk. He picked at the bark, crumbling the fragments that came free between his fingers. Finally he said, "So it was you. Not Rezhyk. My mother fell in love with you. Well, it does not seem quite so impossible that way." His fingers clawed against the tree, scraping bark under his nails. "Do you deny it, Gildrum?"

She made no sound.

"He should have instructed you to deny it. He shouldn't have merely forbidden you to speak of it. You could have lied to me then." He looked down, leaning the crown of his head against the trunk. "I can almost see you charming her, Gildrum. You are so much more . . . *human* . . . than he is. How did it make you feel to deceive her so, demon? You have feelings, I know." He tipped his face sideways, to see her. "But of course you can't tell me."

She sat on the moss with her head bent, her face

buried in her hands, the butter-yellow braids falling forward over her shoulders. "I have feelings," she murmured, her voice muffled by her fingers.

"Are you ashamed of what you did?" He reached out suddenly, jerked her hands away from her face. On her cheeks he saw two wet streaks, demon tears. "Do you weep for shame, Gildrum?"

"Set me free," she whispered, "and you shall know everything."

He pushed her away, tumbling her backward over the exposed roots of the tree. "Freedom, freedom!" he shouted. "That's all I hear from you—freedom! You're freer than I am, demon! You do as you will, even to betraying your master, cunning creature. Your silence has told me as much as words could."

"I would that were truly so," said Gildrum, propping herself up on her elbows. "There is too much that you do not know, Master Cray. Believe me."

"What will you do with your freedom, Gildrum? Kill him?"

"No. I care nothing for *him*."

"You have some other target, then."

"Not for death."

"For what?"

Her eyes pleaded with him.

"What a mad discussion!" Cray cried, throwing his arms out to the forest as to a jury. "I keep finding myself carrying on both sides!" He glared down at her. "Your plans for life after gaining your freedom involve me?"

She shook her head.

"Who, then?" His brows knit tight. "My mother?" Silence.

He took one step toward her and reached down to clutch hard at her shoulder. "You shall not harm her!"

"I shall harm no one," said Gildrum.

"What, then? You want to explain? You want to apologize? Better you stay away from her, Gildrum. Better she should never know what happened. She has her memories, and they, at least, are only bitter with loss. She loved you." He ripped his fingers away from her and straightened, still looking down at her deceptively human shape at his feet. "Oh, my poor mother; how she loved you."

"Free me, Master Cray," she whispered. "You shall not regret it."

"Do you promise me that?"

"Yes."

"But you have made promises before and broken them."

"Not to you."

"To her." He shook his head. "How can I trust your promises?"

"Sometimes," said Gildrum, "a demon makes a promise and the master prevents the keeping of it."

"Prevents the keeping of it?" He crooked his elbows and set his hands on his hips. "Come, come, Gildrum—am I to believe that you meant it when you told her you would return when your duty was done? Perhaps five hundred more years of slavery to Lord Rezhyk was the duty you meant, or however much time remains until he dies. Do you take me for a fool?"

"Sometimes . . . promises are made from the heart, not the head." She lifted a hand to him in supplication. "Set me free, Master Cray. You are my only hope."

His frown deepened. "Hope for what?" he said.

She groped for his near hand, found it, slid her fingers into his palm, levering it away from his hip. "Please," she said. "My throat is thick with words that will not pass my lips. Set me free. You must know what I will do with my freedom. You *must*."

He curled his fingers loosely around hers and then looked down at the two hands, one broad and hard, the other as fragile as a child's, with delicate nails and rosy palms. "You . . . will keep your promise to her?"

"Please," she said.

"This is madness," he muttered. "With silence and just a few indirect remarks, but mainly silence, you have led me to a conclusion I can scarcely credit. Do you love my mother, Gildrum? Have you loved her all this time?" To her firmly closed lips and tightly clutching hand, he added, "But no, you will not tell me that. That is part of the secret that Rezhyk has forbidden you to reveal to me. So I shall not know, for certain, until I free you. And even then . . . how can a demon love a human being?" He covered their two entwined hands with his free hand. "I feel flesh here, but I know you are made of fire. You can appear as you choose, as squirrel or pebble or old man, but still, you are a flame. Gildrum, has demon ever loved a human being before?"

"I don't know," she said. "I think it is not a thing that we would talk about. But it did happen once the other way around, when a master gave a slave a fair form. It was a great joke, for a time, in my world."

"Do they make many jokes, in your world, about human beings?"

"Some do."

"Will they laugh at me . . . when I am there?"

Her unencumbered hand grasped at his tunic. "You will go then?"

He nodded slowly. "I will go. I haven't much choice, have I? Stay and die or go and learn. I will go, and I will work until I have no need to fear him. And I shall gain your freedom."

She scrambled to her knees. "Master Cray, I cannot thank you enough."

"I'm not doing this for you. Just for me. And for her. I trust you will think of a suitable evasion for Lord Rezhyk."

"I have one already."

"Very well. When shall we leave?"

"Now."

"And what of my horse?"

She smiled slightly. "Still thinking of your horse after all these years?"

"I can't leave him uncared for."

"I'll arrange for him to wander back to the lady Helaine and your friend."

"Will they know where I have gone? Will they read my fate in him?"

"I think not," said Gildrum. "He saw nothing but the first moments of the fight. Your lives parted then, and a Seer would know no more than that."

"They will think that something terrible has happened to me."

"So much the better," said Gildrum, "in case my lord should make inquiries."

"Would he doubt your word?"

"I think not, but why take the risk? Now, let us depart so that I may settle you and lay out your further course of study."

Cray nodded, and before the gesture was complete, the demon turned to flame and engulfed him. This time her fire was not a tenuous veil but an opaque sheet through which he could not even see his own limbs. His eyes closed against the intolerable glare and then he squinted hard at the fierce redness that penetrated his eyelids. A heartbeat later, he lost his balance and tumbled, flailing, into nothingness. There was no ground beneath his feet anymore, no grass, no shrubs, no trees to clutch at. He screamed. He opened his eyes, but the dazzle was too much for him and he had to shut it out again. Then something tugged at his hand, as a dog tugs at the leash, and he felt his body straightening, streaming out behind his fingers like hair in a high wind. He flew.

"Don't be afraid," said Gildrum's crackling demon-voice. "You are safe with me. But you cannot stay here. I will take you to a more suitable place."

"Where are we?" Cray croaked.

"This is Fire, my home. Without my protection you would char in an instant. But we'll be out soon; the boundary is quite near."

Abruptly, the bright light dimmed, and Cray's eyelids unlocked themselves almost by reflex. Gildrum's flame was about him still, but faint now, as the first time she had enveloped him, and beyond the pale yellow of her glow he saw that he was surrounded by smoke. Gildrum kept it from him—it did not powder his skin with soot or make him cough or burn his eyes, nor did it roil from his passage through it.

"This is the boundary between Fire and Air," said Gildrum.

Cray craned his neck to look back the way they had come, toward his feet. Even veiled by smoke, Fire was a terrifying sight. Its beating dazzle was damped, but its violence showed clearly—raging flames of red, orange, yellow, white; nothingness ever burning, never consumed. Cray felt sweat break out on his forehead, though no heat touched him.

"What is it like to live there?" he wondered.

"If your eyes were strong enough to bear the sight," said Gildrum, "you would see that it has a wild beauty all its own. Rivers of molten lava flowing without banks, without the tug of the earth to restrain them. Demons of every shape and shade of flame, like living jewels. And never darkness. Never." Even her sigh crackled. "I spend so little time there, it is twice as beautiful to me as to any other native."

"A terrible beauty," said Cray.

"Well, we will come upon a different sort presently." The smoke thinned until Cray thought he could see a trace of blue in the direction they traveled. Then they emerged from the last wisps, and he saw that it was blue, blue everywhere, as far as the eye could see, the deep azure of a cloudless summer sky. There was no sun visible, yet there was light; the very air seemed luminous. Gildrum withdrew from him, to a ball of pale yellow near his elbow, leaving him to float, perfectly warm and comfortable, in the vast blue. A light breeze played about him, ruffling his hair as his mother had ruffled it when he was a small child; he breathed deep, expecting some scent to be borne upon the wind, but there was neither the green perfume of vegetation nor the heartier smell of animals, nor even the taint of the smoke that lay behind him. The air was odorless, flat, as it brushed his nostrils.

He heard laughter, soft, breathy laughter just behind his right ear. He turned his head sharply to find the source, and his body tumbled toward the flame that was Gildrum. The demon flowed toward him, wrapped about his arm to steady him.

"You must learn to move more slowly in this world," she said.

"Who laughed?" said Cray.

"An air demon, of course," said Gildrum. "Behind you. No, don't turn. You can't see it just now. I'll ask it to come around to your face and show itself."

Some silent message must have passed between the demons, for in the emptiness before Cray's eyes a dark cloud began to coalesce, like a man-sized thunderhead. It laughed, the same laugh as before, and filaments of cloud broke free from the main body with that laugh-

313

ter, floated around it like honeybees around a flower, and settled back into the mass.

"Accept my greeting," said the cloud, "O human being. You are a silly sight indeed, in Air."

"I'm sure I must be," said Cray. "Please accept my greeting in return, O cloud. I am Cray Ormoru."

The cloud laughed again. "Will you call us all 'O cloud,' young Cray? I'll wager he doesn't call you 'O flame,' Gildrum."

"I haven't told him your name. Cray, this is Elrelet, an old friend of mine."

"An old fellow slave is what you mean, Gildrum. Shall I take my true form and shake your hand, young Cray, following human custom?"

"If you wish," said Cray, extending his own hand.

Elrelet laughed once more, and the cloud collapsed to a ball no larger than a fist; it sprouted two long, ropy tentacles, smooth on the upper side, exuding slime on the lower. It thrust one of them toward Cray, grasped his hand like a snake constricting its prey, and pumped so vigorously that his whole body bounced back and forth, as if it were a dusty rag being shaken out.

"Enough," said Gildrum, and she flowed about Cray's body just long enough to damp out the wild motion.

Elrelet withdrew the tentacle. "He has some courage," it said, absorbing the tentacles into its spherical body and then expanding once more to the thunderhead. "Another human would have shied away from me."

"I was raised with snakes," said Cray. "Things that resemble them do not repel me."

"Well, we have things here," said Elrelet, "that by human standards are even uglier in their true forms than I am. Don't be surprised if some of the Free try to startle you with them."

"Elrelet will look after you while I am back at Ringforge," Gildrum said to Cray. "If you trust me, you can trust Elrelet. Ask for whatever you need—food, clothing, advice; Elrelet will provide them."

"Advice especially," said Elrelet.

"I must return now. My lord will be wondering why

I have taken so long; he will call soon and perhaps alter the command, and I must forestall that. I'll return whenever I can. Here are duplicates of your books." Several thick notebooks floated from the depths of her flame, arrayed themselves before Cray's eyes. "You will find that I have written your next few lessons in the latest of them. Study hard, Cray. Farewell to both of you." She streaked past Cray's shoulder, and he turned his head very slowly to watch her dwindle toward the smoke. She entered the grayness that extended as far as the eye could see in the directions that Cray arbitrarily designated as up and down, left and right, a curtain across the whole sky. Swiftly, her flame vanished. Yet beyond the curtain, tingeing it with a ruddy glow, Fire was still faintly visible, a conflagration beyond human imagination.

Cray shuddered once, at the thought of himself in the midst of that vast furnace, then he looked back at the dark thunderhead. "Friend Elrelet," he said, "I have my first request of you."

"Yes?"

"Supper."

Rezhyk sat crouched over his notebook, meticulously inscribing the details of his most recent incantations on a blank page. He did not look up as Gildrum appeared in the workshop, shedding yellow light upon his ring-laden hands before coalescing into the shape of the young girl.

"The deed is done," she said. "I met him on the road as a knight, and we fought. Though he wore no armor and begged me to cease, I would not let him yield. The death blow was a sure one."

"Quite sure?" murmured Rezhyk, his eyes still on the page before him.

"Quite sure," said Gildrum, remembering the cool slice of steel through her inhuman head. Never before had she allowed her fleshly form to seem vulnerable, and the memory of it was strange and lingering, like the flavor of an unusual spice.

"Very well, my Gildrum. I worried this day past, but now you have set my mind at rest. Lean close here and look at this new figure I have devised. I think I shall need a carbuncle for this one, deep, blood-red, perhaps the size of my thumbnail. And you shall find it for me in the East, my Gildrum. Yes."

Gildrum leaned close and looked at the words in that familiar cramped script and nodded to the rhythm of Rezhyk's voice. As he spoke, she wondered at his coolness and his easy displacement of interest. Already, the murder of his son was unimportant to him. There was not a touch of remorse in his demeanor.

Gildrum focused her eyes on the back of his neck for a moment, at the white linen collar of the shirt he wore over the cloth-of-gold. Between the collar and the base of his skull, the thick hair parted, exposing skin that had never seen sunlight.

I would stab you there, she thought, *if I were not a slave. And I would feel no more sorrow than you do at this moment.*

❦ CHAPTER FIFTEEN

From nothingness, Elrelet had produced a roast fowl, and Cray ate it, floating. "Is there nothing more in Air," he said between bites, "but empty space? No vegetation, no buildings, nothing solid?"

"There are buildings," said Elrelet. "You are within one now—my home."

Cray looked about, frowning perplexedly, as if doubting the evidence of his senses. "I see nothing."

"That's because it's made of air. Your eyes are not good enough to see that air can be as solid as many other things. For example, there is a wall behind you. Reach back and touch it. Careful, though; remember you're not accustomed to moving in this world."

Cray stretched out a tentative hand and encountered a surface before his arm had straightened entirely. Invisible, the wall seemed to roil and bubble beneath his fingers, like a spring gushing forth from a mountainside. He pushed against the pressure and could not penetrate it; instead, his own body moved backward as his elbow stiffened.

"How, then, did we get in?" he asked.

"I seem to recall that you have doors in the human world," said Elrelet.

"But I can't see it. How shall I get out?"

"Follow the breeze," replied the demon. "It enters at one door and exits at the other—surely that won't be too difficult for you. But you shall not be going out much at first, not until you've learned how to travel among us. A pity you have no wings."

"Few humans do."

"Well," said Elrelet, "then you shall have to swim. I hope you're acquainted with swimming."

"Not really. I've splashed through a river or two in my travels, but my horse always swam better than I did."

"A pity again. Well, you'll learn here, or you'll be very frustrated. At least you don't thrash wildly about; you have a fine talent for keeping still."

"I learn quickly, I hope."

"If you're quite finished with that poor bird, I'll give you some instructions in swimming."

"I'm finished." The bones disappeared.

"You must think of the air as a tangible thing, as tangible as water," said the demon. "Your arms are your oars. Your feet, too, for that matter. You can just wave the feet to give yourself a bit of forward motion, and the arms control your direction. Try it."

Awkwardly, Cray scissored his legs, and his body began to tumble.

"You have to straighten yourself out," said Elrelet. "Your head is the prow of your ship; it has to face toward your destination."

Cray straightened out and bumped into the invisible wall. He pushed away from it with one hand, stroked tentatively with the other, and soared with some grace until he struck another wall and rebounded in a flurry of limbs. "At least the walls aren't hard," he muttered, reflexively grasping for support but finding none and continuing to tumble in a slow arc.

"Stretch all your arms and legs out as far as you can," said Elrelet.

Cray did so, and his rotation slowed.

"You will stop eventually that way," said the demon.

"I wish I could just stand up," said Cray. "Or lie down. I feel a bit dizzy. Is all the demon world like this?"

"You mean without weight?"

"Yes."

"Then, yes. You'll get used to it. Personally, I prefer it—nothing to drag you down to that hard, lumpy surface. Of course, I can fly in your world, but it's so much more tiring."

"Well, I can't fly there, but I don't mind walking."

"You'll enjoy flying here, I'm sure. You'll miss it when you get back."

"Have you ever walked, Elrelet?"

"Oh, yes, I've done my share. My master used to like traveling. He gave me a horse's form, and I did quite a bit of walking with him. Slow travel it was; I tried to suggest that we fly, but he'd have none of that. A very leisurely fellow."

"What happened to him?" asked Cray.

"Happened? Why, nothing. He's still there, settled into a huge castle with all the souvenirs he picked up in our wandering. I don't see him very often. He has everything he wants and little use for a slave these days."

"Oh. I thought perhaps you had been freed."

"Why would you think that?"

"Because you have a home here. Because Gildrum gave me into your care. I supposed from that that you were here all the time, not enslaved by some human."

"There are many of us here most of the time. We're slaves still, but we have masters who don't call for our services constantly, not like my poor friend Gildrum. We have homes. Gildrum has a home, too—you passed through it on your way here, though I suppose you wouldn't have noticed with your human eyes. We

318

have a whole way of life which is occasionally interrupted by some human whim."

"Are there many like Gildrum?"

"I am at one extreme, Gildrum is at the other, and
there is everything in between, Cray." The demon
made a sound like a human being clearing his throat.
"And now, Cray, I must warn you about the Free."

"The Free?" said Cray, lying quite still in the middle of the air, his arms at his sides, his eyes closed.
Now that he had stopped moving, the dizziness was
passing away. "Who are they?"

"They are the demons who have never been slaves.
They spend their time amusing themselves, and I suspect they will consider you a great source of amusement very soon. They live in fear of the summons,
and fear makes their jesting bitter. I hope you will
not be offended by anything they may say. In any
event, you would be wise to be polite to them at all
times."

"I always try to be polite to those who are stronger
than I am."

"Well, I will protect you, of course . . ."

"But you would prefer not to be given the opportunity. I understand. Is there anything special that I
must not say to the Free?"

"Don't ask their names. Only a slave will admit to
a name."

"And what of those former slaves whose masters
are dead? Where do they fit in? Will they acknowledge
names?"

"Some will, some won't. Some rejoin the Free, some
stay with the more relaxed society of the slaves. We,
at least, though we are compelled by rings, no longer
live in the fear of the unknown."

"And those whose masters have freed them—where
do they go?"

"There are only a few such fortunate creatures.
They alone can live their lives completely as they
choose, for a slave who has been set free can never be
enslaved again." The cloud contracted suddenly, loosing a very human sigh. "I asked my master for that
boon once, but he put me off. He said he might need
me sometime. He'll die without freeing me, I know,

and then I will wait in suspense, wondering if and when another sorcerer will find me. Be glad you're not a demon, Cray Ormoru."

"The Free are not the only bitter demons," Cray said softly.

"No, they are not. To be a demon is to be bitter, at least since the first sorcerer made the first pair of rings to catch us. Even I—and I am one of the lucky ones. I had a better humor than most, before the summons, and my slavery has not been so hard that I have lost it all. Still, even I cry out sometimes. Especially when he calls me. Which reminds me: should I be called, should I disappear suddenly without telling you, it would be best, at first certainly, if you did not wander too far from the house."

Cray bent his legs, clasped his knees. "I should be afraid even to go out. I'd never find it again."

"I'll mark it for you."

"Well, I don't expect to go out much. I have my studies."

"So Gildrum told me." A thread of cloud extruded from the thunderhead that was Elrelet, stretching out and out, past Cray till it curled against the invisible wall beyond him. There the notebooks huddled, like sheep on a cold winter's night. The strand of cloud retracted slowly, depositing the books beside Cray on its way back to the parent body. "Here are your lessons. Whatever else you might need, you have only to ask, and I will bring it."

Cray clutched the books. "I'll just read right now, thank you, while there's still light."

"There is always light," said Elrelet.

"You haven't any night here?"

"None. Nor do we sleep."

"Well then, I'll need some sort of mask if I'm to sleep."

"I can darken the walls for that."

"Good. Later I'll ask for that favor." Cray opened one of the books to the last page he remembered writing on. There were six beyond it, filled with minuscule script that even he might have mistaken for his own. He set a finger at the beginning of the new section and looked back at the thunderhead. "Oh, and if it's possible, I'd like to get my belongings back—the saddlebags on my horse and the sword and shield which lie where Gildrum spirited me away from my own world. Can you do that, Elrelet?"

"Nothing simpler, if Gildrum approves," said the demon. "But I can find you clothes and even a sword and shield if you really want them, all better quality than those you left behind. I don't know what you need them for, though—there's no one to fight with those weapons, and you can go naked, it's warm enough."

"I'm not really accustomed to going naked," said Cray. "My clothes are good enough for me, and the rest . . . well, call it sentiment that makes me want them."

"I see that there is a ring among your belongings." The thunderhead sent a tendril of cloud to Cray's hand, delicately touching the smallest finger, where the slim, inconspicuous band of gold rested. Cray felt a faint dampness at that touch, nothing more.

"There is a ring," he replied, "but it is not important."

"Yes, yes," said Elrelet. "It means you have another ally here, and one who will be more faithful to you than either Gildrum or I could ever be. Don't underestimate the value of a slave."

"Just a small one. I have no further need for his services; I may as well set him free." He twisted the ring on his finger. "Except that I don't know how to do that yet. Perhaps you could instruct me, Elrelet?"

"How refreshing," said the demon. "A master who wishes to free a slave without any prompting. Oh, I could instruct you, never doubt it. Any of us could. But I would suggest that you put the notion aside for now. You may find yourself needing a slave in the near future, even a small one."

"It is my turn to be surprised, Elrelet. I never expected to hear a demon advise me to keep another in slavery."

"I told you I would give you advice, Cray. I hope it will always be useful advice."

"And I thank you for it."

Elrelet left to consult with Gildrum on the matter of

the saddlebags, sword, and shield and returned with the items themselves and with the large counterpart of Cray's ring as well, which Cray had left behind in Ringforge. The demon spewed them into a space which seemed as open as any within the invisible walls; Cray's questing hands discovered it to be an alcove sealed by a cushiony door that yielded to strong pressure.

"One object—you—is enough to be floating freely in my house," said Elrelet. "I trust you will not leave your belongings scattered everywhere. The books can go in here, too, when you're not using them."

"I shall try to be neat," said Cray. "But remember, I am not accustomed to all this floating."

"You will learn."

And he did learn. The mild dizziness passed quickly, as if his two flights with the great bronze bird had inured him to the vast openness of sky all around. After some initial floundering, he developed a smooth swimming stroke and a technique of turning corners by rebounding off an invisible wall. He found that he could read without touching the book save to turn the pages but that he could not write in it without using both hands—one to press the writing implement against the page and the other to keep the book from sailing away under that pressure. Elrelet gave him a silverpoint for the writing instead of quill and ink, saying that the ink would not flow properly in the demon world. Ink was not the only fluid that would not flow without weight, Cray soon determined, and he became adept at shaking globules of wine and water from their containers and sucking them into his mouth before they could spread all over his face and hair.

He learned incantations, he learned procedures. He practiced gestures and tones of voice, rhythms and phrasing. He invented a scheme of notation that would recall details beyond the mere words when his teacher was not near to answer questions. Gildrum visited infrequently, testing him each time on the material he had been given before, leaving more—pages and pages of lore that he must commit to memory. Cray began to wonder how long it would take to make him Rezhyk's equal.

"Time passes differently here," said Gildrum. "Without night to separate the days, time stretches out, and not just for us, who never sleep, but for you, too. If I took you back this instant, what season do you think you would find at Spinweb?"

Cray shook his head. "I have lost track completely. If you told me I had been here a century, I would believe you. Yet my beard hasn't grown an inch."

"And will not," said Gildrum. "Nothing grows here. Nor do you have to eat, Cray, except that you are used to it."

"And will I age?"

"No."

"Then it scarcely matters what season it is at Spinweb. Except . . . I wonder if my mother is worrying about me."

"I think not. You haven't been gone very long."

"She has a magical tapestry that shows her my travels. When she looks at it next, will it tell her I'm here."

Gildrum hesitated. "I should think not. No earthly eyes but yours have ever seen the demon world, Cray."

"What will it show then?"

"I don't know," said Gildrum. "I don't know."

Delivev looked down at the weaving, at the glinting bronze that represented the feathers of a great bird, at the green-fringed darkness that was the entry to the Seer's cave, at the crimson threads that marked Cray's route westward from there. It ceased abruptly in the forest. A sword was woven in silver beside that end point, to mark a fight, but there was no red of blood to show that Cray had been injured. There was simply an end to the line, as if he had settled himself in that spot to wait out the season or the year or eternity. Delivev wondered whom he had fought, but she would not allow herself to call to him to ask. In his own good time, she thought, he would tell her.

Some Free came at last, to view the first human to visit the demon world. Various slave demons had passed by already, according to Elrelet, but had not chosen to shed their invisibility and disturb him. The Free were not so courteous. They cut off the light that poured through the transparent walls of Elrelet's house, great dark clouds crowding close, like a sudden summer storm. Cray closed his book and let it float away; he could not see well enough to deposit it in the alcove where his other possessions were. Elrelet had gone out earlier, leaving Cray with instructions not to go out alone.

Elrelet had told him he was completely safe inside the house, but Cray felt a chill creep up his back anyway, and it was not from any change in the warmth of the air. He touched the ring on his hand and whispered its demon's name, Yra. Presently, a gap showed among the dark clouds, and a ball of mellow light squeezed through the throng. It did not enter, could not without Elrelet's own permission, but it pressed against the invisible wall, shedding yellow light in the gloom. Cray took up his book once more, though he could only pretend to read.

"So you are the human," came a deep voice, like distant thunder. "A puny creature indeed. I expected something greater."

Cray turned his head toward the voice. He could not guess how many demons surrounded him; there seemed to be no clear divisions between individuals. He thought, in fact, that the cloud might be one vast demon until another voice spoke in a different timbre, and he decided that, like a gang of children, they would find no pleasure in approaching him singly.

"Hard to believe," said the second voice, "that one such as this could enslave one of us."

Cray executed a slow bow in mid-air, tumbling completely head over heels till he arrived at his original posture, where he stopped himself with a flick of his leg. "Good day," he said.

"I could tear him apart with a light crosswind," said the voice that had spoken second.

"Come out," said the first voice. "Come out, little human, and play with us."

Cray smiled, swiveling his head slowly so that most of them could glimpse his face. "I thank you for the invitation, but my host has forbidden me to go out of his house without him."

"Forbidden?" said another voice. "A demon forbids a human something?"

"He is afraid of us, this human," said someone else. "And he does well to be afraid." The voice laughed gustily, rippling the clouds all around it like a sudden gale. "This paltry little fire demon would do you little good if we chose to be unfriendly."

"I hope you will be friendly," said Cray. "I mean you no harm."

"No harm?" The voice laughed louder than ever. "What are you doing here, then? No harm! You can't lie to us, human. We know all about you."

"Then you must also know that I plan to free one of your number."

"So you say. But you'll change your mind once you've enslaved a few of us. Gildrum is a fool to believe you."

"Fire demons are all fools," said another voice.

"I will keep my pledge," said Cray.

"Come out, come out," called another voice. "Come out and play with us, human."

"When my host comes home," said Cray, "I will ask for his permission to do so."

The clouds moaned and whispered among themselves, and they pushed at Cray's fire demon until its light flickered like a candle in a drafty room. Cray feigned attention to his book again, only smiling whenever the air demons repeated their invitation, until a rift broke in the darkness, like sunlight pouring through disintegrating storm clouds. Elrelet, small and sharply defined—in contrast to the Free—had arrived.

"Back off!" Cray's host shouted in a voice as large as any of theirs, far larger than mere size betokened. "I'll have no crowding around my house. Back off or suffer!"

In response, the clouds broke apart, and Cray was able to count ten individuals, each as large as a dozen horses together.

"This human is my guest!" said Elrelet. "Any affront to him will be an affront to me."

The demons muttered, and one of them said, "Are you afraid we'll harm him, Elrelet-slave?"

"If any harm comes to him, I shall tell my master the name of the guilty one, and *he* shall exact punishment."

The demons fell silent on a gust of air like an indrawn breath.

"Come out, Cray," said Elrelet. "Let them look more closely upon the enemy."

Cray found the door and swung himself through it. He called Yra to his side, a ball of pale light in the sky-glow.

"My lord," said Yra, "I am no match for such a crowd in a fight. I would be overwhelmed and unable to help you."

"Go home, Yra," Cray replied. "I only needed you for light."

The fire demon flashed away, like a spark spit out from a crackling log.

The air demons crowded close. "So this is a human," said one of them, sending a tendril of cloud to touch Cray's foot. A puff of air ruffled his hair; a stronger draft set him tumbling slowly, a leaf before the autumn breeze. Elrelet expanded into a ring of cloud and encircled his waist like a fat belt, halting his rotation. "Enough of that," Elrelet said. "Play your games with something else."

"We came here to invite him to play," said one of the demons. "Just for amusement, you understand, nothing serious."

"He has no time for amusement," replied Elrelet. "He has much work before him, and you shall not interfere. Begone now you've seen and touched him. Begone!"

Like mist evaporating before the morning sun, they thinned away to nothing, leaving only a single sigh behind, the merest sough of wind. "You, too," said Elrelet, and even that was gone.

Back inside the house, Elrelet said, "They only wanted to frighten you. They wouldn't have shown themselves to your eyes if they had meant real harm."

"Well, they succeeded in their intention," replied

Cray. "I thought the walls would give way any moment."

"Not these walls," said the demon. "Stay inside, and none can touch you. They'll be back, I'm sure."

"For what?"

"To coax you into playing. They have a game, you see—a rather rough one it would be, too, for a human being. That's how the Free spend their time—playing."

"What of the slaves? Don't they play in their leisure time?"

"Not like the Free. Not with such single-minded devotion. The Free wager on their game. And because material goods like gold and jewels have no value for demons, they wager with their names."

"With their names? How?"

"Each round of play pits two demons against each other, and the loser must add the winner's name to its own, and answer the sorcerous summons directed at that name if its own is not called first. The more often one loses the game, the more names one carries, the more likely one is to be summoned. Conversely, a frequent winner is protected against the summons by the many who carry its name. There is a demon among the Free whose name is carried by more than a dozen others, while it carries only its own."

"A dozen?" said Cray. "How do they decide which of them answers the summons?"

"The one who lost longest ago answers, unless it has already been called to some other name."

"And when that demon answers, what happens to the other names that it might be carrying?"

"They stay with it. After its master dies and it is Free again, it is bound to them still. The game is costly, you see, Cray, and the cost does not diminish with time. Only a winner can afford to stop playing, one who has won often enough not only to pass its own name to a number of other demons but to get rid of the names it may have acquired by earlier losing. One who loses more often than it wins can escape only one way: when it is given its freedom by a sorcerer, given the ring that summoned it, that commands it. Only then does the compulsion of the game disappear."

"Compulsion?" said Cray. "But what if a demon refuses to answer a summons for one of the names not its own?"

"Impossible," replied Elrelet. "We are trapped by names, Cray; they are as real and tangible to us as your flesh is to you. When a demon accepts the wager of a name, it is bound by that; if it loses the game and must take the name, it can only rid itself of the name through the game. Of course, one is never rid of one's own name."

"But why would they want me to play, Elrelet? *I'm* not bound by any name compulsion. Winning from me wouldn't do anyone any good."

"Perhaps not."

"What do you mean, 'perhaps'?"

"You are in our world now, Cray. You live by its rules. Perhaps some sorcerer could enslave you, if you bore a demon name. That would amuse the Free greatly—a poor weak human answering a sorcerer's call."

"I can't believe it's possible."

"Don't play with them, Cray. I'm sure you don't want to find out."

"I'm sure I would be terrible at the game anyway, not having a demon's powers. And I haven't the time, as you said yourself."

"They will taunt you and tease you," said Elrelet. "Today's visit will not be the last, in spite of my anger. They will wait till I am gone again."

"I'll try to ignore them."

"I hope you can. Gildrum will never forgive me if something happens to you."

"You two are very old friends, aren't you?"

"Very old."

"Did either of you ever play the game?"

Elrelet hesitated. Then the cloud that was the demon's body darkened. "A long time ago, when I was young and foolish, I played and lost. That was the summons that I answered, not my own. My own name has never been called. If I hadn't played, I would still be Free."

"And Gildrum?"

"Gildrum advised me not to play, and many times

I have wished I had taken that advice. Gildrum has never played. In our youth, you see, the game had not yet taken hold so strongly among the Free. We were less foolish than the Free are today, or so we like to think. Perhaps it isn't true. Every demon born is a fool; only a few have time to learn wisdom before they are enslaved."

Cray pursed his lips. "Demons are born?" he murmured.

Elrelet laughed that light breathy laugh. "Did you think we come into existence out of nothingness, Cray?"

"Well . . . I don't know. Flame, air . . . they seem to partake of nothingness."

"We have a legend—and it may be the truth—that, ages ago, the first demon coalesced from nothingness where the four worlds meet. It was a creature that combined all four demon aspects—air, fire, water, and ice—and immediately after its inception, it separated into those aspects, and each of the four parts retreated to the appropriate dwelling place, to become ancestor to all demons of that sort that came after. But we no longer come into existence in that fashion. We mate, we bear our young alive, we raise them until they can fend for themselves. It is not so different from what humans do."

"Do you have any children, Elrelet?"

"Quite a long time ago I chose to have one. We are long-lived and do not breed very often."

"Elrelet . . ." Cray smiled somewhat sheepishly. "How does one tell, with demons, which are the males and which the females?"

Again, the breathy laughter. "One doesn't, Cray. Those are human distinctions that do not apply to us. Our masters may give us the forms of men or women, but those are just outward semblances. Inside, we are still . . . as we are."

Cray's smile faded, the corners of his mouth sagging, his brows tightening. "Elrelet," he said, "do you know about Gildrum and my mother?"

Elrelet's sigh was a breath of warm wind. "We are old friends," the demon said. "I know, but I confess that I do not understand. Gildrum has been among you

329

humans more than most of us. Gildrum was always sensible, but I suppose that one cannot be sensible in all things." The cloud contracted a trifle and expanded, a pulse like a shrug. "We slaves are compelled to do so much against our own wills, sometimes we have none left. Not Gildrum, though. Not Gildrum. For myself, the threat of the master's punishment would be greater than any desire I might have for anything. Or anyone. I would have killed you, Cray. I tell you that honestly. I would have killed you rather than play this dangerous game with my master. And *he* is far softer than Lord Rezhyk. Disobedience is the greatest crime a demon can commit, Cray . . . because it must be done by being cleverer than the master. Sorcerers don't accept such cleverness with very good grace."

"You think Lord Rezhyk will find out eventually?"

"How can I know? Eventually, yes, of course, when you are ready to combat him. Sooner than that? Study hard, Cray, that you may cut his thinking time as short as possible."

Cray nodded. "I feel like I've played the Free game and lost."

"Something close to that," replied Elrelet.

Cray opened his books once more.

The Free came back, as predicted. This time they did not blot out the light. They appeared, instead, as white cirrus clouds, feathery and evanescent, darting about Elrelet's home as if there were a wild windstorm going on beyond the walls. Cray could not help watching them. After a while, he noticed that they were bouncing a small object about among them, but even with his nose pressed against the cushiony wall, he could not determine the nature of the thing. Once, while he observed, it ricocheted off the outside of the wall, missing his face by only the invisible thickness of the surface, and he recoiled reflexively and tumbled a moment before he could right himself, to the rhythm of mocking, booming laughter. The cirrus clouds scattered abruptly shortly afterward, at Elrelet's arrival.

"They were rather amusing this time," Cray said to his host. "They were playing some sort of game, I think."

"Yes," said Elrelet. "The only game they ever play."

"You mean that was *it*, the terrible game? It seemed so simple. Like children tossing a ball."

"When one's future hangs on the outcome, such a game is never simple. The ball, as you call it, is a cube with a different number of dots on each face. The two players each choose a face as their own, and between them they start the cube spinning and soaring; each must touch the cube at least twice or the game is disqualified, but in fact they generally touch it far more often, and so it tends to make mad gyrations. The object of the game is to strike the cube against some surface, and the player whose symbol is opposite the surface wins. When the cube strikes face-on it sticks tight; striking with edge or corner will cause it to bounce away. And there is a certain minimum distance from the surface, within which neither player is allowed—about three of your body-lengths, Cray. Some games last quite a long time before they are decided."

Cray asked, "Were they using your wall as their surface, or were they just passing by on their way to somewhere else?"

"They were using my wall," said Elrelet. "They were trying to annoy you."

"Like children."

"Some of them are."

Cray smiled. "It's hard for me to imagine a cloud as a child. Are they smaller when they're younger? This lot seemed small."

"No," said Elrelet. "They are born as large as they will ever be. These only appeared small because they wanted to."

"I've seen fire demons and air demons now; what are the other two sorts like—water and ice?"

"Ah," said Elrelet. "Curiosity."

"Well, yes. Why not?"

"I spoke to Gildrum recently, Cray, and have more lessons for you."

"I wasn't thinking about that kind of curiosity."

"You have much studying left ahead of you."

"I know that," said Cray. "But if I'm to be a demon-master, wouldn't it be appropriate for me to find out what the different kinds of demons are like, so that

I may choose wisely among them? Unless . . . the compulsion of the game extends so far that if I summon a water demon I may get an air demon instead, in spite of the considerable difference in procedure for the two."

"No, it does not extend so far," said Elrelet. "And for that reason, the game is played only among one's own kind. Otherwise there is no meaning to winning or losing. There are different variants of the game, too, in the different domains, each suited to the nature of the place. Ice demons, in particular, have an extreme variant because objects do not float freely, unobstructed, in their area."

"I should like to see an ice demon," Cray said.

"Are you thinking of enslaving some of them?"

"I don't know. I know almost nothing about them. Gildrum has given me very little information on them."

"Well, fire and ice, Cray," said Elrelet. "They mix poorly, and so that is not a place that Gildrum frequents."

"Do you know much about them?"

"Some," said Elrelet. "But I thought you were going to concentrate on fire demons."

"I don't know. Any of them would be valuable, I'm sure."

"You'll begin casting your rings soon. You must choose."

"Fire demons would be the easiest, of course. Gildrum has taught me more about them than all the others combined. Still, I would wish a few of each."

"Each? No human being has ever commanded more than two kinds; few more than one."

"I think I will need all four kinds for my purpose."

"I would think . . . fire demons."

"Fight like with like? No, I think that would be a mistake."

"You'll not snuff Rezhyk's fire demons with your water demons, nor freeze them either."

"Perhaps not, but I will be flexible, and Lord Rezhyk will not. That may turn out to be my one advantage. Can you persuade some ice and water folk to visit me?"

"I don't think they'll require my persuasion. They'll

come to see the human at last. You have only to be patient and to continue your studies."

Cray grinned, fingering his book. "You are an un-relenting taskmaster, Elrelet, and a true friend to Gildrum."

The cloud sighed, like a soft breeze rustling leaves. "I try to be."

⋖§ CHAPTER SIXTEEN

They did come in their own good time—spheres of liquid large as bears, milky, opalescent; and giant snowflakes like stars made of glittering openwork lace, with needle-sharp spicules sprouting in every direction. And not only ice and water demons came, but fire as well, blobs of flame from candlelights to roaring conflagrations passed by the house with invisible walls. Cray could hardly look up from his books without seeing some unhuman being floating in the blue, glowing by its own light or reflecting the luminosity of Air from a pearl-smooth or crystalline surface. Elrelet told him that all these visitors were Free, not a slave among them. And the Free of Air continued to pay their visits, more frequently than ever, skittering about the other demons, bumping into them sometimes, and starting what Elrelet referred to as "differences of opinion." These arguments were silent, to Cray's ears, but they involved considerable wild motion.

"They're an unruly company, our Free," Elrelet admitted. "Perhaps that is one of the reasons why we see so few travelers from the other domains."

Cray tried to keep to his studies, but sometimes,

watching the cloudlike Free, he yearned to go out and join them. They still called to him, laughing, caroming their cube off the invisible walls. They seemed more curious now than dangerous, like playful puppies tumbling and yipping in the summer grass. Cray smiled at them as they puffed in and out of visibility, chasing the cube, each other, and any other demons that happened to be near. And when one of them executed a particularly intricate maneuver in his full sight, Cray understood that it was flaunting itself especially for him.

"Do they never tire of me?" Cray said to Elrelet. "I know it's the same group over and over again. I recognize their voices."

"It is the same group. Don't you realize that they're trying to distract you? They don't want you to have a chance to capture any of them."

"I would not keep them long, if I did capture any of them."

"You might possibly convince me of that," said Elrelet. "But not them. They would never trust a human's word."

"Haven't I convinced you already, Elrelet?"

The demon hesitated and then very softly said, "I'm not sure. Truly, Cray, I understand that you mean well now, or you think you mean well, but who can say how you will feel when your hands are covered with rings?"

"I have convinced Gildrum!"

"Gildrum does not care about anything but Gildrum right now. If freedom meant the enslavement of a thousand demons, Gildrum would accept that gladly. And what demon, with the opportunity for freedom, would think differently? Not one of the players of the game, certainly."

"But you. You feel differently."

"And so did Gildrum once. We thought that helping to enslave our fellow demons was the most terrible part of our own slavery. Yet now I help Gildrum to help you enslave." A gust of air was Elrelet's sigh. "I can't say what is right and what is wrong, Cray. Only that my friend asked for aid, and I am able to give it."

"I swear to you, Elrelet—"

"Don't swear. You will do what you will do. I only hope that you are able to accomplish what Gildrum wishes."

"I shall try," said Cray. He smiled ruefully. "After all . . . my life depends on it."

Yet, though his life did depend on it, he grew restless with the study of sorcery, with the seemingly endless supply of information that Gildrum provided him. He saw Rezhyk's fire demon rarely now, only long enough to receive a few scant words of encouragement and fresh volumes of lore. Often even these were transmitted through Elrelet. Rezhyk, Cray was told, was keeping his servant busy.

One day—as Cray had come to think of those periods of time in which he was awake—he threw the books aside and summoned Yra, who had been given Elrelet's permission to enter the house at its master's command. The Free were at play outside, Elrelet was away on some errand, and Cray felt a great need for activity.

"Come, Yra," he said, "I have been too long lazing with these books. My muscles grow flabby and weak with disuse. Bring me some clay and I shall give you another form to suit my need for a sporting companion. And borrow me a kiln, too, from some potter of my world, big enough to house a man. And mark you it has never been used for sorcery before."

"A kiln, my lord? Where will I find such a thing? I am not traveled in the human world, my lord. You must instruct me."

Cray frowned at his servant. "Well, I must confess that I cannot. I know only Lord Rezhyk's kiln, and of course that is not available to us. We shall have to wait for Elrelet's return, I suppose, and ask for one then, but I can tell you of the clay. Do you know what clay is, Yra?"

"No, my lord."

"Well, the kind I am thinking of is reddish in color, a sort of soil that has a sticky quality, of which pottery is made. There is a considerable amount of it exposed in the east bank of a river that runs near Spinweb. I saw it often as a child. Do you know where Spinweb lies?"

"No, my lord."

"What landmarks *do* you know in the human world?"

"Ringforge, my lord, where you summoned me."

Cray's brow knit tighter. "Even I would be hard pressed to find Spinweb from there. You would be flying, though . . . if you went eastward you would strike the river, surely, and then need only follow it south till you sighted the towers of Spinweb." He nodded, more to himself than to Yra. "Yes, do that. Go east from Ringforge to the river and then follow it south. But don't be fooled by smaller streams; you will know the river from its width—twenty humans with joined hands would scarcely span it. When you see Spinweb near, begin searching the east bank of the river for reddish soil, and bring me back enough of that to make a person of my own size."

"My lord . . . what is 'east'?"

"Why . . . east, toward the rising sun."

"And what is the rising sun?"

"The sun, Yra, the sun at dawn."

"What is the sun, my lord?"

Cray stared open-mouthed at the blob of light, so like a sun itself in miniature. "Have you never seen the sun?"

"No, my lord."

"But how can that be?"

Very softly, Yra replied, "I am very young, my lord."

Cray crossed his arms, tapping with one index finger on the large muscle of his left shoulder. "Yra," he said, "how often have you been to the human world?"

"As often as you summoned me, my lord."

"And . . . inside the walls of Ringforge only?"

"Yes, my lord, only there."

"Do you know what a tree is?"

"No, my lord."

Cray sighed. "You have never seen a tree, or a rock, or a river, or any other human beyond me?"

"I have seen rivers, my lord, in Fire."

"Not rivers of water?"

"No, my lord. Are there such things in the human world?"

"Oh, yes. But they flow upon the ground, not through the sky." He shook his head. "Never 'mind, Yra. Never mind about the clay. We shall both wait for Elrelet's return. Perhaps some other time . . . perhaps when I am back in my own world, I will teach you about it."

"Yes, my lord."

While they waited, Cray pulled his sword and shield from the saddlebags where they had nestled since his arrival in Air and began very carefully to practice his swordsmanship. He discovered that while he was adept at moving his own body about in a world without weight, the use of the sword and shield was not as simple as he had expected. Still, he learned to compensate for their bulk, for the way they changed his balance and set him tumbling. And he learned that the shield made an excellent oar.

The Free crowded about Elrelet's house while Cray slashed at nothingness, their cloud forms small as cabbages, looking like so many children peeping from behind curtains at their elders' business. The game had halted, as well as the noise that usually marked their presence. Cray ignored them.

When Elrelet returned, the demon was perplexed at Cray's activities. "In what way will the sword and shield help you make rings and conjure demons?"

"In no way at all," Cray said, his breath coming fast from much exercise. "But they will keep me from going mad with study. Even at Ringforge I took them up when I needed a change from the exercises of the mind."

"Gildrum, I think, would not be pleased seeing you thus."

Cray grinned. "Very well, my host. I have some sorcerous work planned and was only waiting for your help before beginning."

"How may I assist you? Fetch ore, the oven, the tools for casting already?"

"No, no, not yet. I would create a new form for my servant here, and for that I need clay and a kiln never used for sorcery."

"Ah," said Elrelet. "And your little demon is too innocent to find them."

"Precisely."

"Very well. This is a skill you will need to practice, and if you wish a change from study, I can think of no more useful one. I shall return shortly." The miniature thunderhead dwindled before Cray's eyes, to the size of his fist, to the size of his thumb, to nothing. It was gone scarcely a score of heartbeats. Reappearing as a mere speck, it grew quickly, surpassed its usual dimensions, pushing Cray aside with gentle bumps, until it was a sphere with volume eight or ten times that of Cray's body. A hole appeared in the surface of the cloud sphere closest to Cray, tiny enough to admit a finger at first but growing steadily till he saw that the cloud was a mere shell encompassing something else: a brick kiln. Elrelet withdrew completely, compact now in the thunderhead shape, and with one slim tentacle of cloud, the demon pulled the kiln door open to expose a mass of red clay—more than enough for the sculpting of a full-size human figure—and a number of sculptor's implements.

"I presumed you might want some tools as well," Elrelet said. "They are my master's, but I think he won't miss them. He hardly ever does any modeling these days, and I left him a few things in case he should change his mind."

"I thank you," said Cray, pulling at the clay, which floated from its container in one large, irregularly shaped mass. It was cold and stiff between his hands.

"Have you ever worked with clay before?" asked Elrelet.

"Only as a child—small things, bowls, toy figures, a fish or two. I recall that my mother praised the fish."

"And do you intend to make a fish form for Yra?"

"No, a human form. Or at least a human semblance."

Elrelet laughed softly. "You would be wise to start with something simpler."

"I don't want something simpler."

"Then this should be most interesting."

Cray broke a small piece off the mass of clay and

rolled it between his hands until it warmed and became malleable. Then bit by bit, following the instructions that Gildrum had left in one of his notebooks, he added to the piece, building up a core of clay, roughing out the form of a human body—trunk, head, limbs. The figure grew quickly at first, then more gradually as he began to tire of kneading and pressing the form between his hands. He paused to eat, to sleep, to glance again at his studies, but only till his arms were rested, and then he resumed work on the clay. He had used up most of it by the time he judged the figure large enough.

"One of the arms is longer than the other," said Elrelet.

Cray nipped the offending extra length away. "That is the least of my worries," he muttered. He had begun to realize how difficult a task he had set himself. The shape was approximately human, but though he had used his own body for reference, he was not skilled enough to copy the contours properly. Nor could he make the face anything but a mockery of humanity, with a blob for a nose, eyes like pits, and hair a squared-off block. The more he worked, the more he had to admire Rezhyk's abilities; he would never have guessed that any of the bodies that Gildrum had worn in his sight could have been sculpture come to life. At last Cray ceased his molding, his carving, his additions and subtractions, knowing that a better likeness did not now lie within his power. He took up the big square wooden frame strung with the single fine wire, the wire that Elrelet's master had probably used a hundred times, and he sliced the body into pieces—the head, the limbs, the torso, all separate. Then he sliced each section vertically into halves and hollowed them out, rejoining them carefully, smoothing the seams out, until he had a whole statue once more. He had left two holes in the figure, one in the right foot and one in the upper back, as vents.

"Now we are ready," he said to Yra, carefully clasping the larger of his rings on the upper arm of the statue. Gently, he pushed it into the kiln. He swam away then, to the farthest wall. "I command you to enter this body."

Yra expanded a trifle, its glow turning to more evident, licking flame, and it swooped into the kiln. The figure began to glow as soon as the demon touched it, red first, then yellow, then white, illuminating the surrounding bricks with a harsh glare. The color faded gradually after that peak, back to red and even dimmer, until the light pouring into the kiln from the luminosity of Air was greater than any radiated by the figure. Yra's new body twitched slightly, as the demon flexed its new muscles, and terra-cotta powder burst from it, bouncing from the walls like so much flour caught in a gust of wind. Some of it floated from the open door, and more followed, trailing after Yra as the demon stepped out of the kiln.

Cray tried to wave the powder away from himself with one hand, but the turbulence caused by his gesture merely brought more powder to him. He sneezed several times, then covered his mouth and nose with the slack of his sleeve. "Get rid of it, Yra!" he shouted.

Behind him, Elrelet laughed. "I suggest you tell your slave to toss the powder into one of the lava rivers of Fire."

"Do that, Yra," said Cray.

The humanlike figure vanished then, as if it had never existed, replaced by the flames of the demon, which raced about Elrelet's house, scooping up the powder like a damp cloth collecting dust. When it was all gathered up, hidden within the demon's flame, Yra soared out the door and dwindled rapidly in the distance.

Cray swam to the kiln. In front of its doorway, where Yra had transformed to the ball of flame, floated the ring that the statue had worn. Cray slipped it over his own wrist to carry it to the alcove and deposit it in one of his saddlebags. By the time he had done that, Yra was back.

"Shall I resume the new form, my lord?" the demon asked.

"Yes," said Cray. "I've barely had a chance to see you in it."

The flame lost its roundness in favor of an elongated spindle shape which sprouted limbs of flame and then coalesced into the solid shape that Cray had fashioned. The flesh, of a reddish hue, was smoother even than the clay had been, and no seams showed where the parts had been reassembled. Cray sighed. Only a heavy cloak with a deep hood, he knew, would allow this creature to pass unnoticed among mortals.

"Well," said Cray, "I was not expecting my first attempt to yield untrammeled success. Come, Yra, let's see how those awkward arms hold a sword and shield." In the alcove once more, at the bottom of one of his saddlebags, well-swathed in cloth, he found the corroded armaments that Gildrum had carried as the young knight. Rust was thick on the steel surfaces; it smeared off on his hands when he touched them, floating like a spray of darker terra-cotta in the still air of the alcove. Cray tossed the sword and shield toward Yra, instructing the demon to catch them. He remained in the alcove a little longer, to gather up his own sword and shield and his suit of chain.

He had not worn it in years, of course. Even the padding felt strange to him, close and warm against his skin. It had no weight, though, nor did the chain, and he was amused to see the skirt, below his belt, float upward with one of his motions, as if it had been made of thinnest gossamer. He found a few leather thongs among his bags and laced them through some links of chain, to keep the flapping hem under control. He donned his helm.

Yra held the sword and shield under one arm, like parcels waiting to be passed to someone else. Cray showed the demon a proper grip on the sword hilt and slipped the shield into place for it.

Yra gazed at its own arms and at Cray's with some curiosity. "What are these things, my lord?"

"This is a sword," said Cray, "and this is a shield. With the sword you will try to stab or slash me, and with the shield you will ward off my stabbings and slashings. It's quite simple, really. Look, I'll show you." Very slowly, he raised his own sword and cut at Yra's shield; the blade met the rusty steel surface and rebounded, driving Cray backward along with it. Scissoring his legs, Cray returned to Yra and stabbed the demon lightly in the stomach. The point did not penetrate the demon's skin but sprang away; this time Cray was more ready and he did not drift as far.

Elrelet said, "You cannot harm the demon body, Cray, but Yra can hurt you."

"That is what my shield and chain are for. Come, Yra, strike me. But gently."

Yra stared at him. "I have heard, my lord, that humans are quite fragile. This blade is sharp as an ice demon. Will you be harmed if it pierces you?"

"I will," said Cray.

"Then I cannot use it, my lord. A slave may not harm the master."

"I don't wish you to harm me, Yra. This is a sport, not a war. We will spar, no more. You will aim your blows at my shield and I will aim mine at yours."

"A sport?" said Yra.

"A game, you against me. You know what a game is."

"Yra knows one game," said Elrelet.

"Well, imagine that game, then," said Cray, "but without any wagers."

"What would be the use," said Yra, "of playing the game without wagers?"

"Just for the joy of playing." Cray shrugged, grinning. "No, I suppose the joy is bound up in the wagering for you demons. Well, there are other kinds of games, and this is one of them. Strike at me with your sword. Go on, strike, Yra."

Hesitantly, the demon made a clumsy sweep at Cray's shield; Cray did not even have to move to deflect it. Yra floated slowly sideways with the force of the blow.

"You can do better than that, demon slave," said Cray. "Try something more like this." He slashed toward the demon's legs, but when Yra made no move with the shield, Cray twisted his arm and let the stroke slide past. "You mustn't let the blade touch you," he said. "If it touches you, you lose the game. That's what the shield is for, to keep the blade from your body. Your turn now."

This time Yra jabbed toward Cray's waist, and Cray

342

tapped the blade away with one edge of the shield. He could see, though, that the jab would have ended short of his skin, far short.

"Better," said Cray. "Better, but it must be better still." He slashed toward Yra's head, and the demon raised its shield clumsily to ward off the blow; chips of rust flew when Cray's blade touched that tired old surface, and the strap that held it to the demon's arm snapped, rotten after fifteen years of rain and snow. Elrelet hastened to the human world for replacements, fresh, shining arms that any knight would be proud to bear. Yra admired their sheen, "like the surface of Ice where Water meets it."

Cray spent the rest of his waking day laboriously instructing his demon in the rudiments of swordplay. By the time he was exhausted, he had learned that the demon could handle a humanlike body without weight far better than he could but that, in spite of such skill, Yra was a dismal failure at single combat.

"Still," Cray said, "it is better than fighting a wooden post."

The Free, who had not left their places at the invisible walls since Cray's strange activities had begun, whose numbers had in fact augmented with the passing of time, were still there when Elrelet darkened the walls for Cray's sleep. And they were there still, or again, scattered about the walls like water lilies on a pond, when those walls waxed transparent with Cray's wakening.

"Human," said one of them with a deep voice like distant thunder. "Human, what is this you do with your demon?"

"You heard my explanation," Cray said, yawning and stretching.

"All humans spend their time in this manner?" asked the demon.

"Many," said Cray. "It has a certain popularity."

"We would see more of it," said another demon.

"Well, you may go to my world and seek it out if you like."

The clouds shrank, drew together into a knot, physically cringing from his suggestion. "Time enough to go to the human world," said one of them in a high-pitched, breathy wail, "when we are summoned."

"Well, I must return to my studies," Cray said. "I can't spend all my time in pleasure, much as the thought appeals to me."

"Will you play this game again soon?" inquired the deep voice.

"I don't know. Sometime." Cray swam to the alcove, selected a book from among the many floating there.

"We would watch again," said the demon.

Cray smiled toward the voice. "I don't believe in overtaxing my slaves. Yra has served sufficiently for now and deserves a rest. Don't you think so?"

A wind, like the night breeze about tall towers, whistled among them, and they said nothing more. Cray focused his attention on the book in his hands, and when he glanced up again, the Free were no longer visible. He inquired of Elrelet soon afterward and was told that they had gone.

"And glad I am to see an end to them, if only for a little while," said Elrelet. "I lived a quiet life until you came to me. The Free have never paid so much attention to my home as they do now."

"Well, they've failed in distracting me," said Cray. "I think, rather, that I have distracted *them*."

"From the game, yes. And that is not a bad thing, Cray. I have often wished the game could be abolished; and there are many other slaves who, looking back on their own lives, wish it had never existed."

"Steal the cubes," said Cray. "They would at least play less often if they had to keep taking time to replace them. They might become discouraged altogether."

Elrelet chuckled softly, and a small piece of cloud detached itself from the demon's body and floated toward Cray's face, halting a short distance from his nose. In a moment it had lost its rounded formlessness and solidified into a fist-sized gray cube with characters on every face. "It is only air," said Elrelet. It turned slowly before Cray's eyes, displaying all its sides and then abruptly swooped back to the demon and merged there, cloud once more, indistinguishable from the parent body.

"You are more versatile than I thought," Cray said.

"We have our bodies, and we have Air itself," said Elrelet. "They are enough for our needs." The demon expanded slightly and streamed toward the kiln, wrapping a tendril of cloud about it. "Will you be using this again soon, or can I remove it to some less conspicuous place?"

"The clutter of material objects doesn't please you, does it, Elrelet?"

"I must confess it does not. I prefer comfortable emptiness, myself."

"Move it, then. I'll not need it soon. In fact, I may not use it again—I'm not sure. A smaller furnace will do for smelting the rings, and I have been thinking of working with the other sorts of demons, that need no kilns for entering their new bodies."

"You would do well to keep it, Cray," said Elrelet. "You may not need containment for the heat if you work with the other sorts of demons, but you will need protection from the violence of their transformations."

"Is there so much violence?"

"Not from water demons. They only soak the clay until it sloughs away as muddy water. But we air demons erode the clay from within, and when we reach the surface, we spray a fine powder of terra-cotta like a desert sandstorm. And the ice demons, who freeze the form until it is brittle, shatter the clay with considerable force, too. You could be injured if you were struck."

"Ah, but what demon would harm its master so?"

"Inadvertently," said Elrelet. "I know of one demon-master who carries scars to this day and curses every time he sees his reflection. Your mother, I think, would also be unhappy if you were scarred. The bricks of the kiln, you see, can protect you from more than heat."

"Very well," said Cray. "I will remember your advice." He grinned. "Your many pieces of advice."

"You were warned," said Elrelet. "I am an endless source."

"No wonder the Free seldom came near your house before I arrived."

"True enough," said Elrelet, "although none of them ever listened as carefully as you." The tendril of cloud tightened about the kiln and swung it slowly toward one wall, pressed it there, slithered across the bricks, and pulled away. The kiln remained still, as if nailed to invisibility. "This is another alcove, like the one you use for your possessions. It will cushion you if you should happen to strike it. Better than bare bricks for soft human flesh." The tendril disappeared into Elrelet's body. "You spoke of smelting rings. Are you near ready for that now? I can fetch the ores and implements immediately, if you wish."

"No, no," Cray said. "I would not have you clutter your house further, with no real need. I am *not* ready. Do you wish I were?"

"I wish this whole terrible business were finished."

"Is it so terrible, Elrelet?"

"It will be, I think. And I am glad that I will not be involved in the battle itself."

Cray sighed. "Perhaps you had best bring me a little ore now, just a little, and a quern. It will take time to grind all I need, and I might as well begin as soon as possible."

"As you wish, Cray."

When the demon had gone, Cray covered his face with his hands. He rubbed at his skin, as if to wipe away the age and exhaustion he felt there. He had lost track of time completely, could not guess how many weightless sleeps he had known, how many days measured only by his own wakefulness. A lifetime? Sometimes it seemed so, especially when he counted the books he had read, the pages he had written, the constant repetition of words and gestures that made the heartbeats that were his only measure of time beyond sleep blur into one another.

He pulled his hands from his cheeks and looked at them. They were smooth and sinewy, not an old man's hands, not liver-spotted or clawlike, no veins standing out like blue ropes. They were young hands, and he had to smile at them, but only softly, only the slightest flick of the corner of the mouth. His hands were young. It was his heart that was old.

Cray had slept by the time Elrelet returned with a canvas bag of greenish ore, the fragments small, about the size of lentils.

"Where did you find this?" Cray asked. "It looks to be of high quality."

"So you know copper ore?" said Elrelet.

"Oh, yes, I know copper very well. For gold and silver I shall have to trust your judgment, but I know copper only too well. And tin, which I hope I shall never have to use again."

"I found this in one of the richest mines of the human world."

"And you have done nothing to alter its purity?"

"Nothing. I merely removed it from the mine floor, where it had been left by human miners as being too insignificant to remove. I then transported it to you. I knew my task, Cray. I served my master in the very same way, and he always made fine rings."

"Very well. I'm sure you know as much about this part as I do. Where is the quern?"

A wooden box, roughly cube-shaped, with a crank handle protruding from one side, floated out of the cloud that was Elrelet. A cord was looped about the thing, and Cray caught at the free end and tethered it to his belt. It was a small quern, of the sort commonly used for grinding salt. He opened its lid and coaxed a handful of the ore inside, slamming the lid shut before the greenish fragments could rebound from the innards of the quern and float back out. He commenced to crank the handle with the slow, steady rhythm that Rezhyk had taught him—one of the few things, he had discovered, that Rezhyk had taught him properly. The ore yielded with less alacrity than an equal amount of salt, and Cray opened a book to read while he kept up the regular circular motion. Occasionally he switched hands.

When both his mind and his arm were tired, he shoved quern and book aside to stretch. Then, to loosen his stiffening sinews, he took up the sword, called for Yra, and lost himself in mock combat. The wider, more sweeping motion required by swordplay limbered muscles tightened up by the close work of grinding, and he cut, slashed, and thrust till he was breathless and sweating, till the pulse pounded in his ears and beat at the inside of his chest. Yra, of course, betrayed no evidence of fatigue, but halted at Cray's command.

He had not noticed when the Free first began to gather, but when he relaxed, opened his hand and let the sword float free of his flexing fingers, he realized that they were crowded about the invisible walls once more. They murmured their greetings, and one of them said, "Will you go on?"

"Sorry," Cray replied. "I've no more strength left right now."

"We would like to see more."

"Well, you shan't. Come back another time."

They withdrew, grumbling, and Cray dismissed Yra and sought the restoration of sleep.

After he woke, after he ate, after he had resumed grinding the green copper ore, the Free returned. They hovered silently beyond the boundaries of Elrelet's house, while Cray devoted his entire attention to his books and the steady cranking of the quern. He knew they were there, saw their movement from the corner of his eye, but he ignored them until something familiar about their motions drew his notice at last.

They had separated into pairs, faced off, and the pairs—though still clouds—had assumed vague human shapes, with puffs for arms and legs. On one arm of each cloud-person hung a rigid form, more solid to a human eye than the cloud itself—a sheet of hardened substance, as the cube had been hardened from the stuff of cloud. A shield. The other arm, which terminated in a stubby fist, grasped a thick rod of dull gray: a sword.

Cray had to laugh at the bobbing air demons pretending to be knights.

"Do we play so badly?" asked one of the demons.

Cray nodded. "As badly as small children with their first wooden weapons."

One of the demons suddenly slashed at an opponent and cut the cloud-body in half; the halves rejoined almost immediately. "We will improve," said the victorious demon. "Like the other game, this one only requires practice."

"True enough," Cray said, and he returned to his books and the quern.

Elrelet brought silver—gray-black pellets without a hint of sheen—and gold-bearing quartz that sparkled and glinted. Cray had ground them all long before he was ready to put them to use. Elrelet's impatience waxed.

"Do you know something that Gildrum is keeping from me?" Cray asked his host. "Some reason that time is growing short?"

Elrelet spewed out a flock of cloudlets that raced around the room, caroming off the walls. "No. No. But I wish *they* would go away."

Cray grinned. "I find them amusing. They are so clumsy."

"There will be no peace for me as long as you are here."

Cray hesitated. "Is there somewhere else I can go?"

The cloudlets flashed back to their parent body.

"Nowhere as safe as this. No, Cray Ormoru, you won't go somewhere else. Gildrum gave you into my keeping, and I must endure that responsibility. But my other friends avoid me now. They won't come here while the Free are so close."

"Then you must go to them."

"I must watch over you! That comes first."

"I am sorry."

The visits from inhabitants of other domains had continued, and Cray had grown used to glancing up from his book and seeing not only a crowd of the Free of Air but the starlike shapes of demons from Ice, the glow of dwellers of Fire, the milky pearls that were the water folk. They had formerly been few, though, no more than one or two at any one time; now that the Free of Air had taken up arms, the others arrived more often, left more seldom. They seemed more interested in the air demons than in Cray, the human being. They would float about the periphery of the battlefield, which was a sprawling territory centered on Elrelet's house. In clusters they would dance through nothingness, moving as the nearest combatants moved, as if to maintain a good view of the fighting.

Once, Cray looked up from his studies, and a pair of ice demons had faced off, all their spurs but one retracted, thrusting and slashing with that one as with a sword. Not long after that, the fire and water demons took on armed shapes and challenged each other. And eventually, the combat became mixed, ice against water, fire against air, every possible permutation. The air about Elrelet's house was filled with motion, as if a dozen flocks of birds had chosen to roost there.

"There's talk of wagering now," said Elrelet. "Of using this to replace the game. The novelty of it appeals to them."

Cray shook his head. "Well, they are all equally bad at it. If their strength and weapons were on a human scale, a decent man-at-arms of my world would lay waste to the whole lot in short order."

A noise quite close to Cray, like a quarterstaff striking the bole of an oak, made him start. He turned toward the sound and saw an air demon floating just beyond the nearest wall, hardly more than an arm's length away; its cloud sword was raised, and as Cray watched, it struck the wall a second solid blow.

"I challenge you, human!" it shouted. "I will use strength and weapons no better than yours. Show me what a decent man-at-arms of your world can do! Or are you something less?"

"I am something more," Cray replied mildly. "But I am not here to accept challenges of any sort."

"I have vanquished half a dozen already," said the demon. "I am ready for you!"

"I think not," said Cray.

"You are afraid of me!"

"No, not if you abide by your offer and limit yourself to ordinary steel and mortal muscle—if you pit your *skill* against mine and not your power."

"I swear it. Come then!"

"Yes, yes!" shouted the other Free, in all manner of voices.

Cray smiled. "You'll need more than this short practice if you mean to face me."

"You *are* afraid!"

Cray's smile faded away. "Very well," he said. "I will fight you."

"No!" cried Elrelet. "Your sword can't harm a demon, but the demon's sword can kill you!"

"Don't worry about me," Cray said, swimming to the alcove where his arms waited.

"I *have* to worry! How will I ever face Gildrum again if something happens to you?"

"Tell her it was my own idea."

"I won't allow it!"

Cray slipped his shirt of chain over his head. "I know what I'm doing."

"No you don't! Even if you win, the others will scramble to fight you next. You'll have to beat every one of them."

"I think I could do that."

"But it will waste so much time!"

"I'll try to be quick."

The miniature thunderhead expanded to twice its usual size and darkened, and tiny flickers of lightning showed in its depths. "I forbid it!" said Elrelet.

Cray held his helm between his hands, staring at it meditatively. Then he raised his eyes to his host. "You forbid it?"

"Yes!"

"Then I shall have to cease my studies, Elrelet, and tell Gildrum that it is your fault."

"Gildrum would agree with *me!*"

"I shall study no more. I shall stay in the demon world forever. Actually, I find it a very pleasant place."

Elrelet's voice was low. "You won't find it so pleasant if you never eat again."

"You told me yourself that I have no need for food here, that I only eat from habit."

"Cray!"

"I must do this, Elrelet. Don't you realize that they will never leave me alone until I do? They'll stay at the walls, trying their best to keep me from my studies, taunting me, shouting. Let me do this and be done with it. Even if I have to beat every one of them."

The thunderhead rumbled like a dog growling at a stranger. "This is foolish."

"Yes," said Cray. "Will you watch for me, Elrelet, and make sure the fight is fair?"

"Yes. Yes." Elrelet shrank, staying dark and ominous. Then it raced to the nearest door and waited there for Cray to gather his arms and come on.

Cray floated from Elrelet's house, and immediately the Free drew back and formed a sphere about him and his challenger. Cray inspected his opposition, a cloud of the approximate dimensions of a heavy-thewed man, tall, broad of girth. The legs were mere stumps at the bottom of the long torso, but the arms were well-proportioned, with three fingers on each hand. The shield was a duplicate in shape of Cray's own, and the sword was the same length, though a trifle thicker and blunter. As Cray raised his own weapon in salute, the demon's sword slimmed and sharpened to a better likeness.

"What are your rules among yourselves?" asked Cray.

"There is only one—that the blow which cuts the demon through wins the match."

"I accept that," said Cray, "only if one or the other of us may also yield if the fight is going against him. I assure you, I would much rather yield than be cut in two."

"You look forward to losing already, human?"

"No, but one can never tell what may happen. I don't want this to be a fight to the death. I *will* die, you know, if you cut me through."

"I have heard that humans are so fragile," said the demon. "Very well—you may yield if you wish, and I will be the winner. But I shall not yield."

"I would not expect it. Shall we begin?"

They circled each other warily, each waiting for the other to strike the first blow, neither willing to make that commitment. Cray fell easily into the proper frame of mind, treating his opponent with the respect due danger, not the lighter attitude of one who participates in a sport. He had trained for this at Mistwell, with seasoned veterans behind the opposing sword and shield, men who were not afraid to deal out maiming injuries to their students. Only the best had dared to fight those teachers, and by the end of his winter season at Mistwell, Cray had won their respect.

He had never fought for blood in a world without weight. There would be no blood on his sword this day, whether he won or not; his only care was that there be none on the demon's either.

He crouched in the blue sphere that was clear save for himself and his opponent. He crouched to make himself a smaller target, to draw his legs out of temptation's way. Scooping air with the shield as an oar, he turned slowly, and the demon turned, too, as if they were two weights at either end of a weathervane.

The demon struck, a sweeping blow at waist level. Cray deflected it easily with his shield, and as he sailed to one side from the force of that blow, he jabbed experimentally at the demon's torso. He did not mean the thrust to be of any significance, just a feint to test his opponent's reflexes, and he was satisfied by the slowness of response to it; he touched the merest surface of the cloud, where thigh would be on human being, before the demon could bring his shield down and slide one edge along the blade to push it away. The sword would have bitten deep had there been any real force behind it. Cray backed off, pedaling with his feet, then ducked low with a sharp jerk of his shield, his body drawn up as small as possible, only his sword arm lifted away, back, for a slash. Before the demon could tilt to meet his attack, he had cloven it in two from groin to shoulder. The two halves floated apart, letting go the sword and shield, which lost their sharp-edged shape and became cloud once more. The four cloud masses united into an irregular form like a sack of cabbages.

"I yield," said the demon.

Cray stretched his limbs slowly. "When I was as new at the art as you are now," he said, "I, too, thought I had some skill. Later, when I was pitted against better fighters, I learned how little I knew."

"Teach me," said the demon.

Cray stripped off his helm and shook his head. "I have no time."

"Yes, yes, teach us!" cried the demons who marked the sphere of combat. So many shouted that Cray could barely make out their words. They moved a trifle closer to him, shrinking the sphere, and Elrelet slid to Cray's side, dark and rumbling, as a warning for them to stop. "Teach us," they murmured. "Teach us."

"I cannot," he said. "My studies are too important for me to spend my time in teaching demons the techniques of human combat."

"Your studies are only important to Gildrum!" shouted the demon who had been Cray's opponent. "Gildrum cares nothing for us! Gildrum will be freed and we will be the ones to suffer!"

"Any demon I enslave will be freed immediately after Gildrum is."

"So you say," said the air demon. "But why should we believe you?"

"I swear it."

"A human's vow. What is it worth?"

"As much as a demon's."

The demons muttered among themselves, and then one of them in the distance, one with the crackling voice of an inhabitant of Ice, said, "And if Gildrum is not freed? If you fail? What will happen to your slaves then?"

"They'll be as free as you are, of course," said Cray, "because I'll be dead."

There was silence then, and after a long moment, an air demon whispered, "You would fight to the death for a demon?"

"I must," said Cray. "Lord Rezhyk ordered my death; when he discovers I live, he won't rest till his wish is carried out."

"But you could stay here," said another demon, a very faint voice. "You would be safe here forever."

"Would you stay in the human world forever if there were some chance of returning home?"

"No, no, no," echoed about him, voice upon voice.

"Then I must do what I must do. And I have little time for play." He glanced at Elrelet. "I have spent enough away from my studies for now. Shall we go in?"

Elrelet swooped toward the nearest door, and Cray, using the shield as his paddle, followed. But at the opening he turned, clinging to the invisible jamb. The demons had closed ranks behind him, edging closer, jostling one another with their swords and shields of cloud; almost, they looked as if they wanted to follow him inside, which was impossible without Elrelet's permission.

"Will you have time later?" asked one of them.

Cray looked out at them, his eyes skimming from one side of the group to the other. The air demons, in their own element, hovered closest; the scattering of ice and fire and water demons danced beyond, like children trying to catch a glimpse of some great event between their elders' legs. They had no faces, but he thought he could read entreaty in their very stance.

"I can teach you," he said at last, "in return for something."

"What?" asked the demon he had fought.

"Your help."

Some of the demons murmured to each other, and then one of them said, "What kind of help?"

Cray felt Elrelet's light touch upon his back, and he knew that the demon was floating behind him, dark and oversized, ready to pull him inside to safety if the crowd became threatening. "I don't want to enslave any of you," Cray said. "I never did. I only wanted an answer to the great question of my life. I never dreamed where that answer would lead. And now I *must* enslave some of you, as many of you as I can, to do what I must do. Unless . . . you will help me of your own free will."

"Help you with what?" asked a demon.

"Help me defeat Lord Rezhyk."

One demon eased forth from the crowd, and in a deep, familiar voice said, "What would you have us do, human—give you our names? Perhaps even make the rings ourselves that would enslave us? So that you may command us for your battle with Lord Rezhyk . . . and ever afterward? Do you take us for fools?"

"No rings," said Cray. "I would not command you, only ask you. You would obey me for the battle only, until Lord Rezhyk was overcome."

"Till he was dead," said Elrelet.

Cray pursed his lips. "I had not planned to kill him."

"If you arrange this bargain with the Free instead of making rings, you dare not let him live. After the battle, you would have no power to prevent him from killing you."

"He would have no rings, either, when I was finished with him."

"But how would you prevent him from making fresh ones? You cannot take his *knowledge* away from him."

"I could imprison him."

"And worry all your life that he might break free?"

Cray bowed his head and sighed. "You are right, of course. I had not planned to kill him . . . yet in my heart, I knew that I would be forced to it. Even with my hands covered by rings . . . my intention was always to free my slaves when their work was done, and that could not be while Lord Rezhyk lived. So I will kill him, or he me." He looked up, out at the gathered demons. "Will you help me?"

The Free held silent, all their attention on the human being. Cray felt their silence beat against his ears, in rhythm to the throb of his own heart. When he had waited for an answer for a time that seemed to stretch past eternity, he pivoted on the hand that clutched the doorjamb and pushed himself into the house. "If you will excuse me," he said, "I have work to do."

He was well inside, had cast away his sword and shield and helm, had stripped off his chain and tossed it, chinking and rattling, into the alcove, when the voice of his demon opponent called after him.

"Teach me, human," it said, "and I will join your war."

He looked over his shoulder, saw the demon, human-shaped again, come forward to float in the doorway. It had re-formed its sword and shield, and now it held them up as in a salute.

Cray smiled. "I thank you for your offer, but Lord Rezhyk has many slaves—perhaps as many as there are Free here before me. And he has a castle of bronze to hide in, while I have nothing. One demon, no matter how powerful, will not suffice."

The demon laughed, a deep, rumbling laugh that

seemed to fountain outward from the cloud body, entering the house and bouncing from wall to invisible wall. The other demons backed off a little from the sound. "Train me," said the demon, "and I promise you these others will not stay away. They will not dare allow me to become the greatest champion of this new game!"

Cray squinted at the speaker, hesitated a moment, and then said, "Yes. Yes, I shall train you, and I welcome whatever help you will give me."

And suddenly all the other demons were crowding forward, demanding training, demanding to be allowed to help Cray in his fight against Rezhyk.

"Tell Gildrum," Cray said to Elrelet, pitching his voice to carry over the tumult. "Tell her I will be ready soon!"

Elrelet sent a tendril of cloud after the sword, shield, helm, and chain. "You'll need these," the demon said, guiding them toward Cray. Then, close to his ear, Elrelet murmured, "You would be wiser to trust to rings."

"You have no confidence in the promises of the Free?"

"I don't know. They have never done a human's bidding before. Perhaps they will balk."

"I hope they will grow used to it during their training," said Cray.

"Ah, yes, the training. They will have to do your bidding there, won't they?"

"Yes." He slipped the chain over his head, donned the helm. "Very well!" he shouted to the gathered demons, his voice taking on the inflection of the armsmaster of Mistwell, his own teacher. "The first thing you must do is form a double line along this wall, that I may observe your progress without difficulty. Go on all of you, go on . . . except one—my friend who volunteered. I shall pair with that one myself, for now."

The demon he spoke of waited by the doorway while the others organized themselves; when Cray emerged from the house, he and that one were quite close together. The demon turned a rudimentary face toward Cray, a face newly formed since their fight—

two depressions for eyes, a lump for a nose, a slit for a mouth. The mouth opened to speak: "Your friend?"

Cray grinned. "I hope so."

Behind them, Elrelet sighed softly.

❧ CHAPTER SEVENTEEN

She turned to spiders at last, to find out why he stayed so long in the forest. She found webs among the leaves and bade their spinners move and spin anew. They showed her trees, moss, mushrooms, and the thick loam of the forest floor. They showed her butterflies and honeybees and squirrels and rabbits, and even a deer, peacefully unaware of watching human eyes. They showed her rain and wind, sun, moon, and starlight. But not her son.

Gildrum found Cray drilling his troops. A flickering candle flame in form, the demon spoke with the voice of the girl with blond braids: "I would feel more secure if you wore rings. We will have only this one chance, Cray; we must make the best of it."

"We're doing well," Cray replied. "Every time I look, there's a new demon in the line. And they know that if anything happens to me, they'll get no more lessons."

The flame brightened a little. "Perhaps that is the best approach—appeal to their greed."

"They are not so different from human beings, Gildrum."

"I suppose not . . . in some ways."

"I have so much to learn about their powers, so much to know before I can use them as well as Rezhyk

358

uses his. But we'll be ready soon, I know it. Sooner than I could ever cast enough rings, Gildrum, especially here, where the lack of weight makes it so much more difficult than in my own world."

"The techniques I explained to you may never have been used before, but I know they will work."

"I don't doubt that. Still, they are complex, and I'm glad I won't need to use them." He raised his voice momentarily: "Fifth along the line—raise that shield higher there!"

Gildrum watched the demons hack at each other for a time, then said, "I can't stay much longer. My lord received a message from your mother today, and I must deliver the reply."

Cray frowned. "What sort of message?"

"She asked if he knew where you had gone."

"And the reply?"

"That he sent you back to the Seer long ago and knows no more about you."

"She'll ask the Seer next. She'll hear about Gallant turning up without me."

"I'm sure of it."

"I must speak to her, Gildrum. She mustn't worry."

"I can't take you back before you're ready for battle. There is too much danger of him discovering *us.*"

"Take me with you when you deliver the message."

"I'll only leave it by the gate," said Gildrum. "You know I can't enter."

"Then leave me there, too. I'll speak to her and you can bring me back."

The flame dimmed, and Gildrum's voice was correspondingly softer. "He keeps a watch on Spinweb these days. No one can enter without being seen."

"A watch? Why?"

"He grows more fearful of your mother every day, Cray."

"But *why?* He thinks I'm dead, he has the golden shirt—why should he fear her at all?"

"I don't know. He has become . . . different lately. More difficult, harder to please, more petulant. He has been conjuring demons more quickly, too, as if . . . as if he knows that some great battle looms. Lately he had me strengthen the walls of Ringforge."

"But he can't know," said Cray. "Or else he would have punished you."

"He knows . . . something. It has to do with your mother, surely, or why the watch on her castle? Beyond that, I cannot guess. His mind is closed to me these days. He used to talk to me as if I were his brother, wife, child; now he rarely says anything, except to conjure or command. He sleeps in the workshop, too, when he sleeps. He never leaves it." The flame wavered, compressed. "Cray, do you know what madness is?"

Cray frowned. "You think Lord Rezhyk is mad?"

Gildrum sighed. "Who am I to judge? Only a demon. Perhaps I am the mad one, at least by my own people's standards. But mad or sane, I would be free of my lord Rezhyk. Learn swiftly, Cray. Now that I know it will be soon, I am impatient beyond belief!"

"I would not cause her grief, Gildrum!"

"Nor would I, Cray. Not again. But it will be short-lived grief, will it not?"

"As short-lived as I can manage."

Under his guidance, the demons became passable swordsmen. Now their matches lasted longer and were noisier, as sword clanged against shield time and again, in fair imitation of steel. The demon whom Cray had called friend had improved faster than most, earning Cray's praise and considerable personal attention. In return, the demon gave Cray instruction in the powers of his kind and convinced ice, water, and fire demons to do the same. Gradually, Cray began to grasp the scope of the battle that was to come, and the extent of the forces that Lord Rezhyk had at his command. And he began to understand why Rezhyk had chosen fire as his province.

"The demons of Fire are the best of us all," said Elrelet, "though you'd find few but them to admit it. Quick, clever, vastly destructive when they wish to be."

"I have few of them," said Cray, scanning the sword-swinging Free along the wall.

"Of course," said Elrelet. "They are much sought after. More of them have been enslaved than any other kind. I think that must be what makes them so melancholy; every fire demon knows what the future holds. Perhaps that is why they play the game even more seriously than we of Air. Lord Rezhyk is well protected, Cray—never doubt that."

"And you have no confidence in my scheme, have you?"

Elrelet exhaled a gust of wind. "I know only that a slave *must* obey the master. But the Free . . . I see only one in all this crowd that has ever known what a master was. Curiosity, I suppose, has drawn that one to try the new game; it rejoined the old one as soon as its master died. But will curiosity lure it, or any of the others, into your battle? I don't know. We shall have to wait till the moment, and hope. Just now, I wish *I* were Free. Well, I wish it for the usual reasons, but in addition because, if I were, I would help you."

Cray gazed at the thunderhead no larger than his own body. "Elrelet, you have given me more than I can ever thank you for. I can think of only one repayment great enough: when your master dies, come to me and show me how to make the rings that summon you, and I shall set you free."

Elrelet sighed. "All the more reason for me to wish you luck."

Rezhyk had called all of his demons, from the tiniest spark that lit a seldom-used storeroom to the blazing glory of Gildrum's like. They filled his workshop with their light, reflected a hundredfold in the polished bronze walls, till the chamber could almost have passed for a corner of Fire itself. In the pulsating illumination, like the interior of a furnace, yet cool as night air, the rings Rezhyk wore glittered and flashed with the sharp, tense gestures of his two hands. In one shaking fist he held a fragment of ivy, its tendrils curling against his wrist.

"Your objective," he said in a high-pitched, strident tone, as if he were speaking to an unruly mob of children instead of a silent throng of slaves, "is to destroy Castle Spinweb and Delivev Ormoru with it!"

And he cast the ivy into the brazier, where it puffed away to ash.

She woke to the acrid smell of smoke. She frowned,

blinking her eyes, rubbing at them with the backs of both hands. The room was dim as with dawn twilight, and she wondered if she had wakened so early to escape her dark, disturbing dreams, of Cray lost and calling for her, of herself reaching for him but unable to cross the infinite gap that separated them. She glanced toward the fireplace, thinking that a sudden draft had driven soot back down the chimney and into the bedchamber, but the ashes were cold, with no signs of disturbance. The smoke trailed in through the window —she could see it there eddying against the pale stone. She threw the bedclothes aside and went to look out.

The forest that surrounded Spinweb was ablaze.

The sun was high, the time full day, but gouts of thick black smoke veiled the bright sky, and the ruddy flames that roared about the trees were faint compensation for daylight. Among the burning boughs, Delivev could make out the wildly dancing forms of fire demons, and as she watched, more than one mass of pure flame leaped to an untouched tree to set it alight.

"Rezhyk!" she shouted, raising both fists to his minions. "Only a coward attacks without warning, Rezhyk!"

She pushed herself away from the window and raced down the stairs to the garden. There, the birds were circling restlessly, reluctant to leave their nests yet anxious to fly far from the smoke. The snakes and spiders were moving, too, clustering, edging toward the pond. In its stall, the pony whinnied, nervous, pacing with clattering hooves. At Delivev's arrival, the loose animals swarmed to her, spiders climbing her legs, snakes twining about her feet, birds alighting on her outstretched arms. They followed her to the pony's stall, where she placed her bird-laden hands on its quivering muzzle.

"Don't be afraid, my darlings," she whispered to all of them, stroking the pony gently and rubbing her cheek against the nearest fluttering wings at her shoulder. "All will be well, I promise. All will be well."

When they had taken some measure of calm from her nearness, Delivev directed the spiders to the outside wall of the castle, to fashion a gossamer cloak for Spinweb, to cover the ivy, which was already shriveling from the heat of the blaze. Then she mounted the longest flight of steps in the building, snakes and birds trailing behind her, until she emerged in the open air at the top of the tallest tower. The burning trees were just below her there, crackling all around like a sea of rippling light, and smoke swirled everywhere, driven by the slight, steady wind. Delivev drew a kerchief of spidersilk from her sleeve and draped it over her head, to keep the acrid fumes away. Gazing out at the world through gauzy protection, she raised her arms and sent out her summons.

Beyond the fire, beyond the forest, where not even the faintest smudge of smoke could be seen, they answered her call. As demons were drawn to rings, so Delivev's creatures responded to her command. Spiders that had never known her touch left their webs, left their meals, left their egg sacs to answer. Snakes came out of their nests, down from trees, out from under boulders, to heed the call. Ivy and morning glories and climbing roses and wild grapevines pulled up their roots and eased along the ground, tendrils plunging like centipedes' legs. Not toward Spinweb did they travel, but to Ringforge, to the attack. Like a living carpet the creatures moved, plant and animal, leafy and scaly and chitinous.

The vanguard of Delivev's army swarmed upon the plain before Ringforge, and the first sprigs of ivy had begun to scale those polished walls before Rezhyk realized that he, too, was under siege.

"But how did it happen?" gasped Cray.

"She sent a cool note in reply to *his* reply," said Gildrum. "Cool, but polite, I thought; she asked him to try to find out what had happened to you. He took it as a declaration of war. He decided she hadn't believed him when he said he knew no more about you."

"Guilty conscience," said Cray. "What about my mother?"

"We can't touch her. in Spinweb, of course. Nor the castle itself. But when the burning trees begin to fall against the walls we can pile more wood on top of them, and more and more. Even stone walls will crumble, eventually, from such heat. And the forest is large, Cray. A large fuel supply."

Cray's lips tightened. "Webs can hold the heat off."

"Forever?"

"I don't know. I've seen flame leave them unharmed, but—"

"But never so much flame."

Cray shook his head. "Will he keep on if he sees that nothing comes of his fire?"

"He said he would not rest until she died."

"All right. We must act now."

"Are you ready?"

"I have to be ready, don't I?" He swam to the doorway, looked out at the demons flailing each other with their swords of cloud. "Hear me, my friends!" Cray shouted. "Hear me!" A moment passed before the clatter of weapons ceased, fighters reluctant to leave off pressing an advantage. They turned to him, though, at last, their weapons still in the clear blue of Air.

"I must ask that you fulfill our bargain," said Cray. "I need your help now, in my own world."

The demons muttered among themselves, and one voice piped, "We've hardly had a chance to practice your lessons. You've hardly given us any lessons!"

"I have done as well as I could in the time I have worked with you," said Cray. "And I promise to return and continue teaching, after the battle is over."

"But you may not survive the battle!" said the demon. "You may be killed, and then what will we have? The empty promises of a dead human."

"I assure you, you will not be more unhappy about that than I."

"A few more lessons, human," said another demon. "I have just begun to understand how this game is properly played."

Cray shook his head. "I must go now. I would wish to believe that demons keep their promises as well as humans do."

The demon that Cray had fought spoke up; Cray recognized the voice immediately: "I'm with you, human. I'll keep my bargain."

"I thank you," Cray said. "And what of you others?"

A few came forward, but not the majority. Most hung back, swords twitching in their hands, as if eager to return to exercise.

Cray crossed his arms upon his chest. "I'll make you all a better bargain," he said. "Everyone who joins me in this endeavor shall be freed. If I survive."

"Freed?" muttered a demon near him but not among those who had given him their allegiance. "To free us you must first enslave us."

"Yes," said Cray. "I will have to make rings for each of you, but if only you will tell me your names, that will not be such a difficult task. And I swear that any demon I summon with a pair of rings shall be freed immediately. Wait—I'll prove it to you." He touched the one ring he wore, and very quickly Yra appeared, streaking toward him from the boundary of Fire.

"My lord?" said the fire demon.

Cray took the gold band from his finger and, laying it on the palm of his hand, offered it to Yra. "I free you, slave," he said loudly. "You are bound to me no longer. Take this as a sign of your freedom."

Yra swooped upon Cray's hand and enveloped the golden circlet with pale, translucent flame. Cray withdrew his hand, and Yra's flame intensified, became opaque and sharp-edged, almost tangible, and heat flowed from it in one sudden blast. Then the glow paled once more, cooled, and Yra bobbed slightly before Cray. All trace of the golden ring was gone.

"Thank you, Cray Ormoru," said Yra. "No slave could have wished for a kinder master."

"You served me well, Yra. You deserve your freedom."

"Serving you has not been difficult. And, if you will allow it, though I am small and weak, still I would stay with you, my former master, and help you in whatever way I can. You said you would show me your world someday."

Cray smiled. "And so I shall, good Yra. I am grateful for your offer and accept it gladly." He shifted his gaze from the ball of light that was no longer his slave to the line of demon combatants, still hanging back. "Well, my friends? Do you doubt me now?"

"It is a small demon," said one of them. "Of little value to you. You lose nothing by freeing it."

"Every demon has *some* value," said Cray.

"And mine is greater than that one's. How do I know you will free *me* when the battle is over?"

"I give you my word."

"Oh, yes, surely. But how do I *know*?"

"I believe you!" roared the first whom Cray had called friend, the one who had joined him before any of the others. "I believe you, and to prove my belief, I will tell you my name, Cray Ormoru." A few of the other demons began to murmur "No" and "Fool," before this one continued, "I am Arvad. Cast you a ring for that name, and I am yours."

"And free as soon as I have done it," said Cray, thrusting his hand toward the demon. When Arvad made no move to clasp the hand with any demon appendage, Cray explained, "We humans often seal a bargain by joining hands."

Arvad laughed lightly. "Well, I will be human for a moment, then." But instead of loosing sword or shield to disencumber a hand, the demon grew another, with five stubby, splayed fingers, and clenched Cray's hand in it.

"Who else will join me?" Cray asked the crowd.

"Free Arvad first," said one of the demons who hung back. "Then we shall give the matter more thought."

"I have no time," said Cray. "I must go now."

He glanced about at the score of demons who surrounded him, the volunteers. "If these are the only ones who will follow me, let it be so." To them he said, "You must obey my orders, but if one of you devises some better plan than I offer, don't be afraid to speak. I am a novice at this."

"And so are we," said Arvad. "Some of us have never even visited the human world."

"Some? Not all?"

"I have been there once," said Arvad. "I know a tree from a rock."

"Good," said Cray. He turned to Gildrum, who

waited with Elrelet just inside the house. "Have we wasted too much time, Gildrum?"

"I think not. Time moves more quickly here, remember. And the battle will rage long. . . . They have very different powers, but they are not so unevenly matched, those two."

"Well, I hope we may make the difference."

"You should have made rings," muttered Elrelet. "Then you would have the lot of them."

"I think you overestimate my speed, good Elrelet. But that's as may be. Now I must take my leave of you."

"Not at all," said Elrelet. "I'm coming along. I may not be able to take part in your battle, but I can watch. I've not come this far to let the rest go!"

"Come," said Gildrum. "I must return to my duties."

"Which are . . . ?" said Cray.

"Burning trees."

Gildrum left him high above Spinweb, supported by a dozen air demons. Nearby hovered the rest of Cray's army—two pearly bubbles, three glittering snowflakes, and two blobs of pale light, one of which was Yra. Elrelet floated by his ear, a dark smudge.

"Look down," said Elrelet.

Cray looked, and the vertigo that he had lost in Air so long ago reclaimed him for a moment, for there was a *down;* he could feel it pulling at him, through the cushion of air demons. *Down* was where the ground lay, beneath the blue sky of the human world that so resembled the emptiness of Air, save for the intolerable bright spot of the sun. *Down* was where the smoke boiled from flaming trees, and birds erupted each time a new crown of leaves caught fire. *Down* was Spinweb, ringed by roiling blackness, untouched in the midst of destruction. It looked like a toy from Cray's distance. He could smell the smoke, like a campfire of green wood.

"That is my home," said Cray. "We will protect it. Within is my mother, and we will protect *her,* even if the home itself cannot be saved." The vertigo was passing now. "Water demons," he said. "There is a river in that direction." He pointed northwestward.

"You can almost see it from here. Fetch water from it and splash those flames." They soared away, giant raindrops falling sideways.

"How much water can they bring?" said Elrelet. "They are far outnumbered by Rezhyk's fire demons. Those will dry the forest and set it aflame again and again."

Cray scanned the ground. "Where are her forces? Surely she has counterattacked by now."

"There," said Elrelet, nudging Cray's head to the right with a gentle gust of air. "That line of black on the horizon. You'll have to move closer for a proper view."

Cray gave the command, and the air demons carried him north, toward Ringforge. When almost there he bade them stop, for the sky was filled with the smoke he had seen from afar. One of the demons enveloped him with pure air that he might observe the fray without choking.

Below was the true battlefield, a forest blaze to make the fire about Spinweb pale in comparision. Ringforge occupied the center of a vast open space, and the whole surface of the space was coated with char, as if soot had dropped out of the sky upon it. Where the forest began, an enormous circle about the castle was burning, a dozen trees deep. And behind that circle, visible through rustling leaves as an intermittent bubbling, churning motion on the forest floor, were Delivev's creatures. Silent, relentless, they pressed against the barrier of heat and flame and demons. A thousand creatures died each moment, snuffed to ash, yet as many joined the rear of their ranks, continually pushing ahead, ready to sacrifice themselves for their master.

"This is a fight she cannot win," whispered Elrelet. "Fire is too powerful for her."

"Then we must make up for some of her weakness," said Cray. He directed the ice demons to skim over a portion of the barrier and send waves of cold to counteract the searing heat, and all but his enveloping air demon to blow the flame in that area back toward Ringforge and keep it from spreading farther. The sky about him, already dark with smoke, darkened still further as his air demons expanded into thunderheads and swooped low upon the fray. Among the clouds and smoke, Cray could see their lightning vying with the redder flares of Rezhyk's hordes. Sparks from the burning trees showered the bare ground that rimmed Ringforge.

Elrelet whispered in his ear: "Now that you have joined the fight, you must hide yourself. You have no castle walls to protect you from Lord Rezhyk's wrath."

"Am I not safe enough up here? He will think I am a bird. If he looks up. I don't see him. I think he's afraid to come out, Elrelet, afraid he might be injured by some chance good fortune of the enemy. I'll ride a higher breeze if you insist, but I'll not leave the battle."

"I cannot command you, Cray Ormoru."

They soared upward.

"He has called demons back from Spinweb," observed Elrelet. "To combat your forces."

"Good. Less to threaten her."

Elrelet sighed. "How much will it matter? One or two or five demons less. The forest about Spinweb still burns."

"Look!" said Cray, pointing downward. "Some ivy has broken through—I can see the green moving against the ground."

"Yes," said Elrelet. "But Lord Rezhyk has held some servants back upon the walls of Ringforge, and the ivy will be brown soon enough. There. There. You see, Cray, how hopeless it is. You should have made rings."

"I'd still be making them," said Cray. "And the forest would still be burning."

A thunderhead rose from the battle, dwindled, and approached Cray to speak in Arvad's voice. "You said if any of us had plans to offer we should tell you."

"Yes. Yes."

"I have one, but it demands that we demons withdraw from the fight for a short time. All of us."

"Withdraw? To do what?"

"To go back to our world."

"Go back? But why?"

"To speak to the others, the ones who would not come."

Cray's brows knit. "You think you can change their minds?"

"I don't know, but . . . Cray Ormoru, friend, this fight is lost. There are foo few of us."

"We mustn't give up!"

"I don't wish to. If my plan fails . . . I will be back. And these others, too, so they have said. But I thought we should tell you, before we leave, that we are not deserting you."

"Thank you," said Cray. "I fear you will fail; if the promise of freedom was not enough for them, what could be?"

"We will do our best. Farewell."

Cray lifted a hand. "Farewell."

Abruptly, all the thunderheads that hovered about the field of battle vanished, and the cushion of air that had supported and protected Cray disappeared as well, leaving him as weightless as in the demon world for the instant before Elrelet enveloped him. He coughed, having inhaled a whiff of smoke in that moment, and his vision blurred as tears welled up to cleanse his eyes. When he had done blinking, he realized that Yra and the other fire demon that had been with him, that he had not known what to do with, were also gone, and he assumed that the ice demons had followed. Below, the fire raged stronger.

"They are fools," said Elrelet. "Sometimes I think all demons are fools. Only fools would play the game."

"You don't think they'll be able to convince the other Free, do you?"

"I don't know. Their offer will be . . . tempting. Foolish and tempting."

"What offer?" asked Cray.

"The one which your human ears couldn't hear them discuss. Each of them intends to offer to take on the names of all the demons of its kind who will join you here. They trust you, Cray Ormoru. If you free them, those names won't matter. A demon freed by a sorcerer never has to answer the summons for any name. As I said, a tempting offer."

370

"And why foolish, Elrelet? It seems bold and clever to me."

Elrelet sighed. "Foolish once because it may yield too little return to win the fight yet still leave them shackled with extra names. Foolish twice . . . because they are trusting a human being."

Cray closed his fists on empty air, on the body of Elrelet surrounding him. "Is it so very foolish to trust a human being?"

"When rings are involved . . . yes."

"I am as good as my word, Elrelet."

"Gildrum thinks so. But Gildrum is desperate. I will wait, and I will hope. I will hope very hard, Cray Ormoru. But I am glad I am not one of the Free who must chance your trust."

"I shall prove myself, I swear it." He gazed down at the burning forest. "We are not all greedy and self-centered."

"Perhaps I know more sorcerers than you," whispered Elrelet.

Amid the beating heat, Delivev waited for death. She had retreated within the walls of Spinweb when the spiders covered the turret she stood upon with webwork. Now she saw that webbing as her shroud. All the windows of Spinweb were covered, all the doors, all the thick stone walls, but still the heat seeped in, like the strongest summer sunshine in the garden.

She sat in the web chamber, a different scene on every side, and fire in all of them. Here, from her own walls, she could see the forest raging and the fire demons bringing ever more wood to throw upon the blazing trees; they were hard against the stone now in some places, making of Spinweb a victim being burned at the stake. In other webs she viewed the battlefront at Ringforge from a dozen angles, and from none of them was that castle itself visible beyond the flaming barrier that held her forces at bay.

So many tiny lives, she thought, *sacrificed for mine.* Would it have been better, she wondered, if she had let herself die without ever calling them, since she would die anyway, at the last. Soon. She could feel the walls of Spinweb beginning to yield about her, bit by bit, to the fiery onslaught. Already cracks were showing behind the webbing, cracks that admitted the terrible heat. *Baked alive,* she thought, *or perhaps suffocated first,* for the air was growing close as well as hot. She lay back upon the velvet coverlet, wondering if she would be able to find the strength and the courage to climb the stairs again, to throw herself from one of the high windows before the heat became too much. She turned her face to one of the webs. Almost, she wanted to give up, disperse her army, and bring the end quickly.

Almost.

She rolled over on her elbow and lifted a hand to the web. She had seen a place along the perimeter about Ringforge where the fire was sparser. She thrust her forces through there, willing them to push and push, willing them to dodge the flames and surge across the open space that was covered with the cooling remains of their fellows.

She shook a fist at the web, a fist glistening with sweat. "Coward!" she cried. "You haven't killed me yet!"

The air was rent with clap after clap of thunder as great dark masses materialized out of nothingness all around Cray. In spite of Elrelet's protective envelope, he was tossed like a leaf in the storm, jerked one way and another by savage winds, spun, tumbled, till he thought his bones would rip apart. And then he was left behind in sudden calm as the darkness descended below him and he saw for the first time that gigantic human shapes of cloud, with cloud-swords and cloud-shields, marched through the summer day. A hundred times larger than he had ever seen them, the Free of Air roared down upon the burning forest, flattening trees and smothering flames with their weapons. They grappled with fire demons, whirling upon them like dust devils and sweeping them skyward till they looked to be so many sparks against the night of smoke.

Water demons appeared then, like a string of milk-white pearls, with shields as big as ox carts, rounded,

372

full of water which splashed down upon the flaming forest, over and over again, while ice demons swooped low, cooling the steaming ground till frost formed on the scorched stumps.

"Spinweb!" shouted Cray.

A rushing sound by his right ear made him look in that direction, where he saw Arvad, man-sized, with that peculiar near-human face. "Done, even as we speak," said the demon, and its slit of a mouth curved upward at the corners. "The fire is fading, and Lord Rezhyk's minions have been wrestled to the sky by Free fire and air demons, and there they will stay until Lord Rezhyk himself is finished."

"And my mother?" Cray demanded.

"Judge for yourself," said Arvad, who waved a sword of steel-gray cloud downward, toward the blackened line of combat.

The living carpet moved again, green and black, plant and animal. It flowed over the crumbling stumps of trees, over boughs that fell to ash when touched, over soot that was the bodies of earlier attackers. It flowed to the walls of Ringforge and began to climb the polished surfaces. The bronze was smooth as glass, but spiders could lay the sticky strands of their silk upon it and mount the bronze as easily as porous stone. Ivy could follow, with spiderweb purchase, and find rivets not set quite flush with the surface as well, and junctures between the bronze plates to pry at with inquisitive tendrils, in age-old plant fashion. Soon vines festooned the walls of Ringforge, which creaked and rippled before the steady, insinuating pressure.

Rezhyk stood in his workshop, his back to the table, to the glowing brazier. All around him, he could hear Ringforge yielding in agony. The very walls groaned from the warping of the structure, and a sound almost like a human scream marked the wrenching of each copper scale from the window shutter; inside the room, the bronze sheet that covered the window opening and made it seem to be nothing more than another portion of the smooth wall bulged with inward pressure. But Rezhyk's attention was focused on the door to his workshop, and he perceived these other things only peripherally. He stared at the door, a panel closely matching the rest of the wall, save for a slit of space beneath, where it was not snug against the floor. It was an impossibly narrow slit, so thin that a hair could just pass through, but as Rezhyk had always known, it was wide enough to admit spiders. And, one by one, they entered now.

He stamped upon them at first, his teeth gritted, knowing they were no ordinary spiders. He suspected there had never been any ordinary spiders in Ringforge. He stamped. But there were too many of them, pouring through the slit now, and from the window, where the bronze plate had given at one corner. Dozens of spiders. Scores. Hundreds. He could not count so many. They swarmed upon him and he tried to hide his head in his arms, but they crawled down his collar and into his hair. He cupped his hands over his nose, to keep them from his nostrils.

They sat on him. They did not bite.

After a time, he raised his head. His breath quieted, though his skin shuddered beneath a coating of dark, scuttling bodies. He glanced at himself in the nearest wall, and all he could see was a man-shape and two dark eyes peering out. His clothing and skin were hidden. Yet they did not bite.

Though Ringforge crumbled about its lord, the spell of the golden shirt held.

He lowered his hands, and the spiders made no move to clog his nostrils. Instead, they milled aimlessly, and after a while they began to fall off. He helped them a little, shaking his arms and legs one at a time. And then he began to stamp on them again, methodically, each blow a little harder than the last, and he began murmuring to himself in a singsong voice, garbled words with no meaning. He was stamping hard enough to make the floor ring, and he was waving his fists about his head when at last he summoned Gildrum.

The demon took some time to appear. When the blond girl had coalesced from the ball of flame, she apologized immediately. "I had to use considerable strength to break away from my opponent, my lord. The fight does not go well for us. Had I not been re-

treating, I doubt that I would have won away at all."
She gazed at the floor, at the spiders milling over the crushed bodies of their fellows, at Rezhyk's booted feet crushing more, ever more. "What will you, my lord?"

Rezhyk looked up from his task, looked into Gildrum's innocent face. "You have advice for me now, my Gildrum?" he rasped. "You have your usual good advice?"

Slowly, she said, "Your demons are stalemated, my lord. We cannot take Castle Spinweb while it has so many defenders. And the lady Delivev's forces are at this moment breaching Ringforge. My advice is . . . that you throw yourself on her mercy."

Rezhyk pointed a finger at Gildrum. "*You* built this castle, demon! Why did you not build it stronger?"

"My lord," said Gildrum, "bronze has its limitations. And so have I."

"You! You! You never told me she commanded demons!"

"She does not, my lord."

"Then where do they come from?"

"She has an ally, my lord."

"And who would that ally be?"

Gildrum pursed her lips against the answer, but it forced itself from her mouth. "Her son."

Rezhyk left off his stamping, and his eyes blazed with a fire hotter than any demon. "Her son! How can that be? You rid me of him. You killed him." He cocked his head to one side. "Did you not?"

Gildrum whispered, "No, my lord."

"But you *had* to! I commanded you to kill him!" He shut his mouth tight, till the lips showed white and cracked, and the chin began to quiver with his anger. "No," he said in a thin, taut voice. "I see now that I did not quite command you to kill him. What was it I said, O clever Gildrum, that you twisted to suit your pleasure, *to betray me?*"

Gildrum's fingers curled at her thighs, clutching the fabric of her dress. "You said to kill him before he found another master."

"But he did find another master."

"No, my lord."

"Then how did he learn the art, Gildrum? How?"

Very softly, she said, "I taught him, my lord—here in Ringforge and after he left."

Rezhyk's eyes were wide, whites showing all around the irises, and his cheeks were sunk deep beneath his sharp cheekbones. "O my Gildrum," he whispered hoarsely. "O my first and best servant. O my youth's companion . . . conspiring with *her son* against me." He leaned back, clutching at the worktable for support, his fingers clawing stiffly. "Why? Why? You were like my own flesh and blood, my Gildrum. Why?"

Her chin lifted defiantly. "That he might free me, my lord."

"Free you? For what?"

"For *her*."

Rezhyk's eyes narrowed. "What of her? What is she to you?"

"My lord, I love her."

"Love?" Rezhyk pointed a shaking finger at Gildrum. "Down on your knees, demon slave! Down on the knees that I fashioned for you with these two hands! There is no human flesh in that body—what would a human woman want with such as you?"

Gildrum sank to her knees among the spiders. "You have found use for this unhuman flesh," she murmured.

"Love, you say?" Rezhyk shouted, and his lips curled back from clenched teeth. "Know what *love* will bring you, demon! I know an incantation that even my death cannot sunder. At the center of the earth, where the very rocks flow like hot pitch—there shall you find a prison for the rest of time!"

Gildrum bowed her head and clasped her hands against her forehead. "My lord, I beg you—"

"But first you shall serve me once more, better than you have ever served me before. You shall go to your beloved Delivev, and you shall kill her, and after that you shall kill her son. And as proof of your work, you shall bring me their heads before the sun sets today! Now go!"

Gildrum lifted a pale face to look at him. "But my lord," she whispered, "Delivev is within her stronghold, where no demon may enter."

"No demon, perhaps," said Rezhyk, "but you, Mellor, handsome young knight—she will not keep *you* out! Go!"

The slight blond girl vanished.

Cray had been alone for some time, save for Elrelet, watching the battle rage about him in the sky and on the ground. Even Arvad, who had been bringing him frequent reports on the progress of the allied Free was busy with some energetic foe—Cray could see them in the distance, spinning and tumbling, a ball of flame entangled with thick, black cloud like greasy smoke. Other, similar dark clouds spotted the battlefield, but the true smoke had nearly dissipated, though fresh gouts occasionally billowed from the forest as one of Rezhyk's minions broke loose of its assailants and plunged into the trees.

Below, the bronze of Ringforge gleamed no more. The walls, turrets, towers were all choked with climbing greenery.

"It shudders," said Elrelet. "It will fall, at the end."

"When?" asked Cray.

"Sooner than Lord Rezhyk hopes. I'm sure."

A flame sprang into being before Cray's eyes, white as the sun, blinding him for a moment, and the familiar girl-voice of Gildrum burst from it, tighter, tenser than he had ever known it: "Cray! He has ordered me to kill her!"

"What? Kill her? No!"

"A direct order, no way to twist it into something else. I must obey. I must! Remember the shirt is proof against metal and weaving!" The demon flashed away, a bright spot against the blue sky.

"Stop! Wait!" Cray shouted. "Arvad, Yra, help! Gildrum mustn't reach my mother!"

From their individual battles, Arvad and Yra heard Cray's call and streaked toward Spinweb, a dark cloud and a ball of fire. They caught Gildrum above the castle and grappled there, rolling and plunging.

"Down, Elrelet!" said Cray. "Set me at the gate of Ringforge!"

They swooped to the ground, and behind them, Rezhyk's forces broke away from their Free opponents and rushed to Gildrum's aid, and the Free followed until the whole battle had shifted to the sky above Spinweb. Cray glanced over his shoulder once, just before his feet touched lightly among the spiders that still swarmed toward the walls, and he could not distinguish Gildrum in the whirling miasma of cloud and mist, flame, snow, and lightning.

The gate was open, the massive panel warped and buckled by the prying vines that choked the aperture. Cray peered inside, tugged tentatively at the greenery; it did not yield.

"I'm going in," he said to Elrelet.

"What will you do? You have no weapons that can touch him."

"I have my hands." And he bent over, fingertips brushing the ground, and shrank and shrank until he was one with the milling spiders. He scuttled out of his tumbled clothing and into the jungle of vines, into Ringforge.

The anteroom was filled with ivy, with morning glories, with the prickly stems of climbing roses. They hid the smooth floor and walls, they encrusted the wooden chairs, they climbed past the sconces, now dark, even those small demons lured away to battle. Cray traversed the chamber quickly, leaping from stem to stem, leaf to leaf, and at the opposite side he found the door that had been flush with the wall ripped open as by a giant's hand. Vines spilled beyond, into the mirror-walled corridor, and he scurried onward, along the interlacing stems. Here he found the ivy moving, prising at the walls in search of doors; many had already been forced open, the rooms filled with vegetation. One of these was Rezhyk's workshop.

Cray launched himself inside, seeking the sorcerer among the myriad leaves. The vines had entered through a window as well as a door—a window whose existence Cray had never suspected. The worktable was festooned with ivy, drawers pulled out, their contents spilled and enveloped; the kiln was full of leafy green; the ever-burning brazier had been overturned, its coals scattered upon the floor, browning a few morning glory blossoms as they died. One sconce glowed upon the wall.

Rezhyk was not there.

The sun was red—too red. Gildrum felt its pull and dropped low over Spinweb, low in the roiling multitude of frantic demons, then slid into the shadow of one tall tower and descended to the ground. There, the pale glow of the demon coalesced into human form, and Gildrum was Mellor once more, dark-haired and lithe, clad only in a light shirt and hose and soft shoes, all well smudged with soot. His back snug against the stone of Spinweb, he edged past charred and broken trees toward the gate and, reaching it, poised upon the threshold gazing in. The wooden panel had burned away, its ashes strewn inward across the polished stone of the gateroom floor. The tapestries that lined the chamber were charred here and there from the sparks that had blown in with that burning. The doorway was now hung with fine spiderweb.

"Delivev," he whispered, "Delivev," knowing that her creatures would bring her word of him.

In the corridor once more, Cray resumed his human form to stand naked among the vines. They were knee deep about him and rustling with constant movement. The main flow from the gate and the smaller masses that had burst through shuttered windows and even wrenched narrow passage through the very seams of the building, had converged in the corridor, and clusters of stems were even making their laborious way up the staircase. Cray followed, overtaking them with his long, human legs, but at the top of the stairs he found that other vines had already entered through openings at that level. He raced upward, and on the third floor, at the base of one of Ringforge's towers, he found Rezhyk.

Even here there was ivy, climbing the walls in narrow ribbons, trailing from the ceiling. As Cray watched, a hanging strand snaked about Rezhyk's neck, but instead of tightening to strangle him, it lay limp and loose upon his flesh; he cut it away with a bronze knife he had formerly used only for slicing meat at dinner. Though they destroyed his castle all about him, Delivev's creatures could not touch the enemy who wore the golden shirt.

As he cast the ivy from him, Rezhyk saw Cray. "You!" he shouted. He raised his free hand, rings glittering in the light that spilled down the tower stairs. Above them, the sound of wrenching metal was a piercing scream that made Cray's flesh crawl, but Rezhyk seemed hardly to notice it. Nor did he notice the light increasing where he stood, as the wall behind him opened to the reddening sky. Ivy eased in through the aperture, cascaded down the stairs to lie limp at Rezhyk's feet.

"Cray Ormoru!" he shouted, the fingers of his outstretched arm pointing stiffly. "Your rings shall turn against you, your demons shall burn you, freeze you, drown you, blast you to pieces!"

"I wear no rings," said Cray, walking slowly toward Rezhyk, his eyes on the knife. He could see that the bronze blade was wet with greenish plant juices, and fragments of ivy still clung to it where Rezhyk had cut through the clutching stems.

Rezhyk backed up the tower stairs. "Stay away." Ivy waved about his feet, but he stepped firmly, surely, crushing the leaves with his studded boots. "Stay back."

"Your castle is crumbling about you, Rezhyk," said Cray. "Call back your demons and give your rings over to me."

Rezhyk's lips curled back from gritted teeth. "I should have had you killed the first day you came here!" He turned and lunged upward, taking the stairs two at a time.

Cray followed, one hand scrabbling at the bronze rail to aid his progress. He was younger, faster; his pumping legs rapidly closed the gap between them. He clawed at Rezhyk's ankle, at his knee. Rezhyk stumbled, falling heavily on the steps, then bent sharply at the waist and swiped at his pursuer with one fist. A gem-set ring caught Cray's cheek, laying it open almost to the bone, and he recoiled from the shock, hands clutching his bleeding face.

Rezhyk staggered on.

He heard her step first, and then he saw her. She wore black, glossy black feathers from neck to knee. *For me,* he thought, and he felt hot tears rising behind his eyes. Involuntarily, his arms reached out for her, but the spiderweb door and the invisible carrier against demons stopped them, leaving him standing with empty, open hands lifted as if in supplication.

Seeing him, she halted, one foot forward, her weight coming down heavily upon it. Her right hand rose to her breast as she stared at him.

"My dearest love," he whispered, and the tears spilled forth upon his cheeks.

For a dozen heartbeats she stood frozen. The ordeal of the day showed in her face, the pouches deep beneath her eyes, the skin pale, lines etched about the mouth. Fatigue was written there, and vulnerability.

She called his name, his human name, a name never inscribed on any ring. And then she went to him, lifting the silken door aside with one hand, to clasp him in her arms and lay her head upon his shoulder and to murmur that name over and over again.

Cray felt dizzy and faint, and his stomach churned at the sight of his own blood all over his hands. He leaned on the bronze steps, breathing raggedly, shuddering at the tickling sensation of liquid oozing across his jaw, down his neck. Then he took a deep breath and pushed himself upright to continue his chase.

Rezhyk was at the next landing, where ivy had broken through a window and choked the stairwell. He was in the midst of it, hacking at the tangled strands. At Cray's approach, he glanced out the ruptured window at the reddening sky. "You haven't long to live, Cray Ormoru. Count your heartbeats."

"Count your own," said Cray, crouching warily, his eyes on the knife.

Rezhyk's lips curved in a slow smile. "I know you have a certain training. I know you think you'll take this knife away from me. But it will do you no good. You can't turn it against me. You'll have to kill me with your bare hands."

Instead of answering, Cray leaped for him, one

hand at his wrist, the other at his throat. They fell, rolling in the vines, which covered them quickly in a green cocoon.

"Come, come to me, Serpit, Anara, Zelabas!" Rezhyk shouted, ripping Cray's hand from his throat. He was strong, thin but wiry, and the fingers that had shaped figures from clay were like metal claws at Cray's own flesh. "Come to me, all but Gildrum!"

In answer to his summons, the sky about Ringforge boiled with demons. The storm of their presence made the weakened walls of the castle creak and moan, and the tower where Cray and Rezhyk fought swayed like a sapling in the wind. About the tower demons surged, air and water, fire and ice, hot drafts and cold, rain, sleet, snow and hail, and dust and char picked up along the way. But none entered the tower to help Rezhyk; they were too busy with each other.

"You see, sorcerer," gasped Cray, "you have no one to depend on but yourself!"

"So be it!" Rezhyk groaned, and he opened the hand that held the knife, letting the bronze blade drop among the vines. Startled, Cray loosened his grip on that wrist for an instant, and Rezhyk jerked it free, plunging the hand to Cray's throat. "So be it!" And then the second hand joined it.

Cray's arms were too short to reach the long-limbed Rezhyk's face, and his legs were too tangled in vines to kick effectively. He snatched at Rezhyk's fingers, managed to insinuate one of his own beneath two of the sorcerer's ring-laden claws and pull sharply. He heard a bone crack, but Rezhyk seemed not to care, only squeezed, squeezed, while Cray's hands scrabbled and ripped at the flesh of his fingers and cut themselves bloody on the gems of his rings. Cray's head filled with a rushing noise, above which he could barely hear the sound of the window beside them, and of windows and seams all through Ringforge, being ripped open farther, ever farther by the tenacious ivy. With each rent, the spell of the castle thinned, and now the attacking demons beat upon the very bronze with all their powers, waiting for the moment of entry. A sudden burst of sleet splashed through the gaping window onto Cray and Rezhyk, followed by gravel-sized hail that rattled and rang against the interior walls. Cray snapped another finger, but still he could catch no breath.

And then there was a thumping and clattering all around him, and voices were shouting his name over and over again. Icicles had replaced the hail that showered through the window—icicles dagger-length and slim, falling on the massed vines by the armload, glinting in the low sunlight. Some shattered as they struck; a few glanced off Rezhyk's back, ripping his tunic but turning aside from the golden shirt as from chain mail. With one hand, Cray still pried at Rezhyk's stony fingers, but he tore the other loose to grope wildly among the icy shards. Above him, Rezhyk's face began to dim, to take on a ruddy tinge, and some small part of Cray's mind found time to wonder if that were a trick of the oncoming dusk or merely the ebbing away of his sight and his life.

His human-seeming hands had tightened on her, though he had willed them otherwise. He felt nothing, not the smoothness of her flesh nor the heat of her body nor the light touch of the feathers she wore, nothing but the solid, steady beat of her heart. *Only ten more beats,* he told himself. She murmured to him, enfolded in his arms, but he could not hear the words, only the imminent breaking of her bones, real already in his imagination and loud as the end of the world. *Ten more beats, ten more.* He could no longer see her hair so close beside his cheek, only the red, red sun of dusk, looming, filling his eyes with blood. His hands tightened again.

Gripping the blunt end of the dagger shape as tight as any sword hilt, Cray drove the icy point toward Rezhyk's throat. It gave him the extra reach he needed, entering the flesh just beneath the chin.

Rezhyk's eyes widened at the impact, and his mouth opened, but no sound emerged. His fingers flexed convulsively, loosened, and Cray caught at them with all his strength and thrust them away, gasping air at last. With both hands, then, Cray began wrenching at the rings, hoarsely chanting the words that Gildrum had taught him. They rolled over, Rezhyk's fingers working spasmodically, not at Cray's throat anymore but at his own, clutching at the frozen blade that pierced him, while Cray fought to gain his demons. Blood came to the sorcerer's lips, frothing pink with saliva as he tried to cry out, as he gurgled instead of speaking. They rolled again, and the vines wrapped tight about them; and at last Cray had collected all the rings, closed his left hand upon them, and found another sharp shard of ice with his right, for the *coup de grâce*.

Release came so abruptly that he staggered and would have fallen if not for her support.

"Mellor?" she cried. "Mellor, what's wrong?"

He covered his eyes with one hand and stood swaying against her. "Nothing," he whispered, and then he clutched at her, encircled her with both arms and held her tighter than before, but of his own free will. "Nothing is wrong, my darling."

Cray pushed the dead body aside, brushed the clinging vines from his limbs, and lurched to his feet. His breath was fire in his throat, and he shook uncontrollably. Over the ringing in his ears, he heard his name being called loudly, insistently, from the window, and at last he turned and stumbled over the high-piled greenery to answer.

Just beyond the window, the Free were massed, clouds and crystals, flames and milky pearls. They pressed toward him, tendrils of themselves reaching through the aperture to touch him.

"Will you come now?" said Elrelet's voice. "Ringforge is falling!"

And all around him, he heard the agony of the bronze giving way, plates screaming as they collapsed against each other. The tower shuddered and quaked, and the floor tilted under his feet. He gripped the window frame and the buckled shutter, heedless of the sharp-edged metal biting at his fingers. With one foot up on the sill, he slid through the opening and stepped into the air, into Elrelet's grasp. When he looked back, the tower was folding in on itself, sagging, beginning a slow slide to the ground. Gray dust puffed upward as the walls of Ringforge settled into a jagged heap of ivy-covered metal.

Cray leaned back on his demon-cushion. His clothes were there; he shrugged into his tunic, then opened his left hand. The rings lay clumped together, the skin of his palm deeply marked by their presence. In the fading light he could not read the demons' names inscribed on their inner surfaces, and he called Yra to him for a lamp. By the soft demon-glow, the gold gleamed mellow, the stones sparkled red, blue, yellow, black. One by one he slipped them on his fingers, leaving one index finger empty till he found Gildrum's ring and set it there. He put the rest on quickly, and then he closed his fists and turned them before his eyes, gold- and gem-encrusted.

"You are a great sorcerer now," Elrelet whispered. "Lord Rezhyk's former slaves await your commands."

Cray covered one hand with the other. "Take me to Spinweb."

The destruction about his mother's home was enormous. A vast open space, once dense forest, surrounded the castle, the naked ground churned up as by a giant's plow; Rezhyk's demons had uprooted all the trees and piled them against the walls for burning. About those soot-coated walls, the intended funeral pyre, blackened and drenched, still steamed in the dusk. The air demons cleared a wide path to the gate, and Elrelet set Cray down there.

The doorway was covered only with spiderweb gauze. Cray brushed it aside and plunged drunkenly across the ash-laden floor, down the corridor, calling his mother's name. He heard an answer at last from the garden, where he found the two of them sitting together among the sooty roses—she in her black feathers and he with the form and features that Cray knew so well from the tapestry. He ran toward them, tears streaming down his face, and they opened their arms to him.

"You're hurt," his mother whispered, her gentle hands touching his cheek, where blood still oozed from the slowly clotting gash. A spider scurried down her arm to seal the wound with sticky silk.

"Lord Rezhyk did that," he said. "I killed him."

"I know. Gildrum told me." She glanced at the demon, his face so close beside her own that his breath stirred the hair at her brow.

"Gildrum?" Cray murmured. "Then you must know."

"Not everything, I'm sure. But enough."

"And you forgive him?"

"There is nothing to forgive. He served his master as a slave must. But he loves me."

"Yes," said Gildrum.

"And I love him. Demon or human, it doesn't matter."

Cray lifted his ring-cluttered hands. "I took these."

"I know," said Gildrum. "I felt it happen . . . my lord."

"No," said Cray. "I will not be your lord." He pulled the plain band from his finger and set it on his upturned palm. "I free you, slave. You are bound to me no longer. Take this as a sign of your freedom."

Gildrum scooped the circlet from Cray's hand and closed it tightly in his own, so tightly that the knuckles showed white with pressure. For a moment, faint heat radiated from the fist. When it opened again, there were nail marks in the unhuman flesh, and the red-gold band was gone. "Thank you," Gildrum whispered.

"Its mate is buried in the ruins of Ringforge," said Cray.

"Let it stay there. I need no new forms. I have no intention of using any but the one I wear now."

"That pleases me well enough," Delivev said, smiling at him. Then she turned her eyes to her son. "Cray, my heart is so full of gratitude that I can't begin to speak of it. For bringing him back to me . . ."

"And to me," said Cray.

She nodded. "You have worked long and hard for this day, I know. Perhaps . . . all of your life." Her gaze flickered from one of his ring-clad hands to the other. "And now you are a mighty sorcerer."

Cray looked at the rings himself, at red gold and white, and gleaming yellow. They cramped his fingers, stiffened them, and slid against each other, scraping, pinching. He felt as if he were wearing a pair of

metal gauntlets without their leather liners. He shook
his head. "I have a bargain to keep—rings to make
and demons to set free. After that, these, too, shall go.
I never wanted demon slaves."

Her eyes searched his face. "What do you want
then, my son?"

He smiled, and the cut on his cheek, though covered with silk, stung—a sharp reminder of the day's
events. "I have everything I want. The two of you. Together." He hugged them both, one with each arm.
"And later, perhaps when I have finished with rings
. . . I might find some time for spiders and ivy and
climbing roses."

Delivev kissed his good cheek softly. "Welcome
home, my son."

And Gildrum echoed, "Welcome home. My son."

ABOUT THE AUTHOR

PHYLLIS EISENSTEIN was born in Chicago in 1946, and except for two years in Germany and one winter in Upper Michigan as an Air Force wife, she has spent her life there. In early student days, she worked as a butcher, grocery clerk, pin-setter, and tutor in English, Spanish, and trigonometry. Now a full-time writer, she still manages to read voraciously and indulge various hobbies, such as needlepoint, crocheting, choral singing, strumming old folk songs on a classical guitar, and yoga. She also suffers addictions to obscure games of solitaire and the watching of old movies on the Late, Late Show (frequently in combination). Quite recently, she returned to college after a twelve-year hiatus, to become a senior studying freshman Archaeology. As Mme. Klein, she sometimes reads Tarot at science-fiction conventions, astounding the skeptical with her results. This is the fifth novel she has written.

DEL REY SCIENCE FICTION CLASSICS
FROM BALLANTINE BOOKS